SO-ABA-212

I Do Love You Still

I Do Love You Still

Mary B. Morrison

THORNDIKE PRESS
A part of Gale, a Cengage Company

Farmington Hills, Mich • San Francisco • New York • Waterville, Maine
Meriden, Conn • Mason, Ohio • Chicago

LIBRARY OF CONGRESS CIP DATA ON FILE.
CATALOGUING IN PUBLICATION FOR THIS BOOK
IS AVAILABLE FROM THE LIBRARY OF CONGRESS

ISBN-13: 978-1-4328-6939-7 (hardcover alk. paper)

Published in 2019 by arrangement with Dafina Books, an imprint of Kensington Publishing Corp.

Printed in the United States of America
1 2 3 4 5 6 7 23 22 21 20 19

To my family
Jesse Byrd, Jr. and Emaan Abbass
Wayne Morrison
Andrea Morrison
Derrick Morrison
Regina Morrison
Margie Rickerson
Debra Noel
Heidi Abbass
Julie Brown
Princess Cole
Julien Edward Brown Perry
and
KingMaxB (our Yorkie)

In Loving Memory
Elester Noel
Joseph Henry Morrison
Elizabeth Morrison

ACKNOWLEDGMENTS

I thank God for every breath I take, each morning I awaken to a new day, the words I write, novels I complete, and the steps I take along my journey of elevation and appreciation. At times, we know that life can be difficult.

I pray for all Americans. My heart goes out to parents separated from their children; Puerto Ricans who were treated as though you were not US citizens at a time when you needed your country the most; Californians who lost loved ones, pets, and possessions in raging wildfires; Texans, Floridians, and North and South Carolinians struggling to start over after natural disasters. The countless individuals who never imagined their daughter, son, husband, wife, sister, brother, cousin, best friend, or teacher would not return to them after a concert, school day, night out at a club or shopping at the mall. I can't profess to know your pain, but I do say unto each of you, I am sorry those things happened. To African-Americans senselessly and shamelessly killed by officers, my spirit is flooded with sorrow and outrage.

The wiser I become, the more I appreciate the people I meet unexpectedly, my friends, fans, and family.

My son, Jesse Byrd, Jr., is a fantastic award-winning author of children's books. You can visit his website at www.JesseB Creative.com. Jesse resides in Dubai with his beautiful wife, Emaan Byrd, a corporate executive for Huda Beauty and a celebrity on *Huda Boss.* I want to travel like you guys!

There are countless spectacular human beings in the world worthy of recognition and praise. I am fortunate to share the same birth mother with Wayne, Andrea, Derrick, and Regina Morrison, Margie Rickerson, and Debra Noel.

To my nieces and nephews: Rachelle Davis, Lauren Davis, Dr. Angela Davis, Dr. Rose Rowden, Omar Gant, Anissa and Dezi Rickerson, Janard, Christina, Marianna, Derrianna, Derrianne, JoVante, Joseph, Eulalia, and Roland (my nephew-son) Morrison, I am proud of each of you.

As always, a special thanks to my editor, Selena James, Steve Zacharius, Adam

Zacharius, Josh Gordon, and everyone at Kensington Publishing Corporation for supporting my literary career.

Kendall Minter, Kenneth P. Norwick, and Alan S. Clarke (my attorneys), Claudia Menza and Andrew Stuart (my agents), Tiffany Irene and Christal Jordan (my publicists), I don't know what I'd do without your support.

McDonogh #35 Senior High Roneagles Class of 1982, bay-bay #WeRock4Life.

I'm honored to be included in the Worldstar Hit Radio family. John Williams, I can never repay you for gifting me the *HoneyB Morrison Show*. Marcus Lamar, I love you for producing my episodes. Grenard Smith, your assistance is appreciated. Colonel Cassandra Guy, I salute you, girlfriend, for believing in me. Looking forward to reading your book.

Wishing each of my readers peace and prosperity in abundance. Visit me online at MaryMorrison.com. Sign up for my newsletter and invite your friends to do the same. Follow me on: Instagram @MaryHoneyB Morrison; Facebook @TheRealMaryB; Twitter Snapchat @CelebHoneyB; and WorldstarHitRadio.com.

There's always one true love that drifts away but is never forgotten.

CHAPTER 1
XENA

Silence gave sound to the voice inside my mind.

Rolling onto my side, I lay in bed facing the open window. Curtains flapped, whipping a summer breeze that brushed my naked body as though I was its canvas. I inhaled the warm air. I didn't want to be here.

Why was I living with one man, knowing I was still in love with my ex? Exhaling, I turned onto my back, bent my knees, placed my feet flat on the mattress, then stared into the darkness of the bedroom.

Remember why you left him, Xena. I know. But I don't want to be here.

In the beginning, I was happy with my new guy. Doubling back to a former boyfriend, I'd never done that. After all the shit my ex had put me through, I should hate him. I really wanted to, but . . . what had I proven by trying to hurt him the way he'd

13

done me?

I touched my stomach. God knew my aching heart was filled with love for my ex and repentance for what I'd done. Couldn't stop thinking about it or missing him. Doubted he'd take me back if I told him the truth of why I'd left him.

4:50 a.m.

A familiar hand caressed my breast. I scooted, hips first, to the edge of the queen-size mattress. Closing the gap between us, he hugged my waist, pulled me toward him. I resumed my previous position. Stared toward the ceiling fan that clicked each time it rotated.

Leaning in, he sucked my nipple. Didn't deny it felt good. My breaths became shallow, wishing it was my ex.

"Not now," I said, facing him, trying to assume a fetal position to create space between him and my parts I knew he wanted to access.

Dragging me closer to the middle of the bed, he crawled on top of me, began licking my areolas. His hand massaged my B-cups, then he twisted my nipple with his fingertips. I didn't want to enjoy his touch right now, but my body could not deny the percolating energy circulating throughout my chakras.

Pop. Crackle. Pop. Noises emanated from the settling of his old colonial home, recently renovated on the inside.

He used his knee to spread my thighs, then penetrated me. Our morning ritual had begun. *Squeak.* Headboard. *Squeak.* Frame. His hips thrust back and forth. No side to side, figure eight, or round and round clockwise followed by counterclockwise the way my last boyfriend used to do.

Our music was the chorus of a love ballad. I liked my current. I had done a good job of separating the sexual act from my feelings for him.

Closing my eyes, I squeezed my vaginal muscles supertight, pretending he was my ex. Shallow breaths deepened into a soft "haaa," as I exhaled into orgasm number one.

"That's my girl. Let it out," he said. Bracing himself on his forearms, he paused, then he sexed me in slower motion. "Give me another one."

The stimulation inside my pussy intensified. I released a bigger climax. For me. Not him.

"Don't hold back, baby. Give me all of my sweet juices," he moaned, shifting his mouth toward mine.

15

Quickly I pivoted in the opposite direction as he kept stroking. In and out.

"Kiss me, baby." This time he slid his tongue from my cheek to my lips — trailing saliva — then forced it inside . . . lizard-style.

Lust transitioned into frustration with each probe. He was never a good kisser. I cleared my mind. Focused on my task list for the day to calm myself.

Meditate. Go to the market. Meet my contract deadline for our client.

5:05 a.m.

His dick moved back and forth, all five inches in, then all the way out. Lightly he circled the tip of his penis at my opening, glided back in, pulled out. Entering me again, he poked my G-spot. Couldn't lie. Our sex was never wild, but he always made me wet.

Imagining he was my ex, I pulled my boyfriend's ass to me, hugged his shoulders, started groaning loud. "Ah, yes." I told him, "Go deeper inside me, baby." With my ex, I wouldn't have to ask.

"Um-hmm. I love you so." Abruptly his words ended midsentence, then he asked, "I'm not hurting you, am I?"

Nice of him to ask, but he didn't have the

proper equipment to inflict vaginal pain. The lump in my abdomen hadn't gotten larger, but it'd been there for almost a year. I shook my head in response to his question. The doctor said it was a fibroid tumor, and that it didn't need to be removed. Nor would the lump prevent me from conceiving.

Escaping into a fantasy of one of the best lovemaking sessions with my ex, I visualized his long girthy shaft snaking up the walls of my vagina. The opening of his penis moved about the depth of my pussy as though it were a searchlight looking for my soul. I'd pretend to hide my pleasure point, and he wouldn't stop fucking the shit out of me until he made me scream soprano . . . I missed him so much. Instantly my pussy became hot and my juices flowed like a waterfall for my current boyfriend. I tilted my pelvis up, granting him total access to Niagara.

5:12 a.m.
"You're making me cum early," he said, then added, "You ready?" Delving to his max, inches shy of reaching my cul-de-sac, my new boyfriend froze.

Suddenly his ass jerked backward. *Squeak.* He paused. Thrusting forward, he paused

17

again. *Squeak.* One. Two. Back. Forth. His rhythm grew closer, becoming one continuous motion until he and the squeaking came to a stop. I felt his throbbing shaft, then he collapsed on top of me. His accelerated heartbeat pounded against my breasts.

5:16 a.m.

After rolling him onto his side of the bed, I pulled the spread up to my neck, stared toward the ceiling. Lying next to my current, not a day went by where I didn't miss my ex.

Was Memphis in a relationship? Had he forgotten about me? Did he crave spooning me the way I longed to cuddle with him? Trying to convince myself I'd made the right decision to break up with him, I told Adonis, "I love you, baby." My head understood what my man needed to hear. My heart knew the truth.

Lifting the plush yellow comforter away from my naked body, I scooted away from Adonis, sat on the edge of the bed, gazed over my shoulder.

I didn't choose him. On our first date at Paula Deen's Creek House, he'd told me he wasn't looking for a girlfriend; he wanted a wife. I wasn't in search of a husband. Desperate, I had to get out of my mom's

18

house. Didn't want to move in with my best friend, Tina-Love. Her pussy had a revolving door. Men came and went. None of them stayed.

Adonis was considerate, generous, and in love with me. From day one I allowed things to be his way. Sighing, I pivoted in his direction, touched his face, traced the front of his neatly trimmed hairline. The dark hairs of his crown had started to thin. The softness of his beard against my fingertips flowed to a mustache that arched over supple red lips, which had greeted mine each day since we'd met a year ago.

Every day I told myself to stop reliving my past, each time I replayed the reel of my walking out of Memphis's house into my mother's. In less than a week I was out of my parents' place, and into Adonis's apartment building. Planting a kiss on Adonis's forehead as he snored deeper and louder, *Please, don't leave me, Z, I'll be back in Savannah twelve months tops* echoed in my mind.

Not wanting to ruin the biggest opportunity of his lifetime, I'd made a unilateral decision. Aborting my ex's baby without telling him we were pregnant was wrong. I knew that.

CHAPTER 2
MEMPHIS

"I know you have to leave, baby, but I wish you could stay with me a little longer," she professed, trailing kisses along my spine.

She was a sexy motherfucker. First time I saw her I knew straight up I was going to fuck the shit out her. Thin lips. Deep throat. Long wavy blond hair. Ice-blue irises. Tall. Six feet. Perfect size ten. Former high school volleyball Hall of Famer, she'd broken the record for the most game-winning spikes during her four years on the team.

Time was almost up for me here on the West Coast. All I wanted was to get back to the South and confront Xena regarding our unfinished business. I had to know the real reason why she broke it off. Tina-Love pretended Xena hadn't told her.

Yeah, right.

I lay facedown across the massage table Natalie had bought me, fixated on my ex. I'd been nothing but good to her for five years. A brotha had recently turned legal when I'd met Z but the fact that Z — my nickname for Xena — was five years older and salivating ova me kept my dick pointing north every day we were together. An athlete like me could have my choice female. But I wasn't average in any department. Also, I wasn't perfect.

Telling Natalie the same thing Z had told me the day Z walked out of my life, I replied, "You'll be all right." Not certain about my future, not caring about hers.

Natalie dug deeper into my quads. I felt her frustrations. She wouldn't understand, I had a lot riding on Z's love for me.

Olympic Training Camp was coming to an end. I didn't want to return to my hometown a failure in search of a nine-to-five, listening to fans reassure me I could beat Usain Bolt, having my IG followers DMing me not to give up. Sports flowed through the blood in my veins. I would become the world's champion; if Z hadn't abandoned me, I would've gotten an acceptance letter by now to represent the United States in track and field. I know I would've.

Venting to Natalie, I lamented, "I can't comprehend why she ended our relationship. I mean, I-I wasn't going to be gone forever, you feel me? Didn't want any other woman securing her spot. Gave her my all. But it's cool."

The hell it was. Blindsided, I hadn't sensed she was unhappy with my performance in or out of the sheets. A few hiccups here and there were the norm for guys, especially a track star like me. Z had issues, but I wasn't the one who'd fucked her up in the head.

Breaking her silence, I had to ask Natalie, "What do women want? I-I mean her mother was the one who abused her. I'd never mistreat her. You. Any female. Most of y'all have man issues. Can't find, keep, or please one. That's not my fault."

Wanted to add, Why do females do everything for a man thinking that's going to make him love y'all, then when he steps to the next woman y'all feel betrayed when what really had happened was . . . you played yourself. But I wasn't that stupid.

Heard from our mutual friend Tina-Love Z had found my replacement shortly after I'd left Savannah. "I took her off the market first date. Something wifey about her that other women can't compete with. She's better than a Willy Wonka golden ticket. She's more like a gold medal only one man can win, keep, and treasure until he dies. I thought I'd won her for life. I —"

Slap! "Shut upppp! Memphis!" Natalie screamed, commanding my attention. "I'm sick and tired of hearing about your precious Z! You don't call *her* name when I'm sucking your dick!"

Actually, I do. You just don't hear me.

Naked and accessible, I was not arguing with Natalie while I was facedown. Xena Trinity was in a unique category. Passion for me was in her voice, her eyes, her touch, her pussy when I tasted my baby. Penetrating her . . . damn. My dick hardened. She'd never disrespect me the way Natalie had done. Yelling out of control. Z had that silent cry that would break my heart when I saw the sad look on her face. I stared at the twenty-pound barbells on the black carpet of my living room as I listened to Natalie sniffle. Teardrops plopped on my legs, trickled down to my shins.

"I told you when we started this was temporary. Please don't cry." I didn't want to hear it.

"I thought you were over her. Now that you're leaving me you're bringing her up again. Are you planning on getting back with her?" Natalie's fingers firmly glided from my ankles up to my glutes. She squeezed my butt hard with both hands.

Verbally. Mentally. Spiritually. I'd never terminated things with Z. I couldn't, even if I wanted to. Circumstances were beyond my capability. Real love secured home plate. No matter how many pussies I hit, Z had my heart on lock. We had history. Z was forever my girl. All the other females were on first, second, third, the mound. I'd never told her, but Natalie was somewhere in the outfield. Spoiled, rich, privileged white female wanted this middle-class black man's dick to continue making her feel good.

If I never saw her again, that'd be okay.

"What are we?" she questioned. "What's our relationship status?"

You don't wait almost a year to solidify your place in a man's life.

Repeating the same motion, foot to cheek, Natalie had gotten better at releasing my tension, not hers. She'd also grown bitter over the year, wanting what I wouldn't agree to: a commitment. I couldn't take a white woman home to my Jamaican mother. I was going to miss all the generous things Natalie had done for me on a daily. Laundry. Cooking. Stroking my ego and sucking my dick at the same time.

Natalie was upgraded from her tryout spot. She was a free agent. If she traded me the way Z had done, I'd miss the perks. Not

Natalie. I hadn't asked her for anything she didn't want to give me. Lifting my head, I readjusted the pillow, lowered my face into the doughnut hole cushion. "What we have is and always will be special."

"Special? And what exactly is my place? Huh?" She stopped touching me.

Sitting up on the table, I placed my hand on her hip, cupped the nape of her neck, pulled her close. "Kiss me." I couldn't lie, she made me feel amazing. "Don't cry. We'll work this out when I get back," I lied.

Slowly she shook her head, then said, "You're not coming back."

"I have to," I lied again. "My things are here."

I'd received an e-mail that boxes were being delivered to my unit. Upon receipt, I was to pack up my personals, print and adhere the shipping labels. Someone would call me to arrange a pickup time and tracking information would be e-mailed to me.

"To get your clothes, Memphis. Really?" Gazing into my eyes, she continued, "I love you. What am I supposed to do without you?"

Natalie sounded like Z, except Z walked out on me. "I've got to get ready for practice. I'll hit you up when I'm done."

Natalie wrapped her arms around my

neck. Smashed her clit against my flaccid dick. "I've invested a lot of time into you. I want to go with you to Savannah."

That was not happening. I glanced around my furnished apartment. "Nah. You need to go on your mission trip to Havana. People in Cuba need you."

"And you don't?" she cried.

"That's not what I'm saying. I have to focus on qualifying for the Olympics. When you get back, we'll see where I am and take it from there."

Natalie was a twenty-three-years-young female who grew up in Beverly Hills. Didn't know what a W-2 with her social security number on it looked like. Post–high school she traveled the world on missions to help people. Most women needed something or someone to care for. I'd become her state-side philanthropic recipient.

"You love me?" she asked, lowering her hands to my thighs.

One bedroom, bathroom, living, dining, and kitchen. I resided in eight hundred square feet. Natalie owned, free and clear, a two-bed, two-and-a-half-bath town house here in Chula Vista. Her parents didn't believe in her renting real estate. If I were the type of man to dog a female, I would've had her have me on payroll making weekly deposits into my bank account.

Puckering my lips tight, I shifted my mouth and eyes far to the left, then nodded, thinking . . . I loved her in an appreciative kind of way, for all she'd done. Yeah, that was it. "I do."

Natalie stepped back from the table, then demanded, "Say it, Memphis."

I stood. "For real. I've got to get ready for practice in a few hours." I accompanied her to my door and opened it. "We'll talk things over tonight. I promise."

Standing in the hallway, she said, "A radio producer named Rick in Savannah contacted me about you. He's trying to get me to —"

Natalie was trying too hard to solidify her spot. Closing the door, I turned the lock, got my cell. Scrolling through photos of Z and me, I bit my bottom lip. Tears clouded my eyes, splattered on my screen. I wasn't a bad dude.

I didn't know if I could ever forgive Z for breaking my heart.

Chapter 3
Xena

A new day gave dawn to my broken heart.

Sitting on the edge of the bed, I picked up my cell, glanced over my shoulder at Adonis. He was flat on his back. His eyes were closed, chest heaved. He inhaled a snore. Exhaled a whistle. Tuning out Adonis's noise and the clicking of the ceiling fan, I scanned my photo album, *M 2 Z.*

I'd stalked his page every day since I'd left him. My album was filled with screenshots I'd taken of Memphis's social pages. (Had most of his videos, too.) Of course, I'd cropped out all the females. The last selfie I'd taken with my ex was of our sharing an ice cream cone curbside at Leopold's. His tongue was on one side, mine on the other. Then we'd shared a cold, sweet French kiss.

Sniffles accompanied my tears as I fixated on Memphis's dashing smile. Some women would kill to claim him. His large brown eyes beamed back at me. Blackberry skin drenched in shea butter, shrink-wrapped tight to his smooth head, lean muscles, and six-foot-two-inch frame.

Opening his Instagram, I told myself again today it was all my fault. *You threw your man away, girl.* Now I understood there was a difference between letting someone go and tossing them out like trash.

A video yesterday of Memphis running the hundred-meter dash in under eleven seconds looped on his IG. That speed was probably good enough to get him into the Olympics. If he'd made it, I was certain the whole world plus Tina-Love would've known. I needed to check in with her. The caption **heading home soon #savannahhereicome** popped up in my feed.

"Oh! Shit!" Dropping my cell, I bent over.

"What?" Adonis said.

"Nothing, baby," I lied. "I stubbed my toe on the nightstand." I picked up my phone. Unlocked it with my thumbprint.

"You all right?" he mumbled, sliding his hand up and down my side of the bed.

No, no, I wasn't. Felt like I was dying inside. Anxious and afraid to see him. Memphis had 236,721 likes and my bestie, Tina-Love, had just commented to his post, come on home baby!

"Everything okay?" Adonis asked. This time he sat up.

I clicked the side button on my phone, sprang to my feet as my screen went black. "Yeah, go back to sleep, baby."

I could've been Memphis's number one. He had sides when we were together, but maybe I should've forgiven him for that. Nowadays most guys, with and without potential, had extras.

"Come lay with me for a moment," Adonis said.

I ignored his request — we'd already had sex. I'd lie if I claimed not to be jealous that Tina-Love's relationship with my ex never changed. I repoened the app, stared at Adonis, entered the closet, closed the door, then texted my bestie, **Are you home? I need a place to stay.**

She replied, **No. In Milan for a runway show**

Three hundred fifty-one days had already come and gone, and although I was in a committed situation, I had to break up with Adonis and position myself to reunite with my ex before some other female snatched him.

Slipping on my fluffy magenta robe, I placed my phone in my pocket, then quietly stepped across the oak hardwood through the living room, into the kitchen. I poured water and fresh grinds into the coffee maker. Inhaling Memphis's favorite, 100% Jamaica Blue Mountain from his mother's hometown of Kingston, I closed my eyes remembering how he'd sip, never gulp, then say, *Just like my Z, this brew is good to the last drop.* I replayed the sound of his voice.

In anticipation of my ex coming home, my lips curved. Greeting the most beautiful part of the day, I slowly opened my eyes, stood at the kitchen door, and stared through one of the rectangular glass panes, waiting for darkness to give way to the light. I covered my mouth with my hand. My cheeks grew full of the love I wanted to recapture.

"Good morning, gorgeous." Moist lips landed against the nape of my neck.

Gasping, I leapt sideways, exhaled, continued staring out the window through narrow eyelids. "Stop doing that. Seriously." This was the third consecutive day Adonis had crept up on me. "I thought you were asleep."

Adonis stood behind me. Spoke into my ear. "Didn't mean to startle you. I was hoping you'd say something, but since you haven't, I can't take it any longer."

My smile slid upside down as I did an about-face on the white ceramic tiles, shoved my hands in my pockets, silenced my ringer. The ten-by-twelve kitchen space where we stood was adjacent to the dining area where Adonis had his contractor set up a design studio for me to work from home so I could spend less time at my alteration shop. Along the kitchen wall was the refrigerator, sink, countertop, and dishwasher. The gas stove was closest to the kitchen door.

One weekend into our relationship, I'd started sleeping over. Any place was better than being at my mom's; another reason was to convince myself I was over my ex. Cohabiting with Adonis was my second biggest mistake.

"Why are you up so early?" I wanted to add, *interrupting what you know is my sacred time?*

Hiding his hands behind his back, Adonis kissed my lips twice. "You tossed and turned a lot during the night. Then after making love you sat on the side of the bed a long time. You okay?"

I took a deep breath, let it out slowly. This was my opportunity to tell him the truth. "I'm good. We need to —" What in the hell was up with him bouncing up and down? "Please stop doing that. What's up?"

"Pick a hand," he said, squaring his broad

shoulders.

Rolling my eyeballs, I questioned to myself, *God, why am I here?* I meant living with Adonis.

"It's too early for games, babe. Hurry up and decide what you want me to see. I don't want to miss the sunrise," I told him, contemplating my exit strategy.

"Okay, but you always watch the sunrise. This is more important." Walking backward, he insisted, "Come with me to the bathroom." He was still hiding his hands.

Adonis was a typical Aries. Playful. Passionate. Dedicated. Loving. Calculating. He consistently put my needs ahead of his. Above all, he strived to keep me happy. Couldn't say I'd done the same. Pretending to adjust my attitude with a fake smile, I decided to give in.

I should celebrate this man every chance I had, but at this moment I was not in the mood to share in his joy. My mental capacity was filled with memories of Memphis that I could not get out of my head. Maybe because I knew my ex was coming home I felt his energy. Did Memphis still love me? That was what I needed to know.

Adonis ushered me into the bathroom.

"Why are we in here?" I wasn't feeling my current right now, but he was totally wired.

Lifting the toilet's lid, he insisted, "Have a seat, honey." Removing my robe, with one hand he let it fall to the floor. Luckily, my phone didn't slip out of the pocket.

I glanced down at the only place to sit. "Humph. You're tripping. For real. Move," I said, shoving him aside.

Bending over, I scooped up my robe, took one step toward the door.

"C'mon, Xena. For me. Just do it," he pleaded, blocking my exit.

Shuffling backward, I stared at Adonis through narrowed eyelids. There was a time when he'd placed an iPad loaded with books by my favorite authors in my purse. Then another occasion when he'd waited until I was on the commode, then rolled me a bottle of Poo-Pourri spray. My shit didn't stink. That deodorizer was for him.

I was literally inches from falling into a puddle of bacteria-infested water. Whatever he had in mind, I wanted to be done with it and him. Soon as I sat, he said, "Bam! Pee on this!"

CHAPTER 4
XENA

When he presented me with his surprise, his other hand was empty. I stood. Tried moving him out of my way. He didn't budge.

"I'm not pissing on that stick." I touched my abdomen, confirming the size of the lump hadn't gotten any bigger. "I keep telling you. It's not a baby, Adonis. It's a fibroid or something."

"You know how bad my parents want a grandchild. Xena, your menstrual is fourteen days late. This could be it." Adonis raised both brows. His dimples appeared, disappeared, reappeared.

Caught up with the wrong timeline, I'd lost track of monitoring the rhythm method, which had served me well, except for that one time with Memphis. I'd wished I'd kept his baby. "That's why you've been ejaculating deep inside of me every morning. You did this on purpose?"

Adonis became quiet. Held my hand. "Don't be scared. I promise to take excellent care of you and our baby. And we have built-in babysitters." His eyes widened with love. "We can rent this apartment and move into my parents' five-bedroom house. Just until our child starts talking."

Pounding on his hairy chest with both of my fists, I cried, "This! Is my body! Not your parents'. Or yours! Get out of my way! I hate you!" This split second, I really did.

Extremely polite, friendly, and hospitable best described his folks. Mine lived twenty minutes away, and I had no desire to visit them, especially my two-faced mother.

He held me close. Spoke with compassion. "I know I sprang this on you, but I've been praying for us to be pregnant. Either way, it's okay." He touched my belly. He felt what I knew was there. A lump. Not a fetus. I moved his hand.

Adonis's life was on an upward trajectory from the day he was born. Because he'd been sheltered from the struggles of poverty and abuse, I doubted my current had experienced any hard times.

At thirty-five Adonis was president of an all-male private club and the homeowners' association in the development where he and his parents held joint title to their property. Adonis was a licensed real estate agent soon to enter the multimillionaires' sales category. Thanks to his parents, he was the sole heir to several single-family homes throughout Georgia, and he was CEO/president/owner of the property management company that oversaw the operation of the building we lived in.

Pressing my knees together, I shook my head. He nodded his.

For the last five years, my application to debut my men's designer clothing at New York Fashion Week was rejected. I was nowhere close to being accepted for the next show. My new goal was to create a niche, an outrageously sexy yet debonair line to submit for the show that was twelve months out.

I didn't want to be here.

If it hadn't been for Tina-Love introducing me to Memphis, I wasn't sure if I should be thankful for or pissed off with her. She loved Memphis almost as much as I did. She was his loudest cheerleader. I'd never try to take her joy, but where was mine? Maybe my broken heart would've been better off never experiencing true soulmate love.

Adonis snapped his fingers twice. "Xena. Xena."

I did not agitate easily, but this charade made me do what I'd never done before. *Slap!* Hitting my man's face, I demanded, "Move. Until my cycle comes, no sex! You hear me? None!"

He slid in front of me. "It's okay, baby. I understand your frustration. Please. It's been two whole weeks. My mama said you are. I promised her we'd confirm whether she was right." Adonis removed the test from the packet.

"We're not married and I refuse to be a statistic." Truth was, I needed an out from this relationship.

"Prove her wrong. Do it for me. For us." His eyes were bright. Dimples deep.

"Fine." I reassumed my position, spread my thighs, and started urinating, which was easy for me due to the gallon of water I consumed daily.

Adonis held the stick under my flow. Minutes later, his smile grew wide. Jumping up and down he pumped his fist in the air three times, then handed me the results.

I slammed the stick to the floor. "Give me the other one," I grunted.

The second one matched the first. Not caring to wipe myself, I looked up at him, then yelled, "Get out of my face!"

I do not want to be here.

Chapter 5
Xena

"Stay right there." Adonis disappeared, then returned dressed in chocolate slacks, a tan button-down collarless short-sleeved shirt, and hard-sole shoes.

As I looked away from him, gazed out the window, my vision became blurry. Memphis was the kind of man that would've given up his dream of earning a gold medal to raise his newborn. Now I wasn't sure terminating Memphis's baby was the right decision.

"Mrs. Oglethorpe," Adonis sang.

Whipping my head in his direction, I saw darkness submitting to daybreak, casting a shadow behind Adonis. After his knee touched the glazed charcoal tile, he asked, "Xena Trinity, will you be my wife?"

Trapped on the only seat in the bathroom with no viable escape route, I faced a white painted door. Inside, an eight-foot-tall hot water heater consumed the entire closet. No fire ladder was outside the window.

Speechless, I stared at the double pink lines next to the word *pregnant.* The diamond shining in my eyes was a huge solitaire. How long had he been planning all of this? Adonis slid the most gorgeous ring on my finger. He stood, kissed my cheek, retrieved his cell from his back pocket, touched the screen, then placed the call on speaker.

"Mom! You were right! We are pregnant! I'm on my way to pick up what we talked about!" His lips touched my forehead. "Xena, do not leave the apartment until I come back," he demanded. "I have another surprise for you." Touching my stomach, he continued, "This one is mine for sure, Mom. I know it. Mom, I'm on my way." Adonis kissed my forehead. "I love y'all."

Clump. Clump. One sound followed another. *Squeak! Slam!*

I heard the front door to our residence open and close. Quickly I put on my robe. Scurrying to the kitchen, I peeped through the glass pane, watched Adonis's taillights until his car was out of my view. A breakthrough of light beamed in my eyes, blocking my sight.

In a quandary, I pretended none of what had happened was real. I twisted the brass lock to the left, turned the knob. Grateful to greet the dawn of another day, I stepped onto the gray-painted wooden planks.

The white rail wrapped around the balcony, boxing me in. From museums, to statues, to surnames, preservation best described my hometown. Tradition had significance in Savannah, including the Confederate statue in Forsyth Park that was less than two hundred feet away.

Family values had to be number one on the list. Unless kids were not allowed, there were almost as many strollers as there were cars. Children were everywhere, including the one growing inside my womb.

Was God punishing me? Was He trying to teach me a lesson? Or was my baby a blessing?

"Ahh!" I screamed, not caring if I'd awakened anyone at the senior complex on the corner. Or Mr. Ben Matthews. He lived on the first floor. Everyone in the building had to pass his unit with each entrance and exit.

As I inhaled the fresh misty air, my view of the opposite side of the street was partially obstructed by the tall mulberry trees that lined our block. Should've taken Memphis up on his offer for me to stay in his house the year he was in training in California. But our relationship ended when I decided to abort our child.

I cried. "Why, oh, why am I here, Lord Jesus?" I felt as though God would never forgive me.

"You okay up there?" I hadn't noticed Mr. Ben was on the sidewalk, staring up at me. "You not planning on jumping, are you?"

"Yes." I shifted my eyes to the left. "I mean no. I'm okay. Thanks."

"I'll bring you back a cup of coffee," he said. "You stay put, lil girl."

"Thank you." My eyes trailed him across Dayton Street.

Mr. Ben was a friendly, wise old man. Most often when he offered to get something, he never did come back with it. I thought he had the onset of dementia. Never saw any family or friends visit him.

We seldom heard the upstairs tenant. There was only one unit per floor. A white man who looked to be sixty, about ten years younger than Mr. Ben, had a long salt-and-pepper beard and a young girl who visited often. Maybe she was his daughter. Or perhaps his companion.

Leaves rustled as an agile squirrel leapt across branches in the direction of Forsyth Park, the same direction Mr. Ben had traveled.

Life was in and all around me.

I sat in the black rocking chair that was almost eighty-one years my senior. I inherited the heirloom from my great-grandmother who was part Native American. She often read what the whites read, the *Savannah Morning News.* The rocker was the only piece of furniture that I took each time I moved.

The white rocker was one Adonis had borrowed from his parents. His white great-grandfather used to sit there when he read the weekly African-American paper, the *Savannah Tribune.*

Planting my feet firmly on the planks, I braced my back, placed my hands on my thighs, and sat motionless. Inhaling deeply into my stomach, I sensed the radiance of the sun cloaking my flesh.

Exhaling, I closed my eyes, as a shadow of light penetrated my lids. A faint piercing hum resounded against my eardrums. Buzzing locusts. The noise grew louder, then gradually tapered off. I cleared all thoughts from my mind, as I'd done most mornings. Today, I waited for the divine power to speak to my soul.

Silence acquired a different tone.

Breath after breath, I prayed for *a voice.* Sometimes I heard the softness of a little girl laughing, an old man grunting, or a woman crying. I opened the chakras to my mind and heart until it registered. "A life-changing blessing is upon you. Listen.

"Listen.

"Listen."

Retreating inside I slammed the door. I bypassed my work-at-home space. Flopping across the plush purple sofa that could unfold into a futon, I was numb. The rectangular coffee table was situated between an identical couch that faced toward me. Closing my eyes, I placed my hand over my navel.

I didn't feel like doing a thing, but I had to put the finishing touches on my client's tuxedo by this evening.

Click. Slam.

"Baby, I'm back," Adonis said, locking the door. "Oh good. You guys are resting. Don't get up. You hungry?"

"No."

"Thirsty? I'll get y'all some water," he said, standing over me.

"Adonis. I'm fine. Please, I don't mean to sound rude. But leave me the hell alone."

"Hormones kicking in already, huh? Okay. Let me know what you guys need." He exited into the bedroom. In a matter of minutes, my body, my life, and my marital status were about to change. Against my will.

I thought, *Memphis will never forgive me if I had another man's baby.*

Unlocking my cell, watching Memphis on social took my breath away. One post at a time, I felt as though I was suffocating seeing him happy without me.

A voice whispered in my ear, *I love you, Z.*

"Xena! You and my baby need anything?" Adonis called out.

This was going to be my longest or my shortest pregnancy. Either way, I'd have regrets.

CHAPTER 6
MEMPHIS

Jerking my shoulders, one then the other, I stretched my neck side to side. Wiggled my body head to toe. Held my foot in my palm, pulled the heel to my glute. Waited thirty seconds. Stretched my other quad.

I stood in lane one, scanned the field. Life without track, I'd be a fish out of water. Worked my ass off for Z! Was rejected. Put my blood and sweat into training for a year. Still wasn't accepted. Why the fuck was I trying this hard? To prove what? I could fail.

Removed my track shoes, then laced up my tennies. Two of my teammates who had received notification they were competing next summer stood on the side with smiles wide enough for me see almost all of their teeth. I turned my back to them, bit my bottom lip to keep tears from falling.

"Memphis Brown."

"Yes! Coach!" I shouted, praying one way or another, he had news.

Against all the odds, I desperately wanted this little boy born in Savannah, whose mother moved to the US from Kingston with the clothes on her back and made it . . . despite my father abandoning us . . . I had to make her proud.

"Afraid I have disappointing news," Lou said.

Ending today's session, I sensed that Coach Lou Richie was going to tell me what I already knew. *Stay ready. Nah.* "Fuck!" I wrapped my arms to my waist. Finishing the hundred meter in 10.24 seconds wasn't good enough to make the cut? I'd worked my ass off to get under ten seconds. Still hadn't happened.

Standing in front of Lou, I said, "Man, there has to be another way. I have to." I broke down crying. For my not being able to represent my team. For disappointing my mother. For Z. If she were here she'd know all the right things to say.

"What's it going to take for me to qualify? I'll do anything to clinch a spot," I told Coach.

Grown men weren't supposed to cry. My mother instilled in me that tears were a sign of weakness. If she could raise me without assistance of any kind from my father, I could achieve greatness for Mom, and my future wife and children. Have a home built for us in Kingston. "Stay ready" was my mother's daily inspirational mantra. I could hear her voice in my head. Strive to be better than the best; only then can you become number one.

Words weren't necessary. The disappointment showed in the way I glanced toward the ground. My lips and face muscles tightened. I exhaled. Looked up at Coach.

Natalie would probably get pleasure from my failure. After the way I'd treated her, I didn't want to see her again.

Handing me a folded letter, Lou said, "You're going to have to work harder. There's always next time."

Fuck this! Ripping the paper in half, I crushed both halves into a ball, threw it on the ground, then stomped on the letter with the heel of my shoe. "Next time. Right."

Coach stared at the ground, then at me. "Make that your last time throwing trash on my field. You might want to pick up your acceptance confirmation. You're in, MB," he said. "I wanted to see how badly you wanted this."

Thoughts in my mind went mute, limbs numb. Felt like my heartbeat was determined to shoot out of my chest, then there was a hard thump. *Boom!* I stumbled backward as though a shot put traveling sixty miles per hour was hurled into my cavity. Had I heard Coach correctly?

Before bending over, I mouthed, *Repeat that.*

Smiling, he patted me on my back. "It's official, MB. You're in, baby!"

"Are you fucking serious?" I leaned back, released a sharp "Yo!" Tears poured as I stood tall and struggled to swallow the lump in my throat.

I was used to seeing him angry and frustrated. Yelling at me was his way of pushing me harder. I had never seen him sentimental. Coach nodded. His eyes became watery. He blinked them dry.

Coach was that beast on my back every day. Six hours a day. Seven days a week. Sometimes we'd travel to the desert to train under sweltering conditions, down south to battle the drenching heavy raindrops the size of gumballs beating and weighing me down. Then there were the days of trampling through snow and chilling gusty winds that felt like I was being sliced with a knife. Some of that shit, I never understood. But now I get it. Nothing stopped him from preparing us for this moment.

My teammates came onto the field. "Congrats, MB," one said.

"Your next tears better be for winning that silver," the other one said. "Gold is mine, baby."

I did a standing backflip, landed on my feet, then shouted, "Fuck, yes! I'm in!" Sounded like someone had covered my mouth. "Hem. Hem," I hacked, spat on the ground. Shouted the words louder. All the animals hundreds of miles away at the San Diego Zoo probably heard me that time.

I dropped to my knees. "Thank you, Lord Jesus! Whew!" I grabbed my torn letter, sprang up.

If it weren't for my coaches and sports, I'd be dead.

Chapter 7
Memphis

All-American in high school. As a college Hall of Famer, I'd placed first in the one hundred, two hundred, and three hundred meter, consistently. Always the relay anchor, there was only one time I'd disappointed my teammates in the four hundred. We'd placed second by fractions of a second. Second, third, fourth didn't matter to me.

I was lit. I pointed to heaven. Shook my finger. Pounded the left side of my chest. If I wasn't first, I was a loser. In the US outdoor, I broke the record in the hurdles. Ranked fifth in the world by *Track & Field News.* Some thought fifth was great. Not me.

"Thanks, Coach. I won't let you down."

Fuck being Superman. I was the Black Panther. All of a sudden, I was through-the-roof hyped and scared shitless at the same time. My stomach knotted up. Started jumping up and down.

"You bet your sweet ass you won't," Coach Richie responded.

What was success without someone I loved to sing my praises? I got it. Rich people married for someone to share their glory with. Bringing home that gold meant as much to me as winning back my ex-girlfriend.

"Don't slack off. Stay focused. Stay hungry, MB. We on some next-level shit now. Run like a winning thoroughbred. Time to go home. See your mom. Eat healthy. Rest well. Hydrate twenty-four seven. Women are going to try to cram pussy down your throat. No trap babies. Wrap it up. The less you have sex the better. I'm setting you up in Savannah for a media blitz and your daily training schedule. No downtime. The only change is location. I'll meet you at the radio station Monday for the big announcement. First stop, *The Shady Café.*"

Balling my hand to a fist, I covered my mouth. "With @DDDShade, yo?"

She had that porn-star hourglass and she was nationally syndicated. But her shade cast a net deep, far, and wide if she didn't vibe with her guests. Alaska twenty-four seven darkness. Yet being on her show signified a person had made it!

"Get ready for superstar mayhem like

52

you've never witnessed," Coach said, slapping me on the ass. "Congratulations. Don't let this go to your heads, Memphis. You have an obligation to do everything right while representing the US of A in the Olympic Games. And that commitment begins right here." He pointed toward the ground. "Right now." Coach hugged me. "You deserve this, son."

I cried on his shoulder.

One year closer to putting on the track uniform I'd envisioned wearing since I was a kid. "Thanks, Coach."

I took off running on the all-weather rubberized surface hearing *On your marks, set . . . pow!* The sound of the pistol firing rang in my ears. Pumping my arms, moving my legs, I felt invincible. My adrenaline fueled every muscle. I pushed myself harder, a turbo boost erupted. It was like I'd lost my shadow. If I moved any faster, I swore I'd take flight. I didn't put on the breaks until I was a hundred feet from my residence.

After entering the code on the keypad, I unlocked my front door. Unplugging the USB cord from my cell, I collapsed onto my back. Sprawled on the living room floor, I stared at the ceiling. Fresh tears streamed down my temples.

"Fuck your deadbeat ass, man."

Why had he crept up on me in the midst of my salivating?

Didn't care if my father was six feet under, cremated, or alive. Hadn't seen him in sixteen years. I prayed he was watching from hell, that son of a bitch. Wouldn't let one thousandth of an ounce of my piss quench his thirst. Spectators could post what they wanted as to why my deadbeat dad wouldn't be in the stadium next to my mother. Mom was my queen. She'd do anything for me, although I wasn't her biological son.

CHAPTER 8
XENA

"Rise and shine, beautiful." Lying on his side facing me, Adonis touched my stomach.

For the first time, the cheery voice chiming in my ear awakened me to the point that I screamed in my head, *Stop it!* I took a deep breath. Tried to relax. Stared at the ceiling. Didn't move.

"I have a surprise for you. Muah, muah, muah." Adonis removed my eye mask, then leaned in for another kiss. I covered his mouth.

"What? You want me to piss on another stick today? You need a confirmation follow-up?" I felt my forehead tightening.

I wasn't sure if the living being inside of me was creating negative energy. Or if it was Adonis's excitement. Or if it was my being disappointed with myself for making the same mistake again. I didn't want his baby. I was clear about that. My rhythm method calendar had become a game of craps where I was the only loser.

I placed my feet on the hardwood floor, sat on the edge of the bed, staring at the sun shining through the sheer white curtains. I'd overslept, and he'd let me. Retrieving my cell from the nightstand, I saw I'd missed five calls. Four were from my business associate Topez Arrington, and one from a "No ID."

I checked my settings, glanced over my shoulder, and questioned Adonis, "Why did you put my phone on 'do not disturb'? Don't ever touch my phone again."

He smiled. "I did it for our baby. Wait till you see what I got y'all."

"I've had enough of your surprises. I need to work on my new client's tuxedo. That and Topez sent me another contract last night for a wedding party of eight groomsmen. She's meeting me at my shop later. We need to go over the designs for the gentleman's suit line that I'm submitting for New York Fashion Week. This baby is not going to stop my dream from coming true."

My small alteration shop was located in a neighborhood strip mall. Six people could fit if they stood shoulder to shoulder in front of the counter. A one-step-up platform surrounded by three full-length mirrors was by the door. I had mounds and rolls of fabric, equipment, and supplies that were visible toward the back of my store. A design table, sewing machine, and there was one roller chair. The best part was the lease had my name, and my name only it. Trinity Designs and Alterations. Soon I'd have to renew the agreement or find a different location.

"The new business contract is great, babe." His tone was more dismissive than congratulatory. "But our baby comes first. I'm going to compare health coverage plans and life insurance policies to make sure we are covered for everything."

Adonis exited the bed on his side, which was near a fireplace we never used. Opening the closet, he put on his robe, grabbed my robe, went to the dresser, opened the top drawer, then dangled a blindfold on his pointing finger.

He came around to me. "Don't sign off on any new work commitments. I'm going to retire you. All I want you doing is taking care of me, yourself, and our unborn," he said, twirling my mask in his hand. "Pretty soon, you'll be a stay-at-home mom like my mother was with me. By the way, we're moving out of here in two weeks. That'll give me time to rent this apartment by the first of the month."

I stood, walked to the window, slid the

curtains apart, inhaled the fresh breeze. Our debating my future was not a discussion worth having. Kid or no kid, I too had a dream and it didn't include burping, feeding, and changing diapers. Moving out didn't mean my moving into his parents' home. I went to the bathroom, splashed cold water on my face. Adonis was right behind me. He handed me my robe.

"Put this on. I promise. It won't take long. My parents bought you a pre-push gift," he exclaimed. After sliding the robe onto my arms, he placed the blindfold over my eyes.

Exhaling, I felt him tie the satin sash about my waist, then he held my hands. A present for a mother birthing a child was warranted after birth, not before. *Click. Slam.* Standing in the hallway, I heard the lock on the door secure. *Click.*

"Careful. We have to go downstairs. We have nineteen steps, beautiful."

Adonis counted each one aloud. I knew how many steps we had. I could navigate my way through the corridor of this building in the dark. We passed Mr. Ben's front door. Twelve more steps, the familiar sound of the tall entry door with the oblong frosted window seemed squeakier than usual. I felt the wooden porch beneath my slippers. I knew to my left there was a square red table and two matching chairs, and an American flag facing the street was mounted to the white post.

"Eight more stairs to the sidewalk, then you can remove the mask, beautiful."

I went from annoyed to disgusted. I wanted to shout, *I don't want to be with you!* before I could see anything. The sound of locusts escalated, then tapered off. This morning I'd missed the squirrels and meditating while sitting in my great-grandmother's rocker. Suddenly, I recalled, I was supposed to listen for a blessing. Maybe this was it.

"Okay, you can take it off now," Adonis said happily.

A brand-new white BMW with a pewter interior had a huge red bow on the roof. Adonis dug into his pocket, then handed me a keyless remote.

Speechless, I had to admit. The car was gorgeous! My thirteen-year-old Lexus — a gift given to me by my father when I graduated high school — was reliable transportation. It was parked on the other side of the street, at the corner. Staring at the luxurious chrome wheels on the latest-model BMW, I shook my head, thinking, *This man is perfect . . . for a different woman.*

"Get in," he said, opening the driver's-side door. Adonis sat on the passenger's seat, opened the glove compartment, handed me the title and registration. "It's in our names. Mother said we can donate your car to the Salvation Army charity."

Stop cheesing like your mother is the boss of us and whatever she wants, she gets.

The interior had that new smell. Staring at the dashboard, I saw that less than twenty-five miles was on the speedometer.

Looking at the title, I discovered that this car was paid in full. Slowly I shook my head. Memphis couldn't afford to gift me a vehicle that cost nearly sixty-two thousand dollars. "This is too much."

"No such thing for my fiancée. I want you to start looking at baby furniture," he insisted. "My mother has arranged for a company to come and pack our things. We can put your sewing machine, design table, whatever you want to keep, in storage. You don't need that stuff anymore. You can stay at my parents' and focus on designing clothes for our child. That is awesome."

Powering off the engine, I handed Adonis the key. "We need to talk. Later. Right now, what I need is space, to get my day started, prepare for my customer's final fitting, and meet with Topez about the new contract." I reiterated the contract part to let Adonis know I was not giving up my business to babysit his unborn child.

"I understand. Just call my parents and thank them for your gift," he said, easing the key in my robe's pocket. "We'll discuss the rest later."

We retraced our path until we were back inside the apartment. Adonis removed his robe, stepped into a pair of black basketball shorts, put on a Falcons T-shirt, tied his tennis shoes. "I have a few homes to drive by, then I'ma see my parents. I'll check on you and our baby in a few."

Weekends were like weekdays. Time off was a luxury I could take advantage of but didn't want to. I hadn't had a real vacation since before I'd broken up with Memphis. I was thirty-one, struggling, and hungry to walk into a department store and see my creations on the racks.

This was my time to shine!

CHAPTER 9
MEMPHIS

I'd gotten the best news of my entire life!

Pacing from my living to my dining room to my bedroom, I secured my Bluetooth in my ear, dialed my mother, then placed my cell on the granite countertop. I opened the sliding glass door and stepped onto my balcony.

"Hey, baby. How you doing over there in Cali?" she asked. The smile on her face resonated in her voice. Mom was my everything.

"I made it, Mama," I said, eagerly anticipating her response.

There was a moment of silence, then I heard her scream, "Hallelujah! Praise God! Thank you, Jesus! I knew you'd make it. From the first time I saw you take off running you haven't stopped. Saw you practicing on Instagram and Snap the other day. I prayed extra for you last night. You getting into that residence was our biggest blessing.

Give me every detail," she said, then shouted, "Hallelujah! God is good all the time!"

Nodding, I glanced at the parking lot below. None of the cars belonged to me. My SUV was at my house in Savannah where Z should've been waiting on me to return. Natalie was my driver in Chula Vista ninety percent of the time for our outings; grocery shopping (which most times she delivered the food and prepared my meals), the mall, and movie theater were her favorite hangout locations. Whatever I wanted, Natalie obliged, including sex.

Mom never made me feel as though I was adopted. "Mom?"

She answered, "I love you too, baby."

That wasn't what I was about to say. "Knowing Dad got another woman pregnant while he was married to you, why did you keep me?" My biological mother died soon after giving birth to me but —

Interrupting my thoughts, Hattie Mae softly replied, "Hush, my son. Everybody has a past. The best gift your father ever gave me was you."

The residence was all expenses included for athletes. I'd been here for a year working my ass off every day with Coach Richie. Had access to some of the best sports medicine doctors. Regurgitating my conversation with Coach, I wiped my tears, then let Mom know, "I'll be home tomorrow."

"Boy, you should've said that right away. What time you get in?" she asked. Her Jamaican accent was heavy. I heard the sound of her feet shuffling. Before I answered, she continued, "I have to get dressed and go to the store and get all kinds of vegetables, and lots of fish. Oh, the fresh market is tomorrow. I'll get up extra early and go there," she said. "Memphis, I've got to get off the phone, baby, and tell your brother and the family how the Lord has blessed us. Make sure you give thanks. None of that standing up stuff. Humble yourself. Get on your knees, you hear me."

She could text a video to the family group, but I know my mom. She was literally going to call all her siblings and friends individually and repeat what I'd told her from beginning to end each time.

Things with Natalie and me weren't ending good. Maybe I should leave it that way instead of peeling the scab off of her sore spot.

"I will kneel, Ma. I get in at six in the evening. Bye, Mama. I love you."

"I love you too, sweetheart. Bye."

Waiting for Mom to end the call, I looked

out over the facility. Champions trained here. I was grateful to be one of the newest shining athletes.

"Oh, Memphis. I almost forgot," Mom said. Knowing most times she had an after-thought, I always waited for her to hang up first.

"Yes, Mama." I was pretty sure I knew what she'd forgotten.

"You back speaking with Xena?"

I was right. "Not yet, Mama."

"She's the one for you, baby. I know y'all been through a rough patch. I went through something similar with your stepfather, may he rest in peace. But I know I'll never love like that again."

After my biological father abandoned my mother and me to live with and provide for another woman and her kids, Mom was fortunate to find a real man who loved us unconditionally. I had an older stepbrother from my stepfather's first marriage. We were never close, but Mom kept in touch with Lionel.

One could say I was an only child, but that wasn't true. Mom and my stepdad had a baby girl. Mom carried full-term, but the baby was stillborn. The tragedy caused my stepdad to have a heart attack. That was what Mom believed.

"I'll call Z when I get home," I promised.

"Ain't no need of loving nobody over the phone when you can hold them in your arms. Don't call that girl. Find her. I've got to call Lionel, my sisters, brothers, and go to the store, Memphis. Get here safely. Love you. Bye."

"Love you too, Mama. Bye." This time I heard three beeps signifying she was gone.

I took in all the fresh air that I could. The next person I wanted to hit up was Z. This was her victory too. She was the one who'd taught me how to channel positive energy through my seven chakras. How if I put positivity into the universe, the same source would return to me tenfold. Although she didn't attend church, she encouraged me to keep going when I didn't have faith in my ability to succeed.

Why not reach out? She deserved to know the deets firsthand. Picking up my phone, I knew what Mom said was best, but I couldn't chance showing up and having Z reject me. Or if what Tina-Love said was true, I wasn't sure to what extent Z's dude might try to challenge me.

Staring at the letter Z, I exited my favorites. If I'd spoken with Xena and she was apathetic about my news, I'd get mad at her for not being excited for me. I knew she'd walked out on me, but I'd never given her closure. I couldn't. I wasn't done with her. Joy was on the verge of becoming frustration.

Z would always be mine.

Chapter 10
Memphis

Didn't sleep last night. Watching the sunrise this morning, I thought of Z. God knew I missed and loved her times infinity.

Walking about my apartment, I was finally on a solid path to getting my shit in order where I could step to Z correctly, engagement ring and all. I'd do as Mom said and wait until I got home to tell Z in person. Holding me in her arms — as I curled into a fetal position — the way she used to was what I needed. I prayed my forgiving her was satisfactory for us to pick up where we'd left off. My chest tightened.

"This shit is dooooope!" I yelled, then did a standing backflip in my living room. Gymnastics wasn't my thing, but I'd mastered a few moves. I taped up the last box, adhered the label, triple-stacked them by my front door.

There was a three-hour time difference between Chula Vista and Savannah. Z was an early riser. Knowing her, she was meditating or working on a new designer suit for some dude who was about to get hitched. If I took her back, she wouldn't have to worry about chasing that dream of debuting at New York Fashion Week. I'd planned on retiring her from all that stitching and make her a stay-at-home mom.

A collage was the one item I had to take with me on the plane. I admired Z's angelic face, my lips curved until my face ached. Reaching up, I removed the framed five-by-seven from the wall. We were made for each other. I unzipped my backpack, carefully placed the picture inside.

Exhaling, I couldn't help but think this moment was fucking surreal. I skipped wearing underwear, folded my boxers, stuffed them in a side pocket. Stepping into a pair of gray cotton jogging pants, I slipped on a black fitted T-shirt. Double-checked my backpack for my laptop, tablet, headphones, license, and passport, then sat my bag on the dining table.

Buzzzzz! Greeting the delivery guy, I stepped aside, pointed at the boxes. "They're all yours, bruh."

"Keep your head up, dude," he told me. "Trust me, I've seen a lot of athletes work their ass off for nothing. I was one of them.

Take my advice. Ditch the disappointment. Get a nine-to-five, and don't fuck with these crazy-ass females."

He'd find out my truth soon enough when gold medals dangled around my neck. "I hear ya."

Closing the door, I stepped onto the balcony, selected the next person closest to me from my favorites.

She said, "Hey, baby. You home yet?"

"Nah, but I get in today. I am one step closer to the gold. Don't tell Z." I paused, then told Tina-Love, "I made it."

"Ahhhh! That's what's up, my nigga!" she yelled. "I knew you would."

Nodding, I smiled. I needed to hear her enthusiasm. She always came through for me.

"I'm exiting a flight from Nice as we speak. Glad to be back in the States. Where're you flying in? ATL?" she asked, all sexy and shit.

"Nah. Layover there. My final touchdown is Savannah. Didn't feel like taking that four-hour drive after being in the air for five." I was hyped. Wish I could press a button and transport myself straight to Z.

"You need a ride?" Tina-Love asked. "And I'm cooking for your ass."

Tina-Love was the sexiest supermodel I'd

ever met. When I worked up the courage to approach her, Tina-Love turned down all my advances. At that time, I was twenty-one, she was twenty-six. Tina-Love claimed I was too immature for her. Something about how she'd ruin me for all other women. In a way, she was right. Found out soon as she let me hit it. I was one and done! First and last time I tapped out during sex. When I asked if she had a friend she could introduce me to — who looked as hot as her — she hooked me up with Xena Trinity.

Z was no Tina-Love, but I swear it was love at first sight. Opening my Uber app, I used a standard address, requested a car. I had one mandatory stop to make before heading to the airport. Nearest driver was thirteen minutes away.

"Rain check on that meal. Mom is stirring pots and inviting every damn body to her house. Come by. I can't wait to get there, man. Make sure you come, but don't bring Z. Don't want it to be awkward. But you can tell her to fire my replacement." I was grinning like a kid, anxious to hold my Z.

Xena was my eclectic melting pot. Native American. African. French. She had shoulder-length black silky hair from her ancestors' Yamacraw tribe. A long face, narrow nose, piercing brown eyes, and mocha skin. She had the warmest smile I'd ever seen. Made me putty in her arms from date one. Her B-cup boobs and hourglass waist drove me insane every time I made love to her. I didn't need all the extra tits, but Z's firm round ass had to be inherited from her people in Senegal.

"I don't have to tell her to fire dude. We both know the second she sees you, y'all gon' be fucking like rabbits," Tina-Love said, shaking me from my daze. "Don't post anything on your socials yet," Tina-Love insisted on what I was about to tell her.

Hanging my backpack on one shoulder, I glanced around the apartment, wishing the next hopeful who will be housed here would rep the land of the brave. As a black man, I was blessed and lucky to have made it this far.

I pressed the lock button on the keypad for the last time.

"I'm your number one fan," Tina-Love admitted.

That was solid. When it came to pleasing me, in a few ways Tina-Love knew me better than Z. Had to make sure that changed. I wanted Z to be the only woman that knew my innermost secrets. Next to my mother being my nonstop supporter, Tina-Love

72

rolled with the unconditional.

"Let's surprise her. I'll work out the deets. We can discuss it at your mom's dinner gathering. I am determined to get you guys back together. And a celebration is in order for my favorite guy. You're going to make history."

"Love you," I said, as my driver parked.

"Love you more," Tina-Love responded, before ending our conversation.

Chapter 11
Xena

I showered, layered my skin with shea butter, then eased into a cobalt lace jumpsuit with wide legs and a plunging neckline. As I turned my back to the full-length mirror, the part of my body that Memphis liked most would make honeydew melons jealous. Adonis preferred playing with my small breasts. If I'd eventually have a baby bump, on top of the nonvisible lump in my belly, I was going to flaunt my perfect figure every chance I had.

All dressed up, thankful I was home alone, I covered my ears with my headphones, played "Saved" by Khalid, sat in my specially handcrafted, oversize pink chair listening to the lyrics. The accessories I needed to hand stitch onto garments were within arm's reach, including a handheld miniature sewing machine. After threading a needle, I added colonial-style wrist cuffs stitch by stitch to the light and airy men's blouse.

Next, I attached a flat tapered collar. I secured nine buttons under a flap that made them invisible. I replayed "Saved." I hung the purple shirt on a hanger, then steam pressed it. Admiring my creation, I was proud. Whatever my client's net worth, he was going to be the envy of the wealthiest men in Savannah.

Meticulously eyeing the jacket, I pinned the sleeves at the shoulders, then the waist-band to the slim-fit pants. I decided to work on the jacket next as it would take more time.

Not wanting to psych myself into eating for two, I tried to ignore the growl in my stomach. I was undoubtedly hungry, but I didn't want to gain weight prematurely. Not from a plus one. After laying the garment across the back of the chair, I opened the refrigerator. Tossed a handful of blackberries into a bowl. Staring at the rich color, I leaned on the counter and started crying. With every word of the song I wept.

"I miss you so much, Memphis. If you only knew how sorry I am," I said.

I dried my cheeks with a napkin and tossed it in the trash. I cracked an egg, separated the white, washed the yolk down the drain. If Adonis were here, he would've eaten it, despite the fact that I'd warned him of the outrageous cholesterol content. Placing the bowl in the sink, I changed my mind about making a scramble, then rinsed the egg white down the drain.

A ring tone registered. It was the one I'd attached to Adonis's number. I shook my head. "Bodak Yellow" by Cardi B drowned out "Love on Top." I hurried to my cell, answered, "Hey, bestie." I crossed my fingers, then continued, "Please tell me you're back in town. Please."

Tina-Love was a real jet-setter. Drop-dead gorgeous. The most keep-it-real person I knew. And I was eternally grateful that she'd introduced me to my one true love, Memphis.

"Just got in. My driver just left. My housekeeper is on her way out. And my dick is dripping wet fresh out of the shower."

That gurl never wasted time spreading for a man. I didn't bother questioning her or inquiring which guy she was getting ready to have sex with.

"Stop scrambling those eggs, put the smoothie in the refrigerator, and let's meet for breakfast. This Italian guy is hot for me. So hot that he wants to fly me back to Rome next week and I insisted that you accompany me." Excitement radiated in her voice.

Stuffing a handful of fruit into my mouth,

I mumbled, "I have a man, remember?"

Tina-Love laughed. "Get your fine naked ass in my bed," she said to whatever man was with her, then told me, "Sorry, girl. You know you have to tell these niggas what to do."

Trying to imagine if he'd dried off first, I could never talk that way to Adonis. Or Memphis. I heard a man respond, "Okay, baby. Whatever you say."

"You don't have the man you want. Adonis is a seat filler until I get you and Memphis back together, chicka. Meet me at Pirates' House in two hours so we can go over the deets for our trip. I promise you won't touch your purse. And you'll be inspired by the fashions. Your designs are going to make it on the runway in New York."

Two hours? Staring at the jacket, I sighed knowing the deadline for the groom's suit couldn't be pushed back. If I didn't need to let her in on my recent catastrophe, I'd pass.

There were times I wished I was more like Tina-Love. She knew how to live in every moment. We'd been friends since birth, but when it came to men, the two of us were complete opposites. I was a serial monogamous dater who'd only had four boyfriends. Tina-Love entertained whomever, whenever she wanted and she'd never committed to a relationship with any man. How come Tina-Love never slipped up and got pregnant? She was the loose one.

"Okay, but I can't stay long. This guy's seamstress messed up. I agreed to finish his tuxedo by this evening. He's getting married tomorrow, and now I'm going to miss picking up my fresh produce from the market." Despite being overwhelmed, seeing my bestie was worth it.

"You a badass, Xena Trinity. You'll get it all done. You always do. I'm super hyped! And you're superwoman! Can't wait to see you! Bye."

I still couldn't believe I was carrying this child. I prayed, "God, please don't let having a baby ruin my career. Please, God. Please."

"Let me see you jack your dick!"

Hadn't realized Tina-Love was still on the line. Pressing mute on my cell, I washed my hands, picked up the jacket, sat in my oversize chair, and decided to eavesdrop.

CHAPTER 12
MEMPHIS

Sitting on the back seat in an SUV, I lowered the rear passenger's-side window. Looking up at my unit, I was ready for the next chapter.

"Drive slow, man," I instructed him.

My phone rang. It was one of my local randoms. Truthfully, I'd completely forgotten about this one. "What's up?"

"Hey! I'm surprised you answered. Aren't you supposed to be training?" she said happily.

If she knew where I should've been, then why was she blowin' me up at o'dark-thirty? Nonchalant, I replied, "Yeah, heading home for —"

She cut me off. "Don't be sad, Memphis. I'm soooo sorry you're leaving. I knew you wouldn't make it. There's always next time."

That spill reminded me why I'd stopped fucking her and with her pessimistic ass. "Listen —"

"No worries. I've got just the thing to cheer you up! I was calling to say I have two VIP packages for the BET Experience weekend. Postpone your trip home. There's nothing happening in Savannah anyways. Getting back to that X to the Z, ex can wait a few more days. I promise to make you forget the disappointment. I —"

Females always jumped to conclude. "No fucking thanks. I can't accept your offer."

"You so crazy. Wait till I give you the lineup," she insisted.

"I'm going to visit my mom." I'd die of starvation before opening my mouth to share my success with this here random. "Gotta catch this incoming."

"Okay, but hit me right —"

I ended her call, answered the other before it went to voice mail. "Hey, I was just about to surprise your sexy ass. I'm on my way to your place. I have some great news."

Natalie was convenient and she knew her way around my dick blindfolded. Hoped she wasn't still holding on to ills about Z. Natalie deserved closure and I wanted farewell sex. Had to fuel up in case Z was holding out on giving it up. I didn't mind waiting on Z, but I refused to hold out. I liked Natalie enough to let her freak me one more time, but no woman could take Z's spot.

They all knew that. Thought about Tina-Love.

"Me too," she screeched. "I have great news. I'll cook you up an omelet when you arrive."

"Cool." She was back to her normal giddy self and I was hungry as hell.

Coach mentioned to be careful when it came to sex, but I wasn't like other guys and Natalie wasn't the conniving type. I understood females and my body well. I had different levels of cumming. Had to refrain from letting Natalie blow me. That female could siphon my nuts faster than I could run the two-hundred-yard dash.

The driver parked in front of her town house. I got out. Before I rang the bell, she opened the door, then stepped on the porch wearing nothing.

"Damn, girl." As I shoved her inside, we stumbled, then fell on the carpet. "What were you thinking?" I shut the door, helped her up. "Go put on something."

"I always sleep in the nude. You know that." Natalie frowned. Headed upstairs toward her bedroom.

Now that I was on the verge of celebrity status, I couldn't risk paparazzi photographing me with a naked white woman.

I placed my backpack near the door, sat

on her couch. Picking up the remote, I turned the channel to ESPN. Changed to the local news. Back to ESPN, hoping there'd be a brief mention of my acceptance with my photo on the screen. Football. Basketball. Golf. Tennis. All got media love. Track stars busted our asses too.

Natalie returned to the living room, sat across my thighs wearing pink boy shorts and a tank top. Her mouth open wide, she suctioned in my lips. I French-kissed her the way she liked it. Aggressive. My shaft hardened as my head began snaking its way to her pussy. I swear my dick was a cyclops. The beast slid from underneath the waistband of my sweats. I pulled Natalie's panties to the side, let them go. Best to save dessert for last.

"What you stirring up for me? Vegetable omelet with grilled chicken breasts?"

"That or a juicy filet mignon with scrambled eggs." Natalie rocked her clit on the head of my dick. "I'll make it in a sec. First tell me your news, babe?"

Hesitating, I stared into her eyes as she continued to sit sideways. "You got to swear you won't put it on social media."

Eagerly she nodded. "Okay, I won't. Now, what is it?"

Calmly I told her, "I made it to the next

level. I'm going to the Olympics."

Natalie straddled my lap, removed her shirt. "I was hoping you were going tell me!" She kissed my face all over, and her smile was wide. "I knew you'd do it!" She leaned toward the end table, grabbed her cell, snapped a few selfies of us.

I gripped her wrist. "Delete that!"

"Why?" she said, then gave me a pouty mouth. "It's for our eyes only."

"I'm serious. Now. I told you, you can't post anything with or about me. Delete it. Now!" Had to put bass in my tone to let her know I meant it. Watching her select the pics, then send them to her trash, I said, "Empty the can. I shouldn't have told you, man."

"You worried about Z seeing us?" she asked, tossing her phone on the cushion. "I already knew."

Women. Always lying to get a reaction. Losing my appetite for breakfast, and Natalie, I considered hitting back the random that was fresh on my list of incomings. I could go to her spot. Take my edge off. Then head to the airport.

Natalie's tongue swept across my face like a windshield wiper redirecting my attention. I loved that about her. She was unpredictable. A real freak. The kind of woman I might cheat with, but there was only one woman I'd ring up and that would never be Natalie. But I was here and her pussy was like a bird in my hand.

"I have good news too," Natalie exclaimed, grinding on my soft sausage.

She was good at getting an orgasm out of me even when I was pissed. My link grew longer. I was down for our last smash, but fortune and fame was my new bitch.

"Spit it out then so we can both be lit. And you can fix me that steak."

Natalie had traveled to every continent, volunteering to do mission work. She believed the world was her backyard garden and she had an obligation to help those in need of nurturing. Cuba. Ghana. Belize. Nicaragua. Baja. All were places she'd made a difference.

"Let me guess. You're heading to a new mission in Puerto Rico or Costa Rica?"

"That's not a guess, Memphis. I do need to go to Cape Town. That'll be my last trip for a while. They're running out of clean water," she said sadly. Then her eyes beamed. Mine started turning up from her shine.

"I'm pregnant!" She cheered as though she was on the sideline for a Lakers game.

"What the fuck did you say?"

Wiggling spirited fingers on my nose, she repeated, "We're pregnant, baby!"

"We ain't shit." Flopping her onto her side, I lamented, "I told you I didn't want any kids. You did this shit on purpose."

Natalie scooted to the end of the sofa, placed her back against the arm. That bitch hugged her knees to her chest, started crying while frantically shaking her head. "Me either. It just happened. I thought you'd be as stoked as I am. I know you have to stay focused. The baby will be here months before the competition."

Ordering an Uber, I was not starting a family with her. What was my mother going to say? If Z had told me that, I'd be on cloud ten, planning a future for my son or daughter. Son and daughter. Running for a deeper cause. Posing for pictures with a gold medal around my neck while rocking my kid on my arm.

"Contraceptives aren't a hundred percent," she explained. "Our child is a blessing."

"Well, I'm a thousand percent. Squash that shit." I couldn't lie. I could no longer stand the sight of her ass. She was probably never on the pill. How in the hell could I tell?

After picking up my backpack, I waited

outside for my ride, went to the drugstore, bought Natalie a Plan B pill and a bottle of water.

Soon as she opened the door, I handed her both. "Swallow it now."

She shook her head.

"Bitch! I'm not asking. Take it now!" I demanded.

Heard a door open. A woman stood on the adjacent porch. "Natalie, you okay? You need me to call the police?"

The pill was still in her hand. Would probably melt from all the tears. She hadn't said no, and I was no fool. "Don't contact me again." Walking away, I thought of my father. Opening the rear passenger door of my Uber, I didn't want to follow his lead.

If Natalie was telling the truth, I couldn't be a repeat. I had to do the right thing. But how was I going to explain the situation to Z? Sitting in the back seat of the car, I thought that kid was a trap baby. Never imagined she'd do that to me.

A few blocks away, I told the driver, "Man, pull over. Let me out."

Strapping my bag to my back, I noticed a cop car heading toward us.

Just got accepted to rep my country. In my mind I was the man. If those guys were looking for me, to them I could be a dead nigga on the street.

"I'm good," I told the driver. "Let's go."

Chapter 13
Tina-Love

Men were necessary for one thing. *Great* sex.

The majority couldn't fuck worth a damn. Moves scripted. Positions on instant replay. Too many men possessed a limited imagination when it came to pleasing me.

Red polyurethane sheets and shams covered my king-size bed. A spotlight attached to my ceiling beamed on Roman's sinful caramel skin.

"I love the way you jack your dick, babe. You're so fucking hot." Zoning in on his large hand as it eased up his shaft, over his head, down the other side and back made me moist.

Relaxing my ass on the heel of my feet, I watched Roman stroke his thick, long, beautiful and shiny dick. I sat in the center of the bed, facing him, spread my thighs wide, then I slid my hand over my wet pussy. Teasing my clit, I parted my lips, inserted my middle finger inside my vagina, then stuffed it in his mouth.

"Damn, your pussy is sweet," he mumbled. Holding my wrist as though it were a stick on a lollipop, he suctioned my finger up to my knuckle.

Smack! Slapping his face, I commanded, "Roll onto your stomach," shoving him at the same time. He knew I didn't believe in asking twice. His other option was getting dressed and escorted out of my house. No man voluntarily departed from the queendom. Too many apparatuses in every room of my house that commanded their curiosity.

Lust consumed me. I could always depend on Roman to fuck me to my satisfaction. That was why he'd held first place in my rotation for the past three months. Ricardo Salvatori — my Italian stallion — was new to the lineup, but I'd instantly promoted him to second after he made me climax without touching me. If he didn't reside five thousand miles away, Ricardo could potentially eliminate his competition.

Roman's body was compact solid. He was the finest FBI agent I'd met. Roman didn't have a six-pack, but he definitely had hard, flat abs. Huge muscular thighs. And a big one!

Roman faced the slick sheet, turned his head toward the sex swing that was across the room, cuddled a pillow under his chest. "Ready when you are, boss lady."

I picked up a spray bottle, spritzed oil on my titties, his back, and the bed. I slid my nipples up and down his torso, glided my pussy along his spine to not just get him hard but also to make Roman excited.

"You miss this pussy," I whispered in his ear.

"Baby, you know I do," he moaned.

Trust no man was my motto. After what some men had done to me, Roman's place of employment did not make him trust-worthy. Why hadn't my mother, Janice Jones, protected me? Was her having a husband more important than my safety? I had secrets that I was ashamed to tell anyone, including Xena.

The hell with men, their sexual assaults, and their double-standard bullshit! My industry was plagued with married and single sleazeballs. Fidelity was nonexistent. I'd experienced the hands and penis of famous men who'd cheated on their wives as they violated me. Trying to make a man be faithful was a waste of my time.

Kneeling beside Roman, *whack!* My palm

rested on his butt cheek. "Say you like it, nigga."

"Ow," he grunted. "I like it. Love you."

I gripped the cat-o-nine-tails that was on my headboard and twirled the handle. The motion was in my wrist as I looped the black leather strands repeatedly, then softly brushed his body head to toe. *Whack!* This time I hit him harder. Burying his face in the pillow, Roman arched his back.

"Damn, Tina-Love! I miss you, too, but take it easy, my baby."

Nobody took it easy on me. No one! Easy was for the weak. "Shut the fuck up. Give me that ass! And tell mama you love her." I separated his cheeks. Had to pull firmly, then hold them apart.

"I love you so much, mama," he quickly professed. Tilting his hips upward, he granted me access to that tight end. "You have no idea." He held his behind higher.

"You know what good dogs get, doncha?" Moving a red pillow underneath his dick, softly I told him, "Relax, baby."

Frantically he nodded. "Give it to me," he begged, panting.

Sex with me was an experience men never forgot. I stimulated his balls with the leather straps. Moving up, I jiggled the tips inside his ears, at the nape of his neck, trailed the feathery light tips of the strap down his spine, then back to where I started.

I grew up feeling like a freak of nature, but one modeling agent saw something in me that my classmates, friends, mother, stepfather, and I hadn't. Rainey convinced my mom I had a one-of-a-kind appeal. Overnight, after graduating high school, I went from looking in the mirror at what I saw as an ugly duckling, to a runway show in Milan. I went from being poor to being a teenage millionaire living more in Europe than the United States.

Money couldn't change the fact that I still hated my mother for not protecting me.

People around the world still did a double-take when they saw my pouty raspberry-chocolate lips; wide, marquise-shaped eyes; crystal blue irises; long, thick, natural lion's mane; Passe Blanc complexion; long torso; longer legs; size-five slender figure; and A-cups. Men who were fortunate to lick my uncommonly black-cherry areolas and vulva instantly wanted to marry my physical. Had to keep my heart guarded. I could travel the seven continents anytime I wanted and I never needed a man to fly me first-class.

Roman may have not known exactly what I was going to do next, but I knew what he liked. Parting his butt cheeks again, I circled the tip of my tongue along the perimeter of his asshole, then softly planted kiss after kiss after kiss in the center.

The longest "mmmmmm" percolated from the pit of his gut.

Fuck my falling in love with any man. No dude was worth the effort of my being his trophy. I got unconditional affection from the best source, my biological dad. My father, may he rest in peace, taught me how a man should treat me. Repeated acts of kindness weren't the same as a man catching feelings for me the way Memphis felt about Xena. She attracted love.

Lust was drawn to me.

Companionship, I was never in one place long enough to build a worthwhile foundation. Being on the run and the runway was the life I preferred.

Lights, cameras, all eyes on Tina-Love Jones.

I powered on a small butt plug, rubbed it on the sheet, then inserted it into Roman's rectum. I massaged his testicles. His breathing became weighted.

"On your back! Now." I wasn't asking. Never wanted a man to get comfortable in my bed.

I pushed Roman's shoulders, then straddled his hips. Rolling on a condom, I forced a pink hands-free vibrating pleasure ring (with a massager for my clit) to the base of his shaft to keep the rubber from slipping off. My throbbing pussy was slobbering and thirsty at the same time. Inserting his swollen head inside my vagina, I began grinding and winding on his shit rough.

I screamed. "Fuck you! Yeah!"

Roman palmed my ass. Matching my tempo, his strong hands yanked my body toward his pelvis. I placed my hands on his abdomen. Shoved. He thrust his hips upward. The vibration of the ring made me hotter, him harder.

"Yes! Roman. Yes! Roman," I shouted, dragging his name out of my mouth several more times. "Yes! Fuck this good pussy. Whose dick is this?" I placed my fingers behind his neck, my thumbs against his Adam's apple. I gently squeezed.

"Do it, my sweet Tina-Love," he said.

I tightened my grip. "Make me cream all over my dick," I demanded, contracting my grip. His neck was wide like a football player's. I choked him until his veins protruded. My pussy started pulsating. My aggression against men helped release my hatred.

"You ready for this shower?" I asked, loosening my fingers.

"Squirt on me," he begged.

"What have you done to earn mama's precious liquid platinum?" Lightly I stroked his face.

"I brought your new credit card. Tina-Love, please, baby," Roman said, thumbing my clit. His finger moved frantically. Up and down, then in a circular motion.

Squirting came easy, but I didn't do it for every man. "What's the limit?" I asked. Pinching his nipples, I prepared to give him what he wanted.

Roman nodded. "Do it, Tina-Love. I'm about to bust, baby."

Slowing my grind, I asked, "How much?"

"Double!" he shouted.

"So I can spend up to fifty thousand dollars?" I asked.

He nodded.

I stood on the sheet. Roman removed the condom and toy. The butt plug was still buzzing in his ass.

Bearing down, I let my pussy juices gush all over his body.

Roman jacked himself off.

I slid off my bed like it was a sliding board, went to the restroom, washed my hands. Retrieving my phone from the floor, I stared at the screen. *What the hell? Fifty-two minutes and counting and Xena was still on the line.*

Closet freak. "Bye, girl," I said, ending my call with Xena. Texted my housekeeper, **Need your services again. Egyptian cotton linen sheets.**

"Your time is up," I told Roman. "I have an appointment in a half hour. Wash your ass and get out."

Chapter 14
Xena

How are you and my grandbaby? Less than seventy-two hours of our knowing I was pregnant with Adonis's child and another text message registered from Mrs. Jennifer Oglethorpe.

I replied, **We're fine, ma'am. Thanks again for the car.**

Placing my phone on the vanity, I peed, washed my hands, then I parted my hair in the center, brushed it flat against my scalp, plaited a braid on each side, and tied the edges into a bow that rested between my breasts.

A call registered. I spoke through my speaker, "Good morning, Topez. How are you?"

"Awesome and highly favored by the Man above! We need to make an adjustment to our recent contract," she squealed.

Staring at my screen, I frowned. "Which one?" I asked, welcoming all new clients.

I'd nearly saved enough money to move out of Adonis's place and buy my own. Financial independence would mean time-sensitive obligations. Rent. Utilities. Cell. Insurance. Had to budget my resources for purchasing the best materials if I was accepted this year. Plus, it wouldn't make sense to create unnecessary debt when my plan to get back with Memphis hadn't changed. Nothing seemed right.

"I e-mailed it to you an hour ago. If you haven't opened it, don't," she insisted.

"I'm listening."

"Instead of making one of your colonial original tuxedos," she said, then paused.

Painting my lips with the only color I'd worn since high school — the perfect blend of brown with a red undertone, cinnamon — I remained quiet. Topez was silent. Slowly I responded, "Okay. What?" Foundation. Shadows. I'd never worn them and didn't care for them.

Topez continued, "You need to make eight! Isn't that great! And they are going to pay us in cash. You ready for this?" Topez's excitement bounced off my bathroom walls. "Five thousand dollars!"

"That's including the groom's tux, right?"

"No. But look at it this way, we are one step closer to New York's Men's Fashion

Week, my dear. Yes!" She shouted this time. "You have three weeks."

"At that price and turnaround, the groom is the only one getting an original design. The others can choose their colors, but that's it. And theirs will not be hand stitched." I pressed on the lump in my abdomen. "Ouch." A good detox was what I needed. Maybe I could rid my body of all foreign objects.

I knew there were men who didn't have a lot of money, but Topez had to stop under-valuing my time and talent. After deducting her twenty percent, paying roughly $2,500 for cloth and accessories, my gross would equal $1,500.

"That's a lot of work for —"

"I'll pick up the tab on my photographer shooting the entire wedding ceremony and comp you the digital portfolio." Topez's camera guy definitely had an undeniable ability to capture breathtaking moments.

My struggle was real. As was my determination.

While she clicked, clicked, clicked, I'd stitch, stitch, stitch each jacket, pair of pants, and my signature blouse.

Processing how I was going to complete this order with less than three days per suit, I thought, *What if I start having morning sick-*

ness like the last time?

"You there?" Topez asked.

Sitting on the toilet, I answered, "Don't think I'm not appreciative. But you have to start discussing details with me in advance."

If I were constantly fulfilling other people's dreams, when was I going to focus on my private collection that she knew nothing about, and stop piecing my creations together with images from Topez's events?

"You don't sound your usual self, darling. We'll discuss whatever is worrying you later today. What time is our client picking up his suit today?"

No enhancements for my brows, no strokes of blush on my cheeks to accentuate my high bone structure. Melancholy coated my response. "Six." Deadlines for me were beginning to overlap.

"See you at five fifty-five. Joy and sorrow. Just remember, Xena, everything is temporary. Your attitude determines your outcome. We're alive. We're healthy. Cheer up, darling," she said, ending the call.

I washed my hands again. "I could use a manicure," I said, checking out my bare nails.

Topez and Tina-Love were "live in every moment" type of women. I always worried about yesterday or tomorrow. Or the past hour or the next. Topez was, in part, right. I needed an emotional adjustment. More importantly, I could also use a temporary break from my obligations to regroup.

How long could I hide my situation from my mom and dad? Three months? Six? Forever? I avoided sharing information with people I knew wouldn't be supportive. Maybe my mother would be nicer to her grandchild than she was to me.

I didn't care for polish of any kind. SNS. Gel. Acrylic. That was twenty-five extra dollars every two weeks that I'd rather invest in building my brand.

The stress of finishing my current client's suit on time lingered as I draped the unfinished jacket over the mannequin. I had to admit, I'd put my Z touch on that design. Memphis was the only one who called me an alphabet. The first shall be last and the last shall be first. *No matter what happens, Z, you and I will forever be one.* He was right. I hated how I still loved him.

After agreeing to meet Tina-Love for lunch, I realized I had more work than time. I set an alarm on my cell to remind me of when I needed to leave the restaurant. To the Pirates' House and back, door to door and back home, I allowed myself two hours. By two p.m., not a minute later, I'd be sitting in my pink oversize chair, sewing. I'd have to miss the fresh market this Saturday, but I'd allotted time to remove the pins and machine stitch the remaining seams before meeting with Topez.

You can get it done, Xena. You always do, I told myself.

With the five-thousand-dollar bag Tina-Love had gifted me from her first runway show in Milan hanging on my forearm, I picked up the key to my new BMW, then opened my front door.

"Oh shit!" I hopped back. Staring in Adonis's light gray eyes, I rattled my head. "Baby, why are you back so soon?"

"I picked y'all up your favorite smoothie from The Sentient Bean." He scanned my outfit. "A better question is where are you going all dressed up this early? Thought you had to —"

Smiling, I said, "Tina-Love is back. We're having a quick bite. I want to tell her the news in person."

Adonis's lips curved high. I almost saw all thirty-two of his pearly whites. "I'll go with you. I'll drive," he said, closing and locking the door.

Standing in front of him in the hallway, I shook my head. "Baby, why don't you" — I paused, thinking of what would keep him busy — "go to the market for us." I touched my stomach. "And get our usual."

A frown consumed his entire face. "You sure you don't want me to drive you and the baby? That way we can make the announcement together."

I couldn't be more certain. "Positive," I told him.

Adonis hunched his shoulders. "I guess y'all need your girl time. Don't forget we're having dinner with my parents tonight, and tell Tina-Love hi for me."

God, I can't take nine months of this.

Caressing his face, I planted a light kiss on his mouth, then trotted down nineteen steps, passed Mr. Ben Matthews's apartment, exited the door to our building, then got in my new car. Sitting behind the wheel, I charted my ovulation dates in my mind. My period was indeed late. I made a quick stop at the drugstore. Purchased a two-pack pregnancy test, then headed to meet Tina-Love.

Before going inside, I removed the stick from the box, placed it inside a compartment in my purse. If I was going to let her know, I had to confirm she'd be an aunt while I was with her.

I placed the trash inside the glove box, slowly exited my BMW, then entered the restaurant. As I approached the hostess stand, a text message registered from Mrs. Oglethorpe. **How are you and my grand-baby?**

Ugh!!! Returning to the car, I replied, **We're fine thanks.** I retrieved the plastic bag to wrap up the stick after urinating on it. I reentered Pirates' House, went directly to the restroom, emptied my bladder.

Awaiting the test confirmation, I texted my bestie, **Hurry up, girl! I need a drink!**

Chapter 15
Tina-Love

Running a lil late. #fuckfest ran ova. Be there in 15 tops. Order a bottle of champagne, I texted Xena.

"Sex with me" . . . My theme blasted through my speakers as I cruised out of my driveway onto the road marked PRIVATE. My pussy was lit and so was I.

Roman had that good-good readily accessible dick, but his wasn't the best I'd had. It was the best I had right now. En route to the restaurant, a call registered. It was Roman. I tapped the decline button on my display. Didn't need to hear the accolades for my pleasuring him. Or tell him I didn't care to see him tonight, tomorrow, or the next day.

Immediately my phone rang again, interrupting Rihanna's lyrics. I reached to switch to mute and restart my song. I stopped, then answered, "Hey! How's my baby?"

"Good. Real good. Waiting to board my

flight. Where you at?" Memphis asked.

"Where you need to be?" I countered.

"You ain't never gonna stop answering a question with one. And before you say, why should I, I can't wait to see you at my mom's tonight."

Something in Memphis's tone was off. "What's on your mind?" I felt his energy. I always connect with his emotions. "You need to talk? Speak."

"I'm good, man. How many dudes you done fucked?"

"What does that matter? What you need to know is, I'm on my way to meet our gurl for lunch," I said.

Dipping on his stick one time, then hooking him up with Xena, didn't count as betrayal. I wasn't the commitment kind. And, I rode Memphis before, not after their connection.

I heard him say, "Dude, I wish I was there." Then he said, "I'd pop up and surprise her ass."

A lot needed to transpire before Memphis and Z got back together. I hated how men thought because everything was right with them, that was all that mattered. I had to see where Xena's heart and head was.

"This is one on one. I got some of that for you, too, but y'all need to get y'all shit together and stop all this back and forth nonsense. When are you going to tell her your good news?"

Ignoring me, he asked, "Where y'all eating at?"

Memphis hadn't seen Xena in a year. His waiting another day or so wasn't changing their explosive reunion. Plus, my gurl needed a heads-up so we could plot her move out from Adonis's boring ass.

"Uh-uh. I'm not saying. But I'll drop your name in her ear after her second mimosa."

"Do more than that. Let her know I'm in transit. Tell her I know I fucked up bad before I left, but I've changed. I'm ready to come correct and put a ring on it under one condition. She comes clean. I want Mrs. Xena Brown sitting in the stands cheering for her husband."

Memphis had a lot of maturing to do. Everything couldn't be about him all the time. I realized he wasn't marriage material yet. He was clueless. But Xena had to lock him down before the vultures started circling. I'd help him focus more on Xena while getting her to understand her sacrifice of breaking up with Adonis was for the greater good down the road. Xena deserved to have her own men's clothing line in department stores around the world as much as Memphis had earned his opportunity to rep the US of A.

"Post on Instagram that you're heading home and I'll show it to her."

"Cool. Done," he said, paused, then continued, "Bruh, that's my seat. Move over. I want to see Xena right after Mom's get together. Invite her to your place."

Damn. Memphis had to slow down. I let him know, "If it were anyone else other than you, I'd say don't go fucking up my girl's relationship. Promise me if I get the two of you back to —"

"Hold the fuck up. Relation-what? She with the same nigga?" The deepest concern I'd heard Memphis express sounded like a megaphone in my ear. "Tell me the truth."

That reaction right there was why I refused to be bothered with a man's bullshit. "He swooped her up soon as you boarded your flight to Cali. You know our gurl got that black girl magic potion." I wanted to say "magic pussy," but that would've drove his ass stupid. "Xena's in high demand. But no worries. This time don't you act almighty and run her off."

"She had to be fucking both of us at the same time. That's the real reason why she walked away from me. Stopped taking my calls." He became quiet. Meant he was processing Xena's actions from start to now.

Seemed as though he was on the verge of crying, but I knew his arrogant behind was too prideful for that. I didn't owe Memphis an explanation. I was on his side. Best not to piss me off.

"She removed herself from the situation in order to allow you to handle your shit. And you did that. I can't wait. I'm going to the Olympics to see your black ass run like Flash."

"I'm faster than him. What's Xena's dude's name? I know him?"

There wasn't many regrets I had. Telling him Xena was not immediately available was becoming one. "Calm down, my baby. You know I've been pulling for your young, fine ass since you were twenty-one. All you need to know is he's a good man and he treats her like a queen. But Xena does not love him."

"Bet? Let's make sure it stays that way."

"I'll talk to Xena when I see her. Bye."

"Hold up. What you doing after we leave Mom's tonight?" he asked.

I knew it was coming. Memphis, like most men, was quick to forget shit. "What you have in mind?" I asked.

The smile in his voice returned. "Netflix and chill at your spot like we used to. And stovetop popcorn popped in olive oil with whipped butter and sea salt."

"Fine, but we're watching my favorite *Girls Trip,*" I said.

Laughing, Memphis stated, "*Black Panther* is the feature. Never gets old. And make me one of your famous Greek salads."

"You'd betta get a to-go from Ms. Hattie. I'm fifteen on top of fifteen minutes late. Bye, boy."

"I love you," he said quickly.

"Love you more." Blushing, I ended the call. I'd find out what was really bothering him when I looked him in his eyes.

I parked near the entrance, picked up my purse and Xena's gift bag, then hurried inside.

CHAPTER 16
XENA

Browsing the gift shop upstairs at the Pirates' House, I'd read all of the bumper stickers, hanging plaques, and T-shirts. A call registered from Topez. Not wanting to explain why I wasn't home finishing up our client's tux, I let her call go to voice mail, then listened to her message.

"*Xena!*" she screeched. "*We have a revision to the contract and you will never guess from whom. This will, if you do an outstanding job on the nine suits, secure us a place at New York's Men's Fashion Week next summer! Call me soon as you get this message.*"

I leapt high, kicked both feet backward. "Thank you, Lord." That was the best news of my entire life. Had to rethink making all of the groomsmen appear the same.

The cashier questioned, "Honey, are you okay over there?"

Nodding really fast, I couldn't stop smiling. "Yes, ma'am."

I glanced at my watch. "Oh no." Anxiety replaced joy.

No updated text from my bestie, I could've at least sewn a thousand stitches. Hurrying downstairs, I saw Tina-Love posing at the bottom of the stairway.

"Girl, I have to go home and finish a jacket and pair of pants by six, meet with Topez, then get started on my next contract. I'm finally getting my big break." Dinner with Adonis's parents could wait.

Tina-Love leaned down, hugged me tight. "Calm down. We're here now."

"Let's meet for breakfast tomorrow," I told my bestie.

Tina-Love was glowing, wearing a cream-colored multilayered bell-sleeve top that was buttoned up to the wingtip collar. She rocked a pair of black high-waist leather short shorts. Her forty-inch-long legs glistened. Gold crescent moons, bright stars, and identifiable planets decorated the hot pants that barely covered her cute buttocks.

"I like your jumper. You look so cute. I miss your ass." Her eyes shined at mine.

"You could've let me know your fifteen was going to be thirty, but I should've known. Outside of business —"

"Hush," she abruptly interrupted with a grin. "You should've known since you were eavesdropping, gurl. Hope you enjoyed Roman too."

Tina-Love kissed then hugged me tighter, rocking me side to side. I was glad when she finally released our embrace. I stepped back.

"You good?" she asked. "Your energy feels off."

Overwhelmed and excited, I was on the verge of crying. One of the reasons we'd bonded was growing up we were both social outcasts. Tina-Love was tall and lanky. I was an introvert being abused by my stepmom.

"Sweet and sour good. But —" My spirit flat-lined midsentence, evoking silence.

My work was arduous. I loved the outcome more than the process. Showing up, having others fuss over making her body a canvas, my bestie was head-to-toe gorgeous. "I'd like to live in your shoes for a day," I confessed. Seemed like fun.

Tina-Love's net worth was eight figures, and she seldom had to spend a dime of her money. I was ready to achieve millionaire status based on my name. But not from living in the air, sexing different men, or being on my feet.

Twirling once, she replied, "I can arrange that. If you're serious this time."

She'd been in the industry almost ten

years. She could make it happen? More from a fantasy standpoint. I fingered the untied gold bow dangling around her neck. Red open-toed stilettoes, six-inches high glided across the wooden floor as though they were on rollers.

"See you tomorrow," I said, stepping toward the front door.

"You're not leaving. Cheer up, honey, I'm late, not dead," she exclaimed, pulling me to the hostess's stand.

No matter what the occasion, she always commanded attention. I did too. Just not when I was with her.

"Call me." A guy my height, bald with a full beard, handed Tina-Love his card, then added, "Anytime."

I watched Tina-Love let the card flutter until it hit the floor. I failed at concealing my smirk.

"Fuck you with that 'anytime' bullshit," she lamented. "Everything here is designer all day."

"Except your mouth," he said.

"Take your disrespectful dick home to your wife!" she shouted.

People lined up behind us clapped. The guy left without looking back.

Tina-Love's perfect-width shoulders, never-ending torso, and giraffe legs got any man she wanted. Most went wild over those plump lips. Her natural hair was parted down the middle like mine, but she had mad volume that fluffed on the sides as though her Afro had collapsed at the top. Tina-Love could go from brunette to red to blond to silky pressed, to Brazilian blowout, to dreads, back to Afro any day of the week.

The maître d' scanned Tina-Love head to toe. "Impeccable indeed," he stated, speaking more through his nostrils. "Your mouth spoke the truth to that man," he said, escorting us to a small room tucked off of the buffet dining area. He passed six occupied tables, then entered a quaint enclave that was more suitable for a private party, but I appreciated the exclusivity.

"Your waiter will be right with you, ladies."

Okay, nasal congestion wasn't his problem, that was simply the way he spoke.

"Excuse me, sir. We don't have much time. Can you put in an order for a bottle of champagne?" Tina-Love asked, adding a friendly, "Please."

Standing taller, he said, "Coming right up, madam," then he retraced his last steps.

"Why do you flirt with every man?" I questioned.

"If you have to think about flirting, it's not flirting. Anyone can achieve low self-esteem. I prefer to build upon perfection." Handing me the bag in her hand, my bestie said, "Compliments of the designer. It's an original."

I sat my lilac Dior aside. If I auctioned all of the originals she'd gifted me, I could lease the space above my storefront for storage and utilize downstairs for designing and sewing only. I removed the tissue, pulled out a tag with a name I didn't bother trying to pronounce. "Pewter. My favorite color. Thanks."

Hues of gray represented all facets of Savannah's history. From the soil to grow rice, to uniforms worn by soldiers who fought and died during the wars, to the pictures hanging on the walls surrounding us of pirates wearing tattered clothing. Guns, gunpowder, moss hanging from trees throughout the city — the one thing I realized was people were not onlyforgiving, many Southerners were forgetful. Ashes to ashes, dead bodies that hung from branches eventually turned to dust. Gray was a blend of black, white, and everyone in between.

"A little something to add to my gurl's collection," Tina-Love boasted.

She sat next to me at the table set for fourteen, placed her purse on an empty wooden chair. I put both of my handbags on the seat closest to me.

"Xena, your face is glowing. I love it. You're finally using the twenty-four-karat gold serum I sent."

Touching my cheeks, I wished that were true. "Thanks."

Tina-Love lowered my hand, shook her head. "Don't touch it." She'd taught me that only freshly sanitized fingers roamed above the neck.

Our waiter appeared, filled our flutes with champagne, then placed the bottle in a bucket of ice. "Since you don't have much time, may I take your orders?"

"Two orders of your shrimp and fries," Tina-Love requested.

"Nothing for me," I told him. "I have to leave soon."

"You also have to eat," my bestie countered, handing him a credit card. "Make hers to go. Mine for here and I'll have two of your Greek salads to go. Close me out."

I smiled. "Entertaining back-to-back today, huh?"

Retrieving her cell, Tina-Love answered, "Something like that." Tapping on her screen, she showed me a photo. "Can you believe how luscious this man is? Oh, my, gosh. If I could eat him through the phone, I'd swallow his dick whole."

I couldn't recall ever witnessing her depressed or disgusted. Didn't seem normal for anyone to be upbeat all the time. I didn't want to dilute my girlfriend's happiness.

Staring at the pic, I gasped. "Impressive, but do you always have to lead our reunion with a man's penis?" I visualized Memphis fully extended. That was the only shaft I longed for.

"No. But since you walked out on our boy, you never have anything exciting to share. You know I don't play when it comes to my grind. It's less stressful when I date like dudes and treat them like dogs. Gots to see the goods up front. Will not get that fake-ass surprise that comes packaged with popcorn between two peanuts. I have them jacking off and everything. Wanna see his cum shot? He's got serious range." Tina-Love's eyes grew wide.

Leaning back, I glanced around, as if someone in the adjacent area heard her, then I shook my head. "No, thanks. Adonis is good to me."

"But is he good enough for you? No. You don't love Adonis."

I wiggled my ring finger. She held my hand.

"Bitch, this is nice, but give it back. Memphis will be able to do better real soon.

Besides, you don't even smile with your eyes anymore."

I didn't have to. "You're the model. You're trained to project fake emotions. I'm not."

"Gurlfriend, you'd best stop wasting time and get back with Memphis before he snatches the gold. Once he announces he's Team USA, those white girls are going to be all over that beautiful black man."

Tina-Love had seen Memphis naked quite a few times when all of us used to skinny-dip in her pool, or relax in her Jacuzzi. At first, I was the only one uncomfortable. Tina-Love reassured me people in other countries had a pure affinity for nudity. Gradually, I became accustomed to the three of us not wearing clothes while at her house.

"He's probably already got situations and I'm sure the Latinas are humping him too." I stared into her eyes. Squinted. Upset that she'd attempted to make me feel desperate.

I knew she kept in contact with him. "He posted on his social he was coming home soon. You know when?"

"If I tell you, what are you going to do with the info?"

Tina-Love made it easier for me to deliver my bad news. "I need a break from men. Seriously, I have to re-elevate my trajectory." What was I doing with my life?

"I have your solution in one word." Tina-Love sang, "Italy."

Taking a deep breath, I exhaled. "Maybe, if I'm not —"

"Not what, gurl?"

"Pregnant." There, I'd said it.

Laughing, she ignored my sorrow. "I thought you had a real problem." Tina-Love stood, tapped on her phone, placed it on the table. "I'm going to the ladies' room. When I come back, I want you to repeat that. If I heard what I thought, Memphis will definitely not accept your having another man's child. We're getting rid of that problem immediately. It won't be your first abortion."

Holding back tears, I watched Tina-Love strut away with confidence about my dilemma. Memphis? His stepdad raised him. Memphis shouldn't have issues paying it forward. Tina-Love didn't have all the answers.

A text popped up from Mrs. Oglethorpe: **Dinner at my home 6pm. We want to celebrate our grandchild's conception with you and my son.**

I replied, **How's 8pm? I have a client coming over at 6.** Plus, I was going to need a nap and another shower.

That's grand. See you then, was her response.

I can't endure her for the next nine months! I screamed in my mind. *Okay, breathe.* I inhaled into my belly, held it for three seconds, then exhaled out my mouth. Eight o'clock wasn't going to work either. I'd forgotten about Topez.

Scrolling through my photo album, I focused on the first picture Tina-Love had taken of Memphis and me the day she introduced us.

Week one we went on a date to the black museum, the Beach Institute. Then we cruised on the riverboat. Not the one tourists purchased tickets to board. That was the one old man Ben Matthews — who had lots of wisdom — told me a black man used to own until white people forced that guy into an early grave. Memphis and I sailed on the free transit ferry. No one could've convinced me we weren't going to be together forever.

Lawd, why did you make Memphis this fine? My bestie's phone buzzed and lit up.

I stared at her screen. Frowned when I saw a picture of Memphis jumping a hurdle. Checking for Tina-Love's return, I didn't see her. I picked up her phone. A text registered, **Coming straight to your house**

121

when I land. Stay posted up . . . Oh, invite your mom to my mom's tonight. She'd love to see Janice. Up to you.

Memphis's text was immediately followed by a call. "Wow" I looked toward the entrance of the dining area. I didn't want to answer; I had to. It was fate.

I replied, "Hey, M."

An absent response lingered. Quietly I sucked in all the air I could. Letting it out, I repeated, "Hey, M."

"Z," was all he mentioned.

Ending our dialogue, I deleted his incoming call from Tina-Love's log, pressed the side button to close her screen, then placed Tina-Love's phone exactly where it had been.

Reclaiming her seat, and her cell, she glanced at her phone, up at me, back at her screen, then said, "Now repeat that."

"You're going to be an aunt." I touched my stomach. "I'm with child. Pregnant. Expecting in almost nine months. Did I make myself clear?" The tears I'd held in, I could no longer. I wept.

The waiter entered with Tina-Love's platter and two to-go bags. Quietly he sat everything down, then quickly exited.

"Hush," Tina-Love said, dabbing my cheeks with a napkin. "You're pregnant, not dead. You can't have it."

She'd said what I was thinking. Maybe the timing of Memphis's text was some sort of sign that keeping Adonis's baby was not right. I felt as though I'd cheated on Memphis.

"I can't get rid of it. Adonis knows I'm having his baby. And his parents bought me that new BMW parked out front. And I've already had —"

Tina-Love interrupted. "You are not for sale, honey. Take the Plan B if you're late." Tina-Love's eyes became glued to her screen. Without moving her head, she shifted her stare toward me. "Or you can take ella."

Plan B wasn't a consideration. My conception was confirmed. Not familiar with ella, I searched online. It worked like the morning-after pill. I could take it up to five days, 120 hours after unprotected intercourse.

"Here it says five days. I was supposed to start my period two weeks ago."

Tina-Love hunched her shoulders as though we were deciding on tiramisu or peach cobbler. "The abortion pill it is, then. Problem solved."

"That's morally wrong," I retorted, secretly regretting my first termination.

"What's wrong is your having another

man's baby when you know you're still in love with Memphis. Stop settling. Your life, your choice."

She was right, but she still hadn't mentioned she knew he was coming home. I didn't bother telling her about my answering his call.

Picking up my gift and to-go order, I said, "I'll hit you later. Don't want to interrupt your plans for this evening." Two of Memphis's favorite Greek salads to go suddenly made sense.

"You're not the only one with feelings. Let's not forget who broke up with whom and why. By the way" — she eyed the gift bag — "you're welcome, Xena."

"Um-hmm. If you want to make me feel bad about my decisions, thanks," I said, concluding our dialogue.

Tina-Love would never ask, but she wasn't getting back the purse. Ever.

CHAPTER 17
XENA

I was disappointed in Tina-Love, not Memphis.

Locking myself in the bathroom, I sat my designer bag on the wicker basket next to the vanity, stared in the mirror. My bestie should've told me she'd made plans to see my ex at her house tonight. Hadn't heard from her since I'd left the Pirates' House.

Adonis jiggled the handle, which was precisely why I'd shut him out. I had no peace with this man on my ass, my heels. My voice mail was full. Next, he'd have to pay for additional storage on my phone. Or I'd delete Adonis's photos before a single one of Memphis.

Tap. Tap. Tap. "Sweetheart, we need to leave in ten minutes. We don't want to be late for my mom's din-din." He sang, "She made gumbo."

Somberly I answered, "Okay." Although I loved her seafood filé gumbo with three types of crab, lobster tails in the shell, shrimp, and a little andouille sausage, the only thing I had a taste for was Memphis.

Opening my purse, I retrieved the second pregnancy test I'd bought earlier. I was supposed to take it at the restaurant with my bestie in the stall with me. Didn't want to go through abortion number two without Tina-Love being there.

I sat on the toilet, peed on the stick to confirm what I already knew. Where was my genie in a bottle to grant me three wishes? One, to not be pregnant. Two, to win back my one true love, Memphis. Three, to find forgiveness in my heart for the awful things my mother had done to me when I was a child.

I should fake an illness, insist Adonis go to dinner, bring me back a big container of food. After he leaves, I could pop in on Tina-Love and Memphis. If Adonis questions my not being home when I get back, I could lie to him. Tell him it was an emergency. Actually, that would be the truth.

Tap. Tap. Tap. "Sweetheart. We're officially late. Are you okay in there?"

Staring in disbelief, I shook my head. One line was clearly pink. The other was faint. Could it be that I wasn't having a child? Relief carried the stress from my head to my feet. I'd buy another test later. Quickly I rolled the test in a paper towel, stuffed it into a side compartment of my purse.

Tap. Tap. Tap.

Exhausted, I washed my face, brushed my teeth, reapplied my lipstick, picked up my bag, then opened the door. "Let's go," I said.

Adonis stepped aside. I reluctantly led the way to his car.

By the grace of God, I'd met my deadline, went over the details for the new commitment with Topez, then electronically signed off. Praying there'd be no need to tell Memphis anything about Adonis . . . OMG! I texted Tina-Love what should've been understood. **Do not tell Memphis I might be pregnant.**

Might? she replied.

I'll explain later. Heading to Adonis's parents for dinner, I pictured his mom's huge pot of gumbo sitting on the stove.

Bet it won't be better than Ms. Hattie's, I thought, wondering if she'd stirred up her special roux for Memphis tonight. Knowing where Memphis was, I decided that after dinner with Adonis I should visit Ms. Hattie. She always liked me.

My heart dropped. How could Memphis's mother give him a welcome home reception and not include me? Why was Memphis going to Tina-Love's? Crying, I wanted to scream, *Stop the car! And take the wheel.*

"Sweetheart, what's making you cry? If it has anything to do with our baby, save your tears," Adonis said, reducing his speed. "I promise I'll be the best dad and husband I can."

"I'm good," I lied. I became quiet.

We entered his parents' home.

"Don't the two of you look adorable," Mrs. Oglethorpe said, escorting us to the dining room. "How's our grandchild?" she asked.

Exhaling, I replied, "Fine," praying there was no fetus.

Adonis continued the conversation. His dad sat at the head of the table. Mrs. Oglethorpe placed our bowls in front of us, each one nearly spilling over its side.

"Oh Heavenly Father, we humble ourselves before you," Mr. Oglethorpe said, then continued, "giving thanks for the new addition to our family. This unborn child will be showered with love . . ."

I zoned out. Speaking as few words as necessary, I shuffled my seafood from one side of the bowl to the other.

"Xena, you've barely touched your dinner," Mrs. Oglethorpe commented. "What's wrong, honey?"

I didn't want to be here.

CHAPTER 18
MEMPHIS

"Look at my son showing off his dance moves," Mom said with a wide smile.

This three-bedroom, one bath I grew up in seemed a lot bigger when I was smaller. Wooden coffee table, sofa with a snug floral cotton cover, and a worn recliner with a long handle on the side were flush against the walls. Unfolded chairs were scattered. Family sat where they could. Some preferred to stand. Only the elders could reclaim their seat.

"Hafta werk off dis here delicious food you filled me with," I told Mom. "Salads starting tomorrow!" Actually tonight.

Holding Tina-Love's hand, I reached high, twirled her twice, a third time, pulled her close to my body, then gyrated. She kept pace following my lead. Lionel escorted his girlfriend to the center of the living room floor.

"All right now. Both of my men are taking

over," our mom said. "Show 'em what I taught you."

Not many women could look me in the eyes without shifting their eyeballs. Tina-Love was my height. Six-two but that was without her six-inch heels. I spun her out, brought her in, twirled her around once, and gyrated against her pelvis.

Lionel and his girl tried to keep up. In one swoop, I leaned Tina-Love back onto my forearm, tossed her forward, spun, gyrated, then did it again. Lionel had a choice to sit or get knocked down. I had enough stamina to go all night.

Tina-Love could too.

Lionel turned off the music from his phone. That was cool with me.

"I need to check on my house," I said, thinking of Z. An escape to see her or simply hear her voice again would do my heart good. A kiss. A hug. A kiss and a hug would lead to our grinding in the sheets if she showed up at my place.

"You're staying here tonight. Your house is fine. Who do you think been caring for it for twelve months?" Mom said, then answered, "Me."

"He's big-time now, Ma. Let him go," my stepbrother commented.

Nothing in my old bedroom was my size

anymore. Where was I supposed to sleep? "I start training tomorrow. And, listen up, fam. I'm going to be on all the local radio stations in the morning, so make sure you stay tuned."

"Dude, you haven't made it until you sip tea in *The Shady Café* with @DDDShade," Lionel said.

"Keep your app locked in," I told him. "Look," I said, and raised my hands. "I thank you all for welcoming me home. Ms. Janice, it's good to see you. Everybody, Mom, you especially. It's like I'm here, but I'm not. Let me reach out. Do not call or text me. I've got to prep for gold."

"Boy, you're not talking to me," Mom said, wrapping her arms around my waist. "You're my world. I love you. And I'll slap anyone who bothers you. Y'all heard me now?" She stared at everyone in the room.

Eyeing Tina-Love, I shifted my gaze to Ms. Janice, then back to my friend. Tina-Love shook her head. Hoped bringing them together would've changed Tina-Love.

Reuniting Tina-Love and her mom, though I'd tried, that was not my battle to fight. I had to find a way to get to Z.

CHAPTER 19
XENA

"Morning, sunshine," Adonis said, kissing my face. He placed his hand on my belly. "Girl, or boy? Which one do you want?"

"Whatever you want." My true answer hadn't changed. I did not want to have his baby.

"I want our first child to be a boy. Then I want us to have a girl, and another boy. In that order."

I touched his beard, caressed the hairs on his head, thinking how easy it was for men to order up babies like pizza with or without sausage. "Okay."

"I've got a long day. Don't want to miss the sunrise," I said to avoid prolonging this undesirable conversation.

Adonis teased my nipple, circling it in slow motion. "You think it's safe for you to give me some loving?"

Extra pussy. Hold his pepperoni please. The faint line on the second test gave me hope the original result may have been a false positive. I wasn't taking any chances until *I* was certain. "Not right now. It's too soon."

"Cool. I'll lie here and read this *Dicks Are Dumb* book you obviously left for me on the coffee table." He laughed. "Never know. Might learn something." Staring at the woman on the cover, he said, "I can go to the grocery store for you guys and pick up your favorites."

Last night had seemed like an eternity. I hated ignoring Memphis's texts and calls. What good would it do for me to talk with him on the phone in my predicament? Hadn't spoken with Tina-Love since our lunch date. It was obvious whose team she favored.

"I'll do it while you check on your properties. I need to get out the house."

I'd decided to work at the apartment today to avoid risking seeing Memphis pop up at my storefront. One suit at a time, I'd do my best on this contract. I hadn't told Adonis about possibly getting my big break in New York.

"You sure, honey? I don't want you carrying anything too heavy. Besides, you said you have sewing to do. Stay here." Adonis reached over me, picked up his ring, then held my hand. "I want you to wear your ring all the time." He slid it on.

"I won't have a finger to put the ring on if I do that. Try hand stitching all day and see." *Lord, please don't let me be pregnant,* I said in my head. After removing the diamond solitaire, I place it on the nightstand.

"I'll be on standby just in case y'all need me," Adonis said. Resuming his position, turning several pages, he added, "Oh, and we're having dinner with my parents tonight."

Aw, hell no! My voice escalated. "Again?" I aggressively tied my robe, stumped away without responding, sat on the porch in my grandmother's rocking chair. Listened to the locusts, watched the squirrels leap branch to branch, wondering how much influence the females had. One thing was sure, once they were impregnated, that was it. We were the one species that had a system for terminating children in the womb.

I felt like shit for wanting to do the same thing. Softly I asked, "Lord, what is my blessing? I'm listening."

Breathing deeply, I cleared my mind of all thoughts. I witnessed dawn submit to daylight. The number of cars driving by went from one or two to dozens. The sound of silence gradually filled with chatter and sporadic laughter.

Opening my eyes, I retreated indoors. Adonis had left. I sighed relief. Home alone felt like I wanted this every day. I fell backward onto the bed, stretched my arms wide. Called out His name. "Lord —"

My cell rang. I could ignore it, but the word *work, work, work* . . . repeated. Retrieving my phone from the nightstand, I answered, "Morning, Topez."

"I'm in the midst of prepping for a wedding. Meet me at your shop at eight o'clock," she said. "Bring the design for the suit you're working on. See you then. Bye."

Long as it wasn't to discuss another contract, I was good. If Topez wasn't the catalyst to my dreams coming true, I'd void this contract, which was guaranteed to consume the next three weeks of my first trimester.

I turned on the shower and stood underneath the dome. My heart was broken, filled with deceit, guilt, and . . . "I don't want to be here," I cried out loud. Afraid people would judge me, I'd confessed what I could only do alone. My truth.

I blow-dried my hair, let it hang free the way Memphis liked. I put on my athletic boy shorts, and a tight tank top. Laced up my tennis shoes, passed Ben Matthews's apartment, then walked to the corner.

I crossed the street, stopped in front of The Sentient Bean and peeped in the window, noticed Mr. Ben inside talking with a man and a lady. The woman was next to him on the sofa, the guy sat in a chair leaning over them, jotting notes on a pad.

"Girl, you know you want this dick," someone whispered in my ear from behind. Then I felt a hand rub the left side of my hip. I jetted like a plane on the runway preparing to take flight.

"I'd recognize this booty anywhere," he said, keeping pace.

And I'd never forget his touch or the sound of his voice. I ran faster. Purposely. He trailed. How had he found me? Tina-Love must've given him my address. I stopped, leaned forward, gasped. That was why she hadn't contacted me. She was determined to get us back together.

A year had gone by since I'd last seen him. His deep voice, his orgasmic caress, the scent of his cologne were unforgettable. My heart raced as I stared up at the silver moss hanging from a line of trees to my left, my right.

Hearing his voice for the second time in twelve months, was it fate? Coincidence? Somehow he knew I'd be here.

Strands of my hair blew from the back to the front, clung to my cheeks. Wet lips pressed against the nape of my neck. I chose not to move.

I shivered at the thought that he was the only man who had made me climax back to back to back. What I liked most about my ex, unlike the other guys, was that he invested time in learning my body.

Memphis spoke low and directly into my ear. "I know you remember what you used to do with *these* nuts."

I watched a couple with a baby in a stroller go by. Two little girls skipped alongside a different couple. Dogs on leashes frantically wagged their tails as they sniffed one another.

Afraid that I was too weak to resist him, I did not turn around.

"Girl, you gon' show me some love or what?" Memphis asked.

I prayed my fiancé wasn't lurking in the park like a private investigator. Adonis had become rather possessive. Some might refer to his actions as protective. I needed but didn't want to be rescued by anyone, including myself. Out of respect for my fiancé and our child, I started walking toward our place on Park Avenue. Maybe if I could make it back across the street to The Sentient Bean,

Mr. Ben Matthews, the wisest man I knew, could shed wisdom on my situation. That was, if he was still there.

My flat stomach would soon have a small curve. Later I'd be rounder than the watermelon I like from the Fresh Market. Having only seen Memphis on social media, I wondered what he looked like now. If I faced him, would I melt?

Memphis scurried in front of me. Blocked my path. "Damn M." For real? I'd never seen him this muscular. Training camp had done wonders for his body.

Smiling, he nodded. Folded his arms across his chest.

Shit! A crowd of people were holding their phones taking pictures of Memphis. I crossed my ankles and did an about-face in the opposite direction. As I stepped aside, my eyes swept the park from the entrance of the Fresh Market to the stage where a live band played every Saturday.

Aw, hell! I noticed Adonis heading toward me. Us.

Memphis announced, "Last picture folks." Memphis began circling me again. This time he stopped, placed his hands on my hips. "You can't deny me, Z." Felt like old times. I didn't want to, but my body couldn't withhold releasing an orgasm. Laughing, he leaned in for a kiss. Quickly I turned my head.

Nothing was truly wrong with our relationship. It was more me than him. Maybe. We had different dreams, which tore us apart. I didn't want having his child to change our lives. Two souls reaching out for each other, at the same time drifting apart. It took all the restraint I had not to place my lips on his.

"Hey, you look amazing," I confessed, eyeing his incredible biceps, his thighs, legs, chest, his neck and face — all of it was more chiseled than I remembered, than the pictures in my phone revealed. His shoulders were wider.

"Told you I was going to get it done. I'm determined, baby. Nothing can stop me. I'm in. I'm going to the Olympics. And you are going to be right by my side when they hang that gold medal around my neck. This is what I sacrificed for, Z," he said with the same energetic, jovial, wide smile and bright eyes that I recalled. "You all quiet. What's up with you? You looking sweet and juicy. And don't be mad at our gurl. I told Tina-Love I wanted to surprise you."

Before I answered, he said, "I'm moving you up outta that spot with that nigga. Pack your shit, Z. Daddy's home."

The market crowd started to dissipate as raindrops fell between us. I looked for Adonis. Prayed he hadn't seen me.

"Damn, girl. Say something. You happy to see me or what?" Memphis held my hand. "Did you hear me? Let's go chill for a minute before all this blackberry fineness melts down to sugar." He slid his hands from his chest to his dick.

I pulled away. More raindrops poured. I shook my head. Memphis took a step back as Adonis walked up and hugged me.

"Oh, so this is that —" Memphis said.

I interrupted, "Memphis, this is my boyfriend. Adonis."

"Fiancé. What's up, man?" Adonis extended his hand toward Memphis, then paused. "You that local dude I follow online. You made it into the Olympics?"

"Yeah, man." Memphis turned his attention to me. Staring at my ring finger, he told me, "Nice seeing you, Z."

"Man, I'ma be rooting for you," Adonis said, darn near cheering.

Memphis stared at Adonis. "Cool. Do that."

"Well, I'm pulling for you, dude," Adonis said. "I'm a fan."

"Gotta make it to Tina-Love's before I get drenched twice." Memphis put emphasis on

141

my bestie's name.

Adonis covered then uncovered his mouth. "Ain't but one Tina-Love and that's my fiancée's best friend. I follow her, too. Man, that's you?"

I was glad I'd left Adonis's ring on the nightstand.

"Hit me later, Z. You know where I'll be." Memphis jogged across the lawn.

I watched until he was out of view. Tina-Love had taught me to never tell my new guy anything about my exes. But why hadn't she told me Memphis was back and he'd made it?

Adonis looked at me. "How do you know him?"

"From social media like you." That was the truth. Just not the whole truth.

Adonis held my hand. We walked in the rain toward home.

"That dude is the real deal. He's on his way up. But your bestie doesn't take any man seriously. We should make plans to go to the Olympics and support him," Adonis said. "You want to go?"

I thought I'd gotten over Memphis. Now that he was on his way to celebrity status, my bestie was right. Women would be all over his fine ass.

Not responding, I had more important

things to focus on. At Adonis's apartment building, a text registered from Memphis.

You ain't marrying nobody but me, Z!! Meet me at Tina-Love's in fifteen minutes!! Get rid of dude!! You don't love his ass.

Chapter 20
Memphis

Tina-Love and I could be a powerhouse, if she were more like Z, and less like me.

I needed a woman who would keep me first always and support me one hundred percent of the time regardless of my hiccups. What man wouldn't want Tina-Love in his bed or on his arm? Including Z's fake-ass fiancé. Nigga seemed envious believing I was holding down Tina-Love.

The next best thing to dating Tina-Love was my being her best male friend, which in many ways was ingenious on my behalf. Having the two baddest females in Savannah love on me, from time to time I had a mental threesome that ended with my having a wet dream.

Super hyped to meet up with Z, I keyed in the code on the app to open the gate to Tina-Love's mansion. I cruised up the never-ending driveway, parked in the space that was reserved for me, then lowered the garage door. I doubted the customized Bentley next to my QX80 had ten thousand miles on it.

No single woman needed 7,300 square feet. Five bedrooms, six bathrooms, an outdoor terrace with a pool and a Jacuzzi that felt like an oasis, and an unoccupied in-law unit. Plus, Tina-Love had a stable out back with two horses that roamed on two acres of fenced-in land.

Entering the living room, I called out, "Babe! Where are you?"

"In the kitchen!" she shouted.

Boy shorts, tank top, barefoot. Damn, admiring the red polish on her toenails made me think about Natalie. Hadn't heard from her since I'd left Cali. I prayed it stayed that way, and that she was lying just to see what I would say. Or if the kid was mine, that her taking the pill I gave her would resolve all my potential problems.

Chilling with Tina-Love, I said, "You are one sexy woman. You know that?"

"Hashtag rhetorical," she sang.

Her hair was smoothed around the edges, then gathered into a big-ass Afro bun that sat on the back of her head. I kissed Tina-Love on the lips, then washed my hands. "My timing is impeccable. All my favorites. What you want me to do?" I asked, grinning like a little boy. "Z will be here any minute. Saw her earlier. I need you to convince her to come back to me."

"Sit your ass down, she can't do that right now," Tina-Love said, shaking a cucumber in my direction. "Tell me why you went to see my gurl after I told you I wanted to arrange something?"

The long sharp blade diced a carrot end to end in a matter of seconds. This chick did everything with passion and precision. I scanned her white kitchen. Cabinets, counter, stools, floor. I could pretend that Z was the one who reached out to me.

Nah, I couldn't lie. When Z didn't respond to any of my text messages or return my calls, I Googled her e-mail address and cell number. She was an early riser. After training, I waited outside her place.

"You know I had to see my Z."

"No, what you had to do was piss on her proposal. Mark her as though she's your fucking territory." Tina-Love threw a carrot chunk at me.

I caught and ate it. I turned the back of the stool to the edge of the counter and straddled it. "I didn't even know she was going to be at the park."

"Didn't know? Or didn't give a fuck about her situation? That's your damn problem.

That's all of you guys' problem. Pissing on women like R. Kelly is your damn role model."

I didn't want to laugh. I had to.

"I'm serious, Memphis. Xena is stressing the fuck out over you. She can't dump Adonis overnight. He pays for everything, including her phone. So don't go sending her naked pictures and messages that he can probably intercept."

Tina-Love rinsed the baby kale, placed it in a bowl that was inside another bowl, then pushed a lever several times.

"After hearing her voice, and seeing her face, I-I —"

"Dammit, Memphis! Are you listening to anything I'm saying? I'm on your side. What are you talking about?" A handful of diced carrots hovered over the juicer. "She needs to block your ass. And you need to stay focused."

I walked to the opposite side of the countertop. Stood beside Tina-Love. "What was up with Z responding to texts I'd sent you while y'all were at the restaurant? Don't lie. You set that up. You wanted her to know I was on my way home before I arrived."

Fast and furious, Tina-Love chopped another carrot. "A message from you when I was at the restaurant did not happen."

After drying her hands on a dish towel, she showed me her text history. I did not see **Hey M.**

"You're wrong," I explained, showing her my history. "I wouldn't lie to you. But squash all this. I can't let Z marry that nigga."

She rubbed olive oil on the foot-long salmon fillet and sprinkled herbs on top, then massaged it into the crevices. Beauty, and she could cook her ass off. I watched her pick up the pan, bend over, put it in the oven.

While the fish was baking, we engaged in candid conversation about Z. I wanted my ex back but moreso I didn't want to imagine another man sticking his dick in Z.

"She needs time. I've planted the seed. I told her to give the ring back, man. Bullying her back into your world is only going to make her feel guilty after leaving Adonis. Here," she said, handing me a tall glass of kale, carrot, and orange juice.

"You can't tell me how to deal with Z. You may have brought her out of her shell, but I'm the one who sexes her crazy."

Nodding, she lowered her eyes, and her lips curved downward. She poured a smaller smoothie for herself. She removed the fish from the oven; the top was lightly brown and crisp. Tina-Love prepared our plates. Mine had a mound of spinach, sliced heirloom tomatoes, red beets, quinoa, and a healthy piece of salmon. She squeezed fresh lime juice on the fish. Sitting next to me at the island, she said grace before we ate.

"When's your next trip out?" I asked, not feeling remorseful about my dick taming Z.

"Soon. I'm taking Xena to Italy," she said, looking at her plate.

"If I didn't have to train six hours a day, I'd meet you guys there. This fish is amazing," I said, chewing with my mouth open. "Xena could use some time away from that dude. What's our plan to win her back?"

"You tell me." Her head tilted over her plate.

I hated pissing off Tina-Love. "I apologize. I need to shut the hell up and listen to your advice."

Silence lingered.

Tina-Love held my hand. "If I tell you something, you cannot mention it to Xena. If you do, don't speak to me again as long as you live."

Damn, like that? Felt as though my stomach dropped to my lap. I placed my fork on top of my fish. Prayed Z was all right. "Look at me." I wanted Tina-Love to know I could keep a secret. "I promise. For real."

Letting go of my hand, Tina-Love said, "Xena is pregnant."

Instantly I heaved, threw up in my plate, wiped my mouth with a napkin. "Are you fucking serious? She's pregnant for that nigga! Is that why he put a ring on it?" Tears filled my eyes. My children were supposed to be the only one inside of Z.

"How am I supposed to keep this to myself? What the fuck, man? I'ma let her know. He can have her whorish ass." I picked up my cell.

Tina-Love snatched it, then tucked my phone inside her boy shorts. She tossed my dinner and the plate in the garbage. "Calm your immature ass down and pray Xena doesn't find out that Natalie Crow girl is having your baby."

She sat a newly prepared meal before me. I shoved it away. I was speechless for a second. "How the fuck you know that?"

"It doesn't matter what blog she put it on, then took it down. Is it true?" Tina-Love asked. Showing me a screenshot of the post, she slapped the back of my head.

"That bitch. If I were in Chula Vista I'd be fucking knocking on . . . I'd knock down her door!" I circled the island, balled my fingers tight.

"Get mad at yourself! And don't do anything stupid. Women are uniting against abusive men. Your ass might be next."

"What the hell?! I didn't sexually assault her. She wanted this dick!" I pulled the stool far from the counter, sat, crossed my arms. Couldn't stop shaking my head.

"There are no secrets anymore. She probably has you on video, and even if she doesn't this white chick could fuck up everything we've worked for. Memphis, what in the hell were you thinking, hitting that raw?" Tina-Love pressed her palms to my face. "Let me guess. Her head game is on point? And you didn't have the discipline to stop after busting the first nut."

More like desire. Inhaling deeply, I feared what Coach would say. I trusted Natalie. She betrayed me. The left side of my mouth curved with memories of how talented Natalie was. Not many women enjoyed devouring my dick and swallowing my seeds. Reverting back to the matter. *Bitch!*

Tina-Love's eyelids closed. I noticed her eyeballs swept left to right and back. She stared at me. A growl rumbled from my stomach. Starved, I relocated to a seat at the counter, slid the second plate closer, started eating. Should've stuck with fellatio and anal with Natalie.

"That bitch sprang this shit on me right

before I left Cali. But you'd be proud of your boy. I bought her the Plan B pill. My innocence will be revealed."

The salmon was cold. I was heated.

Tina-Love picked her filet apart. Shoveled it around. Mixed it with the quinoa. Her long slim fingers with red painted nails hugged a tall glass of water. "News flash. Plan B doesn't work after conception. She's claiming she's three months. Even if she swallowed the pill you gave her that won't change shit. Neither would an abortion pill if she's more than seventy days. She's saying she's keeping it, which is a no-brainer. Why would she get rid of her meal ticket? All you can do at this point is hope that chick is lying or that it's not yours."

Men just wanted to fuck. Women were treacherous. "You're the best at scheming. Come up with a game plan. How should I handle Natalie? I'm listening."

"You have only one real option. Ask her to marry you."

I spat salmon in my second plate. "What the hell kinda plan is that when you know I was going to propose to Z?" The one woman I trusted after this conversation was my mom.

"Don't be stupid. You are going to marry Z. But first, pick up your cell, tell Natalie you're going to make her Mrs. Natalie Brown, then convince Natalie to abort the baby. Tell her you want to start a family with her after the Olympic Games are over. Do not text her. Call. Right now you're earning what? Forty thousand?"

Sticking out my chest, I proudly said, "Fifty."

"Exactly. She's banking on your endorsements to kick in, which may put you in my income bracket," she said, dropping my plate and food in the trash.

I was looking forward to building a ridiculous mansion with the largest swimming pool and Jacuzzi in Georgia so I could swim and chill in the nude whenever I wanted. Why did Z have to get pregnant?

"Listen, baby. You can't take Natalie at her word. You've got to go with her to the clinic. Speak directly with the doctor afterward to confirm she didn't change her mind while she was on the table. After it's done, stop fucking with her on every level. Let her keep the engagement ring. Get a nice one. One better." Tina-Love snapped her finger. "I'll give you one of mine."

She slid her plate in front of me. "Eat." I shook my head.

She left, returned with a little black box. Opened it.

My jaw dropped. "Damn! You be milking dudes. This rock is sweet. How you get him to come up off of this?" I asked, allowing her idea to marinate.

"The same way you got got. Pussy. I know my worth. Models play the baby card and get Bentleys, houses, yachts, and most of us were never pregnant. Most men use us to impress their boys. Dicks depreciate. Diamonds do not."

"And y'all say we scandalous?"

I texted Natalie, **what's up. i apologize. miss you. call you soon.**

She texted back, **I don't have shit to say to you. Too late now.**

"Enough staring at your phone. I already know. Natalie is still pissed. I would be too," Tina-Love said.

I frowned. She just told me how the models run game. "What the fuck?" What did Natalie's text mean?

"Get your ass upstairs. If Natalie don't fall in line, I'll personally pay her a visit. Nothing and no one is going to keep my guy from bringing home the gold."

While Tina-Love popped a bottle of champagne, her cell rang. Xena's name and picture registered on the screen.

"Like I said. Nothing, and no one." Tina-Love pressed decline, picked up her phone, then headed upstairs.

I was no fool. Leaving the china on the counter, I exited the front door and headed to the gym to lift weights.

CHAPTER 21
TINA-LOVE

Angry pussy.

Disappointing dick.

Disappointed pussy.

Angry dick.

Was anyone sexually satisfied?

Two perfectly good people who were madly in love with each other took a stupid-ass break from their relationship, and despite my best efforts, Memphis and Xena may never get back together.

That wasn't my fault. Nothing pertaining to those two was my fault.

"Hey, what happened to you earlier? Memphis said you were coming over. I gave him your fish," I said, laughing. I didn't want Xena dropping in unannounced thinking Memphis was here.

Her crying, "I may need a place to stay," caught me off guard.

Xena could live with me, but I refused to support her or any adult. Nor did I want to raise her man's kid. Wasn't scaling back on my fuckfests — Hal's fine ass was in transit — to appease a houseguest. No part of my living space was either off limits for entertainment or welcoming to my mother. She could wear off brands the rest of her life. I did not care!

"When, gurl?" Jokingly I said, "Memphis told me he ran into you at the park and that you were supposed to come by, not move in," but I was serious. "He didn't say you were homeless." Any roof over Xena's head was better than mine. "You sure you're ready to move out of Adonis's place and give up your sponsorship?" I had to add, "There's no free rent here."

She hesitated. Sniffled. I thought, great, hoping she was considering all of her options. Her mother would charge her too. That evil and possessed woman should've been a drill sergeant. Janice wasn't mean. She was emotionally absent.

Xena deserved to be in the top fashion shows, but she relied too much on Topez to support her. Allowing Topez to get her every contract was one thing, but depending on a user was next-level failure. Xena worked her ass off while Topez snatched a fifth of her earnings. Once Memphis's cash flow hit his account like a tsunami, Xena had best get a head start and secure home plate before blondie.

"I'm saving my money for N-Y's Men's F-W. Where am I going to go *and* take my work-at-home sewing machine, designing table, chair, and accessories? Huh? I'm thirty-one and done living with my parents." She cried, "Don't make me move to my mother's. Please."

Business was serious. I shook my head, asking, "Is Adonis beating you, gurl?"

Sniffling, she answered, "No. He wouldn't do that."

"Oh, good." I loved my bestie, but she'd set that trap. Her negative comments regarding my lifestyle wasn't happening in my domain.

Couldn't lie. She was better at keeping secrets. Quickly I stated, "Leave that shit. Move in on Memphis. Don't ask. Just do it. Today."

If a man left anything at my house, I'd instructed my maid to put it in a trash bag, then drop it off at the Goodwill and bring me back my tax-deductible donation receipt. Suits. Shoes. Jewelry. Phones. I did not care. If they inquired about their belongings, I told the truth. *I'll check with my maid.* I didn't say when.

"Oh, no, I can't do that to him in my situation."

Possession was still nine-tenths of the law, and the longer Xena waited, the harder it would become for her to get back with our guy. But I couldn't live for her.

Speaking to myself, I notably mentioned, "I really should use this space more often. There are so many choices."

"What?" Xena asked.

I let her know, "I have company coming in a few."

Xena may have forgotten she'd confided in me she'd tired of being the background to Memphis's larger-than-life goal digging personality. Again, that was how she permitted their relationship to begin. Interesting how she'd left out the parts of Memphis's cheating, yet I knew more deets than her. But the solution was not for my bestie to settle for financial security when she could have endless resources and love. Taking the easy path converted speed bumps into road-blocks.

Scared money never made money. People quick to use others' cash and credit, reluctant to invest their own, chased paper, not dreams.

There were words not worth sharing. Memphis told me he felt Xena's designing clothes for men needed to end. He didn't want his wife around dicks all the time. Claimed no man did.

Maybe if they'd confided in each other, Xena wouldn't have ended her relationship with Memphis and he wouldn't have let her.

"There's something I haven't told you and I'm feeling guilty. Memphis texted your phone when we were at Pirates' House. You were in the restroom, so I responded. Then I deleted the messages."

"Cool." I wasn't tripping.

I'd done that many times backstage at runway shows. When I'd done that, I erased the incident from my memory and moved forward.

"Did you tell him I'm pregnant?" she whispered.

"No, girl," I lied. Hal needed to hurry. "That's on you."

"I might not be," she said. "This baby situation is driving me insane. I need to talk with you in person."

I remained quiet.

"But can I tell you why I'm scared to terminate this pregnancy?" The tone in her voice shifted to melancholy.

Damn, she was starting to make me depressed. Sighing heavily, I agreed. "Sure."

"I left Memphis because I was pregnant

with his baby." She yelped like a puppy whose foot was stomped on by accident, then added, "I had an abortion."

"What the fuck?!" Who was Xena? That was a year ago.

"Let me catch this. That's my company calling."

Ending the conversation, I yelped too. Threw my phone on the bed.

Picking it up, I texted Xena, **Take that shit to your motherfucking grave!!**

Pregnancy fucked up too many women's lives while men moved on to the next female. The first time it happened to me, I was thirteen. Doubted the rapist ever knew. But my mother did.

I splashed cold water on my face, cried. Splashed. Cried. Watching my company enter the code I'd given him, I dried my eyes. Laughed out loud. Smiled. Had to shift my emotions.

Thigh-high snakeskin gladiator stilettoes. Red thong. Short sheer black robe. Untamed Afro, spiked at the edges. I opened my front door, then hollered, "Hey, baby! Leave that bitch right there."

Hal parked his cerulean Bugatti Chiron in my driveway. As he rose out of the driver's seat, I watched in sheer amazement that his six-nine frame fit. He retrieved a dozen of the longest-stemmed red roses and a bottle of Dom champagne.

Greeting Hal with a sloppy one on the mouth, I took the flowers.

"Wow!" Hal spun me around the way Memphis had at his welcome home party. "All this sexiness for me, ma?" He slapped my ass.

On the verge of crying, I escorted Hal through the kitchen to the east side of my house into what would soon be our obstacle course. The onyx room.

"Get your dick-hangin', swangin', slangin' ass in the shower. Wash all up in that crack," I demanded, not understanding why some women were afraid to take control. Men loved that shit.

"Skyscraper. Chill," he said. "Got a lil something else for you. Come here."

I did.

He smirked. Spread his feet. "Choose a pocket."

As I emptied all of them like a crack addict, we laughed.

"Skyscraper. You greedy. Keep it all. You're worth more," he said, made an about-face, stumbled into the en suite where he needed to be.

Hal was a professional basketball player.

Married. Four kids. Winning with his $20 million contract. Willing to trade his starting lineup in exchange for me. I dropped the three racks of hundreds in my pleasure chest.

We met on a flight to Trinidad. Shit! I needed to make arrangements to get back to Italy. Without Xena.

"How much time we have?" Hal asked.

"Man, don't creep up. Two, starting the second you enter the room." Lowering my voice, I added, "I'm going to get this ambience lit."

Kneeling, Hal pulled my thong aside, licked my sweet pussy. "I'm going to need at least three."

"Just tonight, big daddy." I fingered his locs. "We'll see."

"One of these times, I'm staying all night." He retreated to the bathroom.

If he weren't married to what he called a mistake. If he didn't almost have enough players to make up his own team, bench included. If he weren't also smashing one of the models I'd introduced him to — Hal could watch the sunrise with me in my Jacuzzi.

Men needed limitations. Hal had to earn extra time hitting this good pussy. Staying overnight was strictly prohibited. Falling asleep was not permitted. Soon as some of my casuals saw my pussy and my place, they were ready to ring me up just to move in.

Memphis was my only exception.

No red slick sheets. No bed. My onyx room consisted of cushions I called my roller-coaster rider, the colossal cheese slice, the vortex, and the eclipse.

Staging the mood for a stellar performance, I'd put seventeen teakwood candles on the mantel, another ten inside the fireplace. I lit each one. In every corner, more teakwood candles sat on warming plates with bright rings at the base. Above the fireplace a nude painting of my sexy body: glowing hair, eyes, lips, nipples, and labia, hung horizontally. After illuminating the track lighting along the crown molding, I turned a knob, and a galaxy of planets rotated slowly. I dimmed the backlight on the sex toy display case, started my bad bitch playlist.

"Hmm." Which items would best show my gratitude?

Opening the glass door, eeny, meeny, miny . . . I selected the short slim black dildo, two blindfolds, held a waterproof triple play (vaginal, clit, and anal) vibrator that had two hundred functions. "And let's see which one is moe? How about . . . ?" I went to the kitchen, placed the champagne and six glass icicle dongs in the bucket. "That'll do."

Removing my clothes, I joined Hal under the dome.

"Woman, I was wondering when you —"

"Hush, baby. I got you."

Warm water drenched our bodies. The night was young and he was clearly ready for my good love-making.

Placing a sponge in my hand, he said, "Wash my back."

I reached up, started on the left side. Small circular motions grew larger. Shoulder to shoulder, I rubbed until I covered the right portion. Up and down, I cleaned his spine, each time delving lower, and a little lower. Gliding my hand between the crevice of his tight buttocks, I eased my finger in and out of his rectum. His erection shifted up, down . . . up.

"I could never ask my wife to do this. What you do to me . . . baby, I feel incredible. I miss you," he moaned. "This is inexplicable. I don't care who else you fucking with long as I'm in your rotation, name your price."

"Hush, my love," I told him. "I'm not going anywhere. And always keep the Mrs. first. Happy wife —"

"You're right. That's why I fuck with your sexy ass," Hal agreed.

Sliding my middle finger inside of him, I reassured Hal, "She doesn't have to do this?" I massaged his prostate with oil. "I got you."

Hal became quiet. Shook his head. He took a deep breath, then exhaled.

"Yes, that's it. Let out all the tension. Open up your chakras."

We fed off each other's energy. I'd taught Hal the biggest challenge of any head game was keeping your mind right.

The churning in my womb moved up to my abdomen, navel, stomach. I closed my eyes, then pressed my nipples against his back, and began breathing in sync with him.

Three inhales, I was ready for this man. All of him! "Get out. It's time to fuck," I told Hal.

We did a sloppy dry-off, flung the white towels to the floor.

"Whoa, Skyscraper. You've outdone yourself. We can't rush this experience," he said, pointing at Mars.

"Hush, Hal." I grabbed the blindfolds, secured his, then pushed him into the vortex. "Don't move."

"Woman!" he yelled, spinning uncontrollably.

I laughed watching Hal hold on to his dick like it was going to fly off. Slowing the pace, I uncorked the bubbly. Doused him with freezing cold champagne. Every time he tried to get up, he couldn't.

"Skyscraper! Stop this madness," he complained.

"You've had ice baths, man. Hush." I switched to my "Fuck Me Slow and Good" playlist.

"Whew! That's better," Hal said. "Ah, yeah."

"I'm coming in with you, baby. Hold on." I opened a condom, placed it in my mouth, covered my eyes with my mask.

Feeling my way to the bucket, I held a massager high above my head. Squatting, I leaned, fell backward on top of Hal. Instantly he caught me.

"Keep that up and I'm going to get you an MVP trophy," I said.

Hal's dick was in perfect alignment with my pussy. "Whoa. Wait." I wiggled. Scrambled. Fast as I could, I shoved the icy massager inside my vagina. Reclined on top of Hal. My modeling contract had a no-pregnancy clause. Stacks of cash was nice, but I had my own.

"Damn, Skyscraper! What's up with all this cold shit? Take that out and let me feel you raw." He cupped my breasts, whispered in my ear, "Just this once, baby."

No man was jeopardizing my livelihood. I handed him the condom. Hal did what he needed to do in order to penetrate me.

His dick traded places with the massager. Hal moaned, "Oh my God, Tina-Love. I think I'm on a stairway to paradise, baby. Your cold pussy feels, aw shit! Fucking stop this spinning top bullshit and let's hit the floor."

I did as he requested. Leaning on my hands, I spread my knees. "Come hit it then."

His hands roamed from my spine to my lower back. Hal slid his engorged head from my clit to my opening. After entering me, he didn't stop until his nuts banged my labia. I let him take charge. Why not? He didn't know, but he wouldn't be back in my rotation for six weeks.

Bam! Bam! Bam! Bam! Bam! Whack!

"Shit! Fuck! Shit! What the fuck, Tina-Love, I love your ass. Give me cold pussy next time and we getting married."

Hal was in the zone. Intermissions were to insert another icy massager. My pussy went from hot to cold and back for an hour. Each time his balls slapped my lips, I clenched my vaginal muscles.

His dick stayed the hardest I'd encountered.

I stayed sexually engaged. Wouldn't stop before him. Hated lazy fucks. Reaching between my legs, I teased his scrotum. When Hal inhaled, I exhaled life into him. He exhaled. I inhaled his breath.

If Hal and I never made love again, my existence would resonate with him on a level that no other female could attain, including his wife. Unless she too understood the tantra.

Xena would thank me for teaching Memphis how to take his time, sustain an erection, prolong his ejaculation, and enjoy sex without feeling the need to cum every time, if she only knew.

Looking over my shoulder, real sexy, I told Hal, "Take your time, daddy. You've got nineteen minutes left."

CHAPTER 22
XENA

"Morning, sunshine," Adonis sang, then smothered my face with kisses.

On the inside, I was screaming, *Stop it!*

He touched my breast. Firmly I placed his hand on his chest.

"You're sexy when you're moody. I see the pregnancy glow my mom told me you have. You get more beautiful every minute. I'll be gentle," he said, circling my nipple with his fingertip. "Give me some."

Kicking the comforter off the bed, soon as I gapped my thighs to roll over, Adonis climbed on top of me. He separated my legs using his knees.

"I don't want to have sex," I protested. Shoving his shoulders.

"It's okay, Xena. We can make love later," he said. "Tonight is date night. Just us. Dinner. A stroll along River Street afterward or a ride on the riverboat. Whatever you guys want to do. Let me know so I can make reservations."

Adonis's lips traveled toward mine. Quickly I moved my head sideways.

"One kiss and I'll let y'all get up," he insisted.

Please quit saying "y'all"! "I'm behind schedule. I have to work. All day," I retorted.

I hadn't gotten my period. Didn't want him ejaculating inside of me ever again. Adonis took advantage of my forgetting to keep track of my ovulating days. I was done with the rhythm method. Before we learned about the human developing inside of me, I wanted out of this relationship. I started harboring disdain for this man. His beard, pale skin, red lips — seeing it, him, disgusted me.

Tears streamed from the corners of my eyes. When I opened my mouth to cry, that fool kissed me.

"It's okay. Let your fiancé make you feel better. I'll be quick," he promised.

"Get off of me!" I cried.

His neck snapped in the direction of the open window. He rolled to his side of the bed. I exited mine.

I went in the closet. Two-thirds of the clothing belonged to me. They'd fit into five garment bags. My heels and flats could go back in my suitcase. All of this would fit in the trunk of my BMW. I could take my belongings, but where? I eased on my robe. Reaching to the shelf above, I slid my hand in the crevice of my folded sweater. When I felt the last pregnancy test, I clenched it. I hid it in my pocket, kept it in my fist.

"I'm going to meditate. Don't interrupt me." I picked up my cell from the nightstand, placed it in my opposite pocket.

Adonis leaned against his pillow, interlocked his fingers behind his head, overlapped his ankles. His dick pointed to the ceiling. "Don't accept any more contracts from Topez. You don't have to work. She does. You'll be an Oglethorpe. I only want to love and make love to you. And for you to do the same. Stop pushing me away, Xena."

Basic as Adonis's request was, I didn't have love in my heart for him. Walking away, I entered the bathroom, locked the door. I hung my robe on a hook, sat on the toilet, held the test stick under my flow. Waiting, I washed my face, brushed my teeth, then I checked the results.

Putting it in the wrapper, I placed the disappointment back in my pocket. "God, why?" I cried out loud. One solid line, the other partial. What did it mean? At this point meditating wouldn't change anything, but I had to do something to maintain my sanity.

Knock. Knock. "Honey, what's wrong?" Adonis jiggled the knob.

He wasn't going anywhere, and thanks to Tina-Love neither was I. How was I supposed to move into Memphis's house without permission? Why wouldn't she let me stay with her?

Not answering Adonis, I texted Memphis, **Can we talk today?**

Nah, I ain't got nothing to say to you Z. You having that nigga's baby and you killed my baby!!!!!!!!!!! Don't contact me again, he responded.

I yelped. Texted Tina-Love, **Why did you tell Memphis I aborted his baby and I'm pregnant? You hate me?** I cried out loud.

"Open the door, Xena. Now," Adonis insisted.

"Go awaaaay!" I slid my back along the wall until my butt was on the floor. I talked into my palms.

"I'm scared. I don't know how to be a mom. What if I can't get it right? Or if I get postpartum blues and can't bond with our child." Banging the back of my head against the wall, I cried louder for those reasons and more. My life was ruined.

Adonis announced, "Xena, I'm taking the

doorknob off."

Listening to the electric screwdriver, hearing screws drop to the floor, I didn't care. I hated myself. Loved Memphis. I had to convince Adonis this wasn't the right time for us to take on such a huge responsibility.

Adonis stepped into the bathroom wearing pajama bottoms and a T-shirt. He extended his hand. "Let's sit on the porch and meditate together."

"I need some time alone," I said softly.

"Xena, you're pregnant not —"

"I know . . . dead!" I yelled up at him.

"That wasn't what I was going to say, honey." Adonis stooped, placed his arm under my bent knees, the other behind my back, then carried me to the bedroom. He laid me on top of the sheets, went to the opposite side, removed his clothes.

Aw, hell no! I got up. "Put your clothes on and meditate with me," I said.

Adonis was all I had.

I didn't share my practice with Adonis often, but I needed his positive energy to overpower Memphis's hatred for me. I stood before one of the most selfless spirits God had embodied inside of human flesh. He would do anything for me. I'd do the same, for Memphis.

I pressed my lips to his. "I'm sorry for

freaking out."

After I put on my robe, our footprints marked the oak wood floor. We bypassed the two purple sofas. I led the way to the kitchen. He opened the door. I sat in my great-grandmother's rocker. He sat in his great-grandfather's.

The back of my left hand rested atop my thigh. His right hand was on his. Adonis interlocked his fingers with mine.

"I don't know what I'd do without you and our baby, Xena. I love y'all to death," Adonis admitted.

That was a first. I was not in the mood to be confrontational or sentimental. I did not want to be here.

I responded, "I know. Let's focus."

We sat still.

Rocking, I closed my eyes. Breathed deeply. Listened. Wasn't sure when the message or messenger was coming to deliver me from mayhem. I exhaled. My thyroid was out of sync, but I didn't have hyperthyroidism. Doctor said the lump in my throat that I could never swallow was caused by anxiety. The stress-induced inflammation had started a little over a year ago.

Tears flowed. The tingling sensation irritated my eyes.

I shivered head to toe as an electric wave

traveled from my feet to the crown of my head.

"You okay?" Adonis inquired.

"Close your eyes and listen," I told him to shut him up.

I could feel Adonis's pulse. I felt, but did not hear, my heartbeat. Opening my chakras from the seventh to the first, I listened.

Nothing surfaced. Getting ready to open my eyes, I heard my grandmother's voice in my ear. "Everybody needs you. Who do you need?"

Kneeling on the gray wooden planks, I leaned on the rocker, placed my head sideways onto the seat, imagined my head on my grandmother's lap.

"You okay?" Adonis asked.

"Hush," I said softly.

He knelt in front of his chair.

I heard squirrels roaming about the branches. Locusts buzzed. Leaves rustled. Wind grazed my skin. Searching for the answer, I knew I loved, appreciated, and cared for others, but I didn't need anyone, including my parents. It was time I tried to make it on my own.

Standing, I told my fiancé, "I have a lot of work to do . . . at the shop. I'll be back in time for the dinner."

"I was having some sorta breakthrough,"

he responded, staring up at me. "The sun is barely up. Stay. Let's meditate a few more minutes."

"A breakthrough is great. You stay. I can't concentrate." Truth was, my gut instinct made me uneasy. I did not want to need Adonis. Not waiting for another reply from Adonis, I left him outside, on his knees.

I showered, dressed, gathered my design materials, trotted down nineteen steps.

"Morning, Xena," Mr. Ben said. "Slow down."

"Good morning, Mr. Ben."

He said, "If it feels right, it usually is," then closed his door.

Thinking about Mr. Ben's words, I glanced upstairs to the balcony. Adonis was staring down at me. No words were exchanged.

Our silence had sound.

I drove my new car to Tina-Love's house.

Bumper-to-bumper traffic gave me time to think of what I'd say to Tina-Love. Definitely didn't want to walk in on her with her legs in the air and a dick in her vagina or her mouth. She introduced me to Memphis, but did she want him for herself? I didn't believe that, but what was her intention? Knowing her, she probably had some strange guy tied to her bed. I'd only freaked out for one man. Tina-Love probably lost count in high school.

"Good morning, Savannah!" the local radio personality shouted through my speakers. "I wanted to get him in earlier this week, but he'll be here today." I turned down the volume. It was too early for all the extra.

With greater enthusiasm, @DDDShade followed with, "Coming up in the top of the seven o'clock hour we have our Olympic-bound track star, Memphis Brown, in *The Shady Café,* joining us to talk about what it takes to make it to —"

Tearing up, I took a deep breath, changed the channel. "Coming up for you in the eight o'clock hour, Savannah, we have the one, the only Memphis Brown! And his coach, Lou Richie, telling us more about the training camp Memphis Brown is starting for kids in our community. Stay —"

Approaching the private road that led to the security gate to Tina-Love's property, I stopped my car on the side of the road, made a U-turn, then drove to my shop.

I parked facing my storefront. Two other cars were on the small lot. Unlocking my front door, I heard, "What took you so long?"

"Shit! What are you doing?" I placed my

hand over my fast-beating heart.

Adonis said, "You never leave the house that early. How did I beat you here? Answer my question, Xena. What took you so long?"

CHAPTER 23
MEMPHIS

As I arrived at the studio with Coach Lou, from the curb to the entrance fans chanted, "Mem*phis*! Mem*phis*!" The noise grew louder from men, women, and school-aged children. Black and white faces were intermingled. Some waved small American flags. Others held homemade posters.

I read, MEMPHIS I'M YOUR #1 FAN! on one board. OLYMPIC TICKETS PLEASE MR. BROWN! FOR ME AND MY MOM! Then there was my favorite, MEMPHIS BROWN THE GOLDEN CHILD!

Sports united people. I, Memphis Brown, united this crowd. The smile on my face could only get wider if I inserted a dentist's lip and cheek retractor and left it there.

One important person was missing. Tina-Love. Z hadn't denied that my text was true. She could've said something before killing my kid. Damn! Best not to tell my mom what Z had done to her grandchild.

"Memphis, I love you!" a tall, fair-complexioned cutie said, extending a piece of paper and pen to me. "Please!"

After scanning her hair down to her feet, briefly, I gave her eye contact. Faces surrounding her blurred.

"Please!" She gave me the praying hands.

"What are you going to do, MB?" Coach Richie questioned.

I wanted to give her more than an autograph. I was, as my mother would say, sniffing a skunk's behind. Thought about the delivery guy in Chula Vista telling me not to trust women. Nodding to my thoughts, I hated Z. Natalie, she'd been too quiet.

I didn't care about females' feelings anymore. Mom had another big family dinner coming up. The ache in my jaw from grinning was a good one. Cutie appeared young, yet legal. Model type. Or she could be IG-famous.

I replied, "I love you more!" and she broke our eye contact, looked down. I scribbled on a blank page. Placing her possessions in her hand, she stroked my middle finger.

Moving toward the door, I declined the mounting pleas for my signature. My life had forever been changed. Virtually every woman here wanted a piece of me, including cutie. Had to give some female that opportunity. I no longer wanted to snatch Z from Adonis.

Spooning with a stranger. Waking up to someone in the morning the way I'd done with Natalie. I wanted that. Z was my soulmate. If she fucking kept that from me, I couldn't trust her. Tina-Love was my soul sister. A lot of chicks wouldn't have told me shit.

Coach Lou was literally on my heels. "This is the beginning of something bigger than you. Get ready for the whirlwind, MB."

I heard, "Sign my shirt! My shoes! My arm! Please!" ringing from all directions. Lil kids tapped, touched, rubbed my fitted black two-piece athletic tracksuit.

"Let the man through. He has an interview to do," the husky security guard shouted, parting the crowd.

A voice behind us screeched, "I love you, Memphis!"

Absorbed by the emotional high, I answered, "Memphis loves —" I stopped mid-sentence, glanced over my shoulder. "Wow." Lowering my shades to the tip of my nose, shit was about to get real, real quick.

I saw her frantically jumping up and down, wiggling spirited fingers at me. Right before entering the building, I heard her unmistakable voice penetrate my eardrums.

"I love you, baby!"

Coach Richie asked, "You know her?"

"Hell, no," I replied.

He said, "Keep walking, MB. Don't say anything to her."

I couldn't move fast enough with husky in front of me.

"Wait." He did an about-face. "That's the blonde from Chula Vista." Talking to my back, Coach Richie said, "What the hell is she doing in Savannah?"

I hunched my shoulders. Kept it moving. Shot Tina-Love a text. **Did you know Natalie was in Savannah? Just saw her in the crowd outside the studio**

Hell no! How would I know that? she replied.

She knew everything else. Hitting her back with, **What should I do?** I got on the elevator with Coach Richie and the security dude.

Lou Richie's voice trembled as he told me, "It's way too early in the equation for stalkers, MB. Keep me posted when you find out her motivation."

Tina-Love responded, **Be yourself on-air. Shine like the black diamond you are. Remember to talk about your starting a nonprofit for kids. I'll handle Natalie. My masseuse is setting up for my 2 hour**

rubdown. Have a lunch date at noon with our gurl. Let's meet up at 2p.

Fuck commenting on Z. Didn't want to come close to running into her ass. I swear Tina-Love was born with inverted dick. **I have to train from 2-8p catch up to you @your place later**

Tina-Love texted, **Cool. Did you have that conversation with Natalie about marriage?**

Hell naw! Head high, chest forward, eyes bright, I entered the suite. A group of kids rushed me. Clung to my legs, arms, and waist. I was a human Christmas tree, and they were my ornaments.

I handed Coach Richie my cell. "Take pictures. I have to post this on all my pages."

Natalie couldn't possibly hurt me like Z. Natalie getting an abortion would be her doing me a favor. She was not going to steal my shine. Following Tina-Love's suggestion to keep the peace, I shouldn't have texted Natalie that "I miss you" bullshit knowing I never meant it. If I had proposed, she'd be swinging from one of my limbs like these kids.

Staff was gathered in the lobby, anxiously awaiting their turn to take photos with me and snag my autograph. I signed a few track shoes and T-shirts. Posed for selfies. The show producer asked Coach Richie to take a group pic of me with his employees for them to frame and hang on the wall.

Staring at the celebrities on display — Drake, Cardi B, Mary J, Eminem — I'd be a local standout. Stardom was made for Memphis Brown and Memphis Brown was made to shine like a diamond. A black diamond. Tina-Love was all the way right.

"Have a seat here, man," said Rick the radio producer, who was also @DDD Shade's husband, as he rolled out a stool with a high back. "Adjust the height to your liking, bruh."

@DDDShade, the most popular female personality in the country, looked up from the computer monitor, nodded at me.

An assistant handed Coach Richie and me headphones. "Put these on. We're going live in sixty seconds."

I hoped Adonis's Passe Blanc punk ass was listening. He was no competition for the blackberry juice. That nigga couldn't touch me, and yes, I was never going to reclaim what was rightfully mine. But I could if I wanted to.

This was my first on-air. I slid my sweaty palms together. @DDDShade didn't move her head, but she looked over at my hands, smiled, resumed focusing on her monitor. I had three more back-to-back in-studio lives to go after this. *On second thought, I should pop in on Tina-Love and Z.*

"This is your gurl @DDDShade! Usually I'm spilling tea up in *The Shady Café* for my 'shade trees,' but today I have a sweet treat for ya! And I do mean dark and delicious! What's up, Memphis Brown?! Huge congrats! He's fine, ladies. I'm sure he can handle any age."

I blushed, but was sure no one could tell but me when my face got hot. @DDDShade reminded me of my ageless cougar crush, Angela Bassett.

"Question number one for Memphis Brown. Are you single *and* available?" she asked.

Without hesitation, I answered, "Yes. And yes." A day prior, I would've answered the opposite.

"Any baby mamas?" she inquired.

I shook my head.

"He's shaking his heads to that one, ladies. We're going to get to Coach Lou Richie in a minute, but first. Memphis. Tell us about your journey and what it means for you to represent the United States of America in next year's Summer Olympics."

I'm downstairs listening to you on my phone, Natalie texted. **Give me a mention.**

They don't have to hear about our baby yet.

Loosening my neck, I thought, *What was the question? Oh, yeah.* Excitedly I answered, "The world. This means the world to me. First, I have to thank my mother, Ms. Hattie Mae Brown. Seeing my mom sacrifice for me to be here is why I have to give back to the single moms and kids in my community. I know what's it's like growing up without a father. Props to my stepbrother, Lionel, aunts, uncles, cousins. Too many to mention by name. Tina-Love, my soul sister. I worked my 'a' off. Deserve to be here, but it's nothing if I can't help the next lil Memphis ride this train."

Yes! Baby, we are going to do incredible work in the community! Natalie texted.

I wish that bitch was on a mission in Costa Rica! Had to find a way to support getting her out of the country.

"Listeners, if you want to hit me with a question for Memphis Brown," @DDD-Shade said, and gave out her Twitter and a call-in number, then repeated it.

"I'm lovin' it and you," @DDDShade said, turning her attention back to me. "What do you eat every day? Hopefully not supermodel Tina-Love. You know my shade trees didn't miss that, right?"

187

I smiled at @DDDShade.

I want to have you for brunch, Natalie texted. **Who's Tina-Love?**

I prayed Natalie would stop. What was her point? "The main things I eat are fish, salads, pasta, red potatoes, fruits. My mama's seafood gumbo. Lots and all types of veggies. So kids," I emphasized, doing what Tina-Love said, keeping the focus off of me, "if you want to be strong and fast like Memphis Brown, eat your vegetables first."

"Hmm." @DDDShade stared at her screen. "Listeners, don't go anywhere because up next in *The Shady Café,* forget spilling the tea," she yelled, "I have quick-saaaaaand! Let's talk about how this television ho, I meant *ho*stess, whose husband allegedly has a mistress of over a decade, allegedly, is going to handle her man after all the *ish*! she's dished about celebs."

Rick peeped in. "The ratings are through the roof! Great job you guys." He closed the door.

After the break, @DDDShade went hard for the TV host. I was never going to be on @DDDShade's bad side, but that was all she seemed to have.

"We're back and we have a caller on the line," @DDDShade said, then answered.

"Who's calling and what's your question?"

"It's an old friend of Memphis's. I just wanted to say, congratulations, baby."

My heartbeat multiplied. I replied "thanks" to Z, but I was done with her!

@DDDShade snarled, "Thanks who?" then adjusted to a friendlier tone. "We have time for one more call before I speak with Coach Lou Richie. Who's calling and what's your question?"

"Hi, my name is Natalie."

Coach Richie coughed. I damn near fell off of my stool. *Lord, please don't let this bitch fuck up a stellar interview for me.* I stared at Coach Richie.

@DDDShade asked, "Natalie, what's your question?"

Coach Richie stood, spoke on-air for the first time since we'd arrived. "Sorry, Natalie. We really have to get going."

Redirecting her gaze toward Coach Richie, @DDDShade replied, "Oh-kay," with curiosity. "Natalie, post your question on our website."

Natalie blurted, "We came all the way from Chula Vista to support you, Memphis," then ended the call.

"Well. We love *you,* Memphis Brown," @DDDShade said. "You are family and can come back anytime you'd like. I'd love to have you."

There she went, dropping the flirtatious double meaning.

Ignoring @DDDShade, I removed my headphones and placed them on the counter. That *bitch Natalie was stalking*!

@DDDShade spread a sinister smile. " 'We'? Oh-oh. Sounds like I might need to invite Natalie to sip tea at *The Shady Café*. Shout it out, shade trees . . . Quick-saaaaaand!"

"Quicksand, my ass. I don't know a Natalie," I lied, then left.

CHAPTER 24
XENA

Steam suspended in the air. I registered each word filtering through my wireless sound system as that radio talent brought Memphis's fourth interview of the morning to a close with the last caller.

As with the previous conclusions, I heard the last caller say, "Hi, my name is Natalie. We came all the way from Chula Vista to support you, Memphis."

Who is she? flooded my brain. I felt her love for Memphis in the sweet tone of a California proper-girl accent. She was committed to Memphis. *We love you, Memphis,* she'd said, four times, to millions of listeners near and far.

In less than four hours, she'd made herself relevant. Natalie's call-ins had gone viral, her followers were in the seven digits, and she had an open invitation to *The Shady Café*.

"I miss you, Memphis." No one could

hear me but me. I texted him, **Is Natalie your girlfriend?**

As I hung the steamer on the pole, I regretted breaking up with Memphis. Wish I could be as happy as my clients and Topez would be when they saw the groom's tuxedo.

Is Adonis your man? You're the one wearing an engagement ring. You need to take that shit off and come home where you belong.

Was there really room for me in his celebrity-driven life? Memphis didn't want me back.

The doorbell chimed. Soon as I saw who was outside, I deleted the message history from my ex, smoothed my hands over the finished jacket on the mannequin, fingered the blouse and trousers on the rack. Smiling, to cheer myself up, I unlocked the door, then greeted my fiancé.

"You could've used your key," I told Adonis, then asked, "How's your day going?" Proud of my accomplishments, I extended my arms for a hug.

He slapped my hands. "What's up with your calling in to @DDDShade's show to congratulate Memphis Brown?" Adonis questioned, standing two inches in front of us with his hands by his side.

Turning off the radio app on my cell, I backed away from Adonis. "Where do I sleep every night? Who do I wake up to every morning?" I moved closer, placed his palm on top of my abdomen. "Whose baby is growing inside of me? I'm not going to entertain an argument where there is no justifiable cause. I said, on-air, that I was an *old* friend."

I picked up a blank page, stood at my workstation, began sketching for my next contract. I'd dreamt of a one-of-a-kind design last night. The jacket I envisioned was lightweight, long-sleeved, tailored to a second skin yet comfortable and flexible. Seamless. No visible buttons. Feeling the animosity in Adonis's attitude was confirmation of what I needed to do.

"Don't leave out the *baby* part," he added. My fiancé stood behind me, placed his hands on the desk, leaned over, then lamented, "First, the market. Now you're calling in congratulating him. What's next? Stop fantasizing about a man that has a harem. You heard the Cali chick that called in to every one of his interviews. She sounded white." Standing tall, he continued, "Look at me, Xena. You are an engaged woman carrying my child. Show respect for the Oglethorpe name. My mama and my daddy heard you too."

I put down my pencil. Faced my reality. "I dated Memphis for five years. You are the first and only man I've been with since *I* left Memphis a year ago. Do I still love him? Yes. Do I love you?" I lied. "Yes. Now, please leave, you're upsetting me. I have lunch plans."

"So now I'm upsetting you." Shaking his head, Adonis said, "You're not going out to lunch with him or any man long as you're mine."

He walked up to my mannequin. *Bam!* It slammed to the concrete floor. "That's what I'm going to do to Mister All-Star when I see him."

I stared at my jacket until my vision blurred. Picking everything up, softly I told him, "Please. Get out."

"No, you get out!" he demanded. "Who paid off the remainder of your commercial lease?"

He'd voluntarily insisted but, unlike his residential properties, Xena Trinity was the only name on my rental agreement. Where was his insecurity stemming from? If I wasn't at the apartment, I was here. Working.

I picked up my cell, texted Tina-Love, **Come soon as you can. I have to get away** from Adonis. He's acting crazy!

?RU, Tina-Love asked.

My shop.

Okay. Have to handle some business for Memphis first. CU@1p, she replied.

Good thing I wasn't dying. That was an hour and a half away. I had to handle this alone? While my bestie went to the rescue of my ex? Calming Adonis, I had to get him out of here before the situation escalated.

"Adonis, what's wrong?"

"I never thought you would lie to me too," he said. Tears coated his eyes. "Is that my baby or his?'

Crying on the inside, I thought, *Am I to blame for whatever another woman had done to him?* "Apparently, your mind is made up about me too. I'm not your ex. Think whatever you want." I should've comforted him, but I didn't want to.

"You slept with him," he said, knocking my sketch pad to the floor.

"I have the absolute most fantastic news for you, Xena!" Topez announced as she sashayed into the shop. She sat in the roller chair at my sewing machine, spun around. "Darling, pack your bags. We are catching the first flight out in the morning to New York City, for not just a, but *the* meeting that will secure our position! Let me see what you're coming up with."

I picked up my drawing. There wasn't much to let her see on paper. The groom's tux was the highlight.

Admiring my creation, she complimented, "Already I can tell this contract is going to be a masterpiece ensemble!" Topez gasped. "Oh, where's my manners. Hello, Adonis."

"Xena is an engaged mother-to-be. She's not getting on that plane with you or anyone else," he said.

Topez stared at me, looked at my garment for the second time. "Darling, how many months are you?"

"Not sure. I just found out about two weeks ago," I told her, shifting my eyes toward Adonis.

"Well, one baby doesn't stop a New York Fashion Week show, darling. This is a once-in-a-lifetime opportunity, and lots of mothers work. By the time that bambino arrives, you'll have more than enough money to hire a traveling nanny."

"You are not Xena's husband." Adonis poked himself in the chest. "I am," he continued, raising his voice.

"In case you didn't know, the Thirteenth Amendment freed you, and women have the right to work."

"Then she can buy her own car and find a

place to live." Redirecting his attention toward me, my fiancé opened his hand and demanded, "Give me my house and car keys."

If he thought I was going to fall on my knees, plead to maintain possession over things that obviously didn't come from his heart, he was wrong. I put his house key and his car remote on the counter.

He wiggled his finger. "And the key to the store."

"No," was all I told him.

"I don't know exactly what's going on here, but I've seen enough. Adonis, you need to leave before I call the police," Topez said.

"You'll have to come home to get your clothes," Adonis said, walked out, then slammed the door.

All the tears I'd held in came rushing out like a waterfall.

"Listen to me," Topez said. "Dry those tears. Crying is for the birth of a baby and the death of a loved one. Not for a man that disrespects you. I don't know what happened and don't need to. Listen to me. You think he would allow you to come between one of his precious real estate deals?"

I shook my head.

"Then why in hell you let him come into

your shop being rude and destructive? Don't answer that. Have you been to the doctor for blood work?"

I'd been super busy. Had put our clients' needs ahead of mine. I confided, "I'm not sure if I want to keep it."

"First, the doctor. Then make a decision. It's your body. But do not abort out of spite."

All of my possessions, a lot of my materials, were at Adonis's house. I'd never given him a reason to be jealous, but I was thankful to learn before it was too late he wasn't the man I thought he was. I went from being the woman he wanted to share the rest of his life with to a person he hated, all in less than twenty-four hours. I was not apologizing for my past.

"The best way to bring a man down is to cut off all communication with him. Show him you can be happy without him. And let him keep everything that he is trying to use as a weapon against you," she said as she hugged me. "You're successful without him. Get yourself together. Meet me at the airport at six in the morning."

"Thank you. I'll be there," I said, sniffling.

Topez added, "The only power a man has over you is the control you give him."

CHAPTER 25
TINA-LOVE

I'd reached out to Xena. It was the right thing to do after putting her in a bad predicament with Memphis. She agreed to meet. If Memphis was my man, baby or not, no woman could intimidate me. Natalie had best not try that nonsense again.

After parking my Bentley in a stall next to Xena's BMW, I entered her storefront. "Damn, do I need to cancel my Italy trip to attend to your and Memphis's problems? I've got my own to deal with," I said, placing the bag with our lunches inside on Xena's small counter.

"Not you, Tina-Love," she said sarcastically while cutting a piece of material. "I'm not hungry."

Looking beyond Xena, I noticed the most spectacular jacket hanging on a mannequin. "Damn, gurl! This is real boss. I could rock this piece on the runway in Italy. Panties, no bra." Easing it on, I told her, "You've stepped it up. Make me a replica."

Xena remained focused on her task. "Maybe I should switch up. Stop confiding in a so-called friend. Fuck any man I want, then never care if I see him again."

My bestie had the right to tell me that. "You can't handle truth. Not even your own." I wanted to add that was why she'd killed my godchild. "I figured you'd change your mind. Lunch is in the bag. What's up that you can't break to eat when you obviously need to?" Xena had more than herself to consider.

Why wouldn't those two do as I'd told them?

If he had proposed to Natalie, he could've sat her down and shut her up. If Xena would've moved in on Memphis, no matter how upset he would've been, they could've had the make-up conversation.

Memphis's situationship had to de-escalate immediately. I'd gotten Natalie's number from him. Using the cell, I'd Googled it. Found her email. Searched images. The chick had enough selfies to collage-wrap my car. Hadn't seen any photos of Memphis with her. Had to find a way to get and keep Natalie out of Savannah and away from Memphis until after she'd had that baby and he'd won his gold medals. Afterward we could have a paternity test.

A text registered on my cell. **Hi it's Natalie. Memphis told me you're his manager and that you'd find a place for me and his unborn baby to stay. You can call me on this number.**

What the hell? He gave her my direct contact number! Men! Was he serious? I checked the time. Memphis was starting training, but when he finished at eight p.m., we had to discuss this b.s. Okay, I was sure he didn't tell her he'd sponsor her stay. Not after the stunt she'd pulled this morning. I was getting on board with her game. Had to. She didn't say where. Atlanta might be a good fit for Natalie.

Somberly Xena asked, "Can we skip lunch?" She placed her scissors on her cutting table.

Oh shit! Tears clouded her eyes. I couldn't be in two places simultaneously.

"Absolutely, something just came up with Memphis," I replied, texting that Natalie bitch, **What's your relationship with Memphis?**

Abruptly she hit back, **Girlfriend status**

Self-proclaimed, no doubt. Men and their dicks! I had to talk this bitch onto a ledge, then push her the fuck off. **Okay, Natalie.**

I'll send you a time and location in a few.

"I meant skip having lunch here. I need to go shopping. Topez and I are on the first flight to New York in the morning for a meeting that will determine if I get my line on the runway for fashion week next summer."

I barely had my arm around Xena before Memphis texted, **Where y'all at?**

Hell to the no! They'd thank me eventually. The power couple I envisioned was about to get their relationship back on track. He wasn't ready to see Xena.

I hit him with, **#stayfocused #workout hard**

"Bitch, you're withholding pertinent information. This is the moment I have breathed for. Soon as Memphis finishes his training at eight o'clock, I'm going to let him know we have to celebrate and claim your acceptance. But you have to watch out for Topez. Don't sign anything with her without a lawyer looking at it first. When will you be back?" I asked.

"I'm not sure when I'll be back, but no thanks to you, Memphis hates me. Adonis is acting strange so I'm staying here tonight. That's why I need to buy everything for my trip today. I'm not going back to his place. Ever."

Tears that were clinging flowed down her cheeks in a stream. What in the universe was going on? I looked around Xena's shop.

"Where are you going to lay your head? You don't have space for a sofa, sofa-sleeper, or an air mattress." If I invited her to my house, she wouldn't understand the struggle. A hotel was an option, but she'd rather try and make me feel responsible for her sleeping here.

"It's only for one night. I have tons of material. I can make a pallet on the floor and crash here until I figure things out. The last place I want to stay is with my parents and listen to my mother drag for Memphis."

More like drag for her if her mother found out about the abortion. At least Xena had gotten pregnant by her man and not her mother's man. Not once, but twice. Mrs. Trinity never approved of my dating life-style, but where was she when I was being raped? Oh, yeah. Beating on Xena while we were in elementary, junior high, and high school.

Standing on cracks in the concrete floor, I had a change of heart. "You'll do no such thing. You can stay with me tonight, girl. We'll figure this out together. The three of us."

Xena shook her head, dried her tears. "I

got myself into this. I'll be fine."

"Cool." Admiring the drawing, I complimented her. "Nice sleeveless jacket-vest. What type of leather is that?" I had to feel it.

Raising my hand, she said, "Don't touch it. You might stain it."

Who did she think she was talking to? I've worn the most expensive fabrics in the world by designers with their own stores. I strutted to the other side of the counter.

"You always take his side. Why?" Xena asked, digging in the bag. She removed all the containers. "I'm famished."

"Me too," I said, avoiding the question. "Put that down."

Xena said grace, then began eating her salad. "You know more about Memphis than I do."

I didn't understand her point; she was wrong. "We know different things about Memphis. I wouldn't have introduced the two of you if I wanted him. Tell me you're not still in love with Memphis Brown, and I'll stop trying to get you guys back together."

She stood on one side of the counter. I was on the other. Xena could've had a bigger space if she wasn't comfortable with Adonis paying for everything. Xena got what he felt she deserved.

"Regardless of what you think or how you feel, I'm never going to quit being Memphis's biggest supporter. Friends don't make friends lose friends."

Xena dropped her fork in her plate. "See, that's what I'm talking about. Why couldn't you have said you're never going to stop being my biggest supporter?"

"I've known you longer. Didn't think I had to."

"I need you to be here for me," Xena said. "Everyone in fashion knows you. Can you go with us in the morning to New York?"

Wow! I wasn't expecting that. I hadn't ever heard superuser say she needed anyone. I wasn't abandoning Memphis to accompany her to New York, but she asked and I could help by making a few calls.

"Who are you meeting with tomorrow? And since you're not staying at my house, at least let me take you shopping at the mall. My treat."

Xena nodded. "I'd like that. I don't know. Topez hasn't told me yet. I'ma text her now."

Sighing heavily, I rolled my eyes. "Girl, let's go." Before I changed my mind.

As we exited the shop, Adonis rushed from the passenger side of Xena's BMW, then announced, "Xena is my fiancée," as though he were auditioning for a reality show.

"What in the hell are you doing here?" Xena said.

"Since you don't know how to call and apologize, I came to get my car," he said. "When you tell me you're sorry and apologize to my parents for tarnishing my family's name, you can have them back."

I stood tall on my heels towering over Adonis. "Boy, bye. Xena is not going home to you."

Xena shook her head. I wondered, what the hell for? This was her out. *Curse and kick him out!*

Adonis moved close to me, then lamented, "You can sit your lonely single behind down and focus on getting yourself a ring from Memphis."

Xena laughed. "She has thirteen engagement rings, Adonis. None of them are from Memphis."

I didn't miss the way Adonis stared at me when Xena wasn't looking directly at him. He might not be a cheater; he may want to blame me for their problems. Whatever he paid for I did not give a damn. This shop was owned by Xena Trinity's Alterations and Designs.

I shoved Adonis hard. He stumbled backward, then fell to the walkway. "You'd best stay out of a real woman's way." I was cute, but he didn't want me to exhibit my skills up in here. My ring count was at twelve. Had to get that one back from Memphis if he wasn't proposing to Natalie.

"Bitch!" Adonis yelled, standing. "I ought to —"

I kicked above his head, stopped inches from his eyes, then lowered my foot to the ground. That nigga could act all mighty, but he'd be calling on the Lord if he made one bad move in my or Xena's direction.

I'd been raped too many times to count. First modeling paycheck, I took self-defense classes. Adonis did not want this I-can't-wait-to-justifiably-beat-a-man's-ass-for-real pent-up frustration.

"Stop it!" Xena yelled. "I'm not having this! You don't love me and I don't want your car! Your ring." She hurled the diamond solitaire at him. "And I'm not having this baby. All I want to do is live my life for me."

Well, it was about time she raised her voice and took the escape route. Being with Adonis needed to end and this was perfect timing. Next, I had to get Natalie out of Memphis's way.

I texted Memphis, **do not give Natalie my ring!**

"You all up in my fiancée's head with your whorish ways. If Xena kills my baby, I swear I'll do the same to both of you," Adonis said.

Adonis threw the house key, remote, and ring at me. Catching them mid-air — I aimed them at his head. "Fuck a BMW, you fuckboy! Xena can roll in my Bentley, bitch!"

He was like most men. Eager to blame someone else for his fuckup. Men did that shit all the time — gave a woman a gift, then took it back — but they knew better than to try that with me. I could buy Xena a car on Roman's credit card. I needed to give him an encore.

After Adonis sped off, Xena said, "That's why I have to handle my business. Topez must be busy. She hasn't responded to my text."

"Text Topez again. I need for you to find out who you're meeting with. I'll reach out to Rainey. She'll take care of you." Forget Topez. "Soon as you get back, we'll terminate your situation. I'll make the appointment for your abortion on the way to the mall." Had to solidify the situation before Xena changed her mind.

Closing the passenger door, Xena told me,

"I feel stupid getting myself knocked up. I can't be mad at you for telling Memphis. I should've been woman enough to do that."

She should've felt dumb for not giving birth to Memphis's baby. Now Natalie had first dibs.

"You know I don't believe in self-pity. Stupidity is for women who keep permitting the same man to fuck them over and keep lying to themselves about leaving. Let's go get some real food, and get you ready for your trip to the Big Apple."

Fuck Adonis!

CHAPTER 26
XENA

Tina-Love was and would forever be my only bestie. Despite her actions, I wanted her friendship more. She lived in a mansion. I had to admit I was afraid to have my own place, be responsible for all my expenses. Committing to a man meant I didn't have to.

"What's it going to be?" I asked. "Savannah Mall? Tanger Outlets? Or —" I watched Tina-Love weave in and out of traffic. She was monitoring her surroundings and occasionally focusing her eyes on me.

She suggested, "Oglethorpe Mall?"

I didn't want to hear that name, but there was no Spanx Mall or Lenox Square in Savannah like there was in Atlanta. Tina-Love wore a size twelve shoe. My feet were an eight. Her inseam was forty. Mine thirty-four. "Don't make me say that name, but that's the one," I answered.

"Honey, we may not wear the same size,

but I will hook you up with accessories that are and will make you look . . . rich!"

What in the world was I going to find at Oglethorpe that didn't embarrass me in the most important meetings of my career? Wait. I wouldn't want people to feel that way about my clothes. At least the designers in department stores had achieved what I strived for.

Tina-Love was unusually quiet. Her eyes kept darting in different directions, but her head did not move. Suddenly she blurted, "Adonis Oglethorpe is not the founder of Georgia. His family simply shares the last name of James Edward, honey."

Not much in Savannah proper was far from my storefront, yet depending on the time of day it could be inconveniently close. Traffic slowed our pace.

An outgoing ringtone escaped Tina-Love's Bluetooth in the car.

I stared at her. "Are you calling Memphis?" My heart pounded. What would I say if he answered?

"Doctor Francis's office. Hi, Ms. Jones. I'm glad you called. You're due for your annual Pap smear. How can we help you?" a friendly female asked.

"I have a best friend that needs to schedule an abortion," Tina-Love said. "Do you have any openings on Friday?"

My eyes widened. I shook my head. She nodded.

The woman replied, "The doctor has one appointment available on Friday, but Dr. Francis would need to examine her first. What's her name?"

"We'd like everything performed the same day," Tina-Love confirmed.

I was mad at Adonis for the way he was treating me, but in my heart, I wanted to make things right with Memphis. I answered, "My name is Xena Trinity."

The woman confirmed me for three o'clock on Friday. If I changed my mind, I could delay my return trip to Savannah.

Tina-Love turned off her engine. "Call Topez. Put her on speaker."

"Why?" I questioned.

"If you want me to ask Rainey to help you, I need to find out who Topez's people are. Otherwise, you deal without my help." She looked at her cell. Tapped on keys. "Okay, let's stop wasting time. Get out. What all do you want from the mall?"

"Wait." I dialed Topez's number. She answered, "We're all set for tomorrow. You're excited, girlie?"

"I am, but I —"

Topez interrupted, "No buts. Everything

is moving —"

"Hi, Topez, this is Tina-Love, Xena's best friend. Whom all are the two of you meeting with in New York tomorrow?" Tina-Love took my phone out of my hand.

"Hi, Tina-Love, you're amazing! We're meeting with all the bigwigs," Topez said excitedly. "Aren't you proud of Xena? We're finally moving in the right direction to get her men's line on the racks."

"Names, please," Tina-Love firmly said.

"Oh, I can't reveal my sources. You know how this business is. But if you have any movers and shakers you'd like for me to reach out to, text them to me." Topez gave Tina-Love her cell number.

I didn't want Tina-Love to ruin my opportunity trying to prove anything to Topez. I spoke up. "I could use a ride to the airport. Can you pick me up from my storefront?"

Tina-Love pressed her lips together. Slowly shook her head. I hunched my shoulders.

"Why, of course. What's happening?" Topez asked with concern.

Tina-Love handed me my phone, got out of her car.

I told Topez, "Adonis tried to give me back the new BMW, then he repossessed it in the next breath."

"You don't need him, Xena," she said confidently.

Topez needed to know some of my material, supplies, and all of my clothes were at his house. And, "I have no place to sleep so I'm staying the night at my shop."

Gasping, she replied, "You can't be serious. Where is the best friend when you need her?" Topez asked. "She can get you to Fashion Week, but she can't put you up for one night. She's not your friend."

"Tina-Love, is that you?" someone called out.

"Listen, I have a gentleman friend who could use a female companion. His children don't check on him. He has a spacious mansion and won't get in your way, but at least you'll have a bed to sleep in. I'll introduce the two of you when we get back from New York."

I wanted to tell Topez about the abortion, but she continued, "I have to catch this. New York is calling. Pick you up in the morning. Bye, girlie."

I approached Tina-Love, and we stood face-to-face. A young, beautiful woman came up to us, extended her hand to me. "Hi, Xena. I'm Natalie. Memphis's girlfriend."

CHAPTER 27
MEMPHIS

"Is Natalie pregnant?" Coach Richie asked, fastening straps around my waist.

A heavy sled was behind me. This was my last run of the night. Daylight savings was fading to an eight o'clock darkness. My interviews earlier would've been perfect had it not been for that bitch. Couldn't wait to brainstorm with Tina-Love on how to get rid of Natalie's ass forever.

"That's what she claims," I answered. "If she is, I don't think it's mine."

"Is there a possibility?" he questioned, standing in front of me.

Natalie was not going to stick me with a kid or become attached to wages I hadn't earned yet. Soon as she dropped that load, I was demanding a blood test, praying to hear, "You are not the father."

"That's what she says, Coach. But you were right. I listened to everything you said about being careful. I believe Natalie was expecting before I got accepted. I haven't fucked any woman since my acceptance. I don't believe her." I shrugged my shoulders. Tilted my head side to side.

Tina-Love and I were in agreement about not giving Natalie the ring. The only person I was proposing to was Z. And I intended to do that soon as I could snatch off that ring dude put on her finger. Couldn't fake it. I was pissed at Z for aborting my baby but . . . damn, she was having dude's kid. Scrap asking Z to take my last name. In the state of Georgia, if I married Z, I'd be legally liable for that dude's child.

"Did you fuck her without a condom?" Coach Lou Richie asked.

Tension grew in my neck, traveled to my already aching shoulders. Tried adjusting the harness. Turning my head left and right, didn't feel like hearing myself admit how stupid I was for an entire year. I nodded.

"We are going to have to clean this one up fast or you may be uninvited to compete. What can you do to make sure she gets rid of the kid?" he inquired.

Wow! A burning sensation settled in my thighs. I'd done extra reps of squats earlier. A real thorough soak in Tina-Love's Jacuzzi would melt away my frustrations. Temporarily. All life had to offer when it came to sexual gratification was bouts of satisfaction. I was taking a break from sex and females.

I said, "I'm listening," in anticipation of Coach bestowing wisdom upon me that my sorry-ass daddy hadn't. If my stepfather were alive, this conversation wouldn't exist. He talked with me all the time.

Coach Richie shouted, "You don't think! I need for you to talk to me, MB! You are about to fuck up everything I've worked for!"

Hadn't thought about how my situation could adversely impact Coach's livelihood. He wasn't married, but he did have four kids depending on him. How did I know Natalie wasn't playing me? I'd done what I could, but obviously that pill I gave her, she didn't swallow it. The weight of the sled caused my lower back to strain.

"If Natalie is telling the truth, she'll give birth months before the Games." We were shy of twelve months out from passing the torch. "I'll stay away from her and request a DNA."

Tina-Love was the only one that could keep my name clear until the results were in. I was calling her soon as we were done. My left knee buckled. Quickly I straightened it out.

"She's not going to go away easily, MB. She's not going to sit in the stands alone for however many more months and keep her mouth shut. What you're going to do is . . ." He paused. "Have her go to our doctor, take a blood test to confirm her status, and we'll do an early DNA but won't let her know. If you're the father, then you'd better sweet-talk her ass into having an abortion."

Damn. Had to let Tina-Love know what Coach Richie had recommended. She'd love that idea.

"Coach, no disrespect, but I need to drag this sled fifty feet, or I need you to unhinge me." My other knee bent, hit the track. "Fuck!"

He didn't motion to assist me in any manner. Started to question whose team Coach was on. Did he have my replacement lined up?

Coach Richie extended his hand. I reached for it. He pulled away and patted me on my back. "A woman scorned will ruin your life faster than a thousand men who hate you. You know why, MB?"

"Coach, please. For real. Feels like something in my knee is tearing." I tried standing. Couldn't.

"I! Asked you! A question!" he yelled.

His shouting, I was accustomed to. His

energy, I was not. It came from a place of anger. Quietly I answered, "No, sir."

Kneeling behind me, Coach unfastened the straps, then said, "Women are smarter than us. We are forever at their mercy. The minute you forget that, the second you penetrate any part of her — heart, pussy, head — she can bring you down to your knees. Natalie knew what she was doing. Your problem is, you were too busy thinking with your dick! I'll help you this time. Don't be the same fool twice, MB." Coach stood, extended his hand.

I latched on. Struggled to get up. Hugged him. "Thanks. See you in the morning." I limped a few steps. "Six sharp."

"We'll go easy in the morning. I'll set up an appointment with the medics in the afternoon to have those knees x-rayed. Your having an injury may be our saving grace. Humble yourself, MB, or you're never going to grab the gold."

I started trotting. Sharp pains hit me behind my knees like lightning bolts. Had to slow my pace to a walk. Felt like a toddler struggling not to fall. Didn't stop until I was in my car.

Come by and eat. I was happier the text came from Tina-Love and not my mom. Hattie Mae's cooking tasted great, but

Mom didn't understand what proteins my body needed.

I drove directly to Tina-Love. Entered my gate code. Parked in my space next to her car. The aroma of fish engulfed my nostrils when I entered the kitchen. I opened my arms for a hug, but she placed her hand on my chest.

Softly Tina-Love said, "Have a seat at the counter."

Damn! Like that?

After handing me a glass of fresh spinach juice, she prepared a plate with sea bass, fresh smashed red potatoes, broccoli, and a side kale salad with cranberries, pine nuts, walnuts, cherry tomatoes, diced cucumbers, and lots of avocado. Set it in front of me.

"You're not eating with me?" I asked.

Sadly, she said, "Not tonight."

Bowing my head, I quickly said grace, then asked, "What's up?"

"Nothing I can't deal with. But you owe me," she said.

Inside my chest, one heartbeat tried to out chase the other. I stood. "You okay?"

"I will be." A single tear escaped one of her eyes. I'd never witnessed such. This woman never cried.

"Eat. When you're done, go to Xena's shop. Don't call her. Don't ask me any more questions. Just go. I'm going upstairs to my bedroom."

CHAPTER 28
XENA

Literally, but not intentionally, I'd regurgitated on Natalie's lilac romper, then apologized. Based on her confession, that meant she and I were both pregnant. Neither of us had a baby bump. I'd heard her on the radio earlier, but I was surprised she was beyond pretty. I didn't know Memphis liked white girls.

Go ahead. I'll catch up, my bestie had said.

Somberly I'd walked away. Tina-Love never made it inside the mall to meet up with me. I'd left her when she started threatening Natalie, demanding Natalie get out of Savannah. I'd shopped alone, then took an Uber back here to my shop. Everything I needed was in the carry-on roller bag near the door except what I was wearing on the plane. To my surprise, there were some impressive off-the-rack items like the black sequined jumper I'd put on in the morning. Fashion never slept. Every designer knew that.

As I sketched the last of the three designs, I thought I'd be done by midnight, get three hours of rest, and be waiting on Topez by four a.m.

Bam! Bam! Bam! "Z, open up the door."

"Shit!" My pencil slid across the pad. The mistake would set me back at least fifteen minutes.

What had Memphis come to say? He had a white stalker girlfriend? I may have not believed her if she hadn't enthusiastically described his dick down to the clipper-shaven pubic area. Added how his left ball was slightly bigger than the right. There was a small raised mole on the underside of his shaft that was only visible when he got an erection, and was most felt when administrating fellatio.

I turned off the lights, wrapped myself in twelve yards of cheap — red, black, and white — flannel I'd bought six months ago to create a unique winter look that I'd be sexy in. I curled into a fetal position on the concrete floor, next to the table. I hadn't responded to any of Adonis's thirty-two texts.

Bam! Bam! Bam! Bam! Bam! Bam! "I'm not leaving until we talk, Z. I know you're in there! I saw you turn off the light. I love you. Not her."

Based on past situations, when he said he wasn't leaving, Memphis meant it. I had to rest. Opening the door, I stood in the dark. He entered, secured the lock.

I told Memphis, "You're involved. I was engaged. I have to figure things out on my own."

"I forgive you, Z. Did you say 'was'? As in you're not anymore?" he asked. Leaning down, his lips pressed against mine.

Gently pushing him, I said, "Memphis, please. Natalie is having your baby. I'm pregnant with Adonis's child. There's nothing for us to discuss. Please go. I'm exhausted, have to correct the design you made me mess up when you banged on my door like the police. And I have an early flight to New York."

Standing close to him, I admitted to myself that Memphis's body was shaped like a black panther's. Lean. Cut. I smelled the salt on his flesh. Tasted it on my lips from the kiss.

"And I have training. But whatever is bothering you can't wait, Z. Tina-Love said I have to talk with you now. Please, don't shut me out," he begged. "Why are you sleeping here? Let's go to my house," he offered.

A nice bed, warm familiar environment, wasn't meant for me. I needed to be uncomfortable. Plus, Topez had arranged temporary quarters for me when we got back. I shook my head, retreated to my sleeping pad, folded my legs. Memphis flipped up the switch, followed me.

"Please, turn it off." I didn't want anyone to see me with him, or know I was inside my place of business at this hour.

In darkness, I told Memphis, "Say what you need to make yourself feel better and then I really need to be alone."

Sitting beside me, he cocooned our bodies as one. "Z, we're going to do this Olympic journey together. Not Natalie. Not Adonis. The two of us."

Sarcastically I mentioned, "Let's not forget Tina-Love. She tells you everything."

"Why you gotta say it like that? She's our friend." Memphis eased his arm behind my back.

I had to take the deepest breath. I held it, counted to ten. Opened my mouth. Slowly exhaled. Inhaled.

"Wow." Memphis leaned in to kiss me.

I moved my lips in the opposite direction. "I heard her voice on the radio four times today."

"Baby, she's a groupie slash stalker. I can't

control that," he pleaded.

Liar. "I met Natalie today. By accident. I know your friend told you." I could've said *our,* but I had no idea how involved Tina-Love was with the situation.

Memphis pinched my chin, pivoted my face toward him.

I stared into his eyes, not blinking once. "Please tell me you're not serious about her being so crazy about you that she traveled over three thousand miles. How and why did she come here? Tina-Love took me shopping. We ran into Natalie at the mall. She introduced herself as your girlfriend, then gave us an oral tour of your genitals."

Memphis leaned back, sat up. His laughter devolved into a gut-wrenching grunt. Squinting, he massaged his knee. "You're kidding me, right?"

"Stop playing stupid." I slapped his thigh. He jerked. Moved my hand.

I'd witnessed that reaction before. "Oh my God. You injured yourself?"

"Nah. Worked out too hard. That's why I need you. Come to my place. We can continue this conversation in the tub."

"Memphis, I . . ." I paused.

He gazed into my eyes. "What is it, Z? That nigga put you out? You need money? A place to stay?"

Standing, I told him, "Memphis, I . . . I have to fly to New York in the morning. You've got your opportunity. This may be my moment. I can't blow it. And I have to finish my last design."

Using his hands to rise from the floor, he stretched. His lips pressed against mine. His tongue penetrated my mouth. He gently caressed my breast. His hand crept inside my panties, down to my vagina. I gasped when his finger strummed my clit.

"I'm going to leave a key under the mat for you tomorrow. When you get back, come home."

I inhaled. He exhaled. He inhaled. I exhaled.

Lifting me, he leaned my body against the counter. Slowly he entered all too familiar territory. The walls of my womb welcomed his shaft.

He cried.

I cried.

CHAPTER 29
MEMPHIS

Limping into the gym, I straightened my leg, braced my hand on a workout bench, then sat down.

Making love to Xena six hours ago was intense. My knee throbbed the moment my dick stopped pulsating. Not allowing my orgasm to extend into ejaculation, my focus was on pleasing Z.

Coach Richie entered the gym. "MB, that injury may be worse than I thought. How are you feeling?"

I massaged my knee. Pain had intensified overnight. "Man, something ain't right." Thanks to Coach trying to prove his point, I might have to take unwanted time off.

"Rather have you take a few days and be one hundred, than to have you risk not bringing home a medal. Let's go." He said that as if I was responsible for my injury, but my current condition was all his fault.

"Yeah, I'ma need to do that," I agreed.

En route to the on-site physician, I sat on the back seat of a golf cart facing the opposite direction from Coach. He said, "This could be an angel on your shoulder," creeping at about five miles an hour.

Or the devil with a pitchfork. Resting my leg across the seat, I sat sideways. My knee was swollen. "How's that? Why would my being hurt be a good thing?" I questioned.

Coach did a rolling stop at the pedestrian crosswalk. "Natalie. Finding a solution to your problem kept me up all night. You can't take a chance on hoping that kid isn't yours. Tell her you're injured. You can't support a family. Convince her to get rid of it."

Hadn't seen her since my last interview. Natalie at the same mall as Z, at the same time, was no coincidence. What I had to find out was what Natalie wanted from me. Time to bypass Tina-Love's assistance and advice.

I texted Natalie, **meet me at my mom's for lunch**, then sent her the address, because I refused to give her mine. No one messed with Ms. Hattie Mae's baby boy!

#spiritfingers we'll be there!

I replied, **#injured gotta see the doc don't post**. When Ms. Hattie Mae Brown handled Natalie, Natalie would gladly take the first flight out of the country for her next mission trip.

Coach Richie offered to help me get off the cart. He'd done enough.

"I'm good." Limping my way through the sliding glass doors, I followed Coach to the X-ray department.

The technician said, "This is pretty common with athletes when they're first accepted. You're elated to have made it, but remember, the competition is over eleven months away." Completing my X-rays, the technician continued, "The doctor will let you know the results. I'll send these right over. You guys can head to her office now."

I'd lucked up. I'd only strained a muscle, but that hadn't modified my performance for Z last night. Hopefully, I stroked her with this d so good I was on her mind all day. I could never hold a grudge against Z. Not for long.

Z had done me a solid. Thankful I didn't have to choose between staying there for Z and my kid during her pregnancy, or going to Chula Vista to chase my dream, I wouldn't have done anything differently.

"You need a ride home?" Coach asked.

Leaning on the crutches the doctor had given me, I didn't think I needed two. I replied, "Nah, but no more sled for a month." I laughed but wasn't joking. Didn't want to be that competitor that never gave themselves the chance to fully recover.

I was no stranger to pain. "I'll get home the way I got here," I told him. "In my car."

When I arrived at my mom's, Natalie's car was parked in the driveway. I escorted the white girl inside, fast as I could.

"Natalie, is it?" my mom asked, then she gave me "the look."

"Yes, ma'am. Natalie Crow. Grew up in San Diego. My parents still live there. I'm an only child. Have traveled all the continents. Had a passport since I was three months. I just love your son, Ms. Hattie Mae," Natalie claimed, redirecting her attention toward me. "Hi, baby. You poor thing. Sit here." She moved a dining chair away from the table, took my crutches. "What did the doctor say about your day-old injury?"

Hell no! I was not letting Natalie know how long I'd be off from practice, but how did she know it was a day ago? I remained standing.

Mom's lips were tight. She did not blink once. "What's your relationship to this white girl, Memphis?" Her eyelids closed to a slither, didn't touch. Mom's entire face squinted.

Aw shit. My mother seldom called me by

my name. Gasping to respond, Natalie said, "I thought he told you." Standing next to me, Natalie beamed with excitement. "I'm Memphis's girlfriend. Thanks for having us for lunch."

"Lil white girl, do not interrupt me when I'm speaking to my son." Mom's Jamaican accent was super thick.

Natalie's eyes bucked. She focused on Mom, opened her mouth. Quickly I covered her lips, shook my head. "She's a friend, Ma. That's it."

Mom stared at Natalie. "No, she's not. Let's try this another way, Natalie Crow. White women always have a hidden agenda when it comes to successful black men. What do want from my son?"

Natalie locked eyes with my mom. "Oh, Hattie Mae, that's easy. For starters, your grandbaby and I need a place to stay."

I despised women who crashed at and never left a man's house. Natalie was that type for sure. The fact that her Lexus was in my mother's driveway was proof.

Shifting my weight, I stumbled, intentionally pushed Natalie into the living room where I'd danced for hours with Tina-Love. The difference now was the furniture was not against the wall.

"Memphis, be careful," she screeched.

Natalie fell face forward onto the sofa.

Snatching Natalie by the back of her dress, Mom said, "You think you can just move in on Memphis and stick him with your baby?"

"*Our* baby. You have a better idea?" Natalie fired back.

Wedging myself between the two of them quickly, I hugged my mother, leaned on her shoulders. Shielded Natalie. "I'll take care of it, Mama."

Mom retreated to the kitchen, stirred her pot. "If you don't take care of her, I will. Tired of these white women hitching a ride to the bank on the back of decent black men."

"I'm not like that. Memphis and I have had a relationship for almost a year, Ms. Hattie Mae." Natalie opened the cabinet, picked up two crystal glasses, pushed one at a time against the refrigerator's water dispenser.

"Memphis!" Mom's voice escalated extending the s. "Keep my name out of that white girl's mouth and keep her out of my cabinets and away from my appliances."

"Here, baby. You have to stay hydrated," Natalie said, handing me one of the glasses.

Closing the door above the sink, I made sure to stay in front of Natalie. This disrespect and back talk to my mother was a shocker. Z would never. What I had with Natalie was a fuckship. Hadn't thought about why if she'd circled the globe, she was single. I knew what Natalie liked and why, but what type of men was she accustomed to before me?

I faced Natalie's crazy ass. "Friends don't drive over twenty-five hundred miles virtually nonstop demanding a place to live."

"Just like I was invited for lunch," Natalie said.

"Liar!" I shouted, filled with anger.

Mom beat me to it. "Now you're uninvited. Memphis, get that lying-ass white girl out of my house, and if you ever step foot on my property, you will be treated as a trespasser." Mom resumed stirring her pot.

Mom wiped her forehead with a towel, stuffed it back in her apron pocket. She poured a container of field peas into an empty cast-iron skillet, added chicken broth, seasoning, placed it on an open flame.

"Natalie, you've got to go. Now," I told her.

"But I have no place to go," she wept.

"I'll pay for your return flight and have your car shipped back to wherever you came from." Mom dug into her bra, peeled off five one-hundred-dollar bills. "Or you can sleep in your car. Lying bitch."

Quickly Natalie took the cash without a thank-you to my mom. Escorting Natalie to the front yard, I advised her, "I tried to be nice and introduce you to *my mother.* It's best not to come back here." I took small steps, stood by her driver's door.

My plan to get Natalie was failing. Thought Mom could intimidate Natalie. Now I realized this girl wasn't afraid of anyone.

She laughed. "I'm not leaving, silly. We're not in Kingston. This isn't nearly enough to book a same-day one-way first-class flight to California *and* ship my car. We're homeless, Memphis. What are you going to do?" Natalie cupped her hand over her navel.

Glancing next door and across the street, I saw there were no cars in our neighbors' driveways. Thirty feet and Natalie could back her Lexus off our property. She stood on the lawn. By the smirk on her face, I could tell this was a fucking standoff game to her.

"Bitch, leave. I'm trying to be nice. Don't make me call the police." I'd left my crutches inside. Shifted my weight to my right leg.

Boldly she said, "Go right ahead. What I

do know is this pregnant white woman in the South will not be behind bars. That reservation has your name on it, nigga. Call 'em. If I scream that you have a gun, bet you can't outrun a bullet."

Pow! Pow! Shots were fired.

"Shit!" I yelled.

"Ahh!" Natalie hollered, ducked, then covered her ears.

"Memphis!" Mom screamed, dragging the s. "Next time I won't miss. Get that white girl away from here."

Natalie was already gone. She was sitting in my car with her backpack on her lap.

Two feet from strangling Natalie, I drove to the nearest gas station, texted Tina-Love my current situation.

She replied, **bring her to me**

That was why I could never stop loving Tina-Love. I texted Z, for the first time today. **Miss. Love. Forgive you.**

CHAPTER 30
TINA-LOVE

A familiar vehicle stopped at my code box. Memphis extended his arm, pushed the buttons, waited for the gate to open. Why in the hell was he involved with this crazy chick?

Before he parked in the driveway, I'd deleted Memphis's six-digit keypad entry. I'd give him a new one. Females like Natalie hawked a man's every move. Hell, she'd followed Z and me to Oglethorpe Mall. What I'd told her should've kept her away from the three of us; I saw she was relentless.

I sipped from a half full 33.8-ounce bottle of water. Greeting them at my front door, I wore red sweatpants and a tapered cropped sleeved T-shirt, no bra. Two steps in my direction, I noticed Memphis trying not to, but he was limping.

"What in the world happened to . . ." My words trailed off as I watched Natalie trip. I jumped out of her way. She stumbled over my threshold, fell to the marble floor in my foyer.

"Ow! My foot! My baby!" she yelled, before she'd hit the imported tile. Memphis maneuvered around Natalie, leaned on the glass circular table where my four-foot vase filled with assorted lilies stood.

"You okay?" he asked. He moved toward her, reached down.

I swatted his hand. "She premeditated that shit." Fuck her foot and her baby that I did not believe existed. "Don't touch her, man."

Surveying my foyer that opened up into a large sitting area with a black sofa, cream leather couch, and two high-backed leopard chairs, Natalie took her time standing. I waited. Sipped. When she was completely vertical, I pushed that bitch where she'd come from. Outside. She fell for real this time. On her ass.

"I think I injured my back!" she screamed, massaging her hip. "I can't move."

"Save the drama. This ain't no reality show you're auditioning for. If you don't get your conniving lily-white ass off of my property, I'll make you regret being here."

She smirked at me, then Memphis. "Why do black people always think racial epithets are more powerful than the law?" She flashed her cell in front of me. Seconds on her video was ticking away, 3:42, 3:43. "You're his manager, make me regret it," Natalie insisted, staggering sideways.

I stared at Memphis. My breasts heaved. I was outraged. Yesterday. Today!

He placed his hands on my waist. "I'm sorry. I'll call you later. I didn't know she'd act like this. I'll handle her. I'll take her to my house, then put her on a plane in the morning."

Quietly I accompanied him across the threshold. I was disappointed in Memphis. What made him gullible? He'd never let Z get away with that foolishness.

"Take her to a hotel." I didn't know all of what Natalie was up to, but she was building up to a climax and finale. "And don't bring that bitch to my house again." Dousing water on her cell phone, I slammed my door, secured the lock from the inside.

"It's water-resistant!" she yelled, then laughed.

Viewing them on my phone, I heard Natalie say, "Your manager is extremely unprofessional and rude as hell. Guess I'll have to sue her for a million dollars to get some respect." She limped three times, sat on the passenger's side of his car.

Memphis drove slowly away.

After all that, I had to fuck the shit out of some guy.

CHAPTER 31
MEMPHIS

"Memphis, do you care at all about me?" Natalie whined.

I was starting to believe Natalie really thought we were a couple. If I didn't have a lot to lose, she'd see a side of me that terrified me. This chick was converting my mental to a criminal's mind. I drove to River Street, parked in the garage.

"I'm hungry. You want to grab something to eat?" I asked her, not giving a damn. River Street was her final destination.

Dating rich white chicks was no longer my thing. They had the coins to make a brotha miserable as fuck. I was not opening or closing Natalie's passenger door the way I'd done my entire relationship for Z.

Natalie hopped out, waved her spirit fingers. "Sure. Long as I'm with you."

"Get your purse. Make sure you have your car keys, too," I insisted. I planned on leaving her ass here.

"Okay," Natalie said, smiling. Tossing her backpack onto one shoulder, she draped her arm around my waist, rubbed my side.

"Don't touch me." I moved away from her, leaving enough space for a line of people to pass between us.

"Memphis. What have I done to make you treat me horribly?" she asked. "You invited me to meet your mother for a reason. You took me to Tina-Love's house. Why?"

Was Natalie for real? She needed to back away from me.

As I entered The Shrimp Factory, a text registered from the woman I wanted to be with.

I'm confirmed for NYFW next year! Landed early at Savannah Airport. Does your offer still stand? Is the key under the mat?

"Tell Xena hi for me. I have to use the ladies' room, babe. Be right back," Natalie said, then bobbed her blond ponytail side to side as she bounced toward the rear.

It's a text message, dummy. Watching Natalie enter the restroom, this was my opportunity to escape from hell. I pivoted and bumped my black ass into @DDDShade. Fuck!

Staring at her, I replied to Xena, **Yes and Yes omw to the house**

"Look-a-here, hubby," @DDDShade said to Rick. "My newest favorite guest. Join us for an early dinner. I think you'll find what we have to say in your best interest."

Glancing over my shoulder, thankfully I did not see the crazy white woman. "I would love to, but I'm running late for another commitment."

"I'm heading to the ladies' suite," @DDD Shade said, handing Rick her purse. "Change our reservation from two to three."

A waiter cleared a table that offered a view of the river. I'd be insane to wait for Natalie to reappear. "Rain check, man." Patting Rick on the back, I rushed out the exit, lightly applying pressure to my left leg. Halfway to the lot near Byrd's Famous Cookies, I thought, what if Natalie sat with @DDDShade and her husband, Rick? I could risk getting dismissed from the competition if I didn't defend my honor.

"Fuck!" I yelled, as tourists pointed their cell phones at me. "My apology." I posed for a minute.

Limping back to The Shrimp Factory, I peeped through the square-paned glass windows. Saw @DDDShade seated at a round table with her husband. Good. Natalie wasn't with them.

@DDDShade waved, giving me a come-hither. Maybe if I offered them an exclusive, they could get me out of my mess.

"Sit here," Rick insisted, moving over a seat. "What happened to your leg?"

I ordered a dozen oysters on the half shell, a chicken Caesar salad, and a glass of ice water. "It's my knee. Overextended it. I'll be all right."

Natalie strolled to our section, tapped me on the shoulder. I snapped my head in her direction.

"Take your time. I'll meet you here in thirty." She winked.

"Join us," Rick insisted, pulling out a chair for Natalie.

Ignoring Rick, she continued her stride out the door.

"Is that her?" @DDDShade asked. "She's extremely sexy."

More like coo-coo. I'd reconsidered volunteering any information regarding Natalie Crow. "I don't know her?" That was the truth.

"She must be the woman that follows you everywhere?" @DDDShade said. She was in the restroom a short while ago, speaking on her phone pleading with someone to make a deposit in her account. I think it was her mother. You should either file a police report or . . ." She paused.

Rick finished @DDDShade's sentence. "Or get a restraining order. That's what I'd do. Weirdos like her are —"

"Dangerous," @DDDShade commented.

Pivoting my head to look at them, I refused to waste my time or money. She'd disappear after she got tired of . . . that was it! Her mother! Why hadn't I thought of contacting Natalie's parents?

"I don't know what you're talking about." Or what I was thinking. @DDDShade was nationally syndicated. I was not giving her the chance to pour quicksand on top of me.

Dinner parties were in a line at the hostess stand. The sunset slowly created a backdrop to the riverboat. I pushed back my chair.

"Memphis, we won't keep you long," Rick said. "We control a significant portion of the media."

@DDDShade chimed in with, "And, we know athletes such as yourself who come into, or have the earning potential of, seven figures or more, have psychos, like Natalie, determined to come up at your expense."

I sat on the edge of my seat. Ate half of my oysters.

Rick added, "We can help you get rid of her in a few ways. Expose her intentions on-air, making her look like the stalker she is. Find out what's her angle and rally our 'shade trees' to shut down her social pages."

"Or just ask her price and if it's worth it we'll pay her. Have her sign a non-disclosure agreement."

@DDDShade commented. "And —"

Rick snapped his fingers. "Make her go away forever. We've done it for other athletes."

I couldn't lie. I would love that shit! But I was potentially worth millions. I didn't have it. Not yet.

@DDDShade added, "Think about it."

Rick handed me a business card. "Here's my personal number."

I sucked the remaining oysters off the shell, placed two twenties on the table, stood.

Rick handed me back my money. "Call me if you want us to bury Natalie."

Quicksand seemed like the only solution and I wouldn't throw her a rope. Let her call me the *n* word again. "Thanks. I'll definitely be in touch."

I blitzed to my ride. Did a 360. And another.

I knew I'd parked here. Standing in the space where I was positive that I'd left my car, all I could do was shake my head.

My whip was gone!

CHAPTER 32
XENA

Memphis lived in one of the most popular zip codes in Savannah, 31405. Tina-Love resided in the most affluent. And I never had a mortgage with my name on it.

The Uber driver turned into Memphis's driveway. The L-shaped home was tucked away in a cove. Shrubs aligned the bay window. His nearest neighbor resided out back on the other side of the lagoon.

When he switched to his high beam, lights reflected against the double garage, which was painted white. Three wide red brick steps paralleled the driver's side of the car. Opening the rear passenger door, he insisted, "I'll wait until you're inside," then sat my suitcase on the front porch between the two white columns.

"Thank you. I'll be sure to add a tip on the app." I felt uneasy. It would've been better if Memphis had picked me up. If he were here, the inside lights would be on.

I missed meditating on Adonis's porch, but thankfully I had cleared my mind in the chapel at the airport before my flight departed from New York. Awakening to tree branches rustling, squirrels scurrying, and locusts buzzing would never happen again on Park Avenue. Adonis could keep all of my belongings, except my great-grandmother's rocking chair. I had to return it to its rightful space where I stood, here in Southbridge.

"I'll be fine. You can go," I told the driver. I was no stranger to this property or the beautiful flickering fireflies.

I picked up the mat, there was no key. I shook it hard, nothing fell. I waved to the driver, but he kept going, so he must've not noticed. It was a dark night, and the sensor lighting fifty feet away dimmed. I knew I should be indoors by now.

I texted Memphis, **There's no key. I'm tired. I'm going to take an Uber to my shop.**

I texted Tina-Love, **I'm back**, not expecting her to respond. We hadn't communicated since Natalie showed up at Oglethorpe Mall.

My Lexus was old, but it was paid for and it was mine. Was. Mrs. Oglethorpe was benefiting from having the BMW and a tax-deductible donation for my . . . the Lexus.

Didn't want to deal with Adonis. I was certain he'd changed both codes on the keypads.

I was getting Memphis a keyless entry soon as possible.

No don't go. I'm handling business, be there in 15 minutes.

That was a long time to wait. The dimmed lights brightened. A faint sound of crunching twigs came from the side of the house. I elected to investigate. My heart raced. I asked, "Hello. Is anyone there?"

Turning on the flashlight on my cell, I scanned my surroundings, stepped backward, looked up. Down. The key was in the keyhole.

Texted him back, **I found it!**

Entering his three-story house felt like I was home again. I left my suitcase near the door, slid the dimmer all the way up. Hadn't been here in over twelve months, but not much had changed. His African statues, drums, and art on the walls complemented his black leather sofa, kente cloth throws, and area rugs. The oak hardwood floors throughout reminded me of Adonis's unit. A life-sized framed poster of Angela Bassett in *Black Panther* accented the dining room wall like a mural.

"You're his number two gurl," I said, smiling.

Turning the knob to the man cave, I went downstairs to the room that was never off limits to Tina-Love and me. I needed to become the bigger person this time.

I sent her another message. **I did it! Your bestie is in!**

A text registered from Topez. **My friend Bailey says his home is open to you.**

Tell him thanks. I'm okay at Memphis's place. At least I had an option.

I missed my bestie. I dialed her number. It rang once, the call dropped. I redialed. Same thing. Praying she was still taking me to her doctor, I'd try her again when I got upstairs.

Admiring all the trophies and awards Memphis had earned, I acknowledged, "This is quite an accomplishment." Guess I didn't see him as the superstar Tina-Love and all of his other fans fanned out over. I would love Memphis the same if he was a black man struggling.

Thump, thump came from upstairs. Next, I heard the basement door creak.

"Baby, is that you?" I asked, racing up the steps.

My suitcase was where I'd left it except it had fallen over. "Memphis!" I yelled loud enough for him to hear if he was upstairs.

I entered the kitchen. A smile grew. "How thoughtful," I said.

Uncovering the Pyrex dishes, I sampled the mackerel. The red smashed potatoes were almost as tasty as Tina-Love's. Opening the refrigerator, I removed the quinoa salad.

"Mmm. This is *de*licious." I'd wait until he arrived before I ate any more, but Memphis had better hurry.

I went upstairs to his bedroom. The framed picture from our first date hung beside his dresser. Soaking in a hot tub of water would be nice. I entered his en suite. Opening the cabinet below the vanity, I retrieved all I needed to clean the oversize jet tub, then turned on the hot water.

Dancing my way back to my suitcase, I stared at the space where I knew I'd left my bag.

It was gone.

CHAPTER 33
MEMPHIS

Struggling to make it along River Street, I traveled one end to the opposite and returned. I was seconds from dialing the Savannah Police Department when I saw a cop in uniform in front of Huey's.

Approaching him, I noticed Natalie rippling her fingers high above her head, skipping in my direction. "Memphis, darling! Here I am."

Had she been trailing me the entire time? Letting me make a fool of myself?

"There you are," she said, wrapping her arms around my waist. "I was looking all over for you, my love."

Watching the policeman out of my peripheral, I bit my bottom lip to keep from literally choking the shit out of this bitch. Holding her biceps, I took two steps back, then asked, "Where's my car and my key?"

"I don't know," she said, hunching her shoulders. "In your pocket would be my

252

guess. That's where I saw you put it."

"It's not in my —" Digging in my pocket, I sucked in my bottom lip, stared at her. Returning to my original parking space, there was my car. I got in, started the engine, left that crazy bitch standing at the passenger door with her hand on the lever, and sped off. She was smart to let go or I would've dragged her.

En route to my house, I looked in the rearview mirror, slowed down. There was a suitcase on my back seat. It resembled the bag at Xena's shop, but knowing — actually not knowing — Natalie, it could've been a bomb. Coming to a complete stop at the STOP sign, I checked the tag. Xena Trinity's name and phone number were listed.

Breaking every traffic law necessary to get to Southbridge, I entered my garage. I waited until it was completely closed before carrying in the bag. I called out, "Z, baby! Where you at?"

"The living room," she apathetically responded.

I was so happy to hear her voice. I held her hand, lured her to her feet, passionately pressed my lips to hers.

"Baby, why are you sitting in here in the dark? You left your bag outside," I lied.

Z resumed her position, folded her arms,

crossed her legs, leaned back on the sofa. Emphatically she answered, "No, I did not. I left *my* suitcase in the living room *by* the front door."

I placed her bag beside her. "Maybe the maid came in, saw it, and moved it to the garage. I don't know what happened, but here it is." I flashed a smile and raised my brows.

Standing, she extended the handle. "You said it was outside. Now it was inside? I can't play games with you again, Memphis. What maid? That explains the meal on the stove?"

What meal?

"I'm exhausted. Going to soak in the jet tub, then I'm going to sleep," she said, picking up her bag.

"Nah, baby. Let me bring your luggage to you," I said.

"I got it, and you, Memphis!" Z rolled her eyes at me.

"You go right ahead. I'll be up shortly." I should've insisted on carrying her luggage, but I had to check out my kitchen. Circling the island, I uncovered the fish, potatoes, and salad, then tossed it all into the sink, filled it with water, then started the garbage disposal.

I texted Tina-Love, **I need to meet with**

you first thing tomorrow.

Can't do that, she responded.

Don't make me beg. I insist!

I gave her ten minutes. No reply. I needed her advice about how to deal with @DDD Shade and Rick. Hoped Natalie didn't fuck that up too. Reaching out to Natalie would not be smart. The same held true if I did. I joined Z, stripped in the bathroom, left my clothes in the middle of the floor, eased my way into the tub, sat behind her. She leaned into my arms.

"This should be the happiest day of my career." Her voice was melancholy.

Had I upset every woman in my life, including my mother? "Is it something I did directly? If it is, I'm sorry, baby. If not, I'm apologizing in advance. Congratulations. I'm proud of you." Kind of.

What if Z became successful and no longer needed me?

"That came from your lips. Not your heart." She became quiet.

Whatever you do, Memphis, do not take ownership of Z's feelings. She left you. She's carrying another man's child.

I had to know. "Did you call off your engagement?" That would allow us to begin over.

She whispered, "Memphis, I can't keep

this from you any longer."

What now? "Long as you come back to me, we can work anything out together." I kissed her crown, then rested my cheek on the top of her head. I loved this woman more than life.

Z inhaled. I felt her cavity expand. I breathed in after her.

"Memphis, I'm having another abortion."

My lungs deflated with relief. One down. One to go. "That's great."

Z's neck almost did a 180-degree turn. She stood. Water and suds dripped down her pretty smooth skin. Her pussy was close to my mouth.

"Baby, I didn't mean to upset you, but that's what you want, right?" I had no idea what women wanted, including the one that I loved. I gently touched her clit.

Her closed lips spread but did not curve. Z exited the bursting bubbles, wrapped herself in a towel.

Z had abandoned and betrayed me, the same as my real dad had, with no explanation. And she returned without an apology. If she hadn't killed my child, it would be the three of us.

Tired of trying to figure out women, I remained where I was. I heard the front door open. Close. It was time for me to let my situations rest. At least for tonight. Getting out of the tub, I had to jack my dick or I was going to explode.

I retrieved my cell off of the vanity. There were no new text messages. Entering my bedroom, my heart filled with joy, as I gazed at my picture with Z.

Suddenly the pain in my knees reminded me of my priorities. Rest and recover. Tossing back the fluffy down comforter, Natalie sat up.

"Bitch!" I yelled at her ass.

"Z left in an Uber," Natalie said.

"Why in the fuck are you fucking with me? Huh?" I threw the edge of the comforter at her face. Wanted to hurl my phone instead.

Natalie volleyed the cover in my direction.

I slapped my hands against the side of my head.

Calmly she said, "For the same reason you fucked me over."

She was certifiable! The pregnancy was her damn problem. "What do want from me?"

At this point, if I had to, I'd pay her to go away. I started to text @DDDShade. Didn't want to seem desperate. Backspaced.

Natalie eased out of my bed fully clothed down to her shoes. Her eyes filled with tears. I did not give a damn about that female!

If humans were sixty percent water, she could cry herself dry to the bones and I would not piss on her thirsty ass. Whatever she was trying to accomplish, Natalie was definitely going about it the wrong way.

"Something that will cost you nothing but to do the right thing. And I won't stop until you do." She took off her clothes, tossed them to the floor, rolled over, pulled the covers up to her neck. "Have a good night, Memphis."

I sat on the edge of my bed, buried my face in my palms.

That bitch is not doing all of this for nothing. She wants something. I just have to figure out what is it?

"FYI, I have an interview in *The Shady Café* in the morning. I'll need a ride."

CHAPTER 34
TINA-LOVE

"Mmh."

"Ahhh."

"Mmh."

"Ahhh."

It was time for Tina-Love to put herself first. Each time I'd said "mmh," my Italian stallion went "ahhh."

Hey Honey candles emitted an aphrodisiac scent in my home spa. As I lay naked on my back atop a massage table, underneath me the one thousand thread count sheet felt like silk.

Simple Serenity meditation music floated throughout the air. Opening my chakras, I exhaled, preparing my body to release all negative forces. Inhaling, I sucked in positive energy.

"Oooh, Ricardo. You have magical hands. I feel amazing. Thanks for coming on such short notice. I promise to visit you in Italy." I moaned, then continued concentrating on my breathing. "Mmh." I needed another one of his touchless orgasms.

"Anything to be a pleasure to you, my sweet Tina-Love Jones," he articulated in a Zen tone, causing my flesh to tingle all over. Ricardo drizzled warm oil onto my genitals. Cupping his massive hand over my vulva, he held it there, interjected a nice long hum. "You have the most beautiful and unique pussy I have ever seen. Muah," he said.

Exhaling a puff of air, I held my breath. Inhaled abruptly. Had to get Memphis out of my head.

"Wow. You're seriously tensed. Relax, baby. Let me take you away. That is why I am here."

Ricardo Salvatori was a different type of pressure release valve. If we had more time, I could submit to a climax that would flow for over an hour without having him penetrate me.

I closed my eyes. Memphis, Xena, and Natalie, thoughts of them consumed me. The moment I erased one from my mind, another appeared. It was unusually hard not to think of anything. Anyone. Janice Jones surfaced.

"Ah, yes. Right there," I whispered. "Finger fuck me nice and slow."

I'd awakened earlier to a text from Memphis saying he was about to be in quicksand and that I had to keep @DDDShade's husband from allowing Natalie to go on-air this morning. What I was in the midst of having done to me was more vital. I'd warned Memphis to stay away from Natalie. I'd agreed to be at the studio before her scheduled time.

"Breathe for me. In. Out. Focus on your breath," he said. Lightly pinching my labia, Ricardo slid his thumb and pointer finger to the bottom of my outer lip, then did the same on the other side. My body shivered as he stroked my clit up, down, clockwise, counterclockwise, then inserted his thumb into my vagina, while covering my pubic section with all four of his fingers.

This man was a rare gem. "Ah. You're a keeper," I said, and meant it.

"I like you, but I don't rotate my energy," he answered. "I'm a one-woman man. Your pussy is so beautiful."

A man's definition of exclusivity was fuck one woman at a time.

Exploring my cervix with his pointer and middle finger, he navigated west, south, east, then with a firm come-hither motion Ricardo stroked my G-spot. Gently his other hand tapped my seventh chakra at the same time. I pushed, then gushed on the massage table.

Ricardo glided his magical hands from my ankles, to my legs, knees, thighs. Skipping my vaginal area, he continued up to my breasts, then circled my areolas.

"How do you feel?" he asked.

"Like getting married." I laughed. Head to toe I was rejuvenated! "God, thank you. That was a great orgasm."

Sitting up, I placed my feet on the floor, slid on my white fluffy slippers and robe. Ricardo snatched the linen from the table, tossed everything into the hamper, smoothed out a fresh sheet, tucked the edges.

"Rain check on your lingam." I gave him a passionate kiss. "I have business to tend to for a friend. Make that friends." I had to check up on Xena.

"Tomorrow?" he asked, adjusting his erection.

"Hopefully tonight. I'll let you know." I could've let him stay at my mansion, being he'd traveled from far away. Not on the first visit.

I escorted a disappointed Ricardo out the door, showered, and made it to the radio station on time to catch Natalie before she entered the building.

Figured she'd be there early.

All suited up, was she a guest or appearing for an interview? Neutral-colored three-inches-above-the-knee Calvin Klein signature dress, mocha platform open-toed high heels. Her hair was slicked into a ponytail.

"Natalie, you have a moment." I wasn't asking.

As I backed her up from the entrance, she folded her arms, tilted her right hip outward. "Oh, good morning, manager. You look fashionable. Maybe you can give me some tips on how to stay cool. It's hot out here. I have to get indoors," she said, moving left.

I shuffled to my right. "How much, bitch?"

"I was in a fun mood, but you ruined it. I hate women like you," she exclaimed. "You support men when most men are dogs. You despise women when we are more alike than different."

I thought about my mother's man. How I felt with my feet in stirrups while a baby was being vacuumed out of my teenage vagina. Not once. Twice. I hated men. I loved Memphis. And I was learning to trust Ricardo.

Memphis was winning. Natalie was hating.

It took time for me to get Memphis to understand the connection, but as an athlete, blasting off, jacking off until sperm shot out of him like a cannonball felt great, but cumming inside the wrong female could take seconds off achieving his best time and destroy his career at the same time. In the end, he had to do it his way.

"Name your price," I told her.

"Two hundred fifty," she said, holding out her hand.

"No problem. Skip the interview, come with me. You're obligated to sign a non-disclosure agreement first. Then I'll wire two hundred and fifty thousand dollars into your bank account."

Natalie's body swayed back and forth. She collapsed.

"Oh my gosh. Is she okay?" a stranger inquired.

If I abandoned Natalie, I'd be cruel. If I touched her, she might sue me. I did the next best thing. "I'm calling an ambulance."

I could've helped Natalie. Perhaps she needed a friend. Why bother, when the truth was I felt no compassion for her. She was on a mission to trap Memphis and I was on one to save his good reputation. Before the paramedics arrived, Natalie stood, brushed off her clothes. Picked up her purse.

"Good Lord, I was only asking for half of what Ms. Hattie Mae gave me. You ready?"

she said. "I'll ride with you."

"The hell you will. Follow me," I demanded.

I waited in front of the building. Natalie drove up behind me in a Lexus.

Starting my Bentley, I texted Memphis, **You didn't tell me your mother gave Natalie money! How much!**

$500.00. Why?

CHAPTER 35
XENA

Memphis could play games with someone else.

I texted Tina-Love, **Are you still taking me to your doctor today?**

"Girlie. Girlie. Look at what we have." Entering the shop, Topez dropped a swatch book on the counter and opened it to the first page.

Red-rimmed rectangular eyewear matched her lipstick. An old soul in a thirty-nine-year-old body, Topez had her slender fingers in many pockets. I wanted my opportunity badly. Tina-Love had hers. Memphis had his. And finally, I had mine. I'd signed the legal agreement to showcase my men's line next summer. Topez and I executed a separate profit-sharing agreement. I had control. She had benefits.

I stayed on the opposite side of the counter. "Ooh. This is gorgeous." Instantly my spirit soared. "Where did you get this?

Please tell me you didn't steal it from one of the designers we met with," I said jokingly. I flipped through, touching all the fabrics.

She was an average-height woman with light skin and round eyes. Platinum hair cropped her full face. Peach witch-pointed nails with colorful stones dazzled in the sunshine. I watched them fade to cream. She wore a white short-sleeved pantsuit, and a wide red leather belt accented her hourglass waist.

"I can't reveal my source, but now that we are confirmed for next summer's show, there'll be a lot more where this came from. A designer offered it to me as a gift for my business." She sang, "It's all made in Italy."

The mecca for everything from furniture, to art, to clothing. I screamed, "I love it!" glad I didn't need Tina-Love's or her agent's help. "But shouldn't it be mine?"

Tina-Love texted, **Yes. I'll pick you up.**

"Girlie, what's yours is mine. I'm sharing it with you, aren't I?" Topez said, spinning the book 180 degrees for me browse.

Cover to cover I scanned every swatch several times. Spasms and sharp pains penetrated my body unexpectedly. I hopped like a jump rope rotated under my feet, but I'd have rather stayed the night here and been in complete control of my future than under a man's roof compromising my integrity. I rubbed my side.

I hated that I loved Memphis. My unchanged feelings for him didn't make sense.

"Are you okay?" Topez asked, staring at the floor beside the design table. "Really, Xena? I thought you had somewhere to stay. I've made an arrangement for you. You don't have to live here. You've made it."

Topez was right. I, Xena Trinity, would never make a man a priority while he used me for a headrest, or worse: a footstool.

"We made it," I countered, giving her credit for organizing our connections.

I should've taken Topez up on her offer to move in with her friend. I'd never lived with a stranger. What if he wanted sexual favors in exchange? How old was this guy? Creepy old? Or in shape? I needed to save my money for upcoming expenses. My head was swarming with ideas of mixing plaid with leather and cotton with suede. The possibilities were endless.

"That was not a sign of excitement," Topez said. "You're hurting."

"I'm good." Starting from the back of the book, I flipped the page.

She shut the book. "Forget business for a moment. Talk to me, Xena. Like I'm your girlfriend. Not your boss."

Correcting her, I responded, "You mean 'partner.' "

Glad that Tina-Love agreed to take me to my appointment, I couldn't fault her for whatever happened with Memphis and Natalie. There was nothing I could do to untangle that situation.

"The floor is super hard," I admitted, stomping my foot.

Topez circled the counter, stomped her heel. "It doesn't get any harder. This is concrete, Xena."

I nodded. "I know that."

Topez embraced me. "Girlie. I know you're dealing with a lot, but whatever is going on, if you don't want to accept my offer, don't let Adonis put you out. Go back."

Adonis entered my shop. "Xena, I sent you forty-eight messages. Now I see why you can't respond. She's all up in your face," he said, confronting Topez. "She's my fiancée. We don't need your help." Adonis approached me. "Here, honey. I brought you your ring."

"Keep it," I insisted, pushing him away. "I can't wear a ring for a man who has threatened to kill me."

Adonis scratched his beard. "You know I didn't mean it. I'm sorry, but I went bananas when you said you were going to kill my unborn child. Forgive me. Come home."

Topez picked up the book, cradled it in her arm. "Xena, whatever you decide, do not spend another night here. Go home to your parents if you have to. Soon you'll have enough money to buy your own domain. Cash, girlie. And start preparing. After the show, we're opening a design studio for students."

What should've made me excited, didn't. Topez had no idea how challenging my day-to-day decisions were. Move in with a stranger. Go back to a madman. Or live in hell with my mother.

"You'd rather sleep here than be in bed with me. Fine! Have my baby, give me full custody, and you can go live your life any way you damn well please." Adonis looked Topez head to toe, then back up. "I'm beginning to think you like Xena more than I do." Adonis slammed the front door. The walls shook.

"Forget what I said earlier. Whatever you do, do not go back to that fool. He's mentally unstable. My friend will adore you. He loves children and I know he'd accept you and your unborn. Or, there's other alternatives," Topez said, then left.

I wondered why Topez hadn't offered for

me to stay with her. Passing time, waiting for Tina-Love to arrive, I sketched. Erased. Started over. Snatching the page from the pad, I ripped it! I kept dividing the paper, until I couldn't anymore. My energy was dark and I was filled with anger.

"Why me?" I cried.

A text followed by a toot came from Tina-Love. **I'm outside when you're ready.**

Turning off the lights, I locked the door. Tina-Love got out of her car dressed runway ready. Black ankle platform boots with a canary tongue were five inches. A sleeveless yellow, black, and white top nearly dragged the asphalt.

She gave me a real loving embrace. "Everything is going to be just fine," she reassured me, not letting go.

"Thanks. I appreciate your taking me to —"

"Hush, honey. I'm exhausted. Let's get this over with so we can all move forward." She released a long exhale.

At every stop Tina-Love pressed hard on the brakes. I was constantly leaning forward, then being jerked backward. Imagining a number of scenarios of what transpired last night at Memphis's house, I shared the strange events with Tina-Love.

"One minute my suitcase was there, then

it wasn't. Then . . ."

"Stop worrying about Natalie. She's taking her ass back to California. Right now —"

Interrupting, I said, "I never mentioned Natalie's name."

"Bestie, you didn't have to. I know you, you were thinking it. After your procedure, you'll —"

Cutting her off again as she drove into a parking garage, I said, "How do you know she's going back to Cali?"

"Stay focused," Tina-Love said. "I don't have to justify my actions. I'm here to help you out."

My bestie was right. I texted Memphis, **Getting ready to have an abortion. Sorry I didn't tell you in person. I love you.**

He replied, **I know. I love you too.**

I admitted how I felt to Tina-Love. "I hate that you tell him everything."

"Why do you keep harping on that?" she retorted. "It's not going to change."

"How well do you know Natalie?" I asked, unbuckling my seat belt.

Tina-Love silenced the engine, started typing on her phone, then opened her door.

My cell rang. Seeing who it was, I placed the call on speaker. "Hey, Memphis."

Tina-Love sat sideways on her seat with

her feet on the ground.

Memphis said, "Listen, Z. I don't care if you're pregnant. We've both made mistakes. Natalie agreed to go back to Chula Vista and she's having an abortion. After you terminate your situation, I want us to move on with our lives. I'm serious. I want you forever. Z, marry me."

Tina-Love nodded, then mouthed, *Say yes.*

CHAPTER 36
MEMPHIS

Trust no one, I thought.

I was repaying Tina-Love all of her money out of my first check. Natalie was gone, but @DDDShade and Rick insisted on meeting with me. Something about I needed them. Had to hear them out. There was no way I was getting played to the tune of a quarter of a million dollars again.

Brought Coach Richie along to help decide if I needed whatever Rick and @DDDShade were offering. Didn't want to get suckered in. I drove up to an estate, parked inside the garage as instructed. The door lowered.

"Hey, Memphis. Glad you made it," Rick said. Peeping inside my window, he told Coach Richie, "This won't take long. Wait here."

"What's up that Coach can't sit in?" I asked, sitting behind the wheel.

Rick pressed a button. The garage door

retracted. "My house. My rules." He nodded his head toward the exit.

"Hear the man out," Coach Richie said. "We're here."

The sunlight was blocked again. Following Rick, I walked a parallel line into a theater room. Six chocolate oversize chairs, three on each row, had aisles on both ends. Rick and @DDDShade had invited me, as Rick said, to listen.

"Sit here," Rick said, patting the top of the recliner next to his wife.

"Cool, man." I left an empty seat between us. "What are the formalities about?" I asked. "I imagined it'd be informative. We'd sit at the dinner table, eat, chat, and I'd make a decision whenever."

"Turn off your cell and put it in the armrest compartment," @DDDShade said, occupying the empty chair next to me.

"What are you guys? Drug lords?" I laughed nervously.

They waited until my phone was secured.

Rick sat directly behind his wife. The room went black. I couldn't see either of them, or my hand waving in front of my face.

"Hey, man. Turn the lights back on," I protested, but didn't stand up, not knowing what to expect.

"Relax. When you can't see, you listen better. This room is soundproof. And the conversation is confidential," Rick explained.

This here reminded me of the time my friend DaBoyDame let me hang out with him in the studio. The only noises I heard inside the sound booth were the ones I'd made. Shit was trippy. But why did Rick and his wife have this setup at home? Wasn't shit being recorded?

"You can come here whenever you need to truly shut the world out, my man," Rick continued. "Sometimes we gotta do that. I'll get straight to it. Memphis, this underground business is bigger than you will ever imagine."

Had no idea what the fuck he was talking about or where the fuck he was going, but I got why he sat where he did. His words resounding in my right ear. I not only heard, I felt them.

@DDDShade chimed in with, "Sometimes all a woman really wants is a sincere apology and respect. If you had treated Natalie Crow with respect, or had been more compassionate when she told you she was pregnant, Tina-Love wouldn't have had to cover your dick's mistakes at the tune of two hundred and fifty thousand dollars."

What the fuck? How does @DDDShade know that?

Rick got on the invisible mic. "The crazy part was Natalie would've accepted two hundred and fifty dollars."

His hearty laugh pissed me the fuck off. "This shit ain't no joke. Y'all messing with my future earnings."

"You got played, MB. And if you don't listen up, you will get replayed like a broken record," he stated.

"That's scratched," @DDDShade added.

Rick cleared his throat. "Our business is not only to create a story where there is none. But also to make it interesting to our audience. It's called ratings."

I leapt from my seat. "Y'all set me up. So, I was blackmailed?" *Fuck.* I palmed my head, recalling Natalie mentioning Rick's name when we were together in Chula Vista.

"What part of 'played' don't you get? Better to be blackmailed than to be black-balled. You can stay and hear us out," @DDDShade said.

"Or leave and see if you can outsmart us," Rick told me.

My knees buckled. Ass cradled on the cushion. "I'm all ears." I wasn't saying shit else. Was Tina-Love in on this too?

"You won't regret it," Rick said. "When

an athlete's bank account has the potential to increase seven, eight, or nine figures, overnight we're all over you dudes."

@DDDShade said, "Dicks are dumb. Read the book."

Rick tagged in. "Women are smarter. Maybe one every five years will get caught up in a sex scandal that goes viral. The WNBA. Golf. Hollywood. Politics. But young male athletes like you have a bull's-eye on your back. Especially the black ones who come from broken or poor families. Most of them believe they've made it before they cash their first check. You don't have to give a fuck about your dad, but you do need to let go of the hate."

@DDDShade cleared her throat. "People make a living taking advantage of ignorant people with money. Pussy is so good a woman will suck the cum and your cash right out of ya!" she said, squeezing my dick.

"Whoa," I protested. Moved her hand. "Don't do that." Nothing about this meeting excited me.

Who would care or believe me if I reported that @DDDShade sexually assaulted me? No one. And even if they did, who would fire her? Surely not her husband.

"Rick, let the record show I was on the money with this one." @DDDShade exhaled. "If you could only have one, pussy or money, which one would you choose, Memphis?"

I thought, try living without pussy and I'd be at the mercy of a woman. Try living without money and I'd be at the mercy of a woman . . . begging for pussy. Damn! I was intrigued. Still wasn't sure what they had to offer me.

"How do you think white athletes stay off the radar?" Rick asked. "If a white guy had taken a knee for any cause, do you honestly believe not one of the thirty-two football owners would've signed him?"

Probably wouldn't have gotten fired in the first place, I thought.

"Exactly," they said at the same time.

What the fuck?

"See how preprogrammed you were for us to be able to know what you're thinking without your saying it? MB, no one is safe in this game of dicks and dollars. Your coach. We had Natalie bang him a few times. He's telling you to make sure she has an abortion, praying the baby isn't his. That way, no matter how much pressure we applied to you, he was going to let you go down by yourself."

"How's your knee?" @DDDShade asked.

279

Rick emphatically stated, "Put us on retainer."

"We'll keep the leeches off your back," @DDDShade said.

"And off your ass," Rick mentioned.

"And out of your pocket," they both said.

I had to interject, "So y'all exploiting me and lying on my coach?"

"Put it this way," Rick said. "Natalie was never pregnant. But by the time you proved that, your career would've been over. She would've faked a miscarriage and the world who loves you would've hated your black ass."

"Forever. Think about it," @DDDShade commented.

The lights blinded me for a moment.

"How much we talking?" I asked.

"Five grand a month," Rick said. "And we suggest you get back with your ex. It'll be good for your image."

That amount seemed reasonable and worth it, but what was my guarantee?

"Sixty thousand. Each year. Up front," @DDDShade demanded.

Opening the armrest, I retrieved my cell, powered it on. "I'll get back to you guys." I had to run this shit by Tina-Love.

Rick looked at me. "Don't do that."

"Keep this to yourself," @DDDShade

concluded.

"This way," Rick said, escorting me to the garage.

Getting in my car, Coach Richie asked, "How'd it go?"

I punched him dead in his mouth, then drove off watching his lip bleed.

Chapter 37
Tina-Love

"I'm not sure I should do this again," Xena whined.

Once I'd made up my mind something should be taken care of, I did it! My doctor agreed to personally take care of Xena. We'd been here over three hours waiting for blood test results.

"Have it!" I blurted.

Two women were on a love seat facing us. One appeared a few years older than us. The young girl reminded me of when I was a teenager sitting and waiting with my mother to have my first abortion.

I lowered my voice, told my bestie, "Keep the kid. There's always adoption."

Rattling her head, she protested. "I could never give my baby away. We have to get the blood test results first and consult with the doctor." She placed her hand on her belly.

Xena needed to stop worrying about what others thought of her. She'd said that for the people on the couch to hear. My doctor was not going to tell my bestie what to do. No professional would. Xena was going to stop wasting my damn time with her indecisiveness.

I could be home fucking. I stood, held my designer bag. "If you don't want to have it, let's go. *You* can figure out your next move later."

This time the older woman stared at us. Nodded. I prayed that girl wasn't pregnant. I looked at the girl. Her watery gaze scrolled toward her lap. The little girl inside of me wanted to hug the little girl inside of her. Reassure her she'd be okay. But I couldn't. When it came to sexual assault, men were wolves and women were prey.

Xena started biting her nails. "What should I do?"

How many ways could I say it again? I gave her another option. "Adonis's momma will snatch that baby before your umbilical cord is tied. Let him raise his kid."

On the outside, Xena was neatly put together. She'd worn a simple black jumper. Xena sat quietly. Her jet-black hair was parted on the right, smoothed to the back, coiled into a bun. Dark cinnamon lipstick was painted perfectly.

I was ready for the doctor to take Xena in

the back, put her on the table, and perform the procedure so I could get back to Ricardo. I liked him more than I'd admit to him. Reclaiming my seat, I couldn't abandon my bestie. I covered her hand with mine. "You're doing the right thing. It'll all be over soon. Don't worry. I'll support whatever you want to do."

"What if God punishes me? I might not be able to have children after this," she cried.

The little girl nodded. I stared at her, then said, "God will forgive you."

I hugged Xena with one arm. Rocked her slowly. Prayed she'd stop shedding tears on my gold shorts. She was considering having an abortion. She wasn't dying.

The assistant opened the door, called, "Xena Trinity."

"Come with me, bestie," she said, gripping my hand.

As I sat in the cold exam room, my nipples protruded immediately. Ignoring them I texted Memphis, **We're here. Waiting for the doctor.**

Immediately Memphis called. I declined. Texted, **can't talk now dude**

I'd gone with Xena to the lab, stayed by her side when the needle went in her arm. I watched her blood being syphoned into four tubes. All we needed was confirmation and the final chapter to close on this saga.

He replied, **Other than my mom, you and Z are the only women I completely trust.**

What happened now? I didn't want to deal with more of his problems. Men didn't need us until something in their life was jacked up.

He texted, **I need a tune-up tonight or I'm going to bust!**

Not tonight, Z will be at my house.

Then you come to me! he texted.

I wasn't sure how he was going to survive getting to the Olympics without being a repeat target for women like Natalie. **Let us get past the abortion, man! damn! Go to the spa and get rubbed on.**

Memphis should've accepted my massage offer the other day. I understood his going to lift weights was more important. I owed Ricardo an orgasmic evening of relaxation. At this pace, I'd need him to take care of me again.

"Am I doing the right thing?" Xena asked.

Impulsively my eyeballs scrolled left to right. Thank God my doctor entered the room. "Hello, ladies."

Afternoon had transitioned to evening.

Doctor Francis sat in front of the computer monitor, typed for a moment, then faced us. "I've witnessed this a few times in my thirty-eight years of practice," she said.

I hated when people led with statements that sounded as though they were preparing you for your last will and testament. I interlocked my fingers with Xena's. "I'm here for you no matter what," I told my bestie. "Doctor Francis, please. What is it?"

Xena tightened her fingers around my hand, held her breath.

Bouncing the heel of my shoe, I reminded Xena and myself, "Deep breaths."

"Poker face" described the look on the doctor's face. "The good news is, you won't have to have an abortion. You're not pregnant."

What the hoax is going on?

The room filled with silence. I thought I had two reasons to tell Xena she wasn't perfect. Secretly, I wanted Xena to have an abortion. Her having to do so would trump all of my indiscretions.

There had to be a mistake. "What's going on, Xena? One minute you're sure, then you might not be. Now you're not. Explain yourself," I demanded.

This was not the time for her to be quiet and stare at the doctor like a deep dark secret had been revealed. The madness of Xena's mess pissed me off!

Letting go of her hand, I said, "Xena," then tapped her bicep. "You did see the results of your home pregnancy test. Didn't you?"

She nodded. "Of course I did," she answered, then asked the doctor, "How can that be? I saw two pink lines each time. Adonis saw two pink lines on the first one. Then on the next ones I had a solid pink and the other was faint. But they were pink."

At some point I was going to see those outcomes for myself. I texted Memphis, **#falsealarm Xena is not pregnant!**

Digging in her purse, she handed a plastic bag with three test strips inside to Doctor Francis.

The doctor leaned close, nodded, but didn't touch the bag. "I see them. You can keep those."

Memphis replied, **That's the best news I've gotten since I've been back! Going to buy Z a ring right now.**

"Just as there can be a false negative if you take the test too soon, there is what's called a false positive," the doctor explained. "It's very rare but certain medications like Valium, Xanax, antihistamines, barbiturates, and methadone, or medical conditions can influence the results of practically any test. I'm going to ask you a few 'yes' or 'no' questions. Have you experienced fatigue lately?"

If the doctor had any insight into what Xena had gone through, personally and professionally, she wouldn't have had to ask. If Xena wasn't pregnant, she didn't need to stay at my place.

I texted Memphis, **I might be able to squeeze you in for sixty minutes tonight. I'll let you know later.**

Xena replied, "Yes, but that's because I've been working around the clock."

"What about pelvic or abdominal pain?" Doctor Francis asked.

"My back is hurting right now but I think the pain is from having a cyst."

Don't forget to tell her you're sleeping on a concrete floor.

The doctor requested permission to examine Xena. She handed my bestie a paper gown, spoke to me. "You may want to wait for her —"

Xena grabbed my hand. "I need her to stay."

"Okay. I'll be right back." The doctor exited the room.

After Xena removed her jumpsuit, I stared at Xena's abdomen. I didn't see anything.

I pressed firm. Oh, wow. Felt as though she'd swallowed a hockey puck. "You've been hiding that for how long?" Gently I touched the lump again. It was hard.

Doctor Francis reentered, examined Xena, typed on her keyboard, then said, "Answer 'yes' or 'no.' Do you have pain during intercourse?"

"Yes. But it's not that bad and it's been over a week since I've done anything," Xena said.

Humph. I texted Memphis, **Have you ejaculated inside of Xena since you've been home?**

He replied, **no but now that she's not pregnant I will**

No you won't! You have to preserve your strength, I responded. **And, she has something growing inside of her!**

"Indigestion. Difficulty swallowing or eating. Do you feel full quickly?" the doctor asked, then told me, "Tina-Love, if you have to keep texting, please step outside."

I put my phone in my purse. Long as I'd known Xena, she never ate much. Xena wasn't pregnant? I was ready to go. She could make an appointment with her gynecologist and answer these questions.

"No to the first two. Sometimes I lose my appetite, but I don't get full fast. I eat lots of fruit."

"Do you urinate often?"

"Yes," Xena answered.

289

That response required deets. My bestie drank darn near a gallon of water a day.

The doctor said, "Last question. Any signs of spotting or bleeding?"

Shaking her head, Xena responded, "No."

"Okay, to make sure you're fine, I'm going to order more blood work and an ultrasound."

"Oh, great, because I know a baby is hiding in there somewhere and I don't want to wait until it's too late to make a decision," Xena replied, then she mumbled, staring at the bag of sticks, "There's no way I cannot be pregnant."

I questioned, "If you're certain she's not having a baby, Doctor, what's the additional test for?"

"I'm ordering a CA-125 and an ultrasound to make sure Xena's ovaries are okay. And I want to evaluate the cyst."

"Why wouldn't my ovaries be healthy?" Xena asked.

"Ovarian cysts and ovarian cancer are medical reasons a woman can get a false positive pregnancy result. It's rare, but something is causing hCG hormones to be present. I've seen this a few times. Your uterus feels fine, but an exam won't detect ovarian cancer."

Xena's leg started trembling. Mine too.

"You think she has cancer?" I asked. I felt like crying at the thought that my best friend might have cancer.

"Additional testing is a precaution. But with ovarian cancer, the only way to discover it is to surgically remove the cyst, then test them. Let's not get ahead of the situation," the doctor told us.

I was not convinced Doctor Francis was disclosing the whole truth. "I'm sorry, bestie. We'll get through this together. I love you," I said. "You can stay with me."

Chapter 38
Xena

Dr. Francis made me more confused. There was no test for ovarian cancer? How could that be? I regretted not having the cyst removed a year ago. I'd agreed to have the surgical procedure. Until I had an appointment date, I'd carry on. First thing I had to do was visit Adonis.

Five o'clock in the morning, I told the driver, "Right here is fine."

After opening the rear passenger door, I stood on the sidewalk on Park Avenue. Inhaled the fresh air. The familiar sound of locusts made my heart beat with joy. I anticipated the squirrels would soon come. I could hardly wait to hear them racing along the tree branches.

I know everybody needs someone, but as large as my bestie's house was, I refused to live with Tina-Love and her revolving door — one man after another in and out of her vagina and her place. I wasn't judging. Just didn't want a man sleepwalking into my bedroom in the middle of the night.

Massaging my lower back, it felt worse than yesterday. The results of another night on the concrete mattress coupled with worrying if I had ovarian cancer.

I sat on the top step of Adonis's front porch. My, I meant *his* BMW was parked in the same space as the day he'd gifted it to me. His car was right behind it.

"Good morning."

"Oh, shit! You scared me." My head snapped toward the door.

Mr. Ben Matthews laughed. "Hey there. I didn't expect to bump into you down here. Change of scenery is good." He occupied the empty space beside me. "Adonis says you guys are starting a family. Says his mom told him it's a boy. Congratulations."

I heard the familiar sound of squirrels above my head. I wanted to be here. In this very space. Not upstairs. "I'm not pregnant." But I did want to make sure what was mine was still there. Grandma's rocker was where I'd left it.

"Hmm. I know better than to question a woman." Mr. Ben patted his thigh, scratched his head. "My condolences. You guys can try again."

I wanted to tell him the truth, but at sixty-eight, he probably didn't know anything about a false-positive pregnancy result. "How many times did you marry?"

"Who said I'd ever done that?" His stomach jiggled as he laughed. "Where she at? I could sure use the company."

Frowning, I reflected on his condolences comment. Had he concluded I'd had a miscarriage? I'd automatically assumed that a man his age had to have married at least one woman. Mr. Ben was nice but mostly a loner. Friendly, but stayed to himself. This was the longest conversation we'd had. I'd never asked. "You have kids?"

"Nope. After getting out of the military, I never wanted a wife or children. Got a bad case of post-traumatic stress disorder. I love my family. Heck, I even appreciate conversations like this. But I stay to myself for a reason."

I wondered who his beneficiary was. Was he well-off or poor?

Mr. Ben was the right man to ask, "Who do you need?"

He nodded, pointed toward the sky. "The Man upstairs. He's enough. If you have faith. I will say you have yourself a good man. Hold on to Adonis; they ain't easy to come by nowadays, and it doesn't hurt that he has the Oglethorpe name," he said, then stood. "Time for me to ease on down to The Sentient Bean and get my morning joe."

They didn't open for another half hour, but Mr. Ben despised being late anywhere. "Have a blessed day, Mr. Ben."

Making a U-turn at the bottom of the stairs, he said, "Again, I'm sorry for your loss."

A squeak came from the door. I gasped.

"I thought I heard your voice," Adonis said, tying his robe. "Baby, I'm so happy you came back. I'm so sorry. I apologize a thousand times over. I was stupid. Please forgive me. I want y'all to come home where you belong. You guys are my lifeline."

"Is it okay if I meditate?" I asked.

"Of course. Anything." Holding the door, he trailed behind me one slow step at a time. "The new code is 0214. That should be our delivery date or close to it."

I entered the numbers and turned the knob. He shoved his hand in his pocket, handed me a door key. Placing it on the kitchen counter, I peeped in the refrigerator. "I can't believe you have all my favorite foods. You don't eat this."

"I do now," Adonis said. "I'm so glad you two are back home. Don't ever leave me again. I was going out of my mind."

He kissed me. I let him. Didn't understand why I might have cancer when I'd eaten well most of the time.

"You want me to make you a berry smoothie?" Adonis eagerly asked.

Shaking my head, what I needed was options of who would best care for me if I had to undergo treatments. Moving back here with Adonis was a good alternative to sleeping at my shop, but I couldn't do that under the circumstances. I missed my at-home setup. Everything was as I'd left it. My handheld sewing machine. Threads. Accessories.

I went to the bedroom, saw my BMW keyless remote on the dresser. I dropped it in my purse. Since his mother donated my Lexus, the least he could do was let me keep his gift. My name was on the title too.

Adonis entered, plopped on the bed. Letting his robe fall to the floor, he said, "Let me hold you guys, honey," stretching his arms in my direction.

Mr. Ben was right. Adonis was the perfect man. Adonis was always horny, and he loved morning sex.

"I'm going to go meditate. Then we're taking the car to the storefront. I have a lot to do. Had to take on additional work to pay my bills. Gotta make good on the contracts."

I left him sprawled atop the sunshine comforter. He didn't need to know I'd made it to New York Fashion Week.

I placed my purse in the oversize pink chair, turned, bumped into Adonis.

"Work here. From now on do everything here. I'll shower and be gone by the time you're done meditating." He pressed his lips to mine three times. "I'm just glad my family is back. I can't wait to tell my mother."

"Give me until three o'clock," I said.

All of my belongings would be out of his house by two p.m.

CHAPTER 39
MEMPHIS

"Fellas, take everything off the truck. Her clothes go upstairs to the master. Furniture and sewing equipment goes in the family room to my right," I eagerly instructed.

"Cool, let me survey right quick," the driver said, entering my home through the garage.

Whew! My baby was home. She wasn't pregnant. I didn't care where Natalie was. Long as she did not hit me up I was good. I never wanted another Natalie in my life. Had to make Z real comfortable.

Standing in my driveway, I wrapped my arms around her. Whispered in her ear, "I'ma make love to you until the sun comes up. I miss her." I kissed Z. Pretended I was sucking her sweet pussy. "Yeah, you gon' get all this dick soon as they leave."

"Thanks for letting me come here," she said.

"It's Memphis, baby! This is our house

for good. I had a locksmith rekey the property and install keypads. Got video cameras installed too. Want you to feel safe when I'm not here with you."

Nothing was separating me from the woman I was now positive I wanted to share everything with. I removed her engagement ring from my pocket, slid it on her finger. It was the diamond Tina-Love gave me for Natalie, but Natalie wasn't getting it and Tina-Love didn't need it.

"We have a lot to discuss," Z said.

"I know I'm not doing this the right way, but don't ever take it off." I had plans to romance Z properly.

Her hair was wrapped in a sexy bun that was at the back of her head. I was fucking that bun up! By the time I finished giving Z my d the way she liked it, she was going to have that stanky leg wobble in her knees.

"Don't put anything downstairs in my man cave, bruh. That setup has award-winning status." Licking my lips, I shook my head. "I guess I should clear it out."

"Memphis, you don't have to do that," Z said.

Yeah, the freak zone was there way before I'd met Z. Snuck a few females down there while Z was here (but not at home). Let the chicks do a smash and dash. I was done with all that. For real. Z could convert it to whatever.

"I know. But I have to solidify with you that I'm one hundred percent legit this time. Can't risk losing you again."

Her grin was priceless. "Can they set up my sewing machine, design table, and oversize chair in the family room?"

"Fellas, clear out the family room, put all that in the empty bedroom off the garage, set my future wife's office up however she wants. Unpack all her shit to the toothbrush, put it where she tells you, then take away the boxes, strips of tape, all that. One more thing."

"What's that, boss?" the lead mover asked.

"After you guys are done, I need y'all to clear out ASAP. You know what I mean."

"Gotcha, boss man," the mover replied.

Looking around, I'd lost track of Z. *Let me go find this woman.* Z was out back by the lagoon, slowly rocking in her great-grandmother's chair. "You haven't been here but a minute and you already one with nature." Whatever was important to Z was to me, too. "Hey, Granny." I massaged Z's shoulders. They were real tight.

"Memphis, we have a lot to discuss," she said. "When do you resume practice?"

"Tomorrow morning. Everything is good.

My knee is feeling one hundred. Baby, I just want to prove that I'm the only man deserving of your love and affection."

"I'm moving so fast I don't know what direction to go in next. I have the unknown and then there's the unresolved with Adonis."

Z was tripping. "Don't mention his name in my house. What do you have to talk with that nigga about? You're not pregnant. We got all your shit where it belongs. What?" I was fucking heated! Felt like jumping into the lagoon to cool off. "I'll buy you another BMW soon as I make this paper."

"Memphis, I let you hire a company to bring all of my possessions from Adonis's place to yours because I was afraid to do it while he was at home. Giving him closure is more for me."

Women needed that closure shit, men did not. Adonis would have Z's replacement in a heartbeat.

"Boss! We got a situation!" the supervisor yelled.

Heading in his direction, I told Z, "Stay here and rethink what you just told me."

I stopped at the front door. Z bumped into me. I kept walking to my driveway. She stood beside me.

"You famous. You ain't God," Adonis said,

rushing toward me.

Wham! Wham! I struck pretty boy across that disrespectful mouth of his, then I dotted his eye.

Adonis stumbled, swayed.

"Get off of my property!" If I left and returned with a weapon, I was using it.

Z screamed. She should've listened when I told her not to come out here.

"That's going to cost you handsomely, Mister Track Star. I used to be your fan." Adonis held up his cell. Pressed the side button several times.

Wasn't sure if he was capturing Z and me, or doing a selfie. *Wham!* His phone screen shattered, I stomped on it twice.

"I'm an Oglethorpe. I can buy another cell," Adonis laughed, then added, "With my settlement."

I noticed Z hadn't spoken a word after that little yell of hers.

Giving her fifty feet, I'd become a spectator.

"You didn't have to do that," Z said to me.

What was she talking about? Giving her space or smashing his face? I didn't answer or move. How did that nigga know my address? The only physical I'd ever used online was my mother's.

"Xena, don't make me call the cops, baby! That's my property on that truck and the only way you can keep it in your possession is to come back home."

For the first time, I saw the love I had for my woman in another man's eyes.

Z stood in front of Adonis. I couldn't ease my hand between them without touching him and her.

"Keep it," she said. "You can have all of it, even my panties. Memphis has enough money to replace all that shit!"

No, Memphis didn't. Not yet. Hell, I owed Tina-Love $250,000.

"All I want to do is love you and do right by you," Adonis confessed. "I acted out of character. I behaved poorly. But Xena, all I've ever done was love you. You are carrying my child and you're going to let another man take away my DNA?" Adonis started crying like a lil bitch. When dude's tears fell, he couldn't hide his desperation.

"What did I do to hurt you?" Adonis asked Xena, sniffling.

"What you want me to do, boss?" the moving supervisor asked.

Obviously, I did not think this shit all the way through. That dude's heart was ripped. What if I were in his position? Xena hadn't mentioned to him she was not carrying his child. I wasn't going to mention it. What if @DDDShade and Rick were setting me up again?

Trust no one.

The pain on Adonis's face, I'd have to be a sociopath to not have empathy for this man in this moment.

"I love you too, woman," I told Z, making a fist. Not to strike Adonis again.

His lip was busted, eye bruised. Light-skinned guys should never put themselves in a position for a physical altercation. My hand was hurting, but not nearly as much as his heart.

I whispered in Z's ear, "I can't have these types of distractions while I'm training." I told the movers, "Yo! Take all her stuff out of my house and back to ole boy's."

"Memphis, please don't do this. I just need a few hours of closure with Adonis," Z pleaded. "To straighten things out properly."

Fuck that. Memphis Brown was second to none. "Take your time, Z. When it's all good for us to be together, I'll be waiting to properly propose to you." Sliding my ring off her finger, I said, "I promise."

CHAPTER 40
XENA

"What in the hell is this?" Tina-Love stood in her driveway wearing a long leopard see-through robe in front of men who shouldn't see her virtually naked.

I'd parked my BMW in her garage, left the door up. "I'm taking you up on your offer. I need to stay with you until I rent a place of my own," I explained. "A week. Maybe two. Please."

I didn't want to be here any more than my bestie wanted me at her house, but I was not going back to Adonis under any circumstance, nor was I living with Bailey, a man I'd never met.

The lead mover got out of the truck. Barefoot, Tina-Love stomped up to him. "Do not unload a thing, you hear me. Take her belongings elsewhere."

Adonis stood beside me. Tina-Love marched to us. He stared at my bestie's pussy forever, as though he was being hypnotized.

Tina-Love untied her robe, pushed Adonis's head below her navel. "Is that a good enough view?" she said, then slapped him three times. Hard. Fastening her belt, she yelled, "Get off of my property, right now!"

Adonis shook his head like he'd awakened from a long nap. I told myself I didn't care.

What did Tina-Love expect? Her chocolate raspberry lips were protruding. I had to stare elsewhere.

"So are you saying I can't stay with you for a short while?" I asked.

Frowning, she responded, "I'm beginning to believe you may have a mental disorder. What normal person shows up at anyone's home unannounced with a truckload of furniture? That's my concern."

I'd seen every room in her place and knew each one was fully furnished and decorated. But she had available square footage in her garage. "How about they put my things in your in-law unit out back?" My belongings wouldn't be here long.

Adonis held my hand. I pulled away. Why was he following me everywhere?

"What part of 'get off of my property, right now!' don't you understand?" Tina-Love announced calmly. "You too, Xena."

Holding back tears, Adonis gripped my

wrist. "Let's go home and work things out for the three of us. I know you're upset, but you don't have to beg her."

Shaking my head no, I said, "I can't. I have to get my own place." Watching him tear up, I was tired of his crying. "I'll think about it. Go."

"What y'all want me to do with this load?" the moving supervisor asked. "I'm late for my next job." His eyes roamed Tina-Love's body. "Damn, woman. You right for that."

"Forget her. Follow me, man," Adonis said.

The mover replied, "Never that."

"Yes, that! Follow him!" Tina-Love waited until her security gate closed. "You, inside. We need to talk. Don't ever let anyone on my premises without my prior consent. Leaving your things here would've given crazy Adonis an excuse to come back with or without you."

That was fair. I trailed Tina-Love inside her mansion. She went to the kitchen, opened a bottle of champagne, filled two flutes.

"You could've called. Texted. You don't show up at my house on a whim with all of your belongings expecting me to invite you in for an undeterminable amount of time, Xena. What's really going on? Start from my dropping you off at the shop after we left Doctor Francis's office yesterday," Tina-Love said, handing me a flute.

Alcohol on an empty stomach was not what I needed. "No, thanks," I said.

"Yes, thanks. Drink up. It's not like you're pregnant." Tina-Love rubbed the side of her face. "I apologize, Xena. But as your friend, you know me better than anyone and you do this?"

There was nothing worth justifying. I'd left the champagne where she'd place it.

"Has the doctor called you to schedule your procedure?"

I shook my head. Tina-Love was right. I knew she wouldn't be happy to see me. I was disappointed in myself. Again.

"Memphis put me out," I told her.

"That's not what he said when he called me. He said that in the midst of moving you into his place, Adonis showed up at his house unannounced acting an ass. So you leave Memphis's and bring that BS to my doorstep. Why?"

Sitting on the counter stool, I had to put Adonis staring at her vaginal lips out of my mind. She was the slut, not me. Tina-Love also had her life in order.

"You have the opportunity of a lifetime in front of you and you're wasting it on a man who doesn't matter." She emptied her cocktail until the last bubble disappeared, then she poured herself round two.

"Oh, hi," a naked guy said, entering the kitchen. There was no reaction to the fact that I was present.

No need for surprise. This was Tina-Love's norm and why I should be grateful I wasn't moving into her home. First thing I noticed was the guy's penis was almost as big as Memphis's. "Hello," I told him, not wanting to be rude.

He filled a water pitcher with ice cubes, kissed Tina-Love. "Ready whenever you are. No rush. I'll be by the pool."

I gulped all the bubbles, covered my mouth, burped. "Excuse me. I didn't mean to interrupt."

"That's Ricardo. My Italian friend we were supposed to visit." Opening the cooler, she held another bottle of Dom. "You're here. You might as well join us."

Oh no! I stood, glad my BMW was in her garage. "No, thanks. You just reminded me why I shouldn't be here."

I had to credit Tina-Love. From modeling to men, she'd always known what she wanted. And I'd always lived in the shadow of a man. Truth was, I was petrified for Fashion Week, and it wasn't until next year.

I stared at my so-called bestie. She could've offered to help me.

"What, Xena?" With the bottle in her hand, she continued, "You showed up on my doorstep. Not the other way. I'm tired of you, too, Xena. Stop fucking judging me!"

Thump! She banged the bottle against the countertop. Holding my breath, I didn't know what to expect, but I was relieved the glass didn't break.

What was Tina-Love tired of? Devaluing her vagina? Recycling disposable dicks? Or damaging one good man after another. Ricardo appeared nice. That situation wouldn't last long.

"Let me remind you. I am self-made." Tina-Love suctioned in her cheeks, popped the cork on number two, drank from the bottle. "My children were for my mother's man, bitch! You've never been raped! You just keep making dumb-ass decisions."

Speechless. What did she expect me to say? I hadn't visited my dad since I'd broken up with Memphis.

Tina-Love stood in front of me and said angrily, "You're thirty-one. Single. Never married. Damaged. And broken. I'll be damned if I'm going to live my life based on what you or anyone else thinks of me."

She jammed her pointer finger to her sternum repeatedly.

To that, I had no response. I was not going to allow her to condemn me anymore. Adonis. My mother. Tina-Love. The cement floor. I didn't have to sleep at my shop. And I didn't need any of them.

I told her, "Wished you had confessed this while we were in high school. I wouldn't be standing here."

"Xena," she said. "Regardless of my sexual behavior, if you have no compassion for the fact that I was raped damn near every day and my mother knew it, just go."

I stretched my arms to my bestie. We embraced each other. "I'm so sorry that happened to you."

"You can stay the night," Tina said. "In the morning, we can restart this conversation. Take a shower, do not put on any clothes, and meet me and Ricardo by the pool."

CHAPTER 41
XENA

Silence. Did it truly exist?

Wind created sound. I sat on a patio cushion with my legs folded, listening to birds chirping. A constant piercing tone penetrated my eardrums. Water in Tina-Love's pool swished.

"Tina-Love tells me you meditate daily," Ricardo said.

Rudely interrupted, I opened my eyes, glanced around the terrace. "Yes, that was what I was doing," I told him.

"You mind if I set up the massage table out here and show you something?" he asked. "Something inside of you is fighting to invade your body."

I'd enjoyed our spiritual threesome in the Jacuzzi last night watching the sunset, but I was not in the mood for a continuation. "No, thanks. I'd like to practice before the sun rises." I closed my eyes.

Plopping. Propping. Snapping. Swishing.

Prohibited me from keeping my mind clear.

I stood. Stared at Ricardo's nakedness. "Do you ever wear underwear?" I hadn't seen him with any clothes on since I'd met him.

"Do you disapprove?" he asked as though he were my man.

Was he involved in some sort of cult practice?

Tina-Love quietly joined us. A robe more sheer than yesterday's hung on her shoulders. The belt dangled at her sides.

"I requested Ricardo introduce you to a different kind of meditation. Trust him. It'll give you a sharper internal image and help you heal yourself. I hope. I'll prepare us a fresh fruit salad and meet you guys here in an hour." Tina-Love left me feeling the session wasn't optional.

I lay on the table and cradled my head in the doughnut, staring at the tiles.

"Let me place this blindfold over your eyes." Ricardo secured the Velcro.

"Relax and breathe." He waved a scent under my nose. "With each inhale, go deeper until you cannot expand your lungs any farther."

On my third breath of eucalyptus, I released the tension from my body. Felt like I was hovering above the table. I heard more birds chirping, near and in the distance. First there were two, then there were four hands stroking my backside in a slow, gliding, top-to-bottom motion.

A slightly heavier pressure pushed on both shoulders. Their hands never lost contact with my flesh as they synchronized strokes from my ankles, calves, thighs, butt. They focused on my lower back.

Heaviness invaded my body. For the first time, I could feel the cyst without touching my abdomen. Sliding their fingers underneath me, they massaged my collarbone, stomach, pinched my Achilles, lifting me. Seemed as though pennies, nickels, dimes, quarters, half-dollars, and silver dollars rained as I was gently shaken. My head nestled in the headrest as they lowered me onto the table.

I was flipped onto my back. Every beat of my heart chased the next one competing to catch the one before. More whiffs of scented oil, menthol this time.

That was the last thing I remembered.

CHAPTER 42
MEMPHIS

"Push harder, MB!" Coach Richie yelled as I raced by him. "Harder!"

Betrayer. Was that what he did when he fucked Natalie? She wasn't my lady. I didn't care that he'd hit it. Made me see her for the slut she was. Coach putting that "watch out for women" shit in my head, when his dick was trespassing on my territory. I was over it. Regardless of my decision, my success depended upon Coach Richie.

I didn't have to like Coach. But I loved him. He believed in me. No way I'd let pussy come between me and my gold medals.

Every time I thought about Z, about the four-hands massage I let Tina-Love convince me to do with Rico Suave, about Adonis showing up at my house, my speed decreased. Refocusing, I pumped my arms faster, stretched my legs longer. I felt my lips, cheeks, chin, and forehead jolting up and down. Sweat burned my eyes. I was used to it. What I wasn't accustomed to was this downturn. My four-hundred dash went from 50.2 seconds to 65.4.

As I leaned into the curve, my left foot skidded, knocked my right from under me. I slid. Jumped up.

"Fuck!" Anger consumed me. I brushed myself off.

"Give me ten more laps! You're looking lousy, MB," Coach Richie said.

He was right. Runners weren't supposed to fall. Models weren't expected to trip. A turbo boost blasted in my mind, but in reality, I struggled to increase my speed.

Shouldn't have deviated from my norm this morning. Tina-Love told me the true meaning of soul-mating was that I had to connect with Z on a Zen level, be patient, allow her energy to find my spirit. When the two united, I had to let my energy penetrate her mind, body, and soul. I thought that was what I'd been doing the five years I was with Z.

Breaking my stride, I came to a stop. Leaning over, I rested my hands on my knees, told Coach, "Don't say it. I know my mind wasn't one with my body today. I'll make up for it tomorrow."

Coach Richie patted me on my back.

"Next time run like you punch."

He laughed. I didn't. Jogging to the bleachers, I reached inside my bag, retrieved my phone and car keys, checked my messages.

When are you going to come get Her?? Tina-Love texted.

Damn, Z hadn't been there twenty-four hours. Rico Suave was the one that had to go. Had to admit, I did not want Tina-Love to settle down with one man.

After changing my shoes, I walked the all-weather track, retracing my steps to where I'd fallen. This could not, make that *would* not, happen again.

I replied, **1 quick stop then I'm omw**

Nothing you've done was for Z. It was all for you, Tina-Love texted.

That's not true, and she knew it.

Everything I'd done was for Z. I'd admit I executed my judgment in a self-centered, egotistical way. But that was what women accepted.

Then why is she here and you're not?

What the fuck? I was just there. I wasn't taking Z off of Tina-Love's hands. "See you in the morning," I said, waving to Coach Richie.

"MB. Everything is going to be okay," he reassured me. "Whatever it is, let it go,"

Coach said, then redirected his attention to his cell phone.

I wanted to. But I couldn't. Had to stop off at @DDDShade and Rick's.

Xena just left. I think Adonis is moving our gurl back in with him, she texted.

Be right over after my stop. Make sure Rico Suave is gone before I get there. He was trying to move in on Tina-Love. I wasn't having that.

I turned onto Rick's private road and parked in their garage. Rick greeted me with an open hand. "My wife is out."

Perfect! "I'll come back."

"Time is not on your side, my brother," he said, closing the garage door.

Following him into his kitchen, he said, "Have a seat," then asked, "How're things with you?"

I'd never seen an all-black kitchen with a gold backsplash. "Why don't you tell me?" I said, standing at the island.

Rick placed two glasses on the counter, filled them with juice from a decanter, handed me one.

"Thanks," I said, sitting down. "Let's get to it." I wasn't here to make a friend.

"Have you made a decision on our representing you? Before you answer, let me show you this. We're protecting you as of now."

A video streamed on the big-screen television hanging on the wall. There I was punching Adonis in the face. All the outdoor footage was clear, voices and images. "I was justified. He was trespassing," I said.

"Well, there's the one of you punching your coach in the face."

Turning away, I'd had enough of their bullshit!

"Wait. I have another one." Rick pointed the remote.

I watched in disbelief. "This can never get out." I was reporting his ass and his wife to the police.

"I wouldn't do that if I were you." Rick powered off the TV, swallowed his juice until his glass was empty. "Ahh. Good nutrients."

Afraid mine might be drugged, I was not touching it.

"Sixty grand cash, you'll be prepaid up to the Olympic Games, and I guarantee you we will not expose Tina-Love or Xena. Consider it a bonus."

Scanning the room, I searched for hidden cameras. "Xena? Now I know you're lying."

Rick nodded. "She's got a secret."

"I already know. She aborted my baby."

He shook his head. "A bigger one."

Nothing shocked me anymore. "I'm listening."

@DDDShade strolled in. "If he told you, it wouldn't be a secret now, would it?"

My quicksand was starting to bury the people I loved most.

Rick commented, "Exactly."

@DDDShade added, "That's why we're keeping your insurance affordable."

They couldn't get what I didn't have.

Chapter 43
Xena

I left last night! I couldn't take another second of Tina-Love and Ricardo roaming her house naked. Sex on the terrace, in the Jacuzzi, in the kitchen, in the pool, meditation sessions with clothes off, random massages throughout the day was all they did.

"Good morning, honey," Adonis sang, then started kissing me all over my belly. "I missed you guys tremendously. Promise me you'll never leave me again."

Adonis pressed his lips to mine. I moved my head to the side. He cupped my breast, traced my areola with his tongue, softly sucked my nipple.

I didn't want to be here. Didn't want to live with my parents. Maybe my mother had mellowed with age.

"Give me some," he whispered. "I miss cumming inside of you."

I said, "Good morning," then sat on the edge of the bed, picked up my cell, went to the bathroom, placed my phone on the vanity facedown. Sitting on the toilet, I exhaled. There was no way I could tell him. Nor was I risking getting pregnant.

He followed me. "It's time for you to start going to our family's OB/GYN for checkups. Mom says she's the best." His pecker was in front of my face.

Pushing his dick aside, I said, "Stop pretending all the things that transpired didn't. You begged me to come back here. All of my belongings down to my toothbrush" — sighing, I ignored his erection — "are back in place."

"You don't own anything that appreciates in value," Adonis said, backing away from me.

Damn. He was right. Soon as I got myself together, I was out of here for good.

Playfully he moved my hairbrush from the left side of the vanity to the right. "Now everything is in place. If it'll make you feel better, I'll shuffle your clothes, and your design area. Hide a few things." He stood in front of the mirror, flexing. "I'm not afraid of Memphis. I have the trophy."

The swelling in his eye had gone away. A splash of purple remained. The split in his lip was healing. I washed my hands, touched his face. "Memphis did not have to fight you."

"I'll take another to the chin if it means winning you back. I hope he breaks a leg for real."

That was rude. Memphis fought Adonis, but he didn't do it to keep me. I had to place reuniting with Memphis on hold until after my show and his competition.

"Don't forget we're having lunch with my parents. My mom will give you all the information for the doctor and go with you to your appointments."

I blurted, "Leave me alone!" Sitting in my sewing chair I covered my face and cried. "I really need you to give me a break. I'm not —"

Adonis yelled down at me, "Is that what you told Memphis? He doesn't care about you. It's a good thing I got to his house before you fucked him with my baby inside of you! I'm trying to show you love and you tell *me* to leave you alone?" Adonis started crying.

I stopped. Seeing tears pour down his cheeks, I should've been sympathetic. I wasn't. My cell rang, giving me an exit. I hurried to the bathroom where I'd left it. "Hey, Topez. Good morning," I said, making my way to the kitchen. I opened the refrigerator, removed a tray of blackberries, placed them in a bowl.

Adonis sat in my sewing chair. Eyes squinted, lips tight, he stared at me.

"Where are you?" she asked.

Chomping on a sweet berry, I was embarrassed to say exactly. Swallowing the fruit, I answered, "Home. Why?"

Adonis nodded. "Yes, you are at home."

"I just arrived at your shop. Did you forget we have an appointment in thirty minutes with our client for his upcoming wedding?"

"Oh, shoot. I'm on my way." Ending the call, I abandoned what would've been breakfast. I returned to the bathroom.

Adonis turned on the shower, stepped inside. "You can skip meditating this morning. Let's rub each other, then I want you to make love to your fiancé."

He knew I had to leave. I threw a bath towel on the floor, lathered my scrunchie. Head to toe I cleansed my body twice, wiped well with a wet towel, dried off, and left him standing under the dome.

Dripping water, Adonis trailed me from the bathroom to the bedroom. "You're going to see him? That was Memphis calling?"

"I have an important meeting with a client," I said, stepping into a jumpsuit.

"Yeah, right. This early." Fast as he could,

Adonis put on shorts, a T-shirt, and house slippers.

"I told —" I didn't have to explain anything to him. I picked up a tote Tina-Love had given me. Why in the hell was I having this conversation? I slammed the door, then stomped down nineteen steps.

Adonis followed me down the stairs. "Where are you going, Xena?"

Mr. Ben was in the hallway. "You guys okay?"

I heard Adonis's footsteps behind me. He was so close I felt his hand touch mine. I answered Mr. Ben. "I'm fine."

He said, "Give her some space. She's dealing with a lot with the —"

Adonis grabbed me by the waist. Turned me toward Mr. Ben. "You're not leaving me again."

"Let me go!" I told Adonis, yanking away. "And you shut up, old man. You don't know what you're talking about." I stared Mr. Ben in his eyes.

Adonis told Mr. Ben, "She's fine. The pregnancy makes her emotionally unstable at times."

Running out of the building, I heard Mr. Ben's door close. Standing on the sidewalk, I faced Adonis. I did not have to defend my sanity against his opinion.

"I don't believe you're going to the shop. I don't believe anything you say anymore." His expression was filled with sadness.

I prayed Adonis did not start crying again. I was sick of it and him. "Then why am I here?" I asked.

"Because I'm the only one who loves you. Not your mother. Tina-Love put you out. And Memphis is playing you for his fool. The man threw you out of his house."

"Don't act like you didn't beg me to come back here. And I left her mansion. She did not put me out. There's a difference." Ricardo pleasuring himself all day was my incentive.

Staying with him wasn't worth it. Adonis was stressing me out.

I wondered if Tina-Love's version of her having two abortions was the real story. If it was, I understood how that man made her the way she was. But she could curb her insatiable appetite for sex if she wanted to.

"Memphis kicked you out," Adonis yelled inches from my face.

Backing away, I could use another massage from Ricardo before Tina-Love screwed things up with him. Women like her never changed. I wished Memphis hadn't given up on me that easily. Waking up to him would've been nice. "Memphis asked me to resolve my issues with you first."

Adonis lamented, "You have no place to go, Xena. Your own mother doesn't want you at their house."

Getting in the car, I lowered the window, then yelled, "I don't want to —" I stopped midsentence. Where in hell was the asshole inside of Adonis hiding the entire year?

"If you need anything, Xena, let me know," Mr. Ben said, then headed toward The Sentient Bean coffee shop.

In transit to the storefront, I called Tina-Love. Soon as she answered, I said, "Bestie, I need another one of those massages. Adonis is driving me insane."

"Forget Adonis. Have you scheduled your procedure?"

"I'm scared." I didn't want to know if I had cancer.

"Scared won't change your outcome, bestie. Look, Ricardo and I are in the middle of something. Can I call you later?" she asked, ending the call before I responded.

It was after six. Memphis was at training. Tina-Love. Memphis. Topez. Adonis. The constants in my life, I could count on one hand and not use my thumb. Parking beside

Topez's car, I tapped on her passenger window.

Hurrying to unlock the storefront door, I apologized to our client for my being five minutes late. When I turned on the lights, I saw there were flower bouquets lined up on my counter. Only one man could've done this. I swear I wanted to do one long swoop and knock them to the floor.

Mental note. Call a locksmith.

"Cute," Topez said, picking up all five vases and lining them on the floor along the wall.

After carrying the roll of materials to the counter, I made three more trips to get the others. Showed them to the client. "The black leather is for your pants and shirt."

This man had an amazing athletic body. My job was to make him the focus. No one was going to overlook him or any of the groomsmen in his party.

"I'm going to insert a one-inch strip of this kente cloth down one pant leg and over the zipper flap."

Clearing his throat, he interrupted, "You don't think that will create too much attention on my privates? I don't want to get divorced before I say, 'I do.' "

Topez glanced down at his dick, looked at me, then nodded.

"I'll add it to the waistband. Your kente jacket will be tailored to perfection. Let me get your measurements one last time," I said. It was easier to work with men. Brides went on crash diets. Bridesmaids gained weight.

He was quiet while I placed the tape from his waist to his scrotum.

Topez told him, "We're on schedule to deliver everything by this Friday."

"Of course," I added, trying to convince myself I could do it all.

"Thanks! I can't wait to marry this woman. I love her so much. My party will come together to pick up our suits. What's a good time?"

"Seven," I answered, beating Topez to a response.

He asked, "A.m.?"

I clarified, "P.m."

"The rehearsal dinner is at seven o'clock that night," Topez said.

Damn. I was messing up like never before. "How's two p.m.?"

"We'll see you then," he said, exiting the shop.

Topez flopped in the chair at my design table. "Xena, you cannot be serious. You haven't started on any of the tuxedos?"

She knew me well. My phone rang. Shaking my head, I held up my hand. "I have to take this call from the doctor's office." Anxiously I answered, "Hello."

"Is this Xena Trinity?" she asked.

"Yes."

"Doctor Francis wants to see you today. Can you come in at four?"

"I'll be there," I replied, then pressed the end button.

"No time is the right time to screw up," Topez said. "I got you this contract. I refuse to let you ruin my reputation. Tell me what's going on so we can fix it and move forward."

I explained the situations with Memphis, Adonis, and Tina-Love. I told her that there was no baby, and I might have ovarian cancer.

"Please tell me you're not using talcum powder in your genital area," she said.

"Not since high school. Why?" I asked.

"Aw, Xena," she said as though I were to blame. "Studies have linked the use of talc to ovarian cancer. If you have a positive diagnosis, you're going to need everyone close to you to be supportive, including your mother." Her comment sounded more like I was dying.

I didn't know that. I used baby powder on my sheets too. "I had no idea."

"We'll pray for the best, but we need a

plan. First, I'm going to help you meet your deliverable for our client. Then, this weekend, you're going out on a date with Bailey. He's a loving, caring, protective man that could use a good woman friend in his life. Forget Memphis, although I'd choose him over Adonis any day. Get the hell out of Adonis's house today and never look back. He's not the one for you."

I texted Tina-Love, **Can you go with me to the doctor at 4p today?**

Adonis entered the shop, stood at the counter. "Topez, get out of my place of business."

Of course honey. Meet me here no later than 3p. I'll drive.

My ex frustrated me. My bestie's response gave me relief. I didn't want to go alone.

Topez stood. "Xena, help me put the material in my car. We'll do this project at my house."

Adonis raised his voice at Topez. "My fiancée can't lift those heavy rolls. Get out of my shop." Then he calmly said to me, "I came to pick you up. We're having lunch with my mama. It's non-negotiable."

Topez stared at me from the corners of her eyes, picked up a roll of cloth, walked out, then returned. On separate trips, she carried the kente and the leather to her car and drove off.

"Adonis, you cannot disrespect my business partner. I need you to get out of *my* shop. I might not own this space, but your name is not on the lease."

"Xena, sweetheart. I'm running out of patience. You can make this easy by doing what I say."

CHAPTER 44
MEMPHIS

I rolled up to Tina-Love's and parked next to her Bentley.

Had to admit that visual clip Rick showed me of her one-of-a-kind chocolate-raspberry was all the way naughty and very nice. Especially the part where she rubbed Adonis's nose below her waist. Once my thang got excited, he needed attention. I was not holding out for Z.

Strolling through her spot, I found her the first place I thought she'd be. Sunbathing poolside. Wearing sunglasses. I surveyed the sky far as I could see. Rick had to have drones zooming in on Tina-Love's and my houses to have personal footage.

"What are you looking for?" she questioned.

"More like whom. Rico Suave. Where he at?" I wasn't interested in where he was long as he wasn't inside. "I don't want to talk." I was ready to take her up on a massage. I tapped Tina-Love on the shoulder, motioned for her to get off the lounge chair and follow me inside.

I went up to her bathroom, removed my soiled clothes, left them in the middle of the tiled floor, then turned on the shower. Steam rose from the hot water, splashing all over my body. I could barely see through the fog.

I played and replayed how to tell Tina-Love about how she shouldn't expose herself. How she shouldn't have pushed Adonis's face down to her pussy. The shocked look from Z was priceless. I bet that image was etched in dude's mind. If that video was released, Tina-Love's career would come to a halt. Or soar. Either way, she'd be labeled a whore, more so by women. No straight man in the world would find Tina-Love repulsive.

Standing under the dome, I jacked my dick a few times. Let go. Lathering my nuts, I massaged my perineum. Tina-Love taught me how to hit the jackpot spot between my balls and anus. That made me holler like a bitch whenever Z did it. Shit I was doing to myself felt good. I took a deep breath. Reaching around behind my back, I slid my finger in and out of my asshole. One, to cleanse myself thoroughly. Two, the sensation was amazing.

Ten minutes had gone by, no Tina-Love. I started jacking off again. Stopped. If I released all of this pent-up cum, clumps of semen would plop under the waterfall and clog the drain. I let go of my dick. Wondered who Natalie was taking advantage of. Or was she off on a mission to do good? The games Rick and @DDDShade were playing had me fucked up for real. Never believed Natalie would set me up.

I quieted my mind. Smiled. Wider. Being in the shower gave me clarity I couldn't channel anywhere else. *That's it! I'm going to find a way to expose their asses.*

Fifteen minutes in — my fingertips felt like raisins — I heard her footsteps.

Excited, I opened the door, the steam dispersed.

What the hell?! Naked-ass Rico Suave stared at my dick, then into my eyes.

Hunching his shoulders, he said, "There are some things I can assist you with that Tina-Love cannot."

"You can't help me with shit." I wrapped a towel around my waist.

"Energy is masculine *and* feminine. Before we are male or female we are one big ball of energy traveling from body to body. When someone dies, someone gets pregnant. During conception, energy enters the mother's womb, and finds its way to the fetus. During birth, it's not the man that is gay or the woman that is a lesbian or one that is transgender, transsexual, or queer. Energy dictates everything in the universe. I say this to tell you, we all have male and female energy."

Rico Suave stood over the toilet. "Excuse me."

Dude urinated in front of me. Why did Tina-Love have this man invading our space? I exited into the bedroom. Relieved Tina-Love was there. Rico Suave needed to go outside and wait his turn.

I lay facedown, took a deep breath.

Tina-Love said, "Memphis, this is only a massage, and you've had sports massages by men. Relax. You need this. Ricardo is going to assist me."

I demanded, "No touching my dick, Rico." If he did, I was going to bust him one where I hit Coach.

The scent of cinnamon floated under my nostrils. I inhaled. I was feeling some type of odd way. My four-hand strokes were a combination of firm and soft. Deep and shallow.

Rico Suave actually knew what he was doing.

CHAPTER 45
XENA

"I do not control what Memphis does with his body and neither can you. It's the same experience you had, Xena. Lighten up."

Tina-Love said that as though Ricardo was a female. "Hearing you say another man's —"

"What?" she interrupted, turning right on red in transit to my appointment. "We were all in the same room? Ricardo is my man, not Memphis."

Her what? That was a first, hearing her claim a guy. I'd give that relationship two weeks before Tina-Love got bored.

I had a problem with her man massaging Memphis when it should've been me. There went my bestie being Memphis's louder cheerleader. "You cannot justify taking Memphis's side this time. You know what I meant. Ricardo was inside of Memphis. That's what I heard you say."

I'd GPS the route from my shop to the

doctor's office on my cell. We were twenty minutes away with traffic. The seat belt pressed against the lump in my abdomen. I prayed the doctor wouldn't tell me I had an expiration date months out. Tina-Love glanced at me. Her ginormous buns, one on each side of her head, she wore them well. Short romper, high heels; I was most envious of her ultra-flat stomach.

"Stop being closed-minded. It's like having a rectal exam," she said, then laughed.

This was not a humorous occasion. Lately, none of our shared moments were fun. I recalled the last time I was genuinely happy was over a year ago. The light took a long time to switch from red to green. Cars traveled in slow motion. "So now you're telling me Memphis wanted Ricardo to stick his finger up his ass?" My head throbbed.

Needing something to drown out Tina-Love's drama, I pushed a button, powering on her audio system. Folding my arms, I tried visualizing what they did. How they'd done it.

Tina-Love lowered the volume from her steering wheel. We had three miles to go.

"I was kidding about Ricardo" she said, holding my hand. "No one knows Memphis better than us. Don't let anyone, including me, tell you about your man. If you're going to listen to outsiders, your relationship with Memphis won't last."

She had a point. I turned up the radio soon as I'd heard, "Hey, my shade trees! This is your gurl @DDDShade. I've got hot quicksand! Join me tomorrow morning in *The Shady Café.* You won't believe who's sinking. You know what to do. When I post my guest's photo, download it. Print it. And break out your shade spray. You decide if it's going to be hot and sweet . . . hot and sticky . . . or hot and stanky!"

"She's a mess," I said. "I don't like her anymore."

"A hot one," Tina-Love added. "I despise her. One day her ass is going to be in quicksand."

When we parked in the garage, our small talk ended.

Silencing the engine, Tina-Love glanced at me, squeezed my hand. "You ready?"

I opened then shut my door. Quietly entered the building.

Stepping onto the elevator, I shook my head. "I'm not close to being ready," I cried. "I'm scared."

"We're going to get through this together." Tina-Love made me realize that I did need her.

Wasn't sure if I wanted to go on a blind

date with Bailey tonight. If Topez's friend was such a great catch, why was he single?

Entering the doctor's office, Tina-Love dried my tears. The assistant escorted us to a private room. This one was different. A desk, three chairs, and a monitor. No exam table.

"The doctor will be with you shortly," she said, then closed the door.

My silence was filled with fear.

Doctor Francis opened the door and sat in a chair facing us. "Xena."

I could tell it wasn't good by the tone of her voice. It was as though she was consoling me. Tina-Love held my hand.

"Yes," I answered, scooting to the edge of my seat.

"We need to set a date for —" the doctor said.

I didn't want to hear the *c* word. "For what?" I cried.

"I received the results of your transvaginal ultrasound and we need to schedule you for a CT scan. We can perform a surgical biopsy, my dear, but I recommend surgery," she said.

Tina-Love said what I was thinking. "Why?"

"I know the thought of not being completely healthy can be scary. Xena, the X-ray indicated in addition to the cyst, there are masses on your ovaries. I want you to let my assistant schedule you for the first two availabilities. First, the CA-125. Soon as I get those results I can pinpoint where the masses are, and we can schedule the operation to remove them."

Why wasn't she giving me confirmation about the cancer? It was bad news.

"Was it the talcum powder? Someone told me about women suing because baby powder can cause cancer." If that was true, I was including my name on a class action lawsuit somewhere.

"There are many studies that support that. As many as those that disagree. Since you don't know your family history, I have no idea where to start in terms of giving you answers to those types of questions."

Tina-Love asked Doctor Francis, "Does Xena have cancer?"

Numbness settled in my hands and feet. Trembling, I didn't want to hear the truth. *Why me? Why not the promiscuous one, Lord?*

I told the doctor, "I'm ready to set my dates."

"Ovarian cancer is the only form of cancer that we cannot detect before we operate," Doctor Francis explained. "Xena, once we remove the masses, then we will test them. But, I must say, there may be more masses than the CT reveals. Again, I won't know until we operate."

Doctor Francis ended with, "Tina-Love, stay by Xena's side. Out of all the people in the world, you have no idea how many patients have no one to depend on throughout this process."

I looked to my bestie. "Drop me off at my mom's. Hopefully, my dad will understand."

CHAPTER 46
TINA-LOVE

Ricardo did what no man had done. He made me fall in love with him.

Watching my bestie enter her parents' house inspired me to consider forgiving Janice Jones. What if one day I needed my mother?

Guys like Roman, I enjoyed, but he never challenged my mind. I never learned anything from him in or out of bed. Hadn't invited him over since Ricardo arrived. *Hmm.* I didn't miss Roman, not even a little.

Memphis was the only male I labeled a platonic friend.

I'd granted Ricardo an all-access pass to my mansion. He was the most consistent with understanding all aspects of my being, including when I was raped. With his wit, wisdom, charm, skills, talent, and awareness came zero judgment. We agreed that sexuality was not defined by gender.

Riding bareback on top of my horse

Peanut Butter — who got his name after being stuck inside of his mother's birth canal — I'd initiated a conversation I'd never had with a man before by sharing with Ricardo, "I'd like for us to have an open relationship."

First time I'd seen a cesarean performed on a mare convinced me to add, "But I don't want to have any children." No doctor was slicing me open.

Peanut Butter trotted alongside his female companion, Faith. I admired Ricardo in his lime yoga pants, no shirt, no saddle.

Patiently I awaited his response. I'd finally met a man that totally understood me. And I was my authentic self. I didn't want to take Ricardo for granted. Nor would he allow me.

"After being here with you, Tina-Love, I'd like to do that," Ricardo said. "Two free spirits, existing as one, while allowing each other to be uninhibited, honest, and giving. From food to sex to spirituality, we have lots in common. So how do we divide this union timewise?" he inquired. "Do I move to America? Or you to Rome?"

Instead of answering right away, I expressed my desire to experience threesomes with him. "Let's never define intimacy or us."

"Let us not," Ricardo said, "We give our heart and soul all-access to love while keeping each other first. We live wherever we are."

So profound. Being free. Enjoying the fruits of our work. I held my hands high above my head. The sunset kissed me all over. I was on my property inhaling the fresh summer breeze. I was queen. I could willingly depart the throne, but never could I be dethroned.

"I knew you were for me the second I saw you in the boutique. I am a lucky man. American men crazy not to love you," he said.

Oh, how well the men in America loved my lips, my pussy, my money . . . they loved everything about Tina-Love Jones. But they didn't know how to love.

Ricardo tugged Faith's reins. I did the same to Peanut Butter, slid down his side. We walked my horses to their stable, where we brushed their manes, then bathed them.

Heading to the mansion, I noticed a fresh stack of hay. I suggested, "Let's kiss ten times. Not on the lips and not in the same place twice." Spreading my arms, I fell backward like a tree in the forest.

"I am your doctor," Ricardo announced, kissing my eye, ear, nose, and throat. "Wait,

I'm not done. I am also your gynecologist."

I laughed as he went for my clit, vaginal opening, and breast.

"I have three more places, but I must let you catch up," he said, assuming an X formation on the lawn.

Ricardo moaned each time my lips touched him. That was fun, I thought. Walking to the house, we held hands.

He asked, "So when we get married we will both have dual citizenship? Yeah?"

Once upon a time being a citizen of another country was of no interest to me. With the current state of affairs, having the ability to permanently reside elsewhere was a good option.

Marriage might be a decade away but I said, "Yeah." Why not?

Ricardo said, "One, thing."

"What's that?"

"We must agree to share Memphis," he said, raising his brows.

Entering the house, I said, "Absolutely," paused, then told him, "not. Memphis is straight as an arrow."

Retrieving my cell from the kitchen counter, I saw I had a number of text messages, voice mails, and missed calls.

Adonis's voice message was, *"Hey, Tina-Love. I'm worried about Xena. She's not* returning my calls or messages. She's not at my shop. What's going on with my fiancée? I don't know who else to contact. You have Topez's number? Can you meet me for breakfast in the morning?"

The next voice was my mother's. "I heard Xena has cancer. I need for you to forgive me. I want to see you, Tina-Love. Call me. Soon as you can."

Memphis's text read, **omw**

Apparently, Xena's mother had told my mother that Xena had ovarian cancer. Whether Xena conveyed it wrong, or her mother misinterpreted the details, a part of me was glad my mom wanted me to call her ASAP.

CHAPTER 47
XENA

God had a strange way of getting my attention.

I'd coasted on my beauty and submissive personality to attract what society referred to as good men. As I rested in my old bed with the door opened, I overheard my stepmom, who insisted I call her "Mom," was on the phone, telling everyone I had cancer. The sun had barely set and I was ready to leave. Being angry with her was not the best use of the good energy I had.

Fearing the outcome of my situation, my entire perspective on love and life had changed.

"Um-hmm. Yes, child, pray for Xena. She's got cancer." My stepmother paused, then continued, "I'm not sure how long the good Lord gon' let us have her . . . Okay . . . All right. We appreciate your prayers . . . Yes, you can drop off the cobbler tomorrow. Bye."

Leave it to my evil stepmom, she'd already pronounced me dead. I had to get out of here. I texted Topez, **Coming over to work on the tuxedos.**

She responded, **Great. I can't sew using the machine. These suits require perfection.**

Entering the living room, Mom and Dad were side by side on the couch. Dad's hand was on her thigh, his head on her shoulder. With each breath, Dad snorted in, snored out.

My mom nudged him. "Get up and go to bed. Let Xena sit over here."

"Okay, honey. Good night, baby girl," he said, dragging the slippers on his feet with each step.

I stood at the door, entered the address to my shop, then requested an Uber.

"Sit, Xena," she demanded.

Sitting in the space where my father was, I told my mom softly, "Thanks for letting me come by. I just thought you'd want to know. And the doctor isn't sure if it's cancer, so please stop telling everyone that it is."

I was uneasy being this close to her with my father out of the room.

"Xena, you can always come home. What type of mother do you think I am? What would family and my friends think of me if I turned you away knowing you were dying." Changing her tone, she stared at me with piercing eyes. "Do you have an insurance policy?"

Really? I should've known. I wanted to lie, but it was easier explaining the truth. I nodded. "Adonis has one on me." If cancer was confirmed, and I didn't have long to live, I did not care that he was the beneficiary.

"Don't worry," she said, forcing me to lean on her the way I used to do with my dad. "I've told all the family and Ms. Jones you're coming back home. They know not to bother you. How long you think you got?"

She'd done it again. Found a way to isolate me from my friends. Found a reason to have everybody calling her and not me. And she'd made her intent clear. Money.

I could tell she was on the verge of warming up to talk all night. Checking my app, I smiled. My ride was waiting. "I have to go."

Mom frowned. "I know you're not going back to that man who hasn't made you an honorable woman. None of them have. Your father never disrespected me," she said. "Men these days ain't worth what's hanging between their legs." Laughing, she'd given me a perfect opportunity to get out.

I stood, stepped over her feet. "I have to finish a few designs for a wedding Saturday. I'll call you." That wasn't a lie, but it wouldn't be anytime soon.

Snatching my hand, she pulled me in her direction, insisting, "You'll do no such thing. You need your strength for the surgery. Sit."

I collapsed on the sofa, stood, picked up my bag. I wasn't a little girl anymore. "I'll be okay."

She struggled to get up, but the way she flopped, it seemed as though the cushion reached up and snatched her by the butt. Same old floral drapes extended ceiling to floor. Pictures of Reverend Dr. Martin Luther King Jr., Al Sharpton, and Malcolm X hung over the sofa. An empty space was where my photo once was.

"What am I supposed to tell everybody when they drop off food?" After she made another failed attempt to get up, I saw the familiar rage in her eyes.

"Tell them I'm going to die doing what I love." This time I didn't get thrown out; I left.

Arriving at my shop to get in my car, I wasn't surprised it wasn't there. I remained in the Uber, entered Topez's address. I thought about my last words to my mother,

Tell them I'm going to die doing what I love, then started crying. First my tears had no sound. Then there was an aching lump in my throat, followed by loud sobs.

"Damn, girl. You scared the hell outta me," the driver said, increasing his speed.

Parking in Topez's driveway, the driver said, "I hope you feel better."

Upon entering Topez's home, I texted Memphis, **I will always love you.**

CHAPTER 48
MEMPHIS

I love you more Z.

Z had no idea how much I needed to see her words.

I apologize for not letting you stay at my house. Have you resolved shit with dude? I want you back, I texted, entering Tina-Love's house.

I called out her name. "Where are you, woman?"

Rico Suave came galloping down the stairs naked, dick swinging low after he'd stopped three feet in front of me.

"Hey, Memphis. She's in the shower." He raised his brows. Smiled halfway.

I opened the refrigerator to put a barrier between us. "What's good, man? Would it be asking too much for you to put on clothes, drawers?" I asked, reaching for the pitcher of fresh-squeezed orange juice. "Damn."

His sightline was at eight o'clock. I didn't

have many regrets, but experiencing intimacy with a man was definitely one. If Rico
thought I was on his team, if he crept up on
me, he'd find out. I'd be busting him ten
times harder than Coach and twenty times
harder than I'd done Adonis's punk ass.

Easing to my left, and over to the cabinets,
I rinsed a glass, filled it with OJ, left the
picture on the counter, went upstairs.

Tina-Love was lathering herself in coconut
oil.

"Oh, hey, Memphis. You saw Ricardo?"
she asked, putting on socks.

"Yeah, too much of Rico's naked ass all
up in the kitchen," I said, loud enough for
him to hear.

Tina-Love laughed. I did not. Wasn't shit
funny.

"You'd better watch out. He likes you,"
she said, opening her arms for a hug.

"I'm not gay and you know it. Keep him
away from me. In fact, why is he still here?
Put that nigga out. His visa should be ex-
pired."

Tina-Love smiled. "I can't do that. We're
a couple."

I followed Tina-Love to the kitchen.

"Hey, baby. Cook us something to eat,"
she told Rico as if he were clothed.

I'd lost an appetite I never had. Sat my

full glass of juice on the counter.

I stared at Tina-Love.

"Oh, baby. Can you put on a robe while Memphis is here?" she asked.

"Please and thank you," I said, watching Rico go where I hoped he'd stay. "Tina-Love, we both know you're not the relationship commitment kind. What are you doing, man?"

"Living my life. And, Ricardo really," she'd dragged out, "really likes you."

"And you're cool with being with a dude like that? He did some weird spiritual shit on me, but I tell you what, it won't happen again." I was not remotely confused about what my dick liked. "I was responding to you. Not his ass."

"That's cool," she said, all casual. "We're platonic."

I knew that. What was the announcement for? Her man? Let's blast it in *The Shady Café,* then. "I'm not gay."

"Neither am I," Rico said, returning wearing a white see-through robe. "Embracing your sexuality opens doors to the innermost part of the soul that people normally keep suppressed. If ever you want to explore further, I'll gladly give you a massage." He wiggled his fingers. Reminded me of Natalie.

"Baby, do me a favor. Go upstairs. I'll call you when I'm done cooking," Tina-Love said.

Shit felt strange hearing her call another man *baby.* Guess she did that with all of us. Tina-Love was going to have to come up with a special name for me.

Glad Rico was gone, I seized the moment. "I need a cashier's check for sixty thousand dollars soon as your bank opens."

Tina-Love removed the lid off of a glass container, held it under the water, began cleansing strips of lean chicken breasts.

"Did you hear me?" I asked, looking up the staircase, expecting Rico to answer.

"I'm not sure what's going on. I don't want to know what it is this time. But Xena has never asked me for a dime. She knows, and you know, I don't loan money to friends. The only reason that Natalie girl got a quarter of a mil outta me was, I too had something to lose," Tina-Love said, dicing red potatoes. "Memphis, I need for you to get back with Xena. Our relationship doesn't work if all of us aren't in harmony."

If I could wave my hand in the air and start over from a year and some change ago, I would. But this tangled web was our reality. "I can't get with her while she's living with him." I showed Tina-Love the recent

"I love you" text messages I'd exchanged with Z.

"Oh, I see you're trying. But that's insufficient." Tina-Love spoke to me with disdain like never before. "I'm your friend regardless, but you men mistreat women, then expect them to sit on the sideline until you're ready to put us back on your team. All Natalie wanted was an apology that was probably well deserved, but no! I had to pay her off for your ass when you're the one who had your dick all up and through every hole you could fit it in."

Wow. What was the rant really about? How long had Tina-Love been holding in all of this animosity toward me? Red potatoes browned in a skillet. Seasoned chicken sizzled. She put her wrist into scrambling egg whites.

"You were wrong for telling Xena to go back to Adonis when you know she wanted to move in with you. You dangled a fucking carat then you changed your mind about everything, including the engagement ring. And make sure you give me that back."

Damn, I forgot I had that. It was probably worth what I needed and more. Problem solved. Tina-Love didn't need that diamond. Ole Rico was going to ice her up.

"If you're such a friend to Z, why is Rico

Suave here?" I asked. "And Z isn't."

"Get out of my face with that. And don't come back unless I invite you." Tina-Love put the cast-iron skillet filled with chicken in the oven, closed the door.

I was hungry as hell. "Listen, I apologize. You have no idea what I'm dealing with. Make me a to-go and I'm out."

"Good-bye, Memphis. When you stop making everything about you, let me know." Her phone chimed. She picked it up. "Ugh! Now Adonis?"

I demanded to know, "What the fuck he want?"

"I can tell you what he doesn't want and that's your fist in his face." Tina-Love looked up at me. Her eyes were a combination of ice and coal.

For the first time in five years, I was in the doghouse with both Z and Tina-Love.

Tina-Love stood at the bottom of the staircase, then shouted, "Ricardo, baby. Come."

She fetched his ass like a dog and he came hangin' and swangin'. She could have him. I left her house, got in my car. Waiting for Tina-Love's gate to open, I did not want to see lover-boy's dick ever again.

Picturing another man's dick disgusted me.

Chapter 49
Tina-Love

Café M, a hidden gem in the heart of downtown Savannah, gave me what I called "A Piece of Paris" at their French bakery. I hadn't been to my favorite shop in a while. Wouldn't be here now, if I weren't waiting for Adonis to arrive.

The quaint space had a dozen round tables, including the two that were outdoors. Best for the conversation that would occur shortly to take place outside, to avoid eavesdroppers. Scanning a familiar menu, I knew that Memphis would've ordered two peanut butter and banana sandwiches.

"I'd like to have the pink almond praline croissant, fresh fruit, and a cup of coffee," I told the waitress.

A text registered from Ricardo, **are you interested in a foursome tonight?**

I replied, **no.** I had to maintain control of who entered my home. Ricardo could choose sex partners when we were in Rome at his place.

"Excuse me, before you leave, I'll have the bacon and cheese quiche with a cup of Bombay chai," Adonis said, then sat across from me. "Thank you for agreeing to meet with me. How's Xena?"

"I'm doing well, thank you for asking." He needed to slow his ass down. I was not Xena.

"Oh, I apologize Mrs.," he sarcastically said. Clearing his throat, he shouted the word, "Ms," then continued in a normal tone with "Jones."

If I dipped his head again, this time it'd be down to the gutter. Ignorant men take cheap shots at women, believing somewhere in their distorted heads, they were superior.

Standing, I picked up my wristlet and strutted in the direction of my car.

Adonis leapt from his seat, scurried in my tracks, then grabbed my bicep. "I sincerely apologize. Please, don't leave. I need to know about Xena."

I guess stalking my bestie wasn't working for him. He had his BMW and all of her belongings in his possession and he still didn't have Xena. Men.

"Make this your last time putting your hand on me without prior permission."

Adonis let go, raised both palms. "You're

right. Let me apologize a thousand times in advance."

Sighing heavily, I returned to the table. Reclaimed my seat. Sat on the edge. Adonis sat, pressed his thighs and knees together. His attire was equally uptight. A pair of khakis, a striped button-down shirt, brown leather loafers. Adonis looked at his phone, then stared at me.

Our waitress placed our beverages and food on the table, then left. I inhaled the robust aroma of the dark roast, took a sip. Closing my eyes, I let the flavor marinate on my taste buds.

"Whew. This is perfection in a cup," I said, then opened my eyes.

His stare was intense, mouth was gapped.

Snapping my fingers, I let him know, "Adonis, Xena is no longer interested in you. I'm not sure she ever was." I added that last part. I bit into the croissant, and it was amazing. "This is award-winning deliciousness with a capital 'd.' "

Adonis's face exhibited no expressions. "Tina-Love. How's Xena?"

"Busy. She'd like to have her great-grandmother's rocker," I said, switching back to my morning joe.

"That's at Memphis's house," he said.

Standing over Adonis, I questioned, "You

sure that's where the chair is located?"

"Okay, wait. Sit. She can have it back. All I want is for Xena to bring my child home. Please don't stop her from doing the right thing," he said, reversing his condescending tone.

I didn't have time for this bullshit. This time, strutting away, I was done. Adonis wrapped his hand around my bicep again. I swung backward without looking at him. This was what disrespect earned him.

"Ow! Damn. You lucky I don't hit females," he said, then yelled, "That's why your pussy is all over the Internet. You're not a model! You're a whore. Stop trying to make Xena like you!"

"And you're why Xena killed your baby!" I told his inconsiderate ass.

Soon as I'd lied on Xena, I regretted it. My ego insisted that I keep walking. Turning on my engine, I checked my social media pages.

Hot and sweet! *The Shady Café* was lit with nude pictures of . . . me?

CHAPTER 50
XENA

Cement mattress or my room at my parents'.

"You're going on a date with a man that's a half century your senior? That's a sin, Xena Trinity," my mom stated, as though I'd need to repent for the age difference if I broke bread publicly with a man older than her.

Standing in the middle of the living room, I refused to sit anywhere. "You're right." As always. "But it's a date and I've been in the house all day. I'll call you when we leave the restaurant."

Somewhere in my mother's mind, I was sure she was more concerned with what her family and friends would think of her, if they saw me out on a date with a man who could've graduated high school with Grandpa.

Although my mom never congratulated me on my accomplishments, I was proud of myself. Our client had the most extravagant African wedding yesterday. Each of the men were fashion-show ready. A few of the guys were single and close to my age. I'd overheard each of them boasting how they were courting multiple women. The best part was, we acquired new business, two more weddings.

I'd decided to lease an apartment prior to my operations. Or perhaps a seasoned gentleman may be exactly what I needed. I could rent space in his house, and I wouldn't have to tend to his manly desires.

"Couldn't get up in time to worship the Lord and pay your tithes, but you have time for a date? That's a sin, Xena. And go get a scarf. Got your shoulders naked. What're tryna do? Get a stranger aroused?"

A shawl covered Mama's thighs, draped over her feet. The duster was the snap-in-front kind. Wig crooked. Her glasses rested on the tip of her nose.

"You're right again." I went to my room. Grabbed the first shawl I saw.

I knew from observing how Dad dealt with Mom, long as I led with "you're right," or "yes, ma'am," my mom would stop yelling and performing sermons.

"Where're you going?" she asked, occupying most of the doorway.

364

Exiting sideways onto the porch, I answered, "The Chart House."

"Oh, so he has a pot to piss in, huh? Chart House closes at nine. Bring your dad and me one of those shrimp, crab, avocado, and mango towers. And a hot chocolate lava cake. We'll share."

On a warm summer night of nearly eighty degrees, she shivered, then added, "I'm not going to wait up for you all night. Be back by ten. Seafood spoils quick and you know your father has a sensitive stomach." She didn't wait for a response. I heard the lock click.

The driver opened the door. I hiked up the hem of my dress, sat next to a gentleman who didn't appear a day over sixty-five. His hairline had a hint of gray, but not his brows. He had no mustache. No beard. That was good.

"You look ravishing. Topez told me you were beautiful. That truly was an understatement," he said, then asked, "Are you cold? I can have my driver increase the temperature."

I'd forgotten I'd draped myself in the cover-up like a mummy. "No, thanks." I removed the scarf, folded it, then placed it beside me on the seat.

"Allow me to formally introduce myself,"

he said, extending a handshake. "I'm Helly."

Frowning, I thought, *What kind of name is that.* "That's not —"

"Now before you say anything else. Let me explain. My government is Bailey Thornton the third. I was a rather mischievous lad. Whenever I was left unattended, I'd have my hands in something." He laughed.

I listened.

"Cooking oil, motor oil, dirt, mud, my parents' naughty toy box. I was quite the curious one. My mom said 'Aw hell' a lot. Then she started demanding somebody watch Helly. How about you?" Bailey asked.

Saved by the driver who'd parked our car on West Bay Street, then opened the doors, I did not have to respond. Bailey walked around to my side, extended his hand. "Shall we, my dear?"

The hostess greeted him by first and last names (no nicknames), escorted us to a table with a water view. "Your waitress will be right with you."

"Where were we," he said. "Oh, yes. Your turn to share a story about your childhood," he said.

Of all the topics to discuss, I was not allowing myself to relive a horror scene. "I don't know. Let me think about that," I said, noticing we were the only two in our section.

"Thinking is all there is to do, unless one meditates. Are you meditating?" he asked.

I laughed continuously, trying to remember the last time a man had made me laugh. I couldn't remember. "My childhood is rather depressing. Can I defer?"

"I insist," he said.

The waitress brought a bottle of champagne, filled two flutes, then whisked away.

Offering me a glass, he held up his.

"A toast." He smiled.

I mirrored his expression.

"I'm eighty. I'm healthy. I don't take any medications. No high blood pressure, cholesterol, diabetes, restless leg syndrome." He paused, smiled. Continued with, "Well, I think I do have restless leg syndrome." He chuckled. "Sometimes."

Knowing that some men in powerful positions were sexually assaulting women, I didn't find humor in his last comment. Plus, Topez said Bailey wasn't interested in having sex.

"To health. Most people don't have it for the same reason most people aren't successful. They don't want to work hard. I like your work ethic, young lady," Bailey said.

Tipping my glass to his, I wondered what

I could've done differently to avoid possibly getting cancer. "To health."

The waiter placed a seafood tower on the table, the kind my mother wanted me to bring home. I was not getting a to-go order on a first date at a five-star restaurant to please her.

According to Topez, Bailey was wealthy and accomplished. Had two sons, and two daughters, older than me. "What exactly are you interested in?" was my indirect way of inquiring about his livelihood.

"Living. Loving. Enjoying companionship with a wonderful woman like yourself. Certain things in life gives me clarity. Aging is one of them. I'm closer to the end than my beginning. I'm not Benjamin Button, though I've outlived two wives. Figured the third one had to be young enough to outlive me. And you?" he asked.

So Bailey was interested in getting married. He was too old for me, but Tina-Love's mother might be okay with it if she were single.

"Can I be direct with you?" I felt my eyes tearing.

Bailey held my hand, bowed his head. "God the Father, all-knowing, all merciful, I ask that you allow this union to grow into a loving friendship that will give me what I need, but most importantly, give me the insight to selflessly give Xena Trinity the love, patience, and understanding that she needs. Amen."

There was a lump in my throat. I picked mango from the bottom of the tower. Bailey went for the shrimp and crab on top.

"You know the difference between a young fool and an old fool?" Bailey asked, breaking our silence.

Squinting, I gave a half smile.

"Well, at least I can tell you're not meditating. That's good. The difference is . . ." He paused, then said, "Nothing."

I laughed. "I get the point, some men are fools forever."

"Never lie with a fool. You'll wake up with fleas," he said, delving into the crab section again. "I was a foolish boy. Never a foolish man. Real men are responsible. I'll be honest with you, Xena. I've done pretty good for myself. Businesswise. I enjoy marriage. I miss both of my wives. I don't like going to bed by myself. With all of my riches, I'm lonely. Lost most of my hair and my teeth are fake. Have gout in both feet."

The avocado was delicious. I mixed the next bite with mango. I was definitely revisiting this restaurant.

"Thankful for toupees and dental implants. I'm well preserved. Xena, look at me. But don't touch. If you break me, I'm all yours."

I was listening. Shifted my eyes from the tower to Bailey. He had a full head of hair and he walked just fine.

"Hear me. I'm looking for a wife. A nice, respectful woman with morals. You don't have to be a Christian, but you must believe in a higher power. All you're picking at are the vegetables. You haven't touched the best part."

"What if I told you, I may have cancer, and I might be dying?" There, I'd said it.

Bailey held then kissed the back of my hand. "I'd say we should've eaten dessert first. And let's get married tomorrow."

CHAPTER 51
TINA-LOVE

How in the fuck! did she get nude pictures of me! I texted Memphis. **I'm going to the station to beat her ass! And you're next!**

After removing my stilettoes, jewelry, and dress, I cornrowed my hair into four braids. I stepped into my sweatpants and Giuseppe sneakers, and put on a wifebeater.

Ricardo's eyes widened. Quickly he dressed in salmon-colored slacks and a polo shirt, then stepped into brown leather loafers.

"Baby, take a deep breath," Ricardo calmly said. "Let's reset and meditate. Let me give you a massage. We don't have all the facts."

Ugh! I snatched my designer purse. What was a fact was the day Memphis returned from Chula Vista, I've been involved in his bullshit. Trying to protect him had cost me a quarter of a million that I might never get back. Then he strolled into my house and asked for sixty thousand. On top of his inconsiderate ass fucking up his life by fucking over Natalie, I was being humiliated.

Xena wasn't in the best situation with Adonis, but she had stability when they were together. My bestie went from a good environment to sleeping on concrete to living with her mother, whom she hated. Meanwhile, Memphis's ass dangled carats without committing to our gurl. Xena may have been about to be diagnosed with cancer and he was clueless.

"You stay here," I told Ricardo. "I'ma handle that bitch."

"If you must go, you're too upset to operate a vehicle. I'm driving," he insisted, following me to the garage.

"Fine! Drive fast," I demanded, thankful he'd taken control of the wheel.

Ricardo drove at and below every speed limit. The first ten minutes in traffic, I was livid. Starting to take deep breaths, I began to calm down.

No response from Memphis.

"Good, my love. Keep breathing. When we get there, remain calm, cool, and collected. I can ask the questions if you'd like," he said, holding my hand.

Anxious, I pulled my hand away. "I'm kicking her ass whenever we get there." I couldn't recall being this angry since I'd been raped. That motherfucker and my mother weren't shit!

An invitation to her radio station was not necessary, when she was responsible for my pussy floating in the cloud. I saw Memphis entering the lobby.

"Stop here," I told Ricardo.

He slowed down, I hopped out the car. Rolled up on Memphis.

"Fuck you, Memphis. You knew about this shit!" I said, shoving him in the chest.

"I swear I had nothing to do with that. I wasn't even at your house!" He grabbed my wrist. "Calm down!"

"Don't raise your voice at me." Breaking free, I was ready to punch him in his face. But doing so, I'd never make it up to where I really wanted to be.

A security guard approached us. "I have to tell both of you to leave. Now."

"I'm not going anywhere, until @DDD Shade bring her bitch ass down here and explain why she's talking about my pussy on her show with her shady stank ass."

"Miss, please," security pleaded.

"What you don't want is for me to expose her trifling ass. Either you let us upstairs or we're coming back with my fans to protest her show. That bitch isn't the only one who could bury someone's reputation. Trust and believe me."

"I'll have to get permission first. Wait here," security insisted.

"Tina-Love, you've got to stop. There's a better way to handle this," Memphis said. "Let's leave."

"When you get a one-point-five million-dollar gig canceled, then you tell me let's go."

I was two seconds away from slapping Memphis. He should've given me all the deets, and I would've gladly gone against my rule and loaned him the sixty thousand.

"Trust me," Memphis said. "Confronting @DDDShade is only going to increase her ratings."

Hell, mine, too. I knew a lot of people were waiting for someone to take this low-life ho down.

"What if your dick was all over the Internet and you got" — I hopped back, kicked up to his face — "out of the competition. You'd see it my way, I'm sure."

Memphis caught my sneaker. Lowering my foot, Memphis reassured me, "I have a plan."

I grabbed my shoe. A guy stepped off the elevator, approached us. "Wait, Memphis. This went wrong. My wife is going to clear

Tina-Love's name in tomorrow morning's segment."

"Who the fuck is this?" I asked Memphis.

"I'm @DDDShade's husband. Rick. We need to talk. This is all one big misunderstanding. Here's my card. Meet us at my house after the show, say two o'clock?" he asked, all polite and shit.

"We'll be there," Memphis said.

"Thanks, man. No worries. We're going to straighten this out, Tina-Love. We love you." Rick jogged to the elevator.

A text registered from Xena, **I met the most amazing man!**

I replied, **Cool. That's a good thing. Let's meet for dinner.**

I'm not ready to introduce him to anyone but I can dine with you later this week. Sorry about the video with you and Adonis and the nude photos of you, she responded.

Memphis followed me outside. "You keep looking down you're going to trip and fall," he said.

Did that shit already. I was not suggesting to Xena I wanted to meet whatever guy she'd met. He, like Adonis, would never replace fucked-up Memphis. I sent another text, **Have you communicated with Memphis since he wouldn't let you stay at his place?**

No. You? she hit back.

I lied, **No.**

Adonis? she asked.

Again, I lied. **No.**

"What's up with all the divided attention?" Memphis playfully reached for my cell.

I pulled my phone closer to my body. Nothing was funny about this situation. Ricardo parked curbside, got out, opened the passenger door.

Staring into Memphis's eyes, I said, "Question?"

Memphis fingered one of my braids. "I'm listening."

"If all you had were Xena, no stardom, no upcoming world competition. And she was the designer every celebrity wanted to wear on the red carpet, would you still love her the same? Be honest."

Staring above my head, Memphis answered, "I've always been my own man. Never thought of our relationship ending up like that."

That was my point. Most men never viewed themselves as the underdog.

"Well, think of your future like that. Exactly like that. Because if I go down, I'm dragging your ass with me. See you at two."

CHAPTER 52
XENA

"Someone had one glass too many." Bailey raised the sheet above my shoulders.

"Oh my goodness. The last thing I remember is eating in reverse. Dessert, first. I'm clear on that. Then there were our entrees. You had steak. I ordered —"

"A loaded baked potato. I've never seen that many vegetables on top of a potato." Sitting on the side of the bed, Bailey laughed.

I did too. "No, wait. I vaguely recall getting in the car and your —" I sat up, braced my back to the pillow. "Thanks for not taking me home intoxicated —"

If only for the moment, I wanted, make that needed, to be here.

"Again," he added. "You're a lightweight. From now on, one glass of red wine is all you can have. I'm getting the impression you don't want to go home."

Bailey was right. His home was peaceful.

Had great energy. Eventually I'd have to have the operation and my parents would care for me or my mom would kill me for insurance money. Sad that I believed that was true. I loved my dad, but Bailey was right. The thought of going back made me feel like my future would be one failure after another.

"That's what friends are for. To do what's best for one another." His words drew me from my thoughts to his presence.

In his opinion, we were friends. If I agreed, I'd have Memphis, Tina-Love, Topez, and Bailey. Four total. Adonis was not my enemy, but he was not on my list of allies.

"I hope I didn't embarrass you." I waved the sheet to the opposite side of the bed. "Oh, shit!" I uncovered then covered my naked body. "Where are my clothes?"

"It's a good thing they're not where you left them, or they'd be in the middle of my bedroom floor. I hung them behind the bathroom door. You get cleaned up. I'll cook breakfast." Bailey exited.

I heard the clicking of his slippers down the steps. Sounded as though tape was on the bottom. I picked up my cell to call my mother. When had I texted with Tina-Love? I read the history, didn't recall any of it.

Read a text from Adonis. **Is it true? You killed our child?**

Instead of calling my mom, I went inside the bathroom that was inside the bedroom, and closed the door. I phoned Adonis.

"I'm tired of playing games with you, Xena," he answered. "Did you or did you not have an abortion?"

Calmly I told him, "No, I did not."

"Somebody's lying! This is no joking matter. Why would your best friend say you killed our child, if it isn't true?" Adonis's outcry startled me.

I lowered the volume, started running water in the oversize oval-shaped tub, hoping Bailey couldn't hear me. "Adonis, I did not terminate my pregnancy."

Sniffling, he said, "So, you are pregnant. That's a relief."

"No, I'm not," I said.

"Bitch!" he shouted. "Stop playing with my mind. What is it, Xena? Where are you?" I heard shuffling noises in the background.

"I can't answer that." Quickly I went into my settings and turned off my location.

Adonis yelled, "You are going to piss on another stick, in front of me! Today! Where are you?!"

I shouted, "I don't have to prove anything to you!"

Knock. Knock. Knock was followed by the door opening, and Bailey saying, "Sweetheart, you okay?"

"Who the fuck is that!" Adonis yelled.

I ended the call. Told Bailey, "I'm fine. I'll be down shortly."

"I don't care who that was. Sweetheart, remember this. A man who does not love himself is incapable of loving you. But a man who loves himself, can love you more than he loves himself. One is suicidal. The other is homicidal. I've prepped everything, I'll cook when you're done. Take your time."

Bailey left the door open. I did too. Adonis called back. I silenced my phone. I'd contact my mother and my so-called best friend later.

Surely, Adonis thought that I was with Memphis.

I begrudgingly put on the same clothes. That was all I had, underwear included.

I joined Bailey in the kitchen. "Your home could use a designer's touch," I said.

"Have at it. My last two wives decorated their way. Won't treat you any differently. Xena, I want you to stay here. Move in whatever, not whomever, you'd like."

"You deserve better," I said.

"It doesn't get any better than you. You're focused. You're on the right track. I want to help support your dream. But I am too old to date a different woman every time I want to go out. If you're not interested in being my companion, I respect that. We can amicably part ways today. But first, I cannot permit you to leave without experiencing my famous cooking."

We held hands as Bailey said grace. I stacked two pancakes, topped with lots of fresh strawberries, and finished it with whipped cream. Bailey doubled his pancakes, drowned them in cane syrup, dropped four strips of crispy bacon next to three scrambled eggs.

"You might be disease-free, but with all the meat you eat, I'm worried about your arteries, and your colon" I said, then added, "No disrespect."

Bailey nodded. Slid a key to my side of the table. "It's for you. If you're coming back, take it. If not, leave it."

If he did this with every woman he went out with, why was I here? "I do like you. I don't want to burden you with my health complications."

"Let me tell you a story. There was a lady, similar to you, who had cancer. Doctor told her she had six months to live. She believed the doctor and proved him right. There was another lady, similar to you, who had cancer. Doctor told her she had six months to live. She believed the only One that knew for certain was God. I heard her say, 'Lord, let thy will be done on earth. But don't fault me, Lord. I'm not going out without a fight.' One died six months later, as she believed her doctor. The other lived for ten years."

I needed to hear that. "Thanks for breakfast. I have to go to the shop. Can I accept the key, and think about it?"

Bailey smiled. "Are you meditating?"

I gave him a warm and loving embrace as though he was my grandfather.

"I'd like more of those," he said.

"Me too, Bailey. Me too."

CHAPTER 53
MEMPHIS

"Coach, you think you can get me transferred to a different training facility?" Too many distractions occurred being home.

Z vanished. Wasn't hitting me back. Must've gone back to Adonis. Tina-Love ain't had no more love for me, but she'd committed to that Rico Suave nigga. Put him first. I would've been better off staying in Cali chilling with Natalie.

Tina-Love agreed to pay Rick and @DDDShade a smooth sixty thousand dollars to clean up her post and do a public apology. How many hush dollas did they need? Damn! I wasn't done with those schemers. Glad that situation was under control though.

"I'm ahead of you, MB. If we stay here, you're doomed. Should get an answer soon. You stay to yourself. The only person you need to be around is your mother. In fact, I suggest you move in with your mother, until we receive clearance to bail out of Savannah." Patting me on the shoulder, Coach Richie said, "See you at six in the morning."

Had to shut shit all the way down.

Practice with Coach had ended at noon. I called out, "Please help me, Lord!" I pumped my arms. My cheeks, lips, every part of my face jolted. Leaning back, my wings spread like an eagle. Planting my feet on the all-weather field, I stood straight, made a U-turn.

Jogging to the starting line, I got down on one knee. In my head I announced, on your mark, get set. Heard the *pow!* Took off running.

Did the one hundred.

"Again!"

Did the two hundred.

"Again!"

Did the three hundred and the four hundred dash, picking up speed as though I were the last one in the relay and everyone was depending on me for each of us to win gold.

I repeated each meter. My mind said *go* again. My body collapsed on the grass inside the track. Interlocking my fingers behind my head, I bent my knees, stared up at the sky. The sun was blazing. Humidity suffocating. I let the sweat roll off my skin. This was the perfect time to bounce out of Savannah before somebody new started kicking dirt in my face.

Splash!

"What the fuck?" I said, going from horizontal to vertical in two seconds.

"So you convinced Xena to get an abortion?" Adonis questioned.

This light-skinned motherfucker had a death wish, throwing ice water on me. "Of course I asked, but I didn't make her do shit."

"Well, she did. And she's already got another man," Adonis said.

Loosening up, I shook my arms, legs. "Good for her." If that were true, he'd shared the unknown with me. "All I need to know is, y'all done? 'Cause he gon' learn like you, ain't no competition when it comes to Memphis Brown."

"If I were done, would I be here?" Adonis walked away. His head hung low.

He may have been bold, but that nigga wasn't stupid. I got in my car, drove to Xena's mother's house. If it was true that Xena had an abortion, she'd done it for us.

I tapped on Mrs. Trinity's door. Saw her moving about. Maybe she hadn't heard. I knocked harder. Heard the lock click.

Waited. Noticed her moving about again.

"See what the boy wants," I heard Mr. Trinity say.

"It's not what, it's whom. She ain't here and I ain't got nothing for him, not even my words."

Damn. Like that? What did I ever do to her?

Mr. Trinity joined me on the porch. "Hey, son. Xena isn't here right now."

"Thanks for letting me know. When will she be home? I'd like to speak with her in person."

"That's the million-dollar question, son. If you find out, let us know," he said, staring at the cars passing by.

"Is she okay?" I asked.

"Oh, she texts to let us know she's doing well. Said he's taking her to her appointment." Mr. Trinity finally looked at me with sad eyes.

"He? Who? And you're sure you don't know where she's at? What appointment?" I asked, pissed that Z would do this to me again.

"Some girl stuff. My wife says Xena has to go see the gynecologist."

Mr. Trinity was kind. He spoke in a soft tone. How he ended up with Mrs. Trinity was obvious. That woman was a boss and a bitch. Not a boss bitch like Tina-Love.

"Thanks," I said, not wanting to be rude. She was doing her thang. Needed to wait on Coach Richie to give me my departure date and new location. Z could find out I was gone the same way I learned she had a new man. A new fucking man already!

If Z had an abortion, she wouldn't have to see her gynecologist. She must've lied to dude to get rid of him. Tired of trying to figure out Z's bullshit, I got in my car. Driving to my mom's, I called Tina-Love.

Got her voice mail, *"Ricardo and I are busy right —"*

I couldn't push the end button fast enough.

I texted her, **Who in the fuck is that outgoing message for! Change it!**

CHAPTER 54
XENA

"This is the hardest thing I've done," I said, holding Bailey's hand.

The room was cold. I was freezing. My body was covered with chill bumps, and I had to drink one more eight-ounce glass of the thickest, nastiest liquid that should not be for human consumption, especially downing and keeping it down without throwing up for one hour.

"You're not doing it alone. Your parents are in the waiting room. I'm going to win them over. By the time you're done, your mother will forget I'm old enough to be her father."

Smiling, I said, "Make her call you daddy."

"That would be weird," Bailey said.

Two weeks ago, I didn't need anyone, but Bailey was my angel, Tina-Love was my bestie, and Memphis would always have my heart. God gave me the right person today. Memphis couldn't handle the thought of my potentially being terminally ill. I prayed Tina-Love hadn't told him.

"I agree, that would sound creepy. I'll be happy if for once I can prove that mean lady wrong."

Mrs. Trinity. She didn't deserve to have me call her Mom. She didn't like anyone, including my dad. She always had a nasty attitude. Had to be right, even when she knew she wasn't. If she didn't acknowledge Bailey was good to and for me, she could not deny seeing how this man was caring for me today.

"Bailey works well. In fact, I insist she call me by my first name." Bailey gave me a lightweight hug. "Don't throw up. Drink up. I'm going to let the specialists do their job. When you're done, I'll be right here waiting to take you home."

I was scared and didn't want him to leave. I wished my surgery was today. Swallowing all of this for a CT. Waiting for the results from the CT knowing the operation was imminent, I wanted to zip-line from start to finish.

"But." Squeezing his finger tight, I said, "I may not to be able to have any babies," I cried.

"Hush now. You can adopt mine. All four of them. And they can call you Mommy," he said chuckling. "I'd get a kick out of that. They're waiting to close my coffin so they can fight over what they didn't earn. And will not inherit."

I whispered, "Oh, shit," then covered my mouth to prevent throwing up. As their stepmother, I'd be younger than them. Now, that was odd.

Bailey eased his finger out of my grip, pointed up. "Remember who's in charge. I love you."

"I love you too." Was I sincere? Or had I said it for the reasons I always said it?

Did I have feelings for Bailey as a result of his generosity? I knew there were good men in the world, but this man was beyond what I'd imagined. He was like my angel on earth. He didn't come packaged in an athletic frame with bulging muscles, like Memphis. Or four years older with controlling ways, like Adonis.

The technician approached me. "Xena, it's time to go to the imaging room. Keep taking deep breaths. That'll help you relax."

Entering another cold room, the technician handed me another glass of berry-flavored chalky substance to drink. "We're going to get started. If at any time you feel overwhelmed, let me know."

"Okay," I responded. "When will you have

the results?"

"In about three days. We'll call you in. Let's get started."

I was not afraid of being confined to small spaces. From five to nine, Mrs. Trinity did not believe in sparing the rod. When I'd become immune to her beating me, Mrs. Trinity would lock me in a dark closet for hours. That was when I began meditating, before I understood what that was.

I believe the only reason Bertha Trinity hadn't pushed me off the porch when I went on a first date with Bailey was Bailey and the driver were watching.

CHAPTER 55
MEMPHIS

Z please respond to my texts. I need to see you baby.

Was I that horrible of a man that the woman I was in love with refused to communicate with me? Had to admit, the past couple of days, staying focused during training, I'd gotten stronger and faster. Every second shaved off of my previous time had me closer to bowing for the bronze. Third place wasn't my goal.

Parking in front of Tina-Love's security box, I no longer had access. I had to text her, **I'm outside.**

The gate opened. The garage was closed. I parked in the driveway, same spot when I'd brought Natalie. I rang the doorbell. Hated this shit. Felt like a fucking visitor. If we didn't have business to discuss, I wouldn't be here.

"Come in. You look and smell good," Tina-Love said, extending a one-arm hug.

"Ricardo prepped the food. We can enjoy a cocktail on the terrace until dinner is served."

Tina-Love's red long-sleeved maxi wrap dress caressed her figure. It wasn't see-through. A decanter of fresh squeezed orange juice and a bottle of champagne were on the table. She filled my goblet with juice only, her flute with bubbly.

"How's it going with Rico Suave?" I asked, wanting yet not caring to hear her response.

Seriously she asked, "Have you heard from Xena?"

Sighing heavily, I shook my head. "You?"

She did the same. "Guess my bestie is upset with both of us."

"What do you think we could've done to avoid this?" Was Tina-Love going to fess up that her fucked-up "I'm going to get y'all back together" tactics weren't working? Tina-Love had hit a new low with me.

"Probably ninety-nine things could've been altered," she said. "But that doesn't mean the outcome would've been different. I miss the good parts of my mother. You ever miss anything about your dad?"

I frowned. Must've been all that chakra exploration that made her ask me some dumb shit like that. "You can't miss what you never had."

She politely responded, "That's not true."

Following her gaze, I noticed Peanut Butter and Faith chilling side by side. She sat quietly as though she was meditating eyes wide open.

Being hard was easy. Being soft was hard. Mom's love wasn't all I needed. I was good with Z and Tina-Love. Never thought I'd have to share either of them. "I-I —"

"Love is the one exception," Rico Suave said, carrying a stack of small plates and a large bowl. Tossing the salad, he added, "Didn't mean to interrupt. But all creatures crave love in the womb."

"Thanks, babe." Tina-Love leaned toward him with her lips puckered.

He could've given her a peck on the mouth, but his lips lingered. I counted to fifteen before he stood tall.

Preparing two servings, he placed one in front of Tina-Love, the other on my placemat, then said, "Even if you've never been loved by your father, Memphis, you still want to love him and you want him to love you. If you could control your desire to love him, you would. It's beyond your control. That's the honest reason that you hate him."

I stared through his fake ass. My daddy

was dead to me.

Tina-Love gently held my hand. "Ricardo has helped me accept that I do want a relationship with my mother. Maybe he can help you admit you want to contact your dad."

What had Rico Suave done to Tina-Love? I looked at him. This was not the Tina-Love that loved me. The shine in her eyes was for that nigga.

"When a person finds out they're adopted, one of the first questions in their mind is why did my parents give me away? What they really think is, why didn't they love me enough to keep me? Love manifests as hate and pain when we either don't receive the love we crave, or we're too angry or hurt to accept love. Deep inside, you want and need your daddy's acceptance."

I didn't need shit! I was good. On my way to getting world recognition. He'd show his ass up soon enough with his hand out. And when that day came, I'd take pleasure in disowning his ass in front of the world.

"If you want to do chakra work before you leave, let me know. I made a fish stew that is awesome." Ricardo's steps made it seem as though he were walking on air. Or was it eggshells?

I was done with my dad.

"Ricardo helped me not to be angry with you," Tina-Love said.

About what? "That's because you ain't got a reason to be mad at me." Yeah, that dude had to take his brainwashing when-in-Rome-do-as-the-Romans techniques back to Italy.

"When my naked video went viral, I wanted to kill you with a million vibrating dildos."

I laughed. She didn't.

"Seriously. Until my following increased by over a million. Women cheered for me. If you hadn't refused to let Xena move in with you as you'd promised, she wouldn't have come here with Adonis, and I wouldn't have shoved his face to my pussy. You follow?"

Hell nah! "Soooo, you're not accepting responsibility for your actions?" Guess dude hadn't taught her everything.

"You still don't get it. You're not accepting responsibility for yours," she said. "I missed out on seven figures because of you. Another two hundred and fifty because of you. And sixty grand. All because of you, and Memphis, you seriously act as though nothing is ever your fault."

"I never said that. You want me to believe I'm the only fucked-up one in this?" Tina-Love had a blemish on her face. Never saw that on her before.

"You're still in love with Xena. Yet you're still blaming her for the two of you not being together. Tell me I'm wrong," she said.

She was? "I'm not the one who aborted my baby. You have no idea how many times I've texted and called Z. You can't hold that against me. I'm taking initiative despite what she done. What is she doing? You know where she's at?"

"No."

"You heard from her?" I asked.

"No."

"Liar." I stood, tossed my napkin on top of my lettuce. "I'm going to my mom's and do like Z. Y'all don't need me. Don't contact me. I'll let myself out." I made slow strides toward the staircase, praying Tina-Love wouldn't let me go.

"You'll be back when you get used," Tina-Love stated. "Unless you want to keep paying Rick and @DDDShade money you haven't earned, that's up to you! But don't come to me to bail you out."

I never wanted to break ties with Tina-Love. There was something more making me return to her.

She knew Z's other secret. It was time I did too.

CHAPTER 56
TINA-LOVE

Rainey and Ricardo were God-sent.

"That's the best news I've received all week!" I told my agent, rejoicing on the inside.

The little girl in me that was abused was a long way from being healed. At times, I wasn't sure if she'd ever breathe again. Smile again. Genuinely love herself or anyone else.

"I'll get back to you today with the details on the runway show in Sydney. Pack your bags today. You're out on the first flight in the morning," she said. "Check your bank account."

Accessing the app on my phone, I was astounded! An eight-figure deposit was pending. I had my millions, a mansion, a man, but none of that would sustain my happiness if I did not have purpose. The little girl — think I'd name her Lovely — needed to stop hiding, she wanted to stop hurting.

My career gave me a reason to be excited, productive. Travel the world. Maybe I should start a modeling agency with Xena for girls like us. First, I had to get my bestie from under Topez's manipulation.

A text registered from Xena with an address of where she was. What did she want me to do?

"Hold on a moment," I said, placing Rainey on mute. Jumping into his arms, I wrapped my forty-inches around his waist, then I kissed Ricardo. "Say yes."

Rainey never managed my money. She taught me how to check and balance my accounts. I didn't believe in bailing people out of their financial hardships. But when their problems created issues for me, loaning Memphis money was necessary, and it came back to me in abundance. Rainey told me to loan and not give away what I'd earned. That way if the person, friend or not, didn't pay back, they couldn't come back and ask for more.

Smiling, he hugged me close. "Yes."

I was in a space where I wanted to share my blessings.

Unmuting the call, I told Rainey, "I'm going to need you to book a companion ticket."

"A what?" Rainey questioned. "Wait. Seriously. You have never."

"I know, right. I can't believe I'm in a committed relationship." Sounded strange hearing myself say that. "His name is Ricardo Salvatori," I said, giving her his passport number, and other pertinent information. "Can I say, I love and appreciate you, Rainey?"

"Go pack," she said, ending the call.

Not wanting to abandon my two friends, I'd reach out to Memphis. My next priority was Xena. I wasn't calling or texting her back. Ricardo and I would arrive at the address she'd given me.

Ricardo parked in the circular driveway near a water fountain with a statue of a naked Greek god. I stared at his thick hair, muscular physique, and small penis.

Was this where Xena was? Was this a resort for healing?

"Holy incredible. That is Zeus," Ricardo said, staring up. "There are no coincidences. Before we enter this place, we have to channel our energy here," he said, holding my hands.

I'd learned not to question Ricardo's spontaneity when it came to universal awareness. I was fixated on the water shooting eight feet in the air, then drenching Zeus's body.

"It makes sense that Xena would be here." Gently squeezing my fingers, Ricardo explained, "Zeus is ruler of the sky and thunder. And ruler of the Olympian gods."

I held on but had to admit, "I don't get it."

"Olympian. Memphis. Omnipotent. Zeus. Xena. Their path to reuniting is rooted here. Close your eyes."

Five minutes later we opened our eyes to a tall, handsome, much, much, much older man in the doorway. "Come in. Xena told me a friend might stop by. She did not tell me it was Savannah's international supermodel, Tina-Love Jones and company. I would've worn my shoes from Paris," he said, pronouncing it *Pear-ree*.

Xena Trinity had landed on her feet again. I was getting all the deets. I said, "You're charming, Mister . . . ?"

"How rude of me. Bailey Thornton. Not the first or the second but third here."

"Shut the front door," I gasped. "*The* Bailey Thornton, whose family owns Thorntonville?" I asked, holding his hand. "This is my significant one, Ricardo Salvatori."

Greeting Ricardo, Bailey whispered, "Let's not tell Xena who I really am," he whispered. "Right this way."

That lucky bitch had struck oil and gold, and she probably didn't know this man's net worth was half a billion dollars. I followed him to a boutique room where Xena was sitting at a machine sewing. He tapped on the doorframe.

"Sweetheart, your friend is here. I'll be upstairs if you need me. Nice meeting you, Ms. Jones and Mr. Salvatori."

"Our pleasure," I responded, then gave Xena a warm embrace. "How are you doing? And is this the man Topez hooked you up with?"

A woman entered the room, set up tea for three. She returned with a tray of crumpets. I told her, "Thank you." She nodded, then quietly left.

Ricardo greeted Xena with a hug. "Good to see you again. You are in the right place," he said. "I'll let you two have your privacy, babe." Kissing me, he exited the room.

I closed the French doors. The crumpets could wait. "You look good, but how do you feel? What did the doctor tell you?"

"Whether I have cancer or not isn't conclusive," she said, sprinkling fresh crushed tea leaves into a tea ball. She lowered the infuser into her pot of hot water. Mine remained untouched.

We sat next to each other on a white Victorian love seat. I was facing her, and our knees touched. She sipped a few times.

"I don't get it." I gazed at her. Her hair was tucked behind her ears. No lipstick.

"Me either. I eat well. I don't smoke. Seldom drink. My CT scan showed a mass on one ovary, but they won't know if I have cancer for sure until after they operate." Xena repeated, "After."

My heart started beating rapidly. I expected her to cry. She didn't. She sipped with her pinky finger extended. That was new. I wanted to smile, but the timing was off.

"I have to leave tomorrow morning for a show in Sydney. When is your operation?"

Calmly she spoke. "A week from today. I'll be okay. Bailey is taking me."

It may have been an inappropriate time, but peeping over my shoulder, then turning toward my bestie, I had to say it. "You must see Memphis before your surgery. I'll set it up. And what's your intentions with Bailey?" Memphis was young, but old money never aged.

Sipping from her cup, Xena gazed up at me. "You think I'll live to make my debut at New York Fashion Week?" she asked. Still not a single teardrop.

I shed a few, sucked in my lips. Had to stay strong for her. "Of course you will. And your bestie will be there cheering you on. One better, if you want, I'll walk your runway."

That was the beautiful smile I wanted to see. The icing was the shine in Xena's eyes.

"Tina-Love, do me a favor." Xena put down her cup, held my hands. "Don't tell Memphis. I don't want him worrying about me. He needs to stay focused on bringing home all those gold medals."

I blinked several times. At a moment when she should be totally focused on herself, she was concerned about our guy. I was too. "Do you still love him?"

Xena looked into my eyes. "I will always love Memphis Brown. God made it that way."

I nodded, thinking me too. God sent me Ricardo. This was my first time experiencing love for a man. I was ready to forgive my mother? Why not?

Standing, I told my bestie, "Don't just sit there, give me a tour of this *Coming to America* estate."

I followed her on a damn near ten-thousand-square-foot museum tour. This bitch didn't know what she had, but I sure as hell did. "Thanks, bestie. We have to pack for our morning departure. I'm a text away, if you need me."

Escorting us to the foyer, Xena softly said, "I love you, Tina-Love Jones. If I can forgive my mother, you can try. Just try. And please, can you respect what I asked of you? Just this one time. Please."

"Honey," Bailey said to Xena, then nodded at me. "A person can never be greater than their character. Whatever it is, if you can't put it in your pocket and take it with you, don't worry about it."

Hadn't thought about it that way. Didn't know why I never held Xena's secrets when it came to Memphis. "Thanks, Mr. Thornton." I shook his hand.

"Call me Bailey," he insisted, giving me a hug.

I requested of Bailey, "Put my number in your phone. If our friend needs anything at all, call me first."

"Thanks for coming by, bestie. I'm going upstairs. Bailey, sweetheart. Can you escort Tina-Love and Ricardo to her car?"

"Anything for you, my love," he said to Xena, then told me, "Have a great show in Sydney."

What was it about Xena Trinity that consistently attracted men who genuinely loved and would do anything for her?

CHAPTER 57
XENA

Tina-Love arranged what I'd wanted before undergoing my procedure. A face-to-face with Memphis.

"You gon' let me eat your cherry?" he whispered.

Tilting my head backward, playfully I shifted my eyes left and right, then slapped his chest. I met him here to tell him my fate. If I didn't, Tina-Love would beat me to it.

"Gurl, you know you want this," Memphis boasted, then mouthed, *dick.* Dropping the change in the tip jar, he placed his hand around my waist.

"Look, guys! It's Mr. Memphis! Can I have your autograph, please?" a little boy with wide innocent eyes pleaded.

"That's Mr. Memphis Brown. I call him Flash," said another boy, who made a swish motion, quickly stretching his arm high above his head. "Can I have your autograph too?"

"Me three!" an adult shouted.

"Me four!" an adolescent girl said.

A second line formed along the wall next to posters of Morgan Freeman, Ben Affleck, *The Sum of All Fears. Paycheck. Bound by Honor.* And, ended at *Bless the Child.* Moms, dads, and children anxiously awaited their turn to get a signature on napkins, forearms, or clothes. Many posed for a photo with Memphis while praising him for starting his nonprofit. An elderly man and woman cut the line, had their minute with Memphis, then eased to the front of the line and ordered their food.

After Memphis patted the last lil boy on the back, the manager graciously remade our orders, then escorted us to a round steel table with two metal chairs curbside on East Broughton Street. I smoothed my nude-colored sleeveless dress underneath my thighs, then sat.

"You not slick. I'm waiting for my answer." His smile gave shine to the sun beaming down on us. He stuck his finger in my sundae, licked it clean. Smiled again. Took a big bite out of his chocolate raspberry sandwich.

Leopold's Ice Cream held lots of fond memories for us. Although it's been here since 1919, the food and prices remained family friendly.

"I want to make love to you, Z. Tonight. Can we make that happen?" This bite was different. Memphis shoved the cookie in his mouth, slowly eased it out. The only thing left was dough.

I laughed recalling the first time he'd attempted that, he spat it in his hands, handed it to me. "Yeah, you'd better stop or we're making love in your SUV," I joked. His car was at the meter in front of us.

It had been over a year since we'd made love until we fell asleep in each other's arms. More than a year since I'd been fucked to sleep. Sometimes me on top of Memphis or him on me. Sex at my shop wasn't close to our norm.

At his house, we'd awaken and pick up where we'd left off. What my ex enjoyed most nights was spooning. In the beginning, he'd ask me to hold him. A few months into our relationship, he didn't have to say it. I sensed his need for affection then and now. Memphis was hurting. So was I. My body could use an explosive orgasm before my procedure. *I may never see this man again,* I thought, blinking repeatedly.

"I would love you if you had one eye and no teeth," I said, making him flash his whitest smile, which didn't accompany a sound.

My sense of humor didn't have the same comedic delivery as Bailey's, but I managed to ease my sorrow.

My stem sunk into the mound of whipped cream that smothered scoops of vanilla, chocolate, and strawberry. Thick chocolate syrup oozed over the side of the boat-shaped dish and onto the table. Picking up my cherry, I held it in front of Memphis's mouth, tickled his lips.

Memphis stroked my hair from the crown of my head to the edges. "That's not the cherry I want, Z."

I relished living in this moment. Dropping the cherry, I covered my face and started crying into my sundae. What if all my hair fell out? Would he love me the same?

A boy, about three feet tall, tapped Memphis on the shoulder, placed a basketball in Memphis's lap. "Excuse me, Mister Brown. You're fast."

Memphis's eyes softened as he focused on me. Embarrassed for crying, I lowered my head. Sniffled. Blew my nose.

"There you go, kid." Memphis said. "Get up, Z. Now. Let's go."

I reached for one last spoonful of my sundae. The taste brought back fond memories. Not knowing if this would be our last time here together, I attempted to savor one more mouthful.

"Leave that shit there," he said.

Picking up my designer bag, he quickly unlocked the doors, motioned for me to sit on the back seat. Memphis opened the driver's door, started the engine, lowered the tinted windows an inch, turned off the engine, then sat beside me.

"I don't care about our past. Are you ready for a life as my wife?" Memphis asked. "The future Mrs. Brown will have to get used to my being a celebrity. This is nothing compared to a year from now when I bring home those gold medals."

He still didn't understand me. "I never needed fortune or fame to love you." Was this the right time to let him know I might not be here to see him win? Or that I was permanently living with a wonderful man?

"Since you didn't give me my cherry, you still owe me," he said. "Too many kids here. You stay put, I'm taking you to our hide-away." Sitting in the driver's seat, he drove off.

I wanted to be here. But not the background to his foreground. *Dear God. Why can't I be with Memphis Brown till death do us part?*

After driving a half mile, Memphis turned left on River Street. "What's the status of your living situation?" he asked.

Did I have a status? I wasn't a freeloader. During my recovery, would Adonis continue to pay the premiums, or would I have to exhaust my finances for health insurance? Medical expenses?

Memphis cruised another six blocks, then parked beside an abandoned warehouse.

My bestie. Always putting my ex first. "You don't have to pretend that Tina-Love didn't tell you."

"I love *you,* Z," he said. Memphis sat beside me on the rear seat and trailed kisses from my lips to my chin. Slowly he traced to my throat, then he licked a saliva necklace along my collarbone. Reminded me of Adonis. That was not good.

Easing his hand up my inner thigh, under my dress, Memphis fingered my vagina.

"Can I?" he asked.

Gripping his wrist, I asked, "What?"

"I know you're not coming over to my house. I want to taste you, Z. Give me something to savor. Please."

Before I could pronounce the *n* in *no,* his mouth covered mine.

"Memphis, stop," I demanded.

"Don't worry. No one can see us." He placed my purse on the front passenger seat. "Lay down," he said, sliding my hips to the center of the leather cushion. "Close your eyes and relax."

Memphis placed his palms on my pelvis, pushed my dress up to my neck. His thumbs lightly touched my clit. He slid up his fingers to my breasts, paused. He whispered, "Submit to me, Z."

Taking in a deep breath, I shivered. Chill bumps covered my skin. I wasn't cold. Hadn't been nervous with him in . . . longer than I could remember.

"I want this to be mine. I don't want to share you, Z." He knelt on the floor, pushed my dress above my waist, removed my panties, buried his nose in my pussy, then he inhaled.

Even if Bailey would do the exact same thing Memphis was doing to me, it wouldn't feel the same. There was only one Memphis Brown. Only one man I wanted inside of me. Eventually I'd have to go home. But I needed this release.

I'd done my research. Cancer wasn't contagious. Placing my hands on the crown of his head, I pushed. I was on the verge of climaxing and screaming with pleasure. Didn't want to become a human siren.

"Uh, uh. I want all of this, Z. Give it to me," Memphis said, sucking my clit soft and fast.

I held my breath to keep from putting his head in a thigh lock. The more he licked, the tighter I clamped. It was the loudest I'd yelled during sex.

Prying my knees apart, he stuck his fingers in his ears.

Laughing, I asked, "You okay?"

"Huh? What? I can't hear you?" he said.

As I pulled down my dress, I thought I hadn't cheated on Bailey. But men were territorial. Would Bailey be offended if I told him I'd sexed Memphis?

"Damn, you need to come home, Z. Can't nobody love you like me."

"Memphis," I said, touching his face with both hands.

"I got you, Z. Trust me. I'm not going to tell you to go stay with dude. I was wrong for that and I apologize. I know I'm not perfect. I have abandonment issues. But I'm ready to deal with all that. Baby, come back to me. I'm begging. Where are your belongings?"

This time he was crying. His tears were sincere. Timing was priceless. I pressed my lips to his and cried too. We dried each other's cheeks.

Before I changed my mind, I said, "Memphis," hoping he wouldn't interrupt me.

"Don't say no. I can't accept anything but

a yes, baby. Tell me you'll come home." He knelt between my thighs. Dug into his pocket, held the same engagement ring he'd almost let me keep.

"Memphis. Listen."

"Stop saying my name like that," he said, then asked, "Z, will you please marry me. I won't renege. Tina-Love told me —"

I didn't care what Tina-Love said to him. He needed to hear this from me.

"Memphis! Shut up!" I had to yell to get his attention. Lowering my voice, I said, "Baby, I don't want you to focus on me. I wasn't going to say anything." Maybe he was asking what he already knew. "Wait. What did Tina-Love tell you?"

"That I needed to connect with you on a higher level. I'm trying to do that. Please say yes." He slid the ring on my finger.

I took it off and put it in his palm. "Did Tina-Love tell you I have to have surgery in three days?"

He sat close to me. "Surgery? For what? Not the abortion? Thought you had that already."

I cried, then told him, "I may have ovarian cancer." There, finally. I got it out.

He backed away from me. "Is that the disease that women get from sleeping with too many men?"

Searching for my panties, I put them on, unlocked the door, reached between the front seats, got my purse. Unlocked my cell. Entered this location in my Uber app.

Cervical cancer and ovarian cancer were two different types of cancers. Cervical cancer wasn't always the result of a woman having multiple partners. Maybe it wasn't a factor at all. Just another way for men to control what women did with their vaginas while guys had sex with as many of us as possible.

A text registered from Adonis, **I had the movers repack your things. Where do you want them delivered?**

Adonis was lying. I was not giving him Bailey's address under any circumstances. Best not to respond.

Another text from Adonis, **I'm canceling everything. You've got 72 hours to switch your cell, insurance, selling the BMW. I'm done with you.**

I was beginning to understand why my bestie treated men badly.

I cried out loud.

Memphis grabbed my forearm. "Z, I'm sorry. That's what I heard. It's not what I'm saying about you." Leaning over me, he closed the door.

CHAPTER 58
MEMPHIS

"Ten, nine, eight . . ." That was how my life was going. In reverse.

Coach Richie tacked on too many extra reps. "Three, two, and . . ." One usually meant I was done. "From the top, MB!"

I couldn't quit. Didn't want to. Fucking the shit out of Z, sending her wherever she'd gone — after I dropped her at Tina-Love's — with my DNA all over her made me beat my chest. Three days later I was still paying for indulging in her pussy for hours in the back seat of my car.

Coach Richie gave me a stern look, folded his arms. "Next time pick up the pace between reps. A tortoise could cross the finish line faster. You gon' learn to stop fucking your legs from under you. Let's go!"

I went from chin-ups to barbell squats. Six sets. Three repetitions. Ending with jump squats, holding a twenty-five-pound plate, I began with, "Twelve, eleven . . ."

When I got to "Done!" I accidentally dropped the plate, barely escaping it falling on my toes.

"Your training sucked all morning, MB! What's on your mind?" Coach held my leg, stretched my knee to my shoulder.

My hamstring was tight. Body tensed. "A little more pressure." I clenched my teeth. "Yeah, right there." I sucked in oxygen long as I could, praying Z's surgery went well. I exhaled.

Why did I have to be a fucking moron making her feel like a whore when I knew she was the type to date one man at a time?

"MB, out with it," Coach said, leaning his shoulder on my other hamstring.

"Nothing new. Trying not to be an idiot." I needed to go back into a residence or I wasn't going to make it. But that would mean not seeing Z, or Tina-Love.

"News flash, MB. Right now, you're that same idiot."

I didn't need a cosigner. He wasn't all that smart. Fucking my Cali girl, then pretending his dick hadn't dipped.

Fuck! Z could've returned one of my calls, or responded to my texts letting me know how she was doing after we parted. She had three days. Hadn't heard her voice since we'd made love, fucked, relished in our afterglow. If everything was on schedule, she was on the operating table.

"What female is it this time? Please tell me you haven't gotten someone else pregnant." Coach Richie had no idea.

I didn't know what hospital she was in. Couldn't send her flowers.

"Like you got Natalie plumped up. Ow!" I sat up.

He'd shoved my kneecap into my face. I grabbed my lip. Blood was on my hand.

Wham! I busted him hard on his pointed nose. "What the fuck you upset about? You fucked Natalie. You let me take that fall, what else you plotting against me, man? Huh?"

I heard @DDDShade's voice echoing, *Trust no one.*

I pinned Coach Richie to the mat, reached back to check that ass again. Someone grabbed my arm. Next thing I knew I was flat on my back with two guys on top of me. What was Coach going to say in his defense?

"I guess this'll end up in *The Shady Café* too, and you'll throw my ass in the quicksand too."

Coach Richie told the guys, "Let him go," then asked me, "You want to talk this out like men, or you want me to request your replacement? I'm not going to accept your laying hands on me. Do it again, you'll end up in ICU, MB. Maybe behind bars. Let's go."

Leaving the gym, I followed Coach to the track. Had to be in the high eighties, not a cloud in sight. I wanted to scream! Cry. Fall on my knees. Pray. For Z. For me.

Thought I was a badass until Coach Richie referenced prison. I'd never been locked up. After watching the documentary series *First and Last* on Netflix, I knew that Georgia's Gwinnett County jail had the most fucked-up system in the country. I didn't want to go that route.

"Okay, idiot. Out with it," Coach Richie said, jogging.

Running beside him, I asked, "What happened between you and Natalie?"

I'd told her to keep her mouth shut. Wondered if Coach had done the same. How many other men wanted to sex and text her? Never take her out on dates. Natalie was the fuck and chill kind. Whose fault was that?

Life was fucked up when you couldn't trust any of the people in your inner circle.

Coach Richie said, "Natalie is irrelevant. What else you got?"

Maybe. Maybe not. She tried to tell me something about a guy named Rick reaching out to her. My fault for not listening, believing I was invincible. Lap three, I opened up regarding my dad. "I hate him because I need him to show me love."

"Now we have something deeper to work with. Channel that negative energy into positive, MB. No one is indebted to us. Most people who have it easy never win the gold," he said, then stopped running.

Hadn't thought about life that way. I heard my cell ringing. "Let me catch this," I told Coach. Creating distance between us, I anxiously answered, "Hey, how's our gurl?"

"She's still undergoing her procedure. I was calling to check on you," Tina-Love said. "How you holding up?"

"I should be there with her. What hospital is she in?" I had to know.

"She doesn't want to see you. After what she told me you said, I can't blame her. But I forgive you and I'm still your biggest cheerleader, man. We're on our way back from Sydney, Aus—"

"We, who? Better not be that nigga Rico Sua—"

"Hey, Memphis," Ricardo interrupted.

I heard the smile in his voice. Coach walked up. "I have Natalie on speaker. We need to talk."

Didn't need Tina-Love to overhear. Ending my call with Tina-Love and Rico Suave, I didn't bother saying bye. "What's this about?" I questioned Coach.

"Hey, Memphis. I miss you," Natalie said.

I missed her pussy and lip service, but I'd never hit it again. I stared at Coach, hunched my shoulders.

"Memphis, I have information on Rick and @DDDShade that I'd like to share with you," she said.

"I'm listening."

Natalie told me, "In person. I can help you expose her and her husband. Under one condition."

I repeated, "I'm listening."

"When I get to Savannah, you'll take me out on a date, on the Savannah Riverboat."

WTF? Checking out the blank expression on Coach's face, followed by a single nod, I agreed. "Done. Let me know when you get here."

Coach had something to lose. I had something to lose. Natalie had everything to gain.

CHAPTER 59
TINA-LOVE

Sydney was nicer with Ricardo by my side.

I didn't have to dine alone in a five-star restaurant. After my runway shows were over, I had a companion and a driver waiting for me. The flight from Sydney to Atlanta, twenty and a half hours, I cuddled in first class with Ricardo. We enjoyed the same movies. Read from the same book.

As I completed my customs form, a text message registered from Bailey Thornton III.

Xena needs to see you.

"What's wrong?" Ricardo asked, studying my expression as he often did.

"It's Xena. We need to go directly to her fast as we can." I swallowed against a lump forming in my throat.

"I'll order a driver. Have them waiting for us when we land in Atlanta. We can make it there in about six hours."

I texted Bailey, **We're landing at Harts-**

field. Will be there in 6 hours. What's the address?

The information Xena had e-mailed could've changed, and I did not want to end up in the wrong place when every second mattered. Finishing itemizing the gifts I'd bought for Xena, Memphis, Ms. Hattie Mae, Bailey, and my mother, I hoped my mom would love the purse and perfume. Best to start small with getting to know her.

Deplaning, Ricardo and I had our back-packs strapped behind us. Briskly we maneuvered the concourse, trying to stay ahead of the other passengers that were still on board. First class and my global entry would save us precious time.

A text registered from Bailey with the address of the hospital. I thanked him.

"Where are we going to store our luggage and gifts?" I worried for the first time on our entire trip.

On the train, we held on to the same pole. Concourse E, international departures and arrivals, was six stops from baggage claim. The train jerked between passenger pickup and drop-off. Ricardo leaned my head on his shoulder. "Breathe," he said. "I'll have the driver deliver our suitcases and Memphis's shoes to your mom's house. We'll keep the other presents with us. It'll cheer

Xena, Bailey, and whomever else is there up."

As I prayed for Xena, my heart actually hurt. From this day forward, insignificant issues were just that.

"She's my closest friend. I never imagined her not being here. What if she doesn't make it?" I cried. "What if she's dead and Bailey didn't want to tell us over the phone?"

In that moment, I thought about Memphis. Bailey was sweet and a godsend for my bestie, but Xena would want Memphis there too. Knowing Mrs. Trinity, she wasn't having any of it. Exiting the train, we hurried to get our luggage.

I had to think this through, but Memphis was going to be there with us. I kept noticing people who seemingly had no place to be; they gave more attention to their phones than moving forward in the line.

"You see this shit!" I said, predicting Ricardo's response.

"We share space, precious. We don't own it." Lovingly he stroked my back.

It was our turn at the window. Ricardo handed the agent our passports. She looked at the photo, stared at me. Did the same with Ricardo's Italian passport. Hesitantly she closed his book, gave them back to

Ricardo, then politely said, "Have a nice day."

The second we were handed our documents, we headed to find our driver. A customs officer in full uniform, gun on his hip, rifle in his hand, blocked our path. We were so close to the exit, I saw "Tina-Love and Ricardo" on the iPad our driver held.

"Come with me," the agent demanded.

Droves of travelers passed us, exiting security. "Is there a problem?" I asked.

"There will be if you don't do as I've asked. We need to check your bags." His tone was threatening.

Another armed agent approached us.

I explained to him, "My friend is dying. Please, we don't have anything illegal. I need to get to Savannah. Our driver is right there." Pointing, I pleaded. "I'm global entry—approved and this is my significant other." I took my boarding pass from Ricardo, showed it to the agent.

"The sooner you cooperate," he said, glancing down at my identification. "You're the supermodel?"

I nodded, believing he'd let us go.

"The sooner you cooperate you can be on your way," the officer said, returning my document.

Ricardo was quiet. He made a left turn

with the cart, which was stacked with six bags. We entered a room off to the side.

"Place all of your belongings on the conveyor," the agent said.

We did as he instructed. There were two agents in uniform sitting behind a bulletproof glass, observing us. I felt uncomfortable. What if Ricardo had drugs in his luggage? Marijuana wasn't legal in Georgia, and if he had possession of a half of an ounce or any illegal substance, they were locking me up too.

One by one, the agent removed our luggage from the conveyor, placed our bags on a table. He opened each one. Swiped the interior with small square swatches. Sifted through my La Perla underwear, removed the purses from the box, took each one out of its silk cover, pulled out the paper stuffing, checked each pocket. Then he reassembled it all like he was a fucking toddler cleaning up his room.

"Searches aren't always targeted. We choose a time window of one minute and everyone that enters during that time has to be searched."

I rolled my eyes so hard at that, liar! If that were true, where was everyone else? I'd traveled alone for thirteen years, and not once had I encountered this. Take one trip with a man, and all my belongings are violated.

After an hour and a half, the agent said, "You guys are free to go."

What the hell? "What was all of this for?" I questioned.

"It's okay," Ricardo said. "Material items can be replaced. Our concern is Xena. Not those agents. They were doing their job."

That was easy for Ricardo say! I paid top dollar for items they'd blatantly disrespected, and the government wasn't reimbursing me one damn dime. On our way out, I wanted to say something to that damn agent.

Ricardo shook his head. "Relax and let it go. It's over."

Lounging on the back seat of the limousine, Ricardo massaged my shoulders. "You are super tense."

"Why didn't you say something to those agents?" I asked. For a moment, I believed Ricardo was traveling dirty.

"I've learned the less you question authority, the sooner they can move on to someone else. I had nothing to hide. You push. They shove. Hope you didn't doubt me," he said.

Memphis crossed my mind. Set a reminder to text him the information on Xena when I was fifteen minutes away from the hospital. Didn't want him showing up or out. I had to be the buffer between Bailey and Memphis.

I felt remorseful for doubting how well I knew Ricardo. Resting in his arms, I loved him more than before.

Chapter 60
Xena

"You did it, sweetheart." Bailey's face was the last and first I'd seen of my family and friends before and after my surgery.

I kept touching my hair. "What do you think about my cutting off my braids and donating them for a cancer patient?" The doctor hadn't confirmed with me that I actually had it, but I was mentally preparing myself.

"You will do no such thing." My mother spoke up first. "That's bad luck if it ends up with a real witch. You know, there are devil worshipers walking this earth."

She'd made letting go of the ill feelings I had for her impossible. "Mother?"

"What?" she answered in her proper voice. "You're calling me a liar, little girl?"

That was how my punishments started. With her false accusations.

"Why did you beat me and lock me in the closet for hours when I was a *little girl*? Was

429

I a bad child?" I was tired of covering for her. If I was going to die soon, I wanted to transition knowing what made Mrs. Bertha Trinity hate me, and I didn't care who heard.

Bailey stood by my side. He did not interject.

My mom's eyes grew wide. Tightening her lips, she scanned the faces of my father, Janice Jones, then Bailey. She settled that terrifying gaze into the core of my pupils. Thanks to Bailey, I was fearless. Against possibly being diagnosed with cancer. And Bertha. I stared back at her. My body was weak, but I refused to blink until she answered.

"You're trying to make a monster out of me, little girl? After all I've done for you." Her mouth twitched.

I hadn't asked to be here. Parents — step and biological — were supposed to care for their children. I was quiet, praying she'd tell the truth.

"I did no such thing." She moved closer to me.

Bailey held my hand.

"You abused my daughter. She deserves to know why." My father stood beside my mother. "But this is not the time or place."

Just when I thought my father was going

to support me, he'd done what he usually did, stayed neutral.

Tina-Love's mom, Janice, commented, "Sometimes it's hard being a mother. We're not perfect, Xena."

I knew she was not going to defend Bertha Trinity. Focusing on Janice, I inhaled.

Bailey stroked my hair. "This is not the time. You need to rest."

I revealed to Janice, "Of course you'd say that. I know all of what you've done and allowed to be done to my bestie."

Tina-Love quietly opened the door and entered the room. Ricardo was behind her with lots of bags.

Janice continued, this time speaking to her daughter. "If I had to do it all over, I would've put him out, went with you to Italy. I'm so sorry."

"How about have him arrested. It's simple. You chose your man over me, Mama. That's the real reason. We can continue this much-needed discussion later. I came to visit my bestie."

"And," Ricardo chimed in, "I came carrying the gifts Tina-Love has for everyone."

He placed a long box across my lap. Bailey helped me uncover all the layers.

I smiled. "Another purse, I'm sure."

Ricardo extended a gift to Janice and the

other to Bailey. He had one remaining gift in his hand that he held on to. I looked at my bestie. She nodded.

"This is extremely thoughtful," Bailey said. "R. M. Williams boots. Impressive. Thank you." He stroked the leather.

Janice expressed appreciation while discovering an assortment of Bondi Wash. "Tasmanian pepper and lavender scented." She unwrapped a box of jewelry, a bottle of wine, and a designer bag, then hugged Tina-Love. "Thanks for thinking about me."

Bailey set his gift aside and focused on me. "Let's see what else you have, sweetheart."

I resumed venturing through layers of decorative tissue. I gasped. Unrolling material I hadn't seen, I extended my arms and insisted to my bestie, "Give me a hug."

"There's more. A lot more. We'll bring it over when you are home and settled."

The door opened. "Hello, everyone. I hope I'm not interrupting, darling. How are you?" Topez handed Bailey a lovely bouquet of flowers she'd brought for me.

"Let me smell them." I inhaled the best-scented lilies ever. "Thank you so much."

"Oh, what do we have here?" Topez picked up my cloth. "I've never seen such perfection. You'd better hurry up and get well, darling. I'm inspired by this hand-woven material."

Bailey placed the flowers on the table. "Since everyone is full of surprises, I have one of my own."

Bailey dug deep into his pocket, then held my hand.

Not again, I thought.

He retrieved what must've been a seven-carat solitaire. Sparkles bounced off the walls whenever he moved the ring. The room was silent, including my mother, who salivated as though it were hers.

"I would get down on one knee, but that would be awkward. Xena Trinity, if you don't mind loving an old man for the rest of his days, will you do me the honor of being my wife?"

CHAPTER 61
MEMPHIS

Stop fucking clapping!

I'd quietly closed the door after hearing the round of applause when old-ass dude asked for Z's hand in marriage.

Pacing the hall outside Z's room, I couldn't believe she'd rejected my proposal and accepted Grandpa's. What I couldn't understand was, why Bailey Thornton III, one of the wealthiest black men in my hometown, popped the question to Z. Why Tina-Love was in on this and had me show up to make a fool out of myself. If it was any other dude, I would've run up on him and made him swallow that block of ice.

I texted Tina-Love, **Come out here or I'm coming in there.**

My jaw dropped when I saw her long luxurious leg, her thigh, then her whole body. She was stunning in a gold sheer maxi dress that wrapped at her waist. The split was lit all the way up to her hip. Each step she'd taken toward me made me hard. I wanted to moonwalk to take in her beauty a little longer.

Tina-Love handed me a box. "Straight from Italy."

Hopefully, they weren't courtesy of Rico Suave.

"Glad you made it." She said that shit as though Z's hand wasn't weighted down. What did Z do with Adonis's ring? If she was playing a game, trying to catch up to Tina-Love, I was not putting my name in no damn hat.

Forget the pleasantries. "What's going on in there?"

Tina-Love ushered me away from Z's room. She hissed, "Grow the hell up, Memphis. All you care about is your damn ego. Where's the 'How's Xena doing?' That's why I gave you the address."

I wasn't letting her turn this on me. "When you grow a dick, maybe you'll understand."

"No." She gripped my nuts. I swore she was trying to crush 'em.

"Ow, damn."

Releasing my shit, she said, "When you stop being one, maybe you'll get women. You keep forgetting I'm on your side. Now our gurl needs all of us, including Bailey.

He can care for her the way you and I can't. He has the resources. He —"

"No shit." I started inching toward Z's room.

Tina-Love put her hand on my chest, balled my shirt into her fist. "Don't go in there with your bullshit. She's recovering. This ain't about you, Memphis. I'm dead serious. If you're going to act an ass, leave."

"I'ma be cool." I hoped that was true. Wanted to ask if Z would be able to nurture my seeds. I had feelings too.

Tina-Love touched the door, then whispered, "Follow me in. If I squint my eyes at you, shut up. You are the only man Xena has ever been in love with. Bailey isn't going to change that."

The door opened from the inside. It was Z's new fiancé. I took several steps back.

Bailey stood six inches from me, squeezed my shoulders, placed his arm around Tina-Love's waist, escorted us away from the entrance of Z's room, all the way to the elevator.

"I'm Memphis Brown. Z's —" Old dude cut me off.

"You're trying to get where I've already been. Let an old man enjoy her for a spell. I'll take excellent care of *our* Xena. I can love her the way you guys can't," he said.

"I'm sure neither of you want her in a nursing home relying on different strangers every shift who may or may not like their job. I was able to get her an insurance plan after she'd told me Adonis took her off of his. Were you aware of that, Memphis?"

In my defense, I said, "Z didn't —"

"Thank you, Bailey," Tina-Love said, then hugged him.

Old dude was sharp. Open collar shirt, buttoned down, with an ascot. Out of respect, I remained quiet. I hadn't considered who was paying for Z's medical. How long of a recovery was Z going to have? That was why I was here. To find out.

Bailey said, "She needs me and I need someone to care for. I've provided for somebody practically all my life. Young man, if you're going to bring home those gold medals, you're going to have to stay focused. And you can't do that if you're worried about Xena. She'll be yours soon enough." Bailey tilted his hat. "You focus on making us proud. I'll be back to collect my wife in the morning. Don't be rude. Go in and visit our Xena."

How could I be an asshole in this moment? "Thank you," I guess. "Mr. Thornton."

"You are very welcome, Memphis Brown."

The elevator doors opened, Bailey stepped inside. I watched until he was no longer visible.

As I entered Z's room behind Tina-Love, Mrs. Trinity greeted me with a grunt. Mr. Trinity with a handshake. Janice with a light hug. Topez with "Hello." Rico Suave embraced me for what felt like an inappropriate amount of time.

"Now our love circle is complete." Rico Suave kissed me on the cheek, took a deep breath, then exhaled in my face.

Weirdo. Realizing dude was a rare kind, I wasn't mad. I slid my hand down the side of my face, fanned the air in front of me. After showing respect to those who deserved it, I stood beside Z's bed.

"Xena, please find it in your heart to forgive your mother," Mr. Trinity said. He bent his elbow. Mrs. Trinity held on to him. "We'll see you tomorrow, Xena. Good night."

No kiss or hug. Where was the affection? Probably burning in hell with my father's love for me. The Trinitys were probably here to snatch the cash that was about to gush Xena's way from Bailey.

Tina-Love said, "Ricardo and I will be back in the morning. Xena, I love you." Giving Z a kiss on the forehead, Tina-Love continued, "Mom. Memphis. Call me to-morrow."

"I love you guys too," Z said.

Following Tina-Love and Ricardo, Janice lightly touched Z's blanket. "I'll call to check on you, honey."

The door closed. It was just the two of us.

"Hey," I said, noticing Z must've lost five pounds since the last time I'd seen her. "Can I stay the night with you? Please."

Her eyes became glossy. A tear dropped.

"It's okay. Bailey gave me his blessings. Said he was taking care of you for me so I can concentrate on winning." I kissed her lips. "You're still the most beautiful woman in the world."

"He really said that?" she asked.

Nodding, I softly smiled, dragged the big cushioned chair next to her bed. Her eyes stretched. "Memphis."

"All they can do is put me out." I wanted to be here with Z. I loved her.

Recalling Tina-Love's spill about my being egotistical, I focused on Z. "If you're uncomfortable with my being here, I'll go." I returned the chair to its original place.

I returned to Z's bedside. Pressing my lips to Z's I looked in her eyes. "I really do love you. One day, you'll be Mrs. Xena Brown. Right now, it's someone else's turn. I'll wait for you. Promise me, after old man dies, you'll wait for me, Z."

Slowly I headed toward the door.

"Memphis," Z said in the sweetest tone.

"Yes."

"Please don't go."

CHAPTER 62
XENA

"Z. Z."

I heard Memphis's voice. My eyelids fluttered. I glanced in the direction of the blinds. It was pitch dark. "Turn on the light. What time is it?"

He whispered, "I have to go home, change, and be at training in an hour. Thanks for letting me stay. I'll text you later. If you can't respond, it's okay," he said.

Memphis was irresistible when he was vulnerable. This was the man I fell for. "Don't get mad at me. But —"

He placed his finger over my mouth. "Get well, baby. I could never —"

"You might be. I want you to forgive your father and release all animosity you hold for him. Pray and meditate every day. I'm not suggesting this due to my condition, or renewed outlook on faith." I was guilty and wanted Memphis to forgive me. "You'll run faster when you release that dead weight that's bringing you down." I had a good reason to feel that in my spirit for Memphis.

"I love you, Z. Go back to sleep."

To his back, I said, "One eye. No teeth. I will always love you, Memphis Brown."

He paused, then continued in the same direction without speaking a word. I sensed his love, and his pain.

Powering on the television, I saw highlights of the news. Back-to-back tragedies. I was thankful for Bailey, Tina-Love, Memphis, Janice and my parents. None of them were obligated to visit me. I was blessed. I unblocked Adonis.

Watching one news program after another, I kept touching my hair. I worried about my diagnosis, going bald, maintaining my place in the fashion show next year. Life was stranger than fiction, indeed. I traded the depressing news for an inspirational podcast. *Oprah's Master Class.*

A text registered from Adonis. **Can I see you?**

I decided not to respond. He was an amazing provider. His intentions with me were good. Mine with him were not. I acknowledged partial responsibility for using him.

Knock. Knock.

I called out, "Come in."

Adonis appeared. I swore I was dreaming.

"Just tell me the truth," he demanded.

No *hello. How're you doing?*

"How did you find me? You need to leave." I reached for the remote to summon the nurse.

Adonis snatched it from me. "I'm taking you home. You are going to have my child. Get up. If you scream a word, it'll be your last."

I wasn't close or strong enough to kick him in the balls or jab him in the eyes. "I was never pregnant. That's the truth. But in a way, you saved my life."

His eyes softened. "I . . . saved . . . your . . . life?"

I nodded. "If we hadn't gotten a" — I made sure to say — "false positive, by the time I would've found out I may have ovarian cancer, it could've been too late for the doctors to help me. I will always love you for rescuing me. It's God's will being done. And you are forever my hero," I lied. I knew Bailey's positive attitude had influenced me.

Adonis quietly processed what I'd said, and I let him. "I want you back. Please come home."

Best not to respond.

"I know you want your belongings. What's your address?" he asked, holding his phone in front of his chest.

Giving him nothing would start another rant. I gave him Mrs. Trinity's location, knowing I wouldn't be there. "Thanks. Deliver my things there."

The nurse rolled in a wheelchair. "You were one of my favorite patients. Oh, I didn't know you had company. I can come back. Ms. Trinity, soon-to-be —"

"No!" I didn't mean to yell, but Adonis? Calm as he appeared, his stare at the ring on my finger, then up at me, could've killed me.

Adonis shouted, "I saved your fucking life and you killed my child!"

"You have to leave, sir," she told Adonis, escorting him out.

I exhaled, "Thank you, Lord. Please have security come." God only knew what Adonis would do next.

Fear of being a victim gave me a different kind of strength. My pain dissipated. The meds deserved credit. I was ready to run out of here and never look back. How did Adonis find out where I was?

Bailey made an entrance dressed in a suit. Perfect timing. I could not praise the man upstairs enough.

A gold chain dangled from Bailey's vest pocket. He placed one foot forward, then shuffled his feet, showing off his new leather shoes.

"That Tina-Love sure has great taste." His smile was contagious.

I picked up my cell. "I forgot to let her know I was going home this morning."

"I spoke with her on my way over. She's stopping by later. Ricardo wants to do chakra work with you. If you're feeling up to it."

Hesitantly I agreed. "Sure." Hopefully, Tina-Love wouldn't dominate my engagement to Bailey the way she'd wedged herself between Memphis and me. She never interacted with Adonis. Never visited me while I was with Adonis. "Hmm."

"Hmm, what?" Bailey stared at me.

My doctor waltzed in. "Look who's going home this morning. You have a great man here." He patted Bailey on the back. "Not everybody can afford the best private accommodations. I still want you to take it easy. We'll have your results in a few days."

That was what I feared most. My test results.

CHAPTER 63
TINA-LOVE

"Bitch, if you fall anywhere on my property, I will drag your ass to the street by your hair, then personally call the police," I told Natalie. She was dressed urban chic.

She had that "white girl trying to be black" vibe. Ultra-low-rise blue denim shorts that barely covered her round shapely butt, which was bigger than mine. Her wavy honey blond balayage was gathered in a high messy ponytail. Her nose was long, thin. Her lips were plumper, coated in a blazing red matte lipstick.

"I'm not your bitch, but sorry about that slip and fall. I didn't know what Memphis was setting me up for. A girl has gotta stay on her toes." Natalie removed her head band, then wrapped the hair tie tighter, twisted the ponytail into a bun, then tucked the edges.

I chuckled. *Setting her up?* She had that in reverse. Memphis was not a scammer.

"Memphis and Ricardo are on the terrace and I'm right behind you." Just in case her ass missed a stair.

"You have a lovely home." She galloped with high, dainty steps like my horse Faith.

I didn't bother thanking Natalie for coming. This was business and our priority was getting to Bailey's to visit Xena.

"This is my man, Ricardo." No introduction was needed for Memphis.

Ricardo's eyes lit up, mouth opened. "Welcome to our humble abode," he said.

Memphis and Ricardo stood at the same time to pull out Natalie's chair. Memphis muscled the seat closer to him.

"Coffee, tea, mimosa?" Ricardo offered.

"Mimosa, thanks," Natalie said. Releasing the band, she swayed, then tossed her hair behind her shoulders. She fingered her ginormous gold hoops.

That chick had no idea. If she fucked up, I'd snatch her under the table by her feet and make good on my promise. I hadn't gotten a close-up on her the first time, but she was model gorgeous. Mental note, cut her off after drink number two. I texted Ricardo to make sure we were in alignment.

"Memphis, you want to start, or shall I?" I snapped my finger in front of him.

Reading a text from Ricardo, **#4some**, I

ignored him.

"Oh —" was the first word Memphis had spoken since she'd arrived.

Natalie interrupted. "If no one objects, I'll go first."

But of course she wanted to lead. I helped myself to a croissant with fresh peach jam I'd bought from the James and the Giant Peach stand. "Go ahead, missy."

Long as her brows were the only thing she raised toward me, we were good.

Natalie pressed the flute to her tongue. Let the bubbles flow into her mouth. Swallowed. "Memphis didn't choose me. I chose him. It would've been nice of Memphis to have asked me to be —"

Who cares about her backstory? "Fast-forward. Ricardo and I have someplace to go."

For the first time since Natalie sat to his right, Memphis turned his head left, and stared at me.

Natalie continued, "I received a call from Rick asking to meet with me when I was in Chula Vista. My Google number is attached to all of my socials, so that wasn't hard. He visited me in Cali. He told me exactly what to say before Memphis left and when I called in to the stations. He coached me on how to play the mind game with you, Memphis. After you left my town house, Rick and his wife flew me in. Put me up in an Airbnb. Basically —"

Memphis blurted, "Did you fuck Coach Richie?" His eyeballs damn near connected into one.

He was never going to learn how to put his damn dick aside. I sighed, sipped my tea.

"Of course" — Natalie paused, then answered — "not." She laughed. "After how you've treated me, I know you're not worried about whom I'm sharing my talent with."

Whether it was true or false, that was the best response. "How much did they pay you?" That was what I wanted to know.

Natalie smiled. "Less than you. Listen, y'all need me. I don't need y'all. I'm not asking for any more money, and not giving any back. Rick and @DDDShade want me to get pregnant by Memphis for real this time. For double what you paid," she said, staring at me.

"Fuck who you want," Memphis said. "Long as it's not mine, I don't give a damn. The only babies I'm going to kiss are gold medals." Leaning back in his seat, Memphis folded his arms across his chest.

"They want me to set you up again and

449

give birth to your baby right before the Olympics. I can fuck whomever I want, and I will, but if I get pregnant and say it's yours, what are you prepared to do besides defend yourself? The sixty grand you gave them was for me not to rat them out to the FBI. Not for them to protect you. Which they have no intention of doing."

"Wow." She was lying. That trick did not get me for $310,000. "Why in the hell did I give Memphis money to give to them?"

A smirk decorated Natalie's pale face.

"It's okay, baby. We're going to handle those losers." Ricardo was calm.

I hadn't realized I'd said that aloud.

"Since you guys have to leave, I'll hurry. Xena is marrying Bailey. Topez hooked them up. Xena will eventually become a widow, inherit a large sum of money, marry Memphis, that's when I am to announce I'm having your baby, and that setup is going to cost you and Xena millions to keep me from going public. Spoiler alert!"

Natalie wiggled her fingers, then continued, "I split all the money with Rick only. He's cutting @DDDShade out. But that's just the first mils and is nothing compared to the child support Memphis will have to pay me after the endorsements you get if you win gold. Oh, and if you're thinking about not paying up, they're planning on finding your father, and having him live on-air and in the stands at your training and competitions."

Memphis stood. Punched the table. Food popped up. Beverages spilled. No one moved. Pacing the terrace, Memphis said, "We have to shut down all of this scandalous shit!"

That bitch was a witch. Had to be. "How do we prevent this?" I asked Natalie, without having to bury her body in my stable. She had to have the solution.

"We let them believe I'm pregnant. I'll send them pictures wearing baby bumps. Then when it's time to go on their show, I tell the truth and expose them."

She was not worth engaging my feelings. I didn't believe or trust that white girl.

"That's not enough," Ricardo countered. "If what you say is true, your solution is too simple. We have to listen to her archived shows, find others whom they've exploited, get them to speak out, while we keep Memphis protected and focused."

More and more I was convinced Natalie was the mastermind and Rick and @DDD-Shade were following her lead.

"I like that shit right there," Memphis said, reclaiming his seat at the table.

451

Natalie helped herself to another mimosa. I cut my eyes to the corner at Ricardo. He took her flute. "Try the tea. It's delicious."

If Natalie left here and got into an accident, I was not going to be held liable.

She didn't pick up the teacup. "Okay, y'all keep me posted on whether you want to proceed with my plan or have a better one. I'll be in town a few more days." Natalie tossed her hair over her shoulder. "I know the way out."

I darted my eyes to Ricardo.

Leaping to his feet, he said, "I'll escort you," following Natalie.

"What are your thoughts?" I asked Memphis, while we were alone.

"I say we follow Natalie's lead. She has the inside deets." He bit off half of a buttered croissant.

"A bitch you fucked over has your best interest at hand? That's why you're out of $310,000. Natalie is the damn ringleader. She orchestrated all of this. We have to devise our own plan." I paused, stared Memphis in his eyes. "Whose side are you on?"

Slowly he shook his head. "What do you mean?"

"How does Natalie know Bailey and Xena are getting married? They just got engaged.

She knows Topez? Really, Memphis?"

Ricardo rejoined us. "Sweetheart, I heard you. We're on the same page. Memphis. Answer the fucking question."

Both Memphis and I stared at Ricardo. I didn't know he had a curse word in his vocabulary. "I have no idea. You know @DDDShade has her ways of burying people in quicksand," he answered defensively.

"If you say so," Ricardo replied.

Memphis pushed away his plate, stood. "If y'all don't believe me, fine. But shit has been suspicious since Rico Suave showed up here." He pointed at Ricardo. "Check that nigga's credentials."

I yelled to Memphis's back, "You're headed in the right directions. Down! And out!"

CHAPTER 64
XENA

"Let's get married this week, Xena. I don't want to delay making you my wife." Bailey sat on the end of the couch.

Admiring him, he was the perfect gentleman. Red slacks. Red polo. Red suede shoes. Huge heart.

I'd barely been at his home three days after my surgery, and already this man was ready and willing to share his last name. I could hold out for and hold on to Memphis the way I'd done when he'd stayed the night with me at the hospital, but there was no guarantee Memphis wouldn't meet another woman, before I . . . I knew I'd better be present in this moment.

Oil paintings of his wives hung on opposite walls. Wife number one was white. Young. Pretty like Natalie. His second bride was black. Regal and refined. With the exception of being a woman, I did not resemble either.

Facing him, I held his hand. "Okay. But we have to do a lot of planning in a short time. Your kids have to fly in. We need a venue, cake, flowers, food —"

"All we need is us. You can invite Tina-Love and Ricardo, if you'd like. Topez can handle the arrangements. My children, I'll let them know after you legally change your last name to Thornton. If we give them a heads-up, all they'll be concerned with is raising hell over the inheritance none of them are getting."

I'd heard of rich people excluding their children from their will. "But why?"

I'd raise hell, too, if my dad were wealthy and some woman younger than half his age came out of nowhere flashing an engagement ring. Meghan, William, Harold, and Chelsey Thornton were not aware I'd moved in with their father. My dad could come to the ceremony but not my mother. Knowing her, she'd show up anyway, which meant neither of them would receive an invitation.

Sharing my truth with Bailey, I told him, "I'm not doing this for your money."

"I know, sweetheart. That's why we're getting married. My first two wives loved me, not my portfolio. I didn't expect to outlive either of them. I'm putting your name on everything. You're so pure. I'm glad Topez connected us," Bailey said. "Your spirit is angelic. Loving an old man just because. I know you can't do anything sexually, but I'd like to snuggle and hold your hand all night. Can I do that?"

Nodding, I said, "I'd like that."

I reclined into Bailey's arm, and we lounged on the sofa in the living room. My cell rang. I showed him the caller ID. My heart pounded rapidly. I didn't want to answer. Some things were better left unsaid. Not this.

"Put it on speaker," Bailey insisted.

"Hello," I spoke softly.

"May I speak with Xena Trinity."

"This is Xena."

"Hi, Xena. Doctor Telfair, here. How are you feeling, my dear?"

"My incision is healing well," I replied, sitting up. "Bailey is taking excellent care of me, but I'm anxious and nervous to hear my results."

Bailey sat on the edge of the couch. "Bailey Thornton here, Doctor Telfair. Give it to us straight. Don't leave out anything. We have to do everything to make sure my soon-to-be wife is around for a very long time."

"Xena, you're okay with my speaking to the both of you?" the doctor asked.

"Not being okay with Bailey hearing isn't going to change anything. Yes, I want him to hear. We're listening," I told him.

"I only had to remove one of your ovaries. So later, you can try to start a family, if you'd like." Doctor Telfair paused.

The widest smile I'd seen spread cheek to cheek on Bailey. I thought he was done with parenthood. I'd heard the older the sperm, the older-looking the baby. I did not want a baby that would be wrinkled forever.

"That's great," I said, having Memphis's child in mind, after the Olympics. If I were being honest, I needed Bailey as my caretaker. I didn't want him as my lover. But he was my blessing, and I was deeply appreciative.

All the what-ifs hit me hard. Maybe the doctor was overly optimistic about my being a mom. What if I wasn't here to be with my child on his or her first day of school? Or if I had Bailey's baby and lost out on a future with Memphis? Or if Bailey outlived me, what woman would be mommy to my . . . I started tearing up.

"What's the diagnosis, Doctor?" Bailey asked.

I appreciated Bailey's take-charge attitude.

"We caught it early. Stage one. Xena, we want you to start treatment next week. After you complete chemotherapy and radiation, we'll do a series of X-rays. But I also have to let you know, there is a possibility the cancer could return at some point, and we may have to remove the other ovary. Best scenario, it won't resurface. Once your treatments are done, we'll continue monitoring. If you want a baby, I recommend you try conceiving soon as you're in the clear and feeling up to it. Do you have any questions for me?"

I had dozens of uncertainties, but no questions for my doctor. "I'll talk it over with Bailey. Can we call you back if we do have questions?"

"Absolutely. The receptionist will contact you to set up your first appointment. Stay positive. Believe it or not positivity is equally important as treatment," Doctor Telfair said, then ended the call.

I was quiet.

Bailey said, "Let's go upstairs and practice working on our new addition."

What happened to holding hands and snuggling?

His words were a reality check. Bailey was fifty years my senior. He looked amazing with his clothes on. Hadn't seen him naked, nor did I want to. I'd enjoyed all the benefits of his caring for me, but never had I imagined having to engage in sex with a senior. Not to accommodate his request would be selfish.

Allowing him to penetrate me might make me regurgitate. "It's too soon."

"Xena, sweetheart. You're losing your sense of humor." He stroked my hair. "I know how to be gentle. By the way, I'm leaving everything to you just to upset my inconsiderate offspring."

I'd never met them, but I didn't create the barrier they had with their father. "Whatever you'd like to do is okay with me."

"I'll get the certificate tomorrow and ask my pastor to perform the ceremony. I've always gotten married in my church. That's where I want you to feel like a princess."

Walking down the aisle to Bailey was not how I imagined my first wedding.

A text registered from Topez. **How are you doing? Are you up to my coming by and our planning for NYFW? When is the wedding? I know Bailey has big bucks so budget 100k for me as the planner. You owe me.**

CHAPTER 65
MEMPHIS

"Pack your bags, baby! Just got the word, MB. We are out of Savannah." Coach motioned as though he'd spiked a football in the end zone after scoring a game-winning touchdown.

I wanted to throw a flag on the play. *Not now, Coach.* Timing for me was terrible. Good thing I'd finished pressing two hundred pounds of steel above my chest as he danced. I sat on the edge of the workout bench. I hadn't seen Coach this excited since the day he'd told me I'd made it into the Olympic competition. His enthusiasm did not uplift me. I had one reservation: Z.

Standing, I pressed my forehead to my knees, stretched my hamstrings. "How soon and where?"

"First flight out in the morning. Back to Cali," he said.

I sat on the floor, resumed the same stretch position. Relocating was not the solution to resolving my problems. "Chula Vista?" I asked, praying I did not have to live there again. The energy in my body drained to my ass like my nuts were two dumbbells.

No part of me desired close proximity to Natalie on a regular. I couldn't lie. Had to stay hunched over to keep my dick from rising in front of Coach. Seeing her in those short shorts and high heels was a picture framed in my mind.

Natalie was sexy as fuck when I met her at Byrd's Famous Cookies on River Street last night. We walked to a nearby restaurant for dinner. Fully hearing her plan on trapping Rick and @DDDShade was part of my motivation to see her. After the date, my SUV was where I'd parked it. Continuing our conversation at my spot, she'd made an offer. I had to accept letting her blow me, but I refused to put my dick anywhere near her pussy. She'd locked herself in my bathroom, freshened up, then she left my house like a champ.

"What about Nat—"

"Way ahead of you, MB. I made a few calls. Natalie will be on a one-year mission. We're splitting your training between different facilities. You'll be up and down the coast from San Francisco to San Diego. By the time Natalie gets back from South Africa, you'll be decorated with gold medals and slammed with endorsements."

Considering my dick was flaccid, I should've stood and done a standing backflip when I heard such news, but I wasn't thrilled. Natalie was still up to her shenanigans.

"Who paid for the trip?" I asked.

"I did it so she'd stop being a distraction," Coach said.

"How much you went in with?" I questioned.

"Ten grand," he said.

Had to shake my head on that one. With that amount, Coach had fucked Natalie. Might've had his dick sucked too. I pressed my forehead to my knees, held on to my feet. Held on for minute. Sat up.

"She told me Rick and @DDDShade are paying her to give me a trap baby. I'm allegedly in one mil deep to make some shit that hasn't happened go away."

Fuck Natalie's lying ass. All I cared about was ending up with Z. And we weren't coming up off of none of our inheritance from Bailey.

"Since we have less than twenty-four hours to depart, let me get outta here, make my rounds, and say my good-byes," I said.

Coach extended his hand. Helped me up.

"Cheer up, dude. Don't look a gift horse in the mouth. You need to get out of Savannah. This place really is your quicksand. See you in the morning." Coach patted my shoulder.

What was I supposed to do? Tina-Love was booed up with free-loading Rico Suave. Z was engaged to rich-ass Papa Smurf.

Sighing heavily, I jogged to my car. Texted Tina-Love, **omw**

Tina-Love replied, **3579.**

I called Z. She replied with the message, **Can't talk now. Will call you back.**

"That's cool." She had to respect the old man. What if that nigga was around another ten, twenty-plus years? No way in hell I was waiting until I was damn near fifty to get my woman back.

Entering my new code on the box at Tina-Love's, I waited until the gate opened, then parked facing the closed garage. I waited again for her to unlock the commoners' entrance.

"Oo-wee," she said, giving me an air hug. "You hit the shower, I'll prepare you something to eat."

"This is my last night here. I'm leaving for Cali in the morning."

I followed her naked body to the kitchen

and stood by the counter. Watched her open the refrigeration, bend over.

"That's great news," she said.

I wanted Tina-Love to protest.

Unwrapping brown freezer paper, she placed the fish in a bowl of water. I was going to miss seeing her remove a container of diced cucumbers, put them in the juicer, pour two glasses of fresh juice, then hand me one.

"You always know what I need and when I need it." The coolness gliding down my throat gave me life.

"I'm considering living in Italy for a few months with Ricardo. Take myself off the radar of @DDDShade and Rick. Stop communicating with Natalie. I believe she's on their team. You need to ostracize her too. With all of us gone, let them pimp somebody else."

Before Coach Richie told me about the ten grand, I wasn't convinced Natalie was the problem. Clearly, she was.

Didn't realize I'd drifted until Tina-Love said, "But I have to wait until after Xena's wedding."

Spit my last mouthful of juice in my glass. "Damn, what's the rush? Is old dude about to die?"

"We all have to die," Tina-Love commented casually.

"I want all the details. When. Where. Time. All that," I demanded.

"Hmm." Tina-Love smiled. "Ricardo is away for the night. You can stay. We'll chill like old times. *Black Panther,* the movie. Popcorn. Champagne."

"Yeah. Back-to-back encore," I said.

"Really? Okay." Tina-Love sniffed the air in front of me.

"All right. I'm going. I hate I might not see you guys until after the competition."

Tina-Love spread the fillets flat on a rectangular glass baking dish, sprinkled seasoning on top. Washing her hands, she stared at me. "At the competition. Nothing is going to keep me away from seeing you win."

On my way upstairs, a lot of shit went through my mind.

It was time for me to let Savannah and everyone in it go . . . except my mom.

CHAPTER 66
TINA-LOVE

Felt like I had already lost my best male friend.

"Thanks for an amazing night," Memphis said.

Dawn was turning into sunrise. This was Xena's favorite part of each day. I escorted Memphis to my front door.

"I have no regrets." Hugging me, Memphis asked, "You?"

One could not live in the moment replaying scenes from their past. I pressed my lips to his. "I love you, my Memphis. You are the one that I gave away but should've kept for myself. Last night proved that."

He kissed me hard. Held me close. His strong hands caressed my back. "Do you love Ricardo?"

I nodded.

"Are you in love with Ricardo?" Memphis asked.

Looking into his eyes, I told the truth.

"Yes. I am."

His brows moved closer together, eyes squinted, mouth tightened. "How can that be real, if you should've kept me for yourself?"

Memphis's youth and innocence may never go away. Had to present love to him in an organic way by asking, "Do you love Xena?"

"Of course. She's my soulmate, you know that. I'll always love Z," he answered.

His response was as though I should have automatically understood what he didn't.

"People are capable of loving and being in love with more than one person at the same time. Most people don't give themselves the permission because they, like you, feel it's wrong," I explained. "Ricardo and I are in an open relationship. He stayed the night at another woman's house."

I kissed Memphis again. His energy had taken a turn south.

He said what I already knew. "I'm confused."

Pressing my naked body to his freshly washed, Bounce-scented clothes from yesterday, I asked, "Do you love me?"

"Yes, I do," he confirmed.

"Are you in love with me?" This time I pressed my lips to his.

The piercing sound of silence rang in my ears.

Memphis answered, "No. I guess. Not like I'm in love with Z."

Athlete, doctor, mechanic, artist — a man's ego needed a woman's love. Sometimes, any woman's love would do.

"Keep this between us," I said.

He responded, "Goes without saying."

"You'd better get going. Ricardo will be here shortly."

Chapter 67
Xena

Avoid lingered in my spirit as I inched my way to the altar. Where was Memphis? What was he doing? Who was he with?

The closer I got to Bailey, the more I shortened my steps. Everything inside of me felt empty. Tina-Love, Ricardo, and Janice sat to my left on the bride's pew. Topez was alone on my right. Bailey was serious about not having any of his children present.

Five, four, a seven-foot train trailed. *Three.* I paused. Took a deep breath. *Two.* My legs trembled. In remembrance of my great-grandmother, I held a bouquet of Cherokee roses — vibrant green leaves surrounded waxy white petals that circled a sunny golden center. My hands rattled hard. Looking down, I could've been the flower girl. All that remained were the stems.

Tina-Love eased the bare arrangement from my grip. Bailey extended his hand.

469

One. I'd made it to my destination, had nothing to hold on to. I interlocked my fingers, let them rest right below my breasts.

Topez's smile was bright. I gave her a soft blink. White lilies and gigantic bows decorated the ends of the benches, including the ones where no one was seated. That was all the rows, minus two.

My store-bought long-sleeved lace gown had a crew neckline that made me itch. I was hot. Scratching would be rude, especially if I started and couldn't stop. I looked at my bestie, Janice, and Ricardo, then gave them a fake smile. I really wanted to be happy. Tina-Love glanced over her shoulder toward the doors of the church.

I held my breath.

She wouldn't dare! I didn't need Memphis's promises to rescue me to happen this minute. *God, help me, please. Give me a sign that I'm doing the right thing. Please.*

"We are gathered here today to —"

"Sweetheart, are you all right?" Bailey asked, vying for what I hadn't given him, eye contact. He lowered his head.

Quickly I nodded. "Just a little upset."

He frowned.

"This is my third. Your first. Both of my wives had butterflies too. That's a good sign." He instructed his pastor to continue.

I didn't intend to say *upset* aloud.

Every word the pastor spoke was muffled, until I heard, "If there is anyone who objects, speak now or forever hold your peace."

I turned to Tina-Love for a reassuring look that I was doing the right thing. She didn't notice me. She was staring at the doors again, which meant she'd invited him, but he didn't show up. It was best. I had to believe things were in divine order.

The pastor continued, "Xena Trinity, do you take Bailey Thornton the third to be your lawfully wedded husband . . ."

"I —"

A faint squeak resonating from the rear commanded my undivided attention. My head snapped toward the sound. A ray of sunshine spread along the carpet to the pulpit, casting . . . two larger-than-life shadows.

Blinded by the light, I gasped.

"What kind of heathen of a child does not invite her parents to her ceremony?" My mother took her time getting to me. Almost as much time as I'd taken to get to Bailey.

If I had walked faster, the ceremony would be over. Topez approached my mother, then hissed. "Sit down and shut up or get out. This is why you weren't welcomed. Let somebody love this child the way you never have."

My mom looked at Janice. Tina-Love's mother placed her finger over her lips. Dad held my mom's arm. Escorted her to the pew behind Ricardo, who was being extremely quiet.

I sensed Ricardo understood why I wasn't comfortable. He touched his abdomen, heart, and between his brows.

Nodding, we both recognized that my chakras were out of alignment. Every place he'd acknowledged signaled for me not to marry Bailey. There wasn't anyone else to care for me through my treatments. I had so much noise in my head at any moment, I could've raced toward the exit.

"I do," Bailey answered.

When had I spoken those two words? *Oh, Lawd. Is it too late? I'm listening.*

"I now pronounce you man and wife." The pastor added, "You may now kiss the bride."

Arm in arm, I exited the church in a daze as Mrs. Xena Thornton. A white SUV with tinted windows was parked in front.

"Thanks for coming, everyone. I'm going to get my bride home and let her rest up for her first treatment in a few days. I'll keep everyone posted on Xena's progress."

Ricardo hugged me, then whispered, "We'll come by tomorrow and I'll work on you spiritually."

Tears streamed down my cheeks. Memphis was somewhere in California. I did not want my bestie and Ricardo to leave me. "Thank you," I said, still holding on to Ricardo.

"She's my wife, not yours," Bailey joked.

"She should be mine."

Releasing Ricardo, I turned.

Memphis stood wearing — a tank shirt, running pants, and shoes.

"Z, we can work this out. You can come to San Francisco. I'll get you the best doctor," he said.

"Let's go," Bailey insisted, leading me to the SUV.

Half of my train was on the last step. The driver opened the door.

"It's not too late," Memphis begged while digging into his pocket.

"I can deal with a lot of things, but disrespect is not one of them," Bailey said, getting into the back of the car. "Xena, sweetheart, get in."

After watching Memphis lower his right knee to the concrete sidewalk, then open the same ring box a third time, I glanced at Tina-Love.

Staring at the diamond, she shook her head. "Boy, get your ass up," she told Memphis.

He didn't move. Neither did I.

"Xena Trinity, will you marry me?" he asked, holding the ring up to me.

Before I answered, I heard Bailey say, "Driver, close the door. Let's go."

"You are the stupidest woman alive. If you weren't sick, I'd slap the taste out your mouth." My mother stomped off. My father quietly followed her.

"For the first time, I agree with your mother," Topez said. "You actually like playing the victim? Memphis has nothing to offer you. You don't marry promise when you already have perfection. Listen. I'm ordering car service for you to go home to your husband. When the driver arrives, get in the damn car, Xena."

I wasn't certain where Memphis was going to put his ring when my finger was already decorated with a much larger diamond.

Tina-Love shook her head at Memphis. Without saying a word to Memphis, she took the ring out of his hand, gave me her cell, whispered, "Zero, nine, two, eleven," then walked away with Ricardo and Janice by her side.

Memphis stood empty-handed.

"Z, all we need is each other."

CHAPTER 68
MEMPHIS

Z was the most beautiful woman in the world to me.

Admiring her Indian, African, and French features, I was hopeful after my soulmate's recovery we would start a family. Z was lying on her back, in the center of my bed. A long train stretched beside us on the carpet. Short-heeled shoes, covered in glitter, never left her feet.

I nudged her. "Z, wake up. I have to take a red-eye flight to SFO."

"Huh? What?" Sitting up, Z propped a pillow behind her back, fluffed her gown.

"You're leaving me?"

She'd been dressed in the same attire an entire evening.

"Nah, nah. I have training every day," I explained. I'll come home often as I can."

If I could stay here, I would. If I could transfer back to the Savannah facility, I wouldn't do that. "Next summer you'll be healthy, we'll get married, and you'll be in the stands cheering for your man."

Z cried. I wiped her tears.

"Don't do that. I'm here for you. Look, my mother said she'll help take care of you. You won't be alone. And I promise, every break I get I'll be right here." I rubbed her hand.

"You don't get it, do you? I have cancer. I have to have chemotherapy. And radiation." She sat sideways on the edge of the mattress.

Z stared at her lap. Her head moved left and right, repeatedly.

"I gave up Bailey, a man who loved and cared for me, to be with your mother?"

Nothing about my situation had changed. "Please, stop. Long as you love me, the way I do you, our time is coming." Holding her hands, I pulled her up to me. "You have to undo what you've done with Bailey before we can be together."

Smack! I could not believe she hit me. Z's stare fixated on mine. I grabbed her wrist as she swung for strike two.

"You selfish bastard!" she yelled.

"You're the one who slept in this." I flipped the veil dangling down to her ass. "And this." I brushed her gown. "I missed practice this morning to show you how much I want us to be husband and wife. This is how you show your appreciation for MB?"

Millions of women would give all they had to sleep in the same bed with me, and Z acted as though I wasn't worthy.

"Get! Out! Of my way! I hate you right now," Z said, then asked, "What time is it?"

She knew where my digital clock was in the bathroom. She uncovered the cell in the bed. I'd forgotten Tina-Love had given Z her phone. Z yelled, "Ten!"

My flight was departing in two hours. Savannah Airport was small in comparison to Hartsfield.

Z paced my bedroom floor. Each time she turned, she became more entangled in that damn dress.

I tried to embrace Z. Immediate contact with that gown made me cringe. I let go.

"You didn't have the decency to buy me a ring."

Undeniably, Z was heartbroken. What difference did the ring make?

"What's more important? Me? Or some stupid ring? I traveled cross country, Z. And take off that dress. I can't even see my shit."

Lowering my voice, I took a deep breath. "You can stop ring hopping. You had two, and what happened? You don't have to move in with Adonis. Move out with him and in with Bailey. I want you to understand this is your permanent home."

Z whispered, "You took advantage of me. You intentionally ruined my life. I trusted you, Memphis."

Nothing I said would make her feel better. "I'm going to go before I miss my flight. You stay here. Your key and my car key are on the dresser. My mom will check on you. Make sure you send her your appointment schedule. Everything is going to work out fine. Trust me."

My luggage consisted of a black leather backpack. I picked it up, got my cell. Checking my messages, I had one from Rico Suave, Coach Richie, and Natalie.

I called off the dogs. Rick and @DDD Shade won't bother you again. Next time you decide to mess over a woman, Memphis . . . DON'T! I really loved you, Natalie had texted.

I ordered my Uber ride to the airport.

Rico Suave let Tina-Love us his phone to text, **Using my guy's cell. It's me. Tina-Love. I can't support you anymore. No longer your #1 fan**

That hurt. Tina-Love never gave up on me. I bet his ass sent that. *Fuck!* I'd read Coach Richie's text later. I had to keep things moving.

Z folded her train over her forearm, quietly went downstairs.

Grabbing her key, I followed her. "Z, where are you going? Are you going back to him? Please, don't do that, Z. Take your key." I uncurled her fingers. She tightened them. "Answer me."

Z let the key fall to the floor. Sat on the sofa by the door.

Seeing the love of my life turn her back on me brought back memories of my dad. No matter what Z thought, I was a good man and I was not letting her get away from me again.

Checked my app. The driver was here. I called his cell. When he answered, I said, "Hey, man, give me a minute." I trotted upstairs, turned off the lights. Z could switch them back on later.

I had to leave, but I'd be back . . . soon as I could. Returning downstairs, I found that Z and my driver were gone. I viewed my app. The destination for my trip had changed.

Chapter 69
Xena

En route to my husband, I called my bestie on Ricardo's phone. "I screwed up major this time. I owe Bailey an apology."

I heard Ricardo ask, "Where is Xena?"

"On my way home," I answered.

Tina-Love insisted, "Do not show up at that man's house at midnight after you've been MIA. Come to my place. We'll figure out something. If he doesn't take you back, Ricardo and I won't leave until you've completed your treatments."

No scolding or blaming me for trusting Memphis. That was a surprise. "I shouldn't have trusted Memphis. He misled me. Big-time. And for the last time."

Sitting in the back of an Uber, I felt like the biggest fool. I told the driver, "Pull over. I need to change directions."

What I really needed was a wardrobe switch. The wedding gown covered the entre back seat of his Hyundai. Part of me wanted to go the airport and humiliate Memphis. Maybe I should take a flight to San Francisco and show up at his training dressed the way I was and ask for his hand in marriage. How would he feel?

"I can't believe how inconsiderate he was. He knew he had —" I stopped midsentence. "How did he know where I was getting married?"

"Bailey was the one who'd said he was borrowing you. Honestly, Memphis was supposed to be in California during your ceremony. Yes, I gave him the deets." Tina-Love was unemotional.

"What? You did what?!" I was livid. "At least you're consistent. Always doing what's best for Memphis."

"You let your husband drive off without you and I can't undo that. Come over," Tina-Love said.

I heard Ricardo in the background. "Let me speak with Xena."

Ending the call, I told the driver, "Take me to my original destination."

Arriving at Bailey's, I stood at his front door. I didn't have my key. I entered the maid's code on the pad, and the door unlocked. My heart thumped; legs shook uncontrollably. It was difficult to see through the cloud of tears. I blinked. I was here now.

Quietly I tiptoed in, expecting him to turn on a light. After entering the foyer, I made my way to the living room. Bailey wasn't there.

Barely above a whisper, I called his name. "Bailey. Baby, it's me, Xena."

No response. I surveyed the design room. Not expecting to find him there, I was reminded of the kindness Bailey had shown me. Unzipping the side of my gown, I let it fall to the floor. The white lace panties and bra were supposed to be replaced with a beautiful bride's negligee that was upstairs laid across the chaise in Bailey's room.

Sighing heavily, I debated sleeping on the sofa, or going upstairs to my husband. I had to face my demons. The sooner I did, I'd know my fate.

Cautiously I placed one foot in front of the other. I held on to the rail. *I hate Memphis Brown so much right now, I wish he breaks a leg. For real.*

Bailey's door was closed. *Tap. Tap.* "Baby, it's me."

Was he here? I pecked on the door twice. No response. Slowly turning the knob, I eased into his bedroom. I used my hands to guide me to the dimmer switch. Sliding it up, I saw that Bailey was asleep.

"Please forgive me." I sat on the side of the bed. "The one thing you asked of me, I failed terribly. Your being so healthy and all I don't imagine you know what it feels like to have a deadly disease. I messed up. I don't want to die. Say something." I wanted to say I'd ended everything with Memphis, but we did not have closure. I had to know why Memphis thought what he'd done was okay.

"Bailey, please. I need for you to forgive me."

Looking over my shoulder, I saw his cell was on the nightstand closest to him. Did he call or text me? I picked up his phone. Bailey's last contact was Topez.

Curious, I scanned their history.

2:09 p.m. Bailey texted, **If she comes home within the hour she can stay.**

2:12 p.m. **I called her. No answer. Went straight to voice mail.**

3:20 p.m. **Her phone is here. I read this girl wrong. Don't want her.**

3:42 p.m. **She's 50 years younger than you. Yes, you do.**

4:11p.m. **You're right. Where is she?**

4:29 p.m. **You married Xena for love. Memphis can't compete with you.**

5:00 p.m. **She's sick. I'm worried about her. I do love her.**

5:29 p.m. Go upstairs. Relax.

I felt horrible. I indulged in a cold shower, moisturized my body. Holding up the nightie, I decided to wear it for Bailey.

Lying beside my husband, I cuddled behind him. Scurrying, I kicked him. Scrambled to my feet. Bailey's body was stiff. I stared at him. "Bailey!" I yelled. "Baillley!" I screamed. "Bailey," I cried, frantically shaking him.

I called for help. "Nine-one-one operator, what's your emergency?"

"Yes, I just got home. My husband is dead," I said.

"Are you sure he's not breathing?" she asked.

"Positive. His body is lifeless." I'd never been that close to death. Prayed my actions weren't a contributing factor.

"We'll send the paramedics and the coroner," she said. "I want you to stay calm and check for a pulse."

I was not touching him again. There wasn't any.

Sirens blared outside the house, then stopped. I watched the paramedics roll Bailey's body into the coroner's van. I closed the front door. Retracing my steps to the bedroom, I saw my phone had twenty percent battery life. There was no way I was sleeping in Bailey's bed.

I wanted to cry tears of grief, not fear.

Text tones connected like a song. I was numb.

Silence had sound and I did not want to be here.

A text registered from Memphis. **One eye. No teeth.**

ABOUT THE AUTHOR

New York Times bestselling author **Mary B. Morrison** believes that women must shape their own destiny. A motivational speaker and relationship expert, Mary encourages women to become their best. She quit her near six-figure government job to self-publish her first book, *Soulmates Dissipate,* in 2000 and begin her literary career. Healing Her Hurt, Incorporated is a 501(c)(3) nonprofit that Mary founded to promote the emotional, physical, and financial health of marginalized women and girls by providing self-empowerment tools, resources, and education. Mary produced a play based on her HoneyB novel, *Single Husbands.* Her wonderful son, Jesse Byrd Jr., is an award-winning children's author, the owner of JesseBCreative.com, and lives in Dubai with his wife Emaan. Mary currently resides in Atlanta, Georgia.

The employees of Thorndike Press hope you have enjoyed this Large Print book. All our Thorndike, Wheeler, and Kennebec Large Print titles are designed for easy reading, and all our books are made to last. Other Thorndike Press Large Print books are available at your library, through selected bookstores, or directly from us.

For information about titles, please call:
(800) 223-1244

or visit our website at:
gale.com/thorndike

To share your comments, please write:
Publisher
Thorndike Press
10 Water St., Suite 310
Waterville, ME 04901